TWISTED INK

ALSO BY A.M. MCCOY

Bailey Dunn & Co.
Bailey Dunn
Christmas with the Camdens

Beauty in the Ink
Twisted Lace

Cedar Bluff Penalties
Overtime Positions

The Kings of Hawthorn
Claiming What's His
Indulging His Desire
Earning His Eden

The Line Walkers
Stalker
Psycho
Bully

Shadeport Crew
Elora Dax
Carly James
Laila Manning

Standalone Novels
Guilty for You
Secrets Within Us
Sinister Vows

TWISTED INK

A.M. MCCOY

Podium

Cover design by Najla Qamber

ISBN: 979-8-3470-2265-6

Published in 2026 by Podium Publishing
www.podiumentertainment.com

Podium

To everyone who found me by chance on social media and took a chance.
To everyone who shared their love for this story with the world.
To every single reader, new and old, I hope you know how much you mean to me.

CONTENTS

CONTENT WARNING

If you're looking for wholesome world-building with complex situations and in-depth problem-solving outside of the issues within a relationship, this isn't the book for you.

This is a book about four consenting adults who dive deep (I mean DEEP) into the pleasures of a poly relationship. Everything has to do with sex and the good and bad that comes with that. Consider yourself warned.

This one is for the sluts.

TWISTED INK

CHAPTER 1

Reyna

"Dallin, stop," I chuckled, biting my bottom lip to hide my moan as his teeth nibbled on the skin beneath my ear. "I'm going to cut my finger off if you keep distracting me."

His large hands slid down my arms and covered my hands where I held the carrot, slicing it for dinner. He pulled both free and pushed the cutting board across the counter before placing my palms flat on the cold marble surface. "All better," he purred against my ear, and my head fell to the side, giving him better access. "Spread your legs."

"Dallin," I groaned, eyeing the clock on top of the stove. "Dinner will be late if I don't get finished."

"They won't starve." He sucked on the lobe of my ear and then kicked my feet apart forcefully, taking what I wouldn't give to him willingly.

Dallin and I had been together for two years, and I was a plain-Jane vanilla lover mostly, and he was okay with that. But then there were times like tonight, when he'd look at me with a predatory stare and my body would react to his, igniting a fire inside my belly that normally stayed dark. Because there was nothing vanilla about my hulking, dominating boyfriend, even if he toned himself down for me most of the time.

Tonight was not one of those nights, though. He was keyed up, wound tight, and ready to snap, desperate for the relief he could only get when he dominated me and made me beg for him.

"It's rude." I was grasping at straws, trying to come up with some defense to stop this before it started. Because once he got me to a certain point, there'd be no turning back. And with my luck, his friends that were visiting would walk in during the middle of it and never want to visit again. My mother taught me to be a better host than that. "Dallin!" I shrieked when his hand slid up under the skirt of my dress and pulled my panties down my legs. With my thighs spread as far as they were, the lace panties only went down halfway to my knees, but it was enough for him.

"Shh," he commanded, as he licked his fingers and then ran them over my clit and into my pussy. "Be a good girl and let me play."

"What has gotten into you?" I panted, even as I arched my back and pressed my ass out further, so he had better access. "We don't have time for this." His free hand spanked my ass cheek, causing me to yelp and pull away from him in surprise as my flesh bloomed with fire. "What the hell!"

"I said be quiet, Reyna." He kissed down my neck and pumped two fingers into my body from behind. "I want your cream covering my fingers when they get here." He said, "So be a good girl and come on them so you can finish cooking dinner. Because I won't stop until you do, I don't care if they're standing right here in the kitchen and watching me play with your body. I want your fucking orgasm, baby."

"Oh my God," I mewed, giving in to him. "Yes." His free hand tightened around the bun at the back of my hair, and he tilted my head back to stare up at the ceiling as he fucked me with his fingers. "Holy shit, babe."

"That's it," he praised me, sucking on the back of my neck and giving me a hickey I'd have to cover up with my hair later. "My good fucking girl."

His dirty-talk game was strong tonight, and the praise and domination in it were doing something to me. "Harder," I begged. "Please, I need more."

"Beg me better than that, Rey. Make me believe it."

"Please, Dallin, I want to come. Please let me come, baby," I purred, making my face flame bright in embarrassment.

A loud knock sounded from the front door, only a few feet away, making me gasp out loud before he covered my mouth with his hand. "Keep going, you're so close."

"I can't!" I hissed, and then groaned when he spanked me again, the loud crack echoing off the silent kitchen. "Dal."

"Give me what I want." He reached around and tweaked my clit as he added another finger, stretching me out uncomfortably. "That's it," he praised me when I mewed and pushed back with each thrust of his hand. "Come for me."

"I am," I gasped, biting my lip and begging for his hand to cover my mouth again as he pushed me over the edge. "Yes!" I whispered. Two more loud spanks echoed around the room, and I knew without a doubt the visitor on the other side of the door would hear them, even if it was hard to tell what they were listening to exactly. "Fuck!" I screeched as I fell forward on my elbows, sagging onto the counter as I came down off the high.

"Good girl." He slid his fingers from my body and turned me around to face him. "You're so fucking perfect, angel," he said before lifting his wet fingers and sucking them into his mouth. A louder, more impatient knock sounded from the front door behind me, but I couldn't care less as he feasted on the taste of me. "Go to the bathroom and clean yourself up, then come on out to meet the boys."

"Yes, sir," I smirked in a daze of arousal and delirium. "Whatever you say, sir." I skirted past him, pulling my panties up, and all but ran to the bedroom. I had barely cleared the doorway when he opened the front door, guffawing loudly with his friends who were visiting.

I locked the bathroom door behind me and ran cold water over the inside of my wrists, trying to cool my overheated body down as I looked in the mirror. My chest over the top of my simple white sundress was red and flushed from my orgasm, and my cheeks were reddened too.

"Troublemaker," I complained in a whisper as I undid the clip holding my hair up and fluffed it, trying to cover the evidence of what we had just done. The dark tone of my skin and hair helped a little, but it was impossible to cover it all.

I could hear the men chatting and catching up loudly down the hall, and I tried to muster up the courage to join them.

Parker Hurst and Trey Myers had been Dallin's best friends since they were in elementary school, and until two years ago, they were inseparable. But something happened between them right before I met Dallin, and they had fallen out of touch.

Until recently.

I knew Dallin was being evasive with details surrounding their friendship, giving me a glossed-over version every time I asked for specifics, but they meant something big to him once upon a time, and I suspected he was hoping to rebuild that friendship with them.

I just didn't know why he put so much pressure on the reconnection. He'd been a ball of anticipation and nerves for the last few days, brushing it off when I asked him about it and choosing to retreat off to his studio downstairs to avoid the conversation altogether.

Dallin Kent was an incredibly talented tattoo artist who had built a shop from the ground up over the last two years, quickly becoming one of the most popular tattoo destinations in all of Nashville. He added other talented artists as soon as he opened up, and before long, he was incredibly busy and booked for months at a time.

He even gained some high-profile clients, including music superstars, professional athletes, and everything in between.

When we met, he had just bought the building the shop was in and had been renovating the large upstairs apartment to live in. I didn't realize it, but apparently he thought pretty highly of me right away because his renovations included an office built specifically for me to work out of before he even asked me to move in. And I was the luckiest woman in the world because he was not only a sweet and kind partner who genuinely loved to love me, but he was the sexiest man to ever walk the face of the earth.

Which was easy to be when he was six foot three with dark hair faded and styled on top with slate-gray eyes that glowed against his tanned skin covered with tattoos. When we stood next to each other, we looked like opposites: him with his bad-boy darkness and me with my prim and proper schoolteacher vibes. When we met, I didn't even have a single tattoo, and even now I only had one, yet I was dating an artist who was completely covered in tattoos from his neck to his toes. It was fun to watch people's reactions when we went out, but it didn't even faze us anymore.

We were in love. Basically, from day one. And that was all that mattered.

It had been a whirlwind romance, and I'd been riding the high of it ever since. This led us to tonight, hosting a dinner party for his two childhood friends like we were hosting the royal family.

"Babe," Dallin called from the kitchen, and I knew I couldn't hide out anymore.

"Coming," I replied, taking one last look in the mirror before walking out into the lion's den.

My heels clicked across the hardwood floor as I entered the large open kitchen and three pairs of eyes locked in on mine.

Holy fuck.

My step faltered when I took in the sight of the three of them, standing together, leaning on the counter and drinking beers, because I'd never seen a sexier trio before in my life.

Dallin was still the sexiest, but Parker and Trey matched his dark and dangerous vibes with sultry good looks.

"There she is," Dallin called, summoning me to him with his hand extended, and I forced my feet to carry me across the space and into the safety of his arms, somehow maintaining a gentle smile on my face the whole time. "Boys, this is Reyna Delacruz." He kissed my temple and slid his hand down my back to rest it on the swell of my ass before turning back to his friends. "Baby, this is Parker." He pointed to the man on the right, who had short black hair cropped close to his scalp and brown eyes so dark they looked black. But his smile was breathtaking, and I could tell right away he was charismatic and outgoing. He had tattoos up one arm under his simple white tee and dark-wash jeans, making him look effortlessly sexy. He was an inch or two shorter than Dallin, but it was easy to tell he was the type of man to hit the gym every single day. He was the biggest out of the three in the muscle department.

"Hi." I nodded as he held his hand out for me to shake. When I took it, the warmth of his palm surprised me, but his touch was gentle.

"Pleasure, Reyna." His voice was deep, and shivers coated my arms.

"And this," Dallin continued, gesturing to the man next to Parker, "is Trey."

My stare finally tore away from Parker and locked on a pair of blue eyes so bright that they looked neon in the bright kitchen lighting. Trey had long dark hair that was tied up into a bun on top of his head and a short beard that was trimmed and neat, covering his wide jaw. He wore a black long-sleeved shirt pulled up on his forearms, revealing matching black ink on both and a few silver rings on the fingers of his right hand. He was as tall as the other two, but standing in the group, he won the contest for darkest disposition as he simply raised one eyebrow at me and smirked, showing off bright white teeth. "Reyna."

"Nice to meet you both," I said breathlessly, leaning further into Dallin's side as their stares stayed locked on me. "Dallin has talked about you two nonstop the last few days." I looked up at my boyfriend, who smirked down at me. "He's so excited to have you visit."

"We were excited to get the invite," Parker replied, lifting his bottle of beer to his lips, and taking a pull as he held Dallin's gaze.

Why was it so sexy to watch a man swallow?

Why was I so affected by them?

"I'll finish up on dinner." I broke through the haze of arousal, filling the air in the kitchen, and pulled off Dallin's side. "Why don't you guys go catch up and I'll let you know when it's ready?"

"We can help," Parker interrupted, but Dallin kissed my temple again, squeezing my ass tenderly, and pulled back.

"Believe me when I tell you she won't let you even try," Dallin joked, slapping Trey on the back as he herded them toward the living room. "She's a magician in the kitchen and likes to have her own space."

The guys walked off into the living room as I forced my hands back into motion to finish preparing dinner. When they made themselves comfortable, lounging around, my body overheated. My fried nerves left me acutely aware of how near they were. Thank God they didn't stay in the kitchen to actually help. I think I would have combusted into flames.

I listened to them chatting about where Trey and Parker had been traveling lately and all the sights they'd seen as I finished the stir-fry and rice I'd made.

As I reached up in the cupboard for bowls far over the top of my head, an ink-covered arm stretched past me and grabbed the stack that was almost out of reach, as Parker said, "I got it. On the table?" He held the stack in front of him after I backed away, so I wasn't pinned between him and the counter any longer.

"I can do it," I stammered, trying to not get lost in the darkness of his eyes. "Go relax."

He rolled those dark eyes and then winked. "You're right, D, she is stubborn," he called over his shoulder as he picked up the silverware I'd already laid out on his way by the island and took them into the dining room. I stood frozen in place, watching his back ripple and move under the white fabric of his shirt as he set the table until I felt eyes burning into the side of my face. When I looked over at the couch, both Dallin and Trey were watching me with unreadable looks on their faces.

I quickly dropped their penetrating gazes and busied myself grabbing the wine and glasses, adding them to the table, but was careful to avoid looking at Parker at all.

What the hell was wrong with me? Was I really drooling over my boyfriend's best friends? Right in front of him.

"Dinner's ready," I called sweetly, smiling at Dallin as I finally met his stare again. I was afraid I'd find anger in his eyes at having caught me staring at his best friend, but there was a twinkle of something else burning in them as he walked over to me. "Can I get you another beer?" I asked quietly as he stepped right into my personal space and pressed the front of his body against mine.

"Yes, you may," he replied, but before I could turn back to the fridge, he leaned down and kissed me. And not just a peck either, but a deep, sensual kiss that left me leaning into him with my hands on his abs for stability before he pulled away. "I'm going to enjoy this," he said with a smirk, and walked away, leaving me confused and panting.

Trey stared at me from where he stood behind his chair, once again with that unreadable gaze until I ducked my head and ran for the fridge.

Holy fucking shit, I was going to be in a puddle by the time dinner was done.

CHAPTER 2

Dallin

"D tells us you're an author," Parker said, trying once again to pull Reyna into the conversation as dinner wrapped up. She'd sat silently for most of the meal, soaking in everything we talked about, and looked like she was enjoying the conversation.

But I knew her better than that. She was deep inside her head, trying to make sense of the bizarre reaction her body was having to the three of us. We were used to turning women into mush, but Reyna was a good girl and not one to let her body run away with her mind.

But tonight, it consumed her.

Which was exactly what I knew would happen. It was also why I'd played with her against the counter, even though Parker had texted me and told me they'd be arriving in five minutes. I wanted her fresh off a sexual high when she met them.

"Uh, yeah." She cleared her throat and took another sip of her white wine. "I dabble a bit in it."

"What do you write?" Trey asked, playing nicely. I had threatened them before they arrived tonight to be on their best behavior, but I didn't tell them why. If I knew my friends, though, they would figure it out soon.

"Uh—" She paused, and a blush crawled up her cheeks before she answered. "Romance novels, mostly."

I clarified with a pointed look at her. "She's a *New York Times* bestseller. Don't let her modesty fool you, she's incredibly talented."

She smiled into her wineglass and dropped her eyes. Reyna was shy and introverted, but something I found out early in our relationship was that she loved when I stood up for her, being bold when she couldn't be. It was something that really clicked us together when we first met.

The night we met, we were both at a bar downtown. She was out with a group of friends for someone's bachelorette party, and I was out trying to drown my sorrows in rotgut whiskey. I found her sitting across the horseshoe bar and staring down into her untouched glass of wine while her friends partied all around her, oblivious to her level of discomfort when I watched a guy push in on her space. She was polite at first, declining his offers for drinks and dances, but before long, his offers became insistent and he made advances that she was having trouble deflecting.

If someone had asked me that night why I bothered to get up and walk around to her side of the bar, I wouldn't have had a suitable answer.

If someone asked me tonight, I'd instantly tell them it was because I knew then that she was my soul mate, and her sadness called to mine.

I walked around the bar and slid between her and a friend of hers, leaning on the bar as she turned on me with rounded doe eyes as I bent down and kissed her temple. I said something like, "Sorry I got tied up on my way back from the bathroom, baby," and then turned to the jack-off, still trying to get her attention as I stood over him. It didn't take him long, though, to realize he was a puppy in a big-dog fight paired against me, and he scampered off into the crowd looking for someone else to bother.

We spent the rest of the night chatting and getting to know each other, and I was pretty sure I was in love with her calm, sweet soul before I put her in the Uber to go home and said good night.

I called her before I went to sleep that night and asked her out for the following night and the rest is history.

She healed a giant part of the hole that had overtaken my heart when I first moved to Nashville and, without her, I know without a doubt I never would have survived that chapter of my life.

The chapter where I walked away from the only two people who had ever mattered in my life because we all wanted different things. We were going in different directions, and I thought walking away to find what I wanted was the best option for me.

I didn't realize at the time that even finding that other missing part of my life wouldn't make me feel whole without them.

Trey and Parker were now the missing part of my life, and I was desperate to get our friendship back, which was why I'd invited them to visit.

It had been two years since I last talked to them, but when I called Parker a few weeks ago, I was surprised that he not only answered but also agreed to visit and convinced Trey to come along.

I just had to handle this whole thing right, or I'd end up fucking it all up.

And then I could lose them all.

"Dallin," Reyna said, looking over at me with her brows pinched together. "Did you hear me?"

"Sorry." I smiled at her, grabbed my bottle of beer, and took a long pull. "I was lost in thought."

She relaxed and smiled back. "I asked if you told them about the expo coming up."

"Ah." I looked across to where Parker had his brows raised and then to Trey, to find his deep over his eyes in a scowl. "I hadn't. But I planned on getting around to it."

"Sorry." Reyna's shoulders deflated a fraction of an inch, and I reached over, sliding my hand under her hair and squeezing the back of her neck.

"You're fine," I assured her, gentling my tone. "I just didn't want to overload them with information on the phone." I looked back at my friends and took a deep breath. "The Nashville Tattoo Expo is next week. Five days straight of opportunity to thicken your portfolio. I'm a host for it, so I'll be there most days."

"Then why invite us to visit you if you're going to be busy?" Trey snapped, and Reyna tensed under my hand.

"Because you're two of the most talented artists I know," I said plainly, looking over to Parker, "and I thought you might want to check it out and see what Nashville could offer you."

"We're nomads." Trey interrupted Parker as he opened his mouth to reply. "You know that, D."

"I know." I nodded and leaned on the table with my elbows as I stared at my empty plate. "I just thought maybe the nomad days were getting old by now."

"And what?" He leaned forward, glaring at me. "We'd settle down in Nashville?" He was keeping what he really wanted to say to me locked down because of Reyna. And while I was appreciative of that for her sake, I missed his rawness. I never wondered what he thought in the past, because he would tell you like he saw it.

"I thought you might consider it." I stared at him, challenging the alpha in him. "It wouldn't hurt to check it out."

He looked away from me to Reyna and back, chewing on a toothpick that he always kept above one of his ears. "I don't understand you."

"Look." Parker stepped in, leaning forward on the table and breaking through the tension. "I want to check it out," he admitted, and Trey snapped his head around to him like he'd been slapped. "I want to check out your shop, too. I want to hear all about your life and what you've made for yourself here."

"Parker," Trey bit out.

"Enough, Trey," Parker said reasonably. "Put your ego away for five fucking minutes and let's just check this place out for a while." He lowered his voice. "It's been two long years, man."

Trey clenched his jaw and kept his mouth shut as he gave Reyna a passing glance. I looked down at her myself and her eyes were wide, her face pale as she looked around at the three of us.

"Fine." Trey sighed, leaning back in his chair and taking another swig of his beer. "But only if Reyna keeps feeding us this delicious food." He gave her a small smile, signaling that he was at least trying.

She relaxed at my side and smiled brightly at him as the tension melted from the room. "I agree with your terms." She held her hand out and his small smile turned into his trademark smirk as he reached across the space and shook it. "Who wants dessert?" she asked cheerily, looking at me. "I made chocolate peanut butter pie."

"Good God, woman," Parker groaned, leaning back in his chair and making a show of loosening his belt. "Marry me. We can go to the courthouse right now."

Reyna giggled and stood up to start clearing the plates. "Thanks, but I'm already spoken for." She winked at me and walked into the kitchen.

"Hmm," Parker smirked, staring right at me. "I'll see what I can do about that."

The boys were on their best behavior through dessert, asking Reyna all about her life and absolutely charming her. And even if she didn't know it yet, that was a big fucking step for Trey, who was the crassest asshole I'd ever met before. But he was trying.

For her.

When we were done eating, she kicked us out, instructing us to go down to the shop and check it out so she could have some quiet time to finish up on some emails before bed.

So we stood in the middle of Twisted Ink, my pride and joy, as Trey and Parker walked around, taking it all in.

I stood back, watching them and trying to see the shop through their eyes as newcomers, hoping that they loved it.

"Wow, man," Parker said, turning to face me in the large, open lobby. "And each artist has their own private room?"

"Yeah." I nodded, putting my hands in my pants pockets. "Each room is equipped with its own thermostat, flat screen, sound system, and visitor's seating. Anything else the artists want in it is available within reason."

Parker smirked. "That sounds like someone asked for something ridiculous."

I chuckled and nodded. "I have one artist that asked for a stripper pole."

Parker's eyes widened as he shook his head. "The balls on that dude."

"Chick, actually," I replied, enjoying the way his eyes widened even more. "Her name is Lex and the guys call her Mrs. Steal Your Girl because she will swipe anyone without a second of hesitation. She looks like an emo Barbie doll and can pretty much get anyone she wants to."

"Damn." Parker whistled with a smirk.

"Let me guess, you keep Reyna as far away from her as possible," Trey said from where he leaned on the reception desk.

"I don't have many rules for my employees, but I do tell them right away that what's mine is off limits," I answered honestly, holding his blue eyes. "I wouldn't think twice about firing someone over her."

"Noted," he replied evenly.

"Well." Parker kicked the toe of his boot into the floor. "Are we going to address the elephant in the room or are we going to ignore it like it doesn't exist?"

"It doesn't exist," Trey snapped, still staring at me. "You heard the man, Park." He turned to our friend. "What's his, is his."

"That's not the same thing." Parker groaned, rubbing his hand over his face in exasperation before ignoring Trey completely and turning to me. "Does she know? About us?"

I clenched my jaw and swallowed. "No," I replied honestly, hating the guilt that burned in my gut as hurt reflected in his eyes. "She doesn't." I paused and sighed. "She's a good girl. Kind as the day is long, selfless, and completely pure in her heart."

"And if you told her about us, she'd what?" Parker asked. "Be tainted?"

"That's not what I meant." I pushed off the wall and walked toward him, but he scowled deeper the closer I got, so I stopped a few feet away. "I didn't want to just *tell* her about my past. She wouldn't understand it like that. She knows I wasn't an altar boy before we met, but she wouldn't understand if the truth were just words to her."

"What does that mean?" Trey lashed out angrily.

I hated how angry he still was about all of this.

"It means I wanted to show her." I raised my voice, turning on him. "I hoped maybe you both would have forgiven me by now and maybe, just maybe, you could stomach the idea of settling down for once in your lives and giving this a shot!" My chest rose and fell with exertion as I spoke my feelings out loud for the first time in two years. "I thought maybe I was worth not seeing a different patch of asphalt every week." I threw my hands up into the air. "But I'm starting to see that will never be the case."

"D." Parker sighed, deflating from his own anger as I cut myself open for them.

"I don't regret walking away," I admitted. "I meant what I said two years ago about needing something more than the open road. I wasn't happy living like that anymore."

"And then you settled down with someone!" Trey shook his head. "I don't get what you think you were going to accomplish by having us come here."

"I want—" I shrugged as anxiety dried out my mouth. I should have been admitting this to Reyna first, instead of to them. I owed her that much.

"What?" Parker asked, walking forward until he was right in front of me. "What do you want, D?"

"I want you guys back in my life."

"How?" He pushed on, forcing me to say it. "As your buddies that you work with? As your childhood friends whom you were once so close to, no one could come between us? As the dark part of your past that you hide and don't talk about?"

"I want you!" I roared, grabbing the front of his shirt and shaking him. "I want what we had." His nostrils flared, but he stayed solid and still. "But I want her too." I shook my head in frustration. "I want us all to have her."

"Jesus fuck, man." Parker shoved me off, shaking his head as he started pacing. "You just said she was a good girl!" Parker hardly ever raised his voice; he was always the levelheaded one out of our trio, as Trey and I constantly butted heads with our alpha personalities. But now he yelled, unable to contain it. "She doesn't even know that you've been with men before! How do you expect her to take it when you tell her you want us *all* to be together?"

"It doesn't matter." Trey closed the distance between us until we stood toe to toe. "Because I'm not interested in playing house with your sweet little Stepford wife. She's not our type. Boring mousy women don't do it for us, and you know that."

"Wait a second." I clenched my fists, feeling my anger rise at the way he described her like her good-girl personality was a bad thing because it wasn't.

"No, you wait a second." He shoved me in the chest and pointed a finger at me. "How dare you call after two years, begging Parker to come to visit you, and then drop this bomb on us? It's not what we want!" he yelled. "*We* weren't good enough for you two years ago, and now *you're* not what we want anymore, Dallin." His voice was lethal as he poked his finger into my chest. "You walked away from *us*, remember that."

He turned and walked away.

"Where are you going?" Parker asked him as he walked to the front door. "We need to at least finish this conversation, Trey."

"I am done, Park." He looked over his shoulder. "Stay and get the closure you want if that's what you need. But I'm going to the bar. Fuck this shit."

"Trey," I called out as he stormed through the front door, leaving the bells dinging in his absence. "Fuck!" I roared, pulling my hair as I kicked a chair in frustration before throwing myself down into it.

I sat with my head in my hands, panting and trying to figure out what to do as I heard Trey's motorcycle roar to life and then tear off down the street. Parker finally spoke from where he had stood the whole time.

"Why would you risk her leaving you over this? It doesn't seem worth it."

I looked up and stared at him, trying to convey my answer correctly. "Because I know she'll be on board," I replied. "Maybe not at first, and maybe not without a little convincing, but I know her better than I know myself some days, man." I shook my head. "It feels right. I didn't just come up with this harebrained idea on a whim. I'm not like that. I wouldn't risk this one shot with you all without weighing the risks first." He just watched me like he was trying to process that, so I continued on. "I haven't felt complete one time in my entire life, Parker. Not when it was the three of us on the road, and not even since falling in love with Reyna and settling down here. It was never just the nomad lifestyle that didn't do it for me before, and you know that. Something else was missing. And when I envision what it would look like with the four of us, together, completely, I feel like that's the closest I've ever come to being whole."

"And what about us?" He dropped his fists from his hips. "What if you were enough for us before without all of this?" He spun around the shop, looking at it. "Without her."

I stood up and walked toward him until we were less than a foot apart. "If I had been enough for you before, you wouldn't have let me walk away the last time. There's always been a missing link between us, it's why we were never exclusive. It's why we always continued to fuck women all across the country when we traveled. I was just the only one brave enough to rock the boat to try to find the one."

"And you think she's the one, for all of us, not just you? She's nothing like the women we date."

"That's the point," I challenged him. "Don't fucking stand there and try to tell me you didn't get hard the second she walked into the room tonight. That you weren't completely entranced by her the whole time. Am I right?"

"You know you're right." He scoffed. "Doesn't mean it'd work out, man." He sighed. "Trey isn't a gentle man, Dallin. He's got sharp edges, and rudeness is his number one character trait."

"And yet we still find the good in him. Maybe Reyna will be the one to soften him up a bit. If anyone can do it, it's her."

"Maybe."

"What about me?" I asked him, feeling like I was betraying Reyna, but I needed to know the answer. "Do you still have feelings for me? Is this something you'd even want to consider?"

His dark eyes stared deep into mine in a way that had always been all Parker. "I wasn't only hard for your sexy little girlfriend, D, even if you were giving it to her in the kitchen when we walked up to the door, knowing we were on our way up," he replied. "I wouldn't still be here if I didn't still want you."

My body ached for his, but I forced my feet to stay still. "I can't cheat on Rey," I responded. "I need to come clean to her first. But I want you to know how fucking badly I still want you."

His eyes closed, and he took a deep breath like he was physically restraining himself as much as I was. "When are you going to talk to her?"

"Tomorrow," I replied. "We're going on a hike in the morning, I planned on telling her then."

He smirked and nodded. "When she's secluded in the wilderness so no one can hear her scream at you?" he said. "Or so she can't run away from you? Though we both know how much you enjoy a good game of hide-and-seek in the woods."

I shrugged, feeling a bit lighter, like perhaps this would all work out after all. "Maybe a little of both."

"Well, I'll leave you to it." He nodded, backing up.

"Where are you staying?"

"I don't know yet. We didn't make any plans."

"Stay here," I said instantly. "There's a king bed in the spare bedroom."

He rolled his eyes and shook his head. "Down the hall from you and Reyna? I don't think that would be such a good idea."

"Why?" I contested. "It will be fine."

"And what about Trey?"

"He's more than welcome, too. If he wants." He nodded as he considered it. "Stay, Parker," I insisted, firmer this time, and his eyelids fluttered closed as he sighed.

"Don't do that," he groaned. "You know I fold when you go all daddy-Dom on me."

My body stirred, hardening as he got closer to being underneath me again after two long years apart. I walked forward like I was going to walk past him and stopped, touching him only with my shoulder as I leaned toward his ear. "Reyna comes alive when she's dominated." He growled deep in his chest as my words affected him. "What I wouldn't give to watch you fold her up with your sweet words and heavy hand."

"Dallin," he groaned, turning his face toward mine until our lips were nearly touching, but not quite. "When you fuck her tonight, make sure you do it good enough so I can hear it down the hallway."

CHAPTER 3

Reyna

Dallin had been acting weird ever since returning from the shop. He and Parker came back upstairs, but Trey wasn't with them. When I asked where he was, they both deflected, giving non-answers and pretty-boy smiles.

I decided to not call them on it; they obviously had some things to work through as a group. Dinner had been tense, to say the least. Trey was a very severe man, from his dark glare to his less-than-sunny disposition, but it was easy to see what caused it.

Pain.

Maybe it was because of my extensive time locked away writing about brooding, damaged villains in my stories, or perhaps just a woman's intuition, but Trey Myers had scars on his heart. Which he combated with walls and boundaries that he didn't want others to cross. It made him feel untouchable and protected, if I had to guess.

But I think it also made him feel a little lonely.

Not that he or the others would ever admit to having feelings past those that were skin deep. That just wasn't their style.

"You okay?" Dallin asked me as I sat in bed, putting lotion on.

"Yeah, why?" I smiled at him as he took his shirt off and tossed it in the hamper in his closet. I absolutely loved his body; every single time he revealed himself to me, it felt like the first time.

The first time I saw it, I literally drooled with my mouth open.

The first time he touched me, I shivered violently.

The first time he kissed me, my foot popped like in that teenage princess movie.

He was a fairy-tale Prince Charming, wrapped in ink and hard edges to look like the villain. But he was all good, wrapped in gold.

Some days I felt unworthy of him and his love because I still couldn't figure out what it was about me that caught his eye.

But I had, and he'd been such a devoted and passionate lover ever since.

"You seem lost in thought." He came back out of the closet in his tight boxers and pulled the blankets back on his side of the bed. "Are you sure you're okay with them staying here? I know I should have asked before I offered."

I waved him off, setting my bottle of lotion on my bedside table and turning off the lamp before removing my robe. "I have no problem at all with them staying here, Dallin. I just worry about you and Trey."

"What do you mean?" he asked, sliding down in bed and lying on his side as I did the same. He lifted my leg over his hip and pulled me close in the darkness. Our custom oversized king bed seemed nice in theory because of how tall Dallin was, but he still ended up wrapped around me on my side all night long.

And it didn't bother me once in the two years that he'd done it.

"What really happened between you two?" I asked. "Between all of you. There seems to be so much more to the story than what meets the eye." I ran my hand down his muscular chest, tracing the tattoo of my name over his sternum. "There's hurt between you all, isn't there?"

"Yeah, baby." He sighed. "There is. But maybe we can heal some of it and move forward."

"Is that why you invited them to visit? I won't lie and say it didn't feel really out of the blue when you told me they were coming last week."

"I battled with myself for a long time before I picked up the phone and called Parker. I didn't know I was going to do it until the phone was in my hand ringing, honestly. And then he agreed to visit." He shrugged. "I want you to know how much it means to me you're so supportive of me trying to mend this bridge."

"Of course I am. They're obviously important to you, and I'll support you in whatever you decide is the best course of action to fix your friendship. I'll even help where I can. Maybe I can bake cookies for Trey and sweeten up his sour mood a little bit." I giggled at the joke but stopped when he didn't join in like usual. I could feel his slate eyes on my face through the darkness even if I couldn't see them, as he stayed quiet. "Dallin?"

"I think if anyone in the world is going to be capable of sweetening up Trey, it's you, baby," he said with a thickness to his voice. He shifted, rolling over on top of me with his thigh still pressed between mine. "I know I've never been able to resist how sweet you are." He rocked his hips forward, drawing a moan from my lips as he hardened against me. He grabbed both of my wrists and pinned them above my head as he pushed his way between my legs completely until I locked my ankles around his back. "It's intoxicating to men like us, Rey. The three of us are like the big bad wolves in a sweet little fairy tale, and you're the innocent Little Red Riding Hood. Ready and ripe for the taking." He rocked his hips again and kissed me.

"Why does that sound so sexual?" I gasped, feeling an inferno light inside my belly from the visual his words were giving me. The three dark, tattooed men standing over me with hungry gazes in their eyes. "God." My brain was twisted to even think of them like that. There was just so much testosterone in the air when they were all three near.

"Because you're a dirty girl." He smiled against my neck where he was nibbling on the flesh, leaving love bites I hated. But they drove him wild to see after we finished making love, so I let him, as long as I could easily hide them in public. "You write all of that dirty smut all day long, crafting deviously sexual scenarios from fantasies in your brain. It's a wonder you aren't bored with me at the end of the day."

I snorted, rocking underneath him. "You're more sexual than I am." I fought against his hold on my wrists to indicate what I meant. "I'm surprised you're not bored with me and my vanilla sex."

He kissed his way down my chest, pulling the lace edge of my nightgown aside with his teeth until my breast was bare to him before flicking his tongue across the tight bud of my nipple. "You're not vanilla, baby, just reserved." He sucked it into his mouth, and I bucked underneath him. "But that doesn't mean I don't love drawing you out of your safe space with my kinks until you're begging for it like such a good girl."

"Jesus." I groaned, biting my lips. "We have to stop, or Parker will hear us." His best friend lay down the hall in the spare bed and I knew the walls were not thick enough to muffle the noises Dallin would force from my body in a mood like this. He was worked up sexually tonight, which meant he would take me hard and mercilessly. There would be no gentle and slow lovemaking if he had his way.

"Would that be the absolute worst thing in the world?" he said, holding my wrists in one hand and using the other to lift the hem of my nightgown over my hips.

"Yes!" I cried in a dramatic whisper. "I'd be mortified."

"You'd be mortified if my best friend heard you moaning my name while I fucked your tight little body?" he asked, and I groaned at how dirty his words were. "You'd be mortified if he heard you coming all over my cock like the good girl you really are?"

"Dallin." I hissed as his fingers slid under the waistband of my panties and pushed deeper until they found my wetness.

He chuckled deviously. "You're soaked, baby." I hid my face in my arm as my cheeks bloomed with a blush, thankful that I'd turned the lights out before he got me this worked up. "That's not all for me, is it?" He questioned, rubbing my clit in small circles as my hips bucked against him.

"Of course it is," I lied, hating myself for it. "You're the only one I want."

The entire bizarre situation was warping my head and making my pussy weep.

"That's a shame." He growled against my chest as he reached between us and freed his cock. He was so thick, with veins that ran the entire length, ribbing the shaft for greater pleasure, and it never ceased to amaze me every time he pushed into my body. "Because I'm the hardest I've ever been thinking about him listening to you right now."

"Dallin," I moaned pathetically, unable to form any other words as he pulled my panties to the side, not even bothering to remove them, and thrust his cock deep. "Oh my God," I moaned, not attempting to silence myself because of how good it felt.

"Good girl," he praised me, widening his knees and rolling his hips with each thrust. "That turns you on, doesn't it?"

"You turn me on," I gasped. "Whatever you do, hard or not hard, turns me on," I answered evasively.

"I know that, baby. You don't have to worry about offending me by being turned on by someone else." He thrust, driving me wild. "I know you love me, regardless."

"I do," I panted, fighting his hold on my wrists until he released me. "God, I love you so much, it drives me nuts." I wrapped my arms around his shoulders and clung to him as he slammed into me. I wasn't sure what spurred him on tonight to turn him into his dominant and hypersexual self, but I loved it. Between the way he fingered me in the kitchen before dinner and the dirty talk he was using on me now, he was primed and ready to go.

"Then be my sweet girl and come for me," he demanded, reaching between us to roll my clit between his fingers. "Come on my cock and show me."

"Yes," I cried, tilting my head back as my body tightened around his. "Don't stop, please, please, please, don't stop, D," I begged, and he grunted in response, going harder until the headboard hit the wall with each thrust. "Fuck!" I moaned as I shot off through a kaleidoscope of pleasure, coming all over his cock as he demanded of me. I was acutely aware of him bellowing out, slamming his hand against the headboard and bottoming out a few more times before he stilled, his cock jerking inside me as he came.

"Fucking hell," he groaned, grinding into me like he was hesitant to end it all before he rolled off onto his back and panted.

I chuckled in the darkness and stared up at the dark ceiling as I tried to tell myself I was horrified at being so loud.

But I wasn't. Not with him essentially demanding it of me.

If he was all right with it, why shouldn't I be?

"I love you," he said finally, sliding his hand across the sheets to find mine as he sighed and relaxed into the pillows.

"I love you too, Dallin." I rolled over and curled into his side, meaning to only relax a bit before getting up and cleaning myself up. But when his breathing mellowed out into a slumbered one, it lulled me to sleep almost as quickly. And I fell asleep thinking about three pairs of eyes staring at me in the darkness, instead of just one.

Dallin's fevered body was wrapped around me from head to toe, and we lay almost sideways across the bed. My bladder screamed at me, so I fought my way out of his hold to get up and get to the bathroom.

I glanced at the clock on my way and groaned when I saw it was almost three a.m. Which meant that I'd probably have trouble going back to sleep. I was an insomniac, usually only able to stay in bed for a few hours at a time without a sleep aid. And I hadn't taken one last night because I never got back up out of bed after Dallin fucked the crazy into me with dirty talk.

And it was far too late to take one now, or I'd be comatose all day from it.

When I got done in the bathroom, I walked back out into the bedroom. Dallin lay on his back sprawled across the entire bed like a starfish with his groin on full display. I paused at the end of the bed, staring at it in the dim light from the alarm clock, and contemplated crawling back in bed and enticing him to fuck me back to sleep. Something I didn't even know was possible, but on nights like this in the past, if I woke him up for sex, he'd fuck me good, and I'd end up falling back asleep afterward for a few more hours.

But he looked so peaceful, and I didn't want to interrupt him. He had been working nonstop the last few weeks to clear up his schedule for the expo in a few days, so he could dedicate time at the convention center all week.

So instead I slid my robe back on over my body to ward off the chill of the air conditioner and slipped from the room. I planned to make a cup of tea and read my Kindle on the couch for a while to settle my mind. Maybe then I'd get back to sleep.

Normally I'd go into my office and work, but it was right next to the spare room, and I didn't want to disturb Parker.

When we went to bed, Trey still hadn't checked in with either of them, and they weren't sure he'd come back for the night. But Dallin gave him the code to the door just in case and left it in his hands.

I rubbed the sleep from my eyes and stretched my arms over my head as I walked into the kitchen and flicked on the small light over the stove. I worked around the space as quietly as possible, getting my kettle out and filling it with water.

When I tried to turn the burner on, it only clicked repeatedly but wouldn't light. "What the heck?" I whispered frustratedly as I tried to remember where the matches were.

"Need a light?" a deep voice asked from the other side of the kitchen, and I jumped, whipping around to find Trey leaning against the counter in the dark corner.

I put my hand over my heart, trying to calm the erratic beating of it as he pushed up off the edge and sauntered toward me. He didn't have a shirt on and wore only a pair of distressed blue jeans that hung so low on his hips that almost his entire Adonis belt was visible. The V above his jeans snagged my eyes and wouldn't let go as he stalked closer.

It wasn't until he slid his hand into his pocket and pulled out a silver Zippo lighter that I could force my eyes back up to his face, quickly scanning the artwork drawn across his impressive abs.

Why was he so fucking hot?

His body was nearly twinned to Dallin's, maybe a little leaner, but covered with ink and muscle. Perhaps that was why I was nearly drooling by the time he stopped next to me at the stove.

"I didn't mean to scare you," he said, setting his beer bottle down on the counter before lifting the metal grate off the top of the stove.

"I didn't know you were here," I answered stupidly as he flicked the lighter open and held it down to the burner.

"Turn the knob for me?" he asked, looking down over his shoulder at me. I reached across in front of him for the knob, but he was standing so close to it, my arm brushed across his bare abs as I gave the burner gas.

The fire whooshed to life, and I quickly stepped away from him and the stove as I tried to calm my body down before I embarrassed myself in front of Dallin's friend. I set the kettle down on the burner and then turned to face him. He leaned back against the island with his arms crossed over his chest, holding his beer.

"Does this bother you?" he asked quietly.

"What?" I whispered, remembering that my silk robe was open, and my nightgown was sheer in a lot of places. I quickly tied the sash closed and ran my hand through my bedhead.

Could he tell that it was sex hair and not bedhead?

Why did I care?

"That I'm here," he responded, dragging me from my thoughts. "I wasn't exactly the best guest at dinner."

I relaxed a little and leaned back against the counter across from him, crossing my arms over my chest like he was. "Well, lucky for you, we weren't grading you on your manners." I smiled, trying to lighten the mood, but he stayed impassive, watching me. My smile fell, and I dropped his intimidating stare. "Right." I turned back around and opened the cabinet with my teas in it, trying to decide which one would give me magical powers so I could disappear from the entire uncomfortable situation.

"You didn't answer the question," he said after a while of me staring aimlessly into the cabinet. "Does it bother you that I'm here?"

"Why would it?" I turned and faced him, abandoning the decision-making process altogether. "You're Dallin's best friend." I shrugged. "You're more than welcome here. This is his home."

"I thought it was your place. Together," he countered with that same stare. His blue eyes didn't lessen the intensity of it at all, even though they glowed in the darkness.

"He already owned it when we met."

"Yet he crafted it specifically for your needs." He nodded to the open cabinet behind me where a custom shelving unit held all my favorite tea boxes, displaying them and making them easier to choose.

Or it should have been easier, anyway.

I looked over my shoulder at the display and then shrugged, turning back to him. "He's thoughtful like that."

His jaw clenched a little, rolling the muscles in his cheek before he lifted the bottle to his lips and took a large swallow. His neck muscles worked with the movement, and his Adam's apple bobbed, but I tried not to notice the way it made the tattoos on his neck ripple enticingly.

He was covered with ink, more than Dallin was from what I could see above his jeans, but it suited him.

Like the darkness of the ink matched the darkness of his soul.

"What happened to you?" I asked on instinct, and then shook my head embarrassingly. "I'm sorry." I hurried on. "Please don't answer that, it was rude of me to ask."

His lips turned up on the edge of his cheek in the slightest glimpse of a smirk, but that was it. "What makes you think something happened to me?" He ignored my desperate request to forget the question, and I groaned.

The kettle whispered behind me, so I turned back to the cabinet, grabbed the first tea I saw, and closed it, busying my hands as I contemplated his question.

Should I answer it and place myself so far out of my lane, or should I move on and ignore it, like he had done to me before?

"Answer me, Reyna." His commanding voice came from behind me, and goose bumps rose on my skin.

I pursed my lips and watched the kettle like it would help it boil faster, even though we all knew the answer to that question.

"You're in pain," I said after a while, like maybe answering him would release me from the awkward conversation. Which was stupid.

"And what do you know of pain?" He challenged me with a hint of arrogance, so I turned back around to face him.

"Nothing," I replied honestly, hating how impassive his face was.

"Exactly." He leaned up off the counter and set his beer down as he stood in the middle of the space, only a foot away from me. "You live here in your perfect little home, with your perfect little job, and your perfect little relationship to a man you don't even know," he said accusingly. "Yet you dare to think you know anything at all about tortured souls." He scoffed without humor.

"Is your soul tortured?" I held my ground against the man that Dallin called a friend yet showed me nothing friendly in return.

He took one more step, pressing the ends of his boots against the tips of my bare toes, towering over me, forcing me to tilt my head to stare up at him. "You'd run for the hills if you knew just how badly."

"You don't know me," I argued, trying to not let him intimidate me. "You don't know what I can handle or not."

He worked his jaw back and forth before licking his lips, and I was oddly fascinated with the move. "I've met a thousand women like you. Fucked more than half of them. Believe me when I say I know what your limits are, even if you don't."

"Trey." Parker broke up the tense stare-off as he entered the kitchen. I tore my eyes away from Trey's and shuddered when I looked over at Parker. He stood in a pair of tight black boxers and nothing else, rubbing his hand over the back of his neck as he glared at his friend, cornering me. "Leave her alone, man."

"She started it," Trey responded, never breaking his stare away from me.

"I'm ending it." Parker walked over and put his hand on Trey's stomach and pushed himself between us. His scent spun around my head from the proximity. I could feel his body heat radiating off his bare back, and part of me wanted to lean into it. "Go to bed, man," he commanded, pushing him toward the spare bedroom again. "You know this isn't on her."

"No." Trey tsked with his teeth as I peeked around Parker's wide shoulder and found his blue eyes locked on me. "It's on her perfect little doting boyfriend." He scoffed and rolled his eyes. "What a joke."

"Go." Parker walked forward and shoved him again. "Bed. Now." Trey shook his head but walked off down the hall to the spare bedroom, mumbling under his breath, as Parker turned and looked at me, sighing. "Are you okay?"

"Yeah." I nodded, turning off the stove and putting the tea back in the cabinet. "Thanks."

"Reyna," Parker called as I skirted around the island back toward my room, making me pause and look back at him. "Take anything he said with a bucket of salt." He cocked his head to the side. "He's working through some stuff."

"Got it." I gave him a weak smile and hurried off to our room, shutting the door behind me and locking it.

My body was alight with energy from my sparring with Trey and the physical reaction of seeing both of their bodies in such undress.

Fuck Dallin's precious sleep, it was his fault I was so worked up. He lay exactly as he had been when I left, and I paused at the end of the bed, stripped off all of my clothes, and climbed up between his legs.

I was feeling bold, brave, and majorly unhinged as I grabbed onto his cock where it lay against his leg, quickly lowering my mouth onto it, sucking. It jerked in my hand and quickly started growing harder as Dallin tossed his head to the side and reacted to the sensation in his sleep. The man could sleep through a hurricane.

"Mmm." He hummed sleepily as I pushed my mouth down further over his thickness, gagging on the end and pulling off, licking up the side of him. "Yes."

I was wet and needy as I brought him to life, not even understanding what had come over me. I spread my knees wide and reached between my legs, rubbing my clit as I worked him over, getting more aroused by the second until I was panting with need.

Dallin was hard as stone in my hand, and I crawled up his body, not even caring that he wasn't fully awake yet. I needed him.

I lined him up with my pussy and slowly sank down onto him, twirling my hips to accommodate his size, and threw my head back in ecstasy as the pleasure mounted inside me from him filling me up.

Nothing ever felt as good as feeling his cock stretch me open.

I rose, pressing my palms flat onto his chest, and then pushed back down, quickly taking him as his brows creased over his eyes, which were still closed.

"Take it," he moaned, grabbing my hips and thrusting up into me. "That's it, Parker. God." He gasped as I froze above him, staring down as I tried to process what he'd just said. My heart stopped beating completely as he pushed me down on his cock and lifted me off again. "Fuck, baby."

I covered my mouth as he moved me on and off how he wanted, shocked and trying to come up with an explanation. My body reacted to his words ferociously, though, even as they moved at a slow speed through my brain.

My body ignited to them, and I chased after the orgasm they induced.

"Parker," he grunted, tightening his hands around my waist painfully, and I came.

"Dallin!" I shook him frantically as I moaned to the ceiling. "Dallin!"

"Reyna?" He gasped, and I looked down at him to find his eyes finally open and confusion filling them. "What—?"

"Shut up," I cried, digging my nails into his pecs and rocking back and forth since he had stopped moving. "Stop talking and fuck me."

His body jerked underneath mine and then he thrust up into me, giving me what I needed as he moaned. "You're fucking soaked again, baby."

"I said, shut up," I huffed, groaning in desperation for that pleasure that only he could give me again.

"On your knees," he demanded, flipping me off him as I scrambled onto all fours. Before I was even settled, he slammed back into me and I screamed from the intensity of it.

Fuck the houseguests.

This was their fault, too.

"Yes!" I cried, clawing at the sheets for leverage to push back onto him with each punishing thrust. "Harder. Please, Dallin. Fuck me harder."

He growled behind me and pushed my knees wide as he lowered himself and started jackhammering into my body. It was punishing and on the edge of pain as his cock battered my cervix. But I deserved it.

I was fucking him like a slut because he'd brought two men into our home that dripped sex appeal and testosterone. They walked around without their shirts on and then he dared to moan one of their names while he fucked me in his sleep.

Fuck them all.

And fuck me too.

"This hard enough for you?" he bit out angrily before spanking my ass, peppering the skin with his hand until it burned like a bright orange flame.

"Yes!" I screamed, burying my face in the sheets until he grabbed a handful of hair and pulled my head back so I couldn't muffle the noises anymore. "Dallin! I'm coming. God, that feels so good."

"Good girl," he panted, and then groaned when I came around him until he roared my name as loudly as I had his.

I fell flat onto my stomach on the bed, gasping for breath as my head spun from everything that had happened in the last twelve hours. The veiled statements and half-truths spoken right in front of me swirled inside my brain like a tornado. Dallin collapsed next to me, staring at me like I was a ticking bomb he didn't know how to deactivate. "Don't look at me," I panted angrily, turning my face away from his.

"What the fuck was that about?" he asked, ignoring my attempt to stop the conversation from starting in the first place.

"Nothing."

"Bullshit," he growled. "Try again."

"I don't want to talk about it right now." I swallowed, closing my eyes and feeling the fatigue hit me again. "I want to sleep. We'll talk tomorrow."

"Rey—"

"No, Dallin," I snapped, and then sighed, disappointed in myself. Pieces of the puzzle were falling into place inside my head and the last picture terrified me. So I pretended not to see it. "Tomorrow. Just hold me tonight, and we'll talk tomorrow."

He was silent for a long time before he shifted, fixing the blankets, and pulled them over me. His lips pressed themselves against the back of my head before he pulled me onto my side against his chest. "I love you, Reyna."

His voice was sad, like that fact hurt him somehow. It cut me so deep.

"I know you do," I replied, as the first tear slid down my temple into the pillow under my head. "I love you, too."

CHAPTER 4

Parker

"What the fuck is wrong with you?" I barked as soon as the bedroom door closed behind me. Trey paced back and forth around the large room and only glared at me as he passed by each time. "Answer me, Trey."

"I don't know," he snapped angrily, throwing his hands up in the air.

"None of this is her fault," I reminded him, waiting for the logic inside his brain to take hold of his unchecked emotions.

"I know that," he groaned as he stopped pacing. He ran his hand over his face and then dropped it to his side. His shoulders deflated a bit, and I saw him for what he really was.

Hurt.

"She doesn't even know. He plans to tell her tomorrow." I looked at my watch. "Today. This morning." I groaned, trying to wrap my head around what time of day it was. I had been sleeping like the dead when Trey came in after his Broadway Street bar crawl. When I went to bed, I lay in the center of the giant king-size bed and stared at the ceiling, letting the events of the evening replay in my head until I was nearly dizzy from it.

I hadn't expected Dallin to do what I told him to do, but not even half an hour after they went off to their own room, I heard the first small noise of pleasure floating down the hallway. And then another, Reyna's sweet melodic voice filling my ears as Dallin fucked her, making her moan and beg for more. I knew she was trying to be quiet because she didn't want me to hear them, but I also knew how good it felt to get fucked by Dallin Kent's thick cock and she didn't stand a chance of being quiet if he wanted her to be loud. So I lay there and stroked my cock, listening to both of their cries of pleasure until all three of us came, and I wasn't the least bit ashamed of it.

And then I passed out and slept the hardest I had in . . . *years*.

When Dallin called me last week out of the blue, he said he wanted to see us. And introduce us to his girlfriend. At first, I'd been enraged that he would call us and expect us to drop everything to come to see him and the woman he chose over us, but then my common sense kicked in and I realized there was more to his request for a visit than just a friendly introduction. And then my wheels got spinning, imagining every worst- and best-case scenario until I couldn't take not knowing anymore, and I told Trey I was coming to Nashville.

With or without him.

I hated giving him that ultimatum, but I knew he was still hurt and angry with Dallin for leaving two years ago and wouldn't be on board for the visit. But I had to come.

I needed to see Dallin again and see the life he was building.

Without us.

With her.

I told myself on the entire ride to Nashville from the campground we'd been staying at in Oklahoma that it was for closure. Maybe if I saw him happy without us, I'd be able to finally move on.

But Dallin had made nothing easy on me one day in his life. So why would he start now?

I was sixteen years old the first time I realized I was sexually attracted to him. And it blew me over like a leaf in a tornado. It wasn't until years later, after a drunken night in Miami, that I acted on it.

I was worried he would cut me off and look at me differently for how I felt, but he'd surprised me when he reciprocated my feelings, just as strongly. We managed to hide it from Trey for all of two days before he walked in on Dallin, balls deep in my ass, in a sleazy motel one night. We both were sure Trey would duck out of our twenty-year friendship and never talk to us again.

Instead, he walked in, locked the door behind him, and let's just say, by the time the morning sun rose in the sky, we were all changed men. Then we found a type of balance in life that allowed us the freedom we wanted with women while maintaining a drama-free, open relationship among the three of us.

Until Dallin decided he wanted more, and Trey refused to commit.

"He should have told her before he ever picked the fucking phone up," Trey complained, pacing again before undoing his jeans and kicking them off. He threw himself down on his back in the center of the bed and stared at the ceiling as I had done earlier alone and sighed.

"You almost sound like you care for her feelings," I said accusingly, leaning my shoulder against the footpost of the bed. "Which makes little sense because you said you didn't even like her."

"I don't," he snapped, then groaned angrily. "She represents everything wrong with our arrangement."

"No, she doesn't." I got onto the bed and lay on my back on the pillows above him. "She represents everything we can't give him."

He scoffed. "Because that's so much better."

"It is, because it's not a competition, Trey."

"How the fuck do you figure?"

"It's like comparing football to baseball," I said, grimacing a bit at the analogy but rolling with it because I was dead-ass asleep ten minutes ago and it was the best I had. "We love both sports, and are big fans of them both, but one can't replace the other because we get different things out of it." He looked up at me with a look of disbelief, so I continued on. "We get violence and adrenaline with football. The team mentality, morale, and excitement, with a sense of camaraderie. And with baseball, we get the full process and individual skills expertly played out at a slower pace, but just as enjoyable."

"Let me guess, you and I are the dumb jocks banging their heads off each other over a pigskin, and Reyna is all elegant grace and brains."

I snorted and shrugged. "Well, when you put it that way, yeah."

"Great."

"Do you get what I'm saying, though?" I asked, wanting to make sure my point sank through his thick skull.

"Sure, we're two things he enjoys, but we'll never be able to replace the other." He sat up on the end of the bed. "And we'll also never get along in the same stadium."

"It's not just him, Trey." I groaned, hating how he was just seeing the negative. "She's the baseball for all of us, not just him."

"Right." He rolled his eyes, tapping his fingers on his thigh. "Because she's ever going to want to give herself to all of us, and in turn, let us fuck each other too." He stood up and took the tie out of his hair, shaking it free like a shampoo commercial. "You're smoking too much weed again, man, utopia doesn't exist for men like us."

I opened my mouth to tell him to fuck off when something caught my attention.

"Dallin!" Reyna's sweet voice made its way through the walls once again with a hint of pleasure at the end.

"Was that—?" Trey asked, with a slack jaw.

My cock twitched in my boxers, and I groaned. "Yep, round number two, apparently." We stayed quiet, waiting for another noise from the other end of the apartment when Dallin's voice carried through, followed by the aggressive slapping of skin. "Jesus fuck." I grabbed onto my cock and squeezed as Dallin spanked Reyna, making her cry out in pleasure. "Must be something got her worked up in that kitchen." I eyed him, getting my point across.

"Good girl, my ass," Trey complained with his hands on his hips as his own boxers started tenting in the front.

"Do you think he has her bent over?" I asked.

"I don't care."

"Yes, you do," I countered. "You know he loves fucking in doggie. And he's good at it, too." He groaned but didn't respond to my bait, so I pressed on, trying to force his hand. "I bet he's got her bent over. I bet he's got his knees spread wide so he can go hard."

As if on cue, Reyna begged for it harder.

"Fuck." Trey moved forward a foot but stopped, grabbing his dick and squeezing before dropping his hold on it as if it burned him. "I can't." He shook his head. "I can't listen to that."

"Come on." I pushed my boxers down and freed my cock, stroking up and down it as his eyes stared hungrily. "You know you want to do more than just listen to it."

His jaw clenched and his nostrils flared as war raged behind his blue eyes. He was torn and fighting his body on its response.

But he was losing.

"Come on, Trey." I pouted. "We both could use the release."

"*Good girl.*" Dallin praised Reyna, and Trey's eyes nearly crossed before he lunged at me, unable to fight it any longer.

He climbed up the bed and wrapped one hand around my cock and the other around my throat, pushing me down into the pillow as I hissed and bucked into his hand. The rings he wore on his right hand clashed against the four barbells pierced into the underside of my cock, ringing like a bell being sounded as he stroked me.

"Not a fucking sound," he commanded against my lips. "If you make one fucking peep, I'll make you regret it."

I smirked at him devilishly. "Whatever you say, big guy," I taunted.

I was bigger than him, but tonight he wanted to top, and I didn't care as long as I had sex.

"Feet on the floor," he ordered as he got off the bed and grabbed the lube from my bag, pushing his boxers down and finally freeing the beast inside. I slid off the bed, kicking my boxers off and bending over the tall mattress, presenting how he wanted me. I didn't bother looking back as he opened the lube and poured it onto my ass; chances are he was envisioning Dallin anyway, and I couldn't even be mad at that. Because I was envisioning how good it would feel to bend Reyna over like D had her, spanking her ass and making her beg for more as Trey pushed two fingers into me aggressively.

The lovebirds down the hall were getting even louder, building up to their big finish as Trey's cock pushed through the first ring of my ass. It burned like it always did, but I grabbed the lube from where he'd tossed it onto the bed, coated my hand, and stroked my cock in time with his as he started fucking me.

He wasn't gentle, hardly ever, but tonight was especially brutal.

"Quiet," he demanded, pushing my face down into the blankets when I grunted louder than I should have. "I warned you, Parker."

"Shut up and fuck me," I threw back at him, and was rewarded by him rotating his hips, burying deep inside me and stretching me out.

"Fuck," Trey grunted. "She's coming again."

Reyna screamed her orgasm out and I bit the blankets as Trey reached under me and covered my hand with his, stroking me harder and faster until I let go completely and just lay there, taking it all.

"Yes," I moaned, as his fingers ran over my balls and taint too. "I'm close."

"Me too," he growled, squeezing tighter. "You feel so fucking good, Park."

"Mmm. Don't you want to call me Dallin right now?" I teased, and then grunted when he changed angles and went harder. "Fuck. Fuck. Fuck. I'm coming, Trey."

"That's it," he hissed, biting my shoulder as his orgasm erupted the same second mine did. He slammed into me repeatedly, jerking my cock until I coated the hardwood floor between my feet and then sagged onto the mattress in exhaustion.

He pulled out and smacked my ass good-heartedly before grabbing a spare shirt from his dirty clothes bag and wiping himself off. He took care of me, and I threw myself up onto the bed, too dead-legged to do anything else.

"Thanks for that," I sassed him as it finally quieted down the hall as well.

"Don't fucking mention it." He rolled his eyes, refusing to joke with me.

Because as soon as the endorphins faded from his orgasm, his anger would return, and we'd be back to square one. But at least I'd be passed the fuck back out when that happened.

He got into bed after cleaning up the rest of the mess and lay on his back with his arm thrown over his head, silently stewing for a while before he finally spoke.

"How would it even work?" he asked uncharacteristically. Trey was always the one with the answers, but the whole thing was taking a toll on him. "What does a relationship between three men and a woman look like?"

"I don't know, Trey," I answered truthfully. "But I'll be honest with you and tell you that it probably looks a hell of a lot more enticing than what we're doing now."

"You want this?" He turned his head and looked at me as I forced my eyes to open back up.

"I want you," I admitted. "I want Dallin, that never stopped."

"And Reyna?" He sighed. "She's so . . ." He paused and looked back up at the ceiling. "Good."

I smirked into the darkness and closed my eyes again. "Think of how good it would feel to let her light shine into our darkness. And to maybe darken her up a bit too."

"I don't think Dallin could ever give her to us completely, though. How do you give a girl like that to someone else and not feel possessive of her?" He sighed again. "How do you just stand back after two years of solo time and watch another man, men like us, have her? With no say in what goes on."

"I think you have to trust those men," I replied. "I think you have to love those men just like you love that woman. But I don't know."

"Love," he grunted, shutting down with toxic masculinity and societal expectations. "I'm not capable of love."

If I were a lesser man, that statement would have hurt deep down in my chest. But I had been at Trey's side since third grade, and I knew he thought himself incapable of love. I also knew that he did love me, in his own way, even if he wasn't willing to put a label on it.

"Night, Trey," I said, rolling away from him and letting the comfort of the bed soothe the unease inside me. Sleep would heal it all, and tomorrow morning would look a lot different.

"Night," he mumbled, rolling onto his other side away from me.

CHAPTER 5

Dallin

Reyna grabbed her thermos of coffee off the counter with a small smile as I held the door open for her. She wore a burgundy pair of leggings that lifted her ass past mouthwatering levels and a matching sports bra. Her long dark hair with highlights of caramel was tied up in a fancy bun on top of her head, and her face was free of makeup as we left the house for our usual morning hike.

She wouldn't meet my eyes as we silently got out of bed and dressed to leave. I told myself it was because we were trying to be quiet, not to disturb Parker and Trey down the hall so they could sleep in. But I wasn't so sure.

As soon as we were done having sex in the middle of the night, she shut down, locking her emotions down so tight, I couldn't see them at all.

I'd woken up in the middle of a hot sex dream to Reyna riding my cock desperately, seeking pleasure. Normally, that'd be one hell of a way to wake up, but behind her desperation was something darker.

Something I hadn't seen in her before when I was inside her body.

Anger.

Maybe even a bit of guilt.

But above all of that was a whole lot of fear.

And then this morning, that shadow in her warm hazel eyes was back, leaving me on edge. Which didn't help, considering I was planning on ripping myself open to her in a way I'd never done with someone else before.

It reminded me of what Parker must have felt when we were young and he came out to me, admitting he was sexually attracted to me and confused by it.

Was he this nervous before he told me?

Did I do everything right to assure him and support him?

Besides fucking him raw for two days straight in some of the best sex of my life. While I had never exactly looked at Parker sexually before that moment, as soon as his words were out into the universe, they eased something inside me. His sexuality or gender didn't matter at that moment anymore, and neither did mine.

He was my best friend, along with Trey, and we had been each other's everything since we were kids. Feelings had grown and morphed over those years past platonic without me even realizing it, and as soon as I knew his true feelings, I just let mine have the freedom they deserved.

And it had been the start of something life-changing.

Until it stopped morphing and expanding with us when we grew and matured. It was like that part of our relationship was stuck in the same place that it had started when we were twenty years old. But we were a couple of thirty-something-year-olds and it didn't complete me the way I once thought it would.

And then I met Reyna.

My God, everything changed inside me that day, too.

"You're quiet," she said from the passenger seat as we neared the little-known trail up one of the mountains. It was our favorite hiking spot because it was quiet, no tourists knew about it, and locals were sparse around the area.

"I wasn't sure if you were ready to let me talk again." I gave her a tentative smile as I put her Jeep in park. "You told me to shut up more than once last night."

"I know." She looked down into her lap, where she picked at a hangnail on her hand. "Did you bring me up here to break up?"

"What?" I twisted my body toward her in shock. "Why would you ask that?"

She swallowed but wouldn't look over at me. "I feel this impending doom hanging over us right now." She let out a shuddering breath. "And it terrifies me."

"Hey." I slid my palm over her cheek, forcing her to look at me. I had to express my commitment to her as efficiently as possible, or she'd doubt it. So I went straight with honesty. "I want to spend the rest of my life with you, Reyna. I'll never leave you."

Her warm honey eyes flicked back and forth between mine in uncertainty. "Then why does it feel like you already have?"

"Because I have to tell you something about myself, that might feel like a betrayal to you." I sighed, dropping her face and leaning back against my headrest. "But I've been nothing but committed to you, and that's how I want to stay." I looked over at her. "Walk with me?"

She nodded and opened the door, sliding her body out onto the ground, waiting for me to grab my backpack of supplies and meet her there.

We headed up the trail in silence for a while, falling into a routine so easy it was muscle memory.

"Does it have to do with Parker and Trey?" she asked after a while.

I nodded and slid my fingers through hers, hoping she would let me touch her, and reveled in the way she tightened her hold on mine and leaned her head against my arm. "Yeah."

"I think I have an idea." She peeked up at me through her lashes, surprising me.

"You do?" I scowled down at her in confusion.

"Last night," she started, staring off down the trail. "When I, uh, woke you up." She chewed her bottom lip in trepidation and my heart stopped beating completely, expecting the worst from her. "When you were still asleep, you called out Parker's name." The air left my lungs in a whoosh of shock, but her fingers stayed tight between mine. She wasn't letting go. "If that had been the only thing to happen, I probably would have let it go. Maybe thought it was an accident or something." She swallowed audibly. "But with the tense comments made during dinner, and then the way Trey acted when he got in last night . . ." She faded off.

"You saw Trey last night?" I asked, then shook my head. "Wait, let's circle back to that. I want to explain everything to you first."

"Okay."

I took a deep breath and let her warm fingers in mine ground me. "When we were twenty years old, we were drunk one night after a day of partying on the beach in Miami, and Parker confessed he was attracted to me," I said. "Sexually." She peeked up at me but remained silent as I worked through it. "He was torn up about it and confused and it weighed so heavily on his shoulders, eating him up."

"Was he afraid you'd reject him?"

"Yeah." I nodded. "He thought our entire friendship would implode, and I'd cut him out of our circle."

"But you didn't," she replied.

"No." I sighed, remembering that day like it was yesterday. "The images that started flooding my head of him that way didn't repulse me." I shrugged. "I was a horny twenty-year-old and said, what the fuck, and told him we could try some stuff out and see where it went."

"And it went . . ." She dropped her head with her eyes locked on me, hoping I'd finish the sentence for her because she was that cute.

"Straight to bed." I gave her what she wanted. I smirked lightly, trying not to gloat about it but remembering it fondly. "We didn't get out for two days."

"Wow," she whispered, swallowing, facing forward as we walked while she tried to absorb that. "Did you—?" She stopped, and I watched as a blush crawled up her cheeks. "Does he—or do you—? You know," she stammered.

"Who got fucked and who did the fucking?" I probed, and she flushed even brighter with a groan. I smiled and kissed her hair, taking a deep breath that at least she wasn't running for the hills.

"Yeah."

"For a while, he was the bottom exclusively. But then we switched it up," I admitted. "And then when Trey joined in—" I shrugged, and she snapped her head up to me with her mouth hanging open.

"Trey?"

I raised an eyebrow at her in question, and she snapped her mouth shut and looked forward again. "Does that surprise you?"

"Yes," she answered instantly. "He seems so brutish and crass and not at all what I would expect in a gay lover."

"Bisexual." I coughed in shock. "None of us are exclusively into men, and I can't speak for them anymore, but I've never been with any others besides them. And until two years ago, neither had they. I don't know since then, but before that, it was just the three of us."

"Wow," she said again, taking a deep breath. "So you three were in a relationship for almost fifteen years, and then you just left them?"

"Ouch." I rubbed a spot on my chest that ached at her accusation.

"Sorry. I didn't mean it like that, I'm just trying to figure this out."

"I know." I squeezed her hand. "We weren't really in a relationship. It wasn't a big thing for any of us to label. We all rode together, traveling across the country and working at expos and pop-up shops. Sometimes we'd settle somewhere for a few months, working for a shop, but we were nomads. We all still hooked up with women when we wanted to, without judgment or fear of offending the others, and when the mood struck, we hooked up."

"All three of you?" She licked her lips before biting on her bottom one. "Together at the same time?"

"Sometimes." I watched her, observing the way her body was reacting to the news. "Sometimes I'd fuck Parker, sometimes I'd fuck Trey." Her breath caught in her throat and her fingers tightened around mine. "Sometimes Parker would fuck me, sometimes Trey would." Her nostrils flared as she stared off into the distance, completely unaware that I was watching her so closely. "Sometimes one of us would be in the middle, taking it and giving it at the same time."

"Jesus." She groaned, closing her eyes and panting.

I pulled her to a stop and then ushered her off the trail into a shaded clearing with a bench and sat her down.

"That turns you on," I said, not asking because it was obvious to me, even if it wasn't for her yet.

"I—" She stopped, looking up at me. "I don't know what it does to me. Tell me how we got here today and then I'll have a better answer for you."

"Fair." I smiled and leaned back against the bench, pulling her tight against my side so I could wrap my arm around her. "Two years ago, we came to a crossroads. I wanted more out of life than to just travel every day and continue the bachelor lifestyle we'd perfected for over a decade. Trey didn't. He loved being a nomad, chasing the sunset wherever he wanted without worrying about mortgages or electricity bills. He loved being free." She looked up at me, waiting for more. "And I wasn't satisfied with them and a random woman from a different town each night. I wanted more, but not with strangers anymore."

"You wanted a woman," she repeated, like she was trying to clarify.

"I wanted a relationship." I tried to explain it. "The nomad life wasn't for me, and having them wasn't enough anymore, either. I begged them to join me in Nashville. I begged them to try it out for a while, to see what we could make of it." The feeling of that same pain from years ago burned in my chest. "But Trey wouldn't even try. I didn't mean enough to him for him to try."

"Dallin." She crawled onto my lap, holding my face in both hands. "I don't think that's true."

"It is." I wrapped my hands around her waist and pulled her flush to me. "Parker was torn, trying to figure out what to do to keep us all together, but in the end, he followed Trey. I think he was afraid that if he didn't follow him, Trey would disappear forever. He knew where I would be, so he went to keep tabs on Trey. I tried to let it go and move on, but I was miserable. For months." I slid my hand around the side of her face. "Until I met you."

"I had no idea you were grieving such a loss when we met."

"I didn't want you to," I admitted. "I wanted to pretend that the entire thing never happened. And it was easy to do because I felt something for you I'd never felt before."

"What?"

"An instant connection." I kissed her nose. "My relationship with the guys evolved slowly over time, leaving me unable to pinpoint the moment that I knew they were mine. But with you, it was like the moment you looked up at me when I slid in next to you at that bar, scaring off the creep that wouldn't leave you alone, you were mine." Her eyes closed, and she leaned into me. "And I was yours."

"But your heart belongs to them." She shook her head, trying to wrap it around everything. "How can you love me when you still love them?" I opened my mouth, but she cut me off. "Don't try to tell me you don't love them, Dallin. I see you. I feel you." She put her hand on my heart with sadness in her eyes. "I don't own you like you do me. I never will."

"You're wrong." I shook her. "Maybe it's because you've only experienced monogamy or maybe it's something else, but my heart doesn't feel torn between you three. It feels like I gave each of you a piece of it and it's not complete without the three pieces put back together." I stared at her as her eyes rounded. "Like I'm not whole without all three pieces."

"What does that mean, then?" she cried, working herself up for what she thought was heartbreak. "Am I supposed to just let you go simply because on my own I'm not enough for you?"

"Shh." I tried soothing her, but she tore out of my arms and paced the dirt clearing in front of me. "Reyna, I already told you, I'm never letting you go."

"It feels like it." She ran her hand over her chest. "In here. It really fricking feels like it."

I stood up and stopped her from pacing, forcing her to stare up at me and focus. "I want you. And I want us all to be together."

"I don't understand." She blinked.

"I want you to let them into your heart, just as you've done for me." Her eyes rounded and her mouth hung open. "This isn't about you losing something or having to give me up to them. I'm asking you to give yourself to them. I'm asking you to be with all of us, together."

Her eyes jumped back and forth between mine like her brain was shorting out. "Why would they possibly want to be with me?"

I let out a breath and smiled down at the woman who had taught me so much about myself, who clearly knew nothing about herself. "Because you're the most incredible person I've ever met before. You're breathtaking beautiful and heart-*stopping*-ly sexy."

She rolled her eyes and groaned, pulling back from me. "You're delusional." She shook her head. "Trey hates me. There's not a single situation in the entire world where he'd be interested in me." I smirked at her, and she huffed, putting her hands on her hips. "There's not!"

"I haven't discussed it with him yet, so I won't lie and tell you what he admits to feeling. But I know Trey." I pulled her back to me and forced her to wrap her arms around my waist so I could hold her. "I know that bad-guy act is just something he puts out when he's scared. And I know you may be far better than any of us deserve, but I also know you're what we dream of and need." I pressed my body into her, so she could feel what this conversation had done to me. "And I know, without a doubt, that Trey and Parker are both physically attracted to you. You just have to decide if you're attracted to them and if you would want to be with all three of us."

"And if I don't?" she asked, staring up at me. "If I said it was all too much and I couldn't survive that kind of relationship? What would you do?"

"I'd spend the rest of my life with you, happy and in love with you, no different from today," I admitted honestly.

"But you'd never be complete," she whispered. "You'd never be whole without them."

I sighed. "No, I don't think I would be. But I'd survive. The difference is, I wouldn't survive without you."

"I don't know what to say," she confessed. "I don't know what to do."

"That's fair, baby." Kissing her forehead, I held her as she clung to me. "I'm not asking you for declarations and promises today. I just ask that you think about it."

"Okay." She sighed and wrapped her arms tighter around my waist. "I promise you I'll think about it."

We stayed like that for a while before I pulled her onto the trail to finish our hike, and I let her stay in silence as she thought over everything. I wanted her to choose the pace that we talked about it.

A while down the trail, she gave in and broke the silence again. "I'm attracted to them."

She said it like she was confessing to murder in the middle of a police station and was expecting to be punished for it.

"They're good-looking men," I replied with a smile, as hope bloomed in my chest.

"They look like you." She looked up under her lashes at me before taking my hand and squeezing it. "I was never attracted to the bad-boy type until I met you. So it's your fault."

I snorted and nodded. "I accept the blame for that."

She gave me a little smirk and then sighed. "Last night I woke up and went to make some tea. But Trey was in the kitchen, I think he had just gotten in."

"Okay." I waited for her to say the rest of what was weighing on her.

"He said he had met a thousand women like me and that he knew I couldn't handle him." She raised her eyebrows. "I obviously didn't know what he was talking about at that moment, but I didn't need to. Parker came out of the spare room and made Trey go to bed before we could finish the conversation."

"He's—" I paused. "Trey's closed off to most people. He doesn't open up easily. He uses anger and meanness to protect himself."

"Classic dark and brooding male main character." She rolled her eyes. "I get that, and I told him that. Which is why he told me I couldn't handle him in the first place." She looked up at me and stopped walking. "I don't want him to make me feel like I'm not good enough." She licked her lips and swallowed. "I know that may sound stupid and juvenile, but I'm almost thirty years old, in a committed relationship with a man I want to spend the rest of my life with. I don't think I want to go backward to a place where a man can make me question my self-worth." She flung her arms out dramatically. "And that guy is exactly the type of man to do that, simply to keep everyone at arm's length."

"But if you know that he's going to be difficult going in, and you have not one, but two other men absolutely smitten with you while he gets his head out of his ass"—I smirked devilishly—"can't you at least admit it's tempting?"

She groaned and kicked her toe into the dirt. "Tempting doesn't begin to describe the appeal here, Dallin." She peeked up at me again. "I came into our room and jumped your cock like that last night *because* I was tempted," she admitted, and my brows rose in intrigue. "Trey was shirtless, and all broken and dark, exactly how the hopeless romantic in me wants to fix and heal him. And Parker came out to save the day all rumpled and sexy in a pair of tight boxers and I—" She groaned again. "I was fucking turned on by them."

She hardly ever swore, so hearing her do it when talking about Parker and Trey excited me even more than her describing how hot they got her.

"So let me get this straight." I put a hand on her hip and pushed her off the trail until her back pressed against a tree and then caged her in. "You sparred with Trey, and were rescued by Parker, and you came in and rode my cock with your dripping pussy to get off because all of it aroused you. And you still think it wouldn't work out?"

She tipped her head back and huffed again in frustration as her body and her head went to war. "Yes."

"I'll tell you what," I said, pressing my hips forward and rubbing my once again hardening cock against her belly before lifting her so she wrapped her legs around me and pinned her to the tree. "In the shop last night after Trey left, I admitted to Parker what I wanted to happen between the four of us." Her eyes rounded and her nostrils flared as I pressed against her pussy, rocking into her to arouse her even more. "He wants you." I closed my eyes and laid my forehead against hers. "God, does he want you, baby. And you have no idea how fucking hot that makes me."

"Dallin," she panted, digging her nails into my neck.

"He told me when I fucked you last night to do it good so he could hear you moan and beg for it."

"Fuck." Her eyelids fluttered closed as I kept on.

"And when I had you bent over at three a.m., drilling my cock into this perfect fucking pussy, I was imagining what it would look like to do that with Parker laid out in front of you, with his cock down your throat." I lifted one hand to her neck and squeezed, drawing another perfect moan from her lips. "I want to screw you so hard your body rocks forward onto his cock, giving you no choice but to take us both. The image of that fucking does something to me, Reyna. It makes me feral."

"Fuck me," she gasped, clawing at my shirt as she rocked against me. "Right now."

"Here?" I asked, looking around. We'd seen a few other hikers on the way up, but none for quite a while. "You want to take my cock where someone might see you?" I thrust against her. "Hear you?"

"Yes." She nodded eagerly. "You've had me so twisted up the last twenty-four hours, I'm desperate."

"I can't have that." Kissing my way up her neck, I lifted her off the tree, walking farther into the woods for a more private spot. I was okay with sharing her with Trey and Parker, but not with anyone else. No one got to see my girl like this but us. I dropped her to her feet and pulled her leggings down as she kissed my lips, biting on them in desperation. "Turn around and hold on, love."

She flipped around and gripped the tree as I pulled her hips back, popping her lush ass out for me. "Please, Dallin," she begged. "I'm so warped in the head, but I'm fucking desperate for it."

"I got you, baby," I purred against her back as I lined my aching cock up and pushed in deep. I had to crouch behind her to get the angle right, but I'd gladly take the cramps in my hamstrings to give my girl what she wanted after a morning like this. "You're dripping wet, never once in our two years together have you been as wet as you've been the last three times I've fucked you."

"Yes," she moaned, pushing back against me. "Oh my God, D." She rolled her neck and moaned as I took her hard.

"Tell me what you're thinking about," I growled into her ear as I reached around and circled her clit.

"No." She shook her head deliriously. "I can't."

"Tell me," I growled, firmer, biting her shoulder to entice her to give me what I wanted. I needed to know what was on her mind. What she was fantasizing about while I fucked her body. I hoped it was about the guys, that they were somewhere in her brain, leading her toward pleasure even without being here. "I need it."

"You," she gasped, digging her nails into my arm where it was buried between her legs, rolling her clit exactly how she liked. "I'm envisioning you, laid out on your stomach, with Parker behind you." She moaned, shaking her head. "Oh my God."

"You're fantasizing about me getting fucked?" I asked, swelling even more inside her. It was so fucking hot to have both sides of my sex life combining right in front of my eyes. "You're thinking about watching Parker give it to me?"

"Yes," she cried. "Do you have any idea how hot you two are? Seeing your bodies together." She moaned and then seized up around me. "I'm coming."

"Good girl." I praised her as she came. "Name the time and place and I'll give you that. I'll make every one of your fantasies come true."

"I didn't even know it was a fantasy of mine until today." She groaned. "And now I'm rabid for it."

I slowed my thrusts down, reaching up and sliding her bra up to expose her large breasts to my hands. "Close your eyes and think about something else for me."

"What?" she whispered, doing it as I played with her body in broad daylight.

"Imagine your pretty legs spread wide in the bed next to us, lying right next to me as Parker fucks me."

"Fuck," she whimpered, tightening around my cock.

"Now imagine looking down your body." I licked my way up her neck and to her ear, nibbling on her lobe as she obeyed me. "With your head tipped back in ecstasy. Your fingers tangled in long dark hair as Trey licks his way up your sweet pussy."

"Dallin." She groaned, shivering in my arms as I pressed her to imagine the man she was convinced didn't want her.

"His fingers are so long, buried deep inside you while he sucks on your clit as you ride his face." She mewed and her legs weakened under her. But I was right there to support her and hold her up as she gave in to desire. "You're going to cream on his face before he crawls up your body and lines his thick cock up with your pussy." I bit her neck, sucking it into my mouth as she purred in my hands, liquid heat coating my cock as she neared another orgasm. "His cock is so thick, baby. Not as long as mine, but so fucking thick. It's going to feel like he's in your chest with how far he's going to stretch you to bury himself in deep."

"Please," she begged, reaching over her shoulder to dig her fingers into my hair, pulling it tight as she fought for control.

"He's going to slam into you, he's not gentle, but you'll never want him to be. You're going to beg for his intensity as he fucks you. I'm right there too," I promise, grounding her. "Parker and I are right there, touching you and kissing you while you take Trey's cock for the first time."

"I can't," she gasped, shaking her head back and forth. "I'm not supposed to want to."

"I want you to," I growled. "I want you to spread your pretty thighs anytime one of them tells you to. I want you to constantly have a cock or a mouth on your sweet little pussy, dragging orgasm after orgasm out of you. I want you to use us all for your pleasure."

"Yes!" she screamed, biting my hand as I covered her mouth so hard, she drew blood from my palm. "Oh . . . my . . . God."

"I want to worship you," I growled, nearing my orgasm, unable to hold off any longer. "I want you to let us all worship you."

"Please." She sagged against the tree as I filled her up. "God," she moaned as I pulled free of her body and laid my forehead against the back of her head, panting.

"You're so fucking perfect, Reyna." I sighed, sliding her leggings up as she fixed her bra, so no one got a free show after the ecstasy wore off.

She turned and leaned against my chest with a small smile of contentment on her face. "I'm deranged in the head," she joked. "But it sounds like you like it, so I guess we'll go with it."

I kissed her forehead and then her lips, softening against her as she melted into my arms. "I more than just like it, baby," I assured her. "Let's get home so I can feed you and clean you up."

"Hmm," she said, "I like the sound of that."

CHAPTER 6

Reyna

I held Dallin's hand in my lap as we drove through town back to our home. My brain was whirling around inside my head, even as my body was relaxed and sated.

Dallin was bisexual.

And polyamorous.

And wonderful.

And loving.

And tender.

And terrifying.

And far more experienced than I was.

And I didn't know what the fuck to do with my hands.

Literally, now, and in every scenario that had played out in my head since he told me his secret, I didn't know what I was expected to do with my hands with so many more partners joining the fun.

Obviously, that was hypothetically speaking, because nothing was going to happen this second. Dallin had told me and the guys what he wanted out of this, and it sounded like Trey refused and Parker was on board but hesitant.

And I was . . . also on board, but hesitant. I loved Dallin, with every single thing inside me, and I was experienced enough through my work as a romance author and the extensive research I'd done over the years for that to know there were relationships out there that looked like the one Dallin was trying to build.

But I also knew there was a high level of skepticism and judgment against people in polyamorous relationships, every single day.

Was that something I wanted to face? I didn't know.

Nashville was a party town, bringing in tourists from every walk of life for its fun atmosphere and exciting adventures, but it was also a southern town that sometimes had small-minded opinions as well.

And we were opening ourselves up for that judgment if we were to build a relationship that had four different sides to it, instead of two.

Luckily, our friends were all open-minded and inclusive of all sorts of orientations. Most of our friends were from the tattoo shop that Dallin owned, or our friends that we rode motorcycles with, so they were just naturally more laid back and loving of all sorts of people.

But still.

What a mind trip.

"I'm not ready to just jump in," I said when we neared our underground parking garage. "I need time to get to know them personally. And you need to talk to them and find out if they're on board or not. I don't want to get invested in something and have them ride off into the sunset with no warning."

"That's fair," Dallin agreed, squeezing my hand on my lap. "Parker texted me a little while ago and said they were headed out for lunch. Maybe I'll go meet them and have a chat."

"Okay." I nodded as more thoughts swirled around inside. "What about sex?"

"What do you mean?" He looked over at me and I was sidelined by how heartbreakingly sexy he was. He wore a pair of shorts and a cutoff T-shirt, with a hat on backward and sunglasses on; he had that powerful man stance with one hand on the top of the steering wheel and one buried between my thighs holding my hand. And it was unfair how easily he made it all look.

"Are you going to—" I swallowed audibly. "Do you want to—with them?"

"Fuck, baby." He looked over at me as we came to a red light. "Say the word *fuck*." I rolled my eyes and groaned. "It's a natural thing."

"I know that. But I've never talked to you about it in the context of you *fucking* other men before. Or anyone, for that matter, since we got together."

"We are together in this endeavor, Reyna. I'm not going to just go out and fuck someone else, male or female, without it being an exclusive thing between us all."

I sagged into my seat, relieved that he would not sleep with them yet. "Okay, good." I watched traffic pass us as we took off again. "But you want to, don't you?" I looked up at him and saw his jaw clench.

He nodded, looking over at me and answering truthfully. "Yeah, baby. I want to."

"You enjoy being a bottom?" I hesitated only briefly on the word, and he smirked. "As much as you like topping?" I struggled to envision him underneath either of his friends because I had only ever known him as the dominant in our relationship. But when I got a flash of what it would look like to see him bottom, my entire body tingled with excitement.

"Sometimes." He shrugged, watching traffic. "I'm more comfortable being a top, but I enjoy taking it as well. The situation just has to be right."

"What does that mean? Right?"

"It means I have to be so fucking horny I'd fuck a light post before I willingly fall onto my knees and submit. I can't just lie down for anyone at any given moment, I need the workup to get me crazed for it, and then I'll take a cock like one of the best out there." I groaned, clenching my thighs as his crude words zapped straight to my clit. "I will admit, I'm a little nervous by the idea of getting fucked again, though, because it's been so long."

"Will you prep?" I kept my eyes forward because I was a hair trigger away from mounting him right there in the front seat from the effect this entire revelation had been having on me. "Like I did when we started doing anal?"

"Maybe." He put the Jeep in park and looked over at me. "Are you offering to help me get ready to be fucked?"

"Jesus, Mary, and Joseph," I whispered, fanning myself. "Dallin. You can't say things like that." I glared at him.

"Why not?"

"Because I'm going to combust into ash. And I'll be really mad if I die before I get to see you with another man."

"Fuck." Now it was his turn to grunt and groan. He reached down with his free hand and adjusted his thickening cock while he watched me. "Fair point."

"Thank you." I smiled softly. "For being honest."

"That's all I'm ever going to be with you." He lifted our hands to his lips and kissed my knuckles. "I promise you, I'm in it for life with you, baby. I just hope to add to our happy life, not separate and categorize it."

I thought that over for a second. "I like that analogy. I understand it all a bit better that way."

"Good. Because you're stuck with me either way." He lifted his sunglasses off and winked at me with his sexy playboy grin.

"Well, when you put it that way." I rolled my eyes and got out of the Jeep.

I sat at my desk in the quiet apartment and stared at my blank computer screen. I was halfway through writing a contemporary romance about a woman who moved to a new town and met the grumpy neighbor next door, but I just didn't have the spark to finish it anymore.

Not when the story I had been crafting felt dull compared to the real-life porno that had been playing on repeat in my brain since Parker and Trey showed up last night.

Suddenly, cutesy romantic comedic banter wasn't doing it for me.

I needed dirty, raw passion to expel some of the building tension inside my own body.

I closed that in-progress book and opened a blank document. I stared at the blinking cursor as I chewed on my bottom lip in trepidation.

Dallin was meeting up with Parker and Trey at a biker bar down the street, and my mind was running rampant, wondering what they were talking about.

What they were deciding.

I felt like I should be there, but I couldn't bring myself to face the awkwardness of that endeavor.

The sexiness of it.

The animalistic excitement of it.

So instead I pushed my fingers down on my keyboard and forced myself to let my creativity set the course and wrote unfiltered and unchecked.

I knew I'd never show it to anyone, not even my agent.

But I had to get the energy building inside me out somehow, and since there wasn't a hard dick laid out before me to ride . . . this was going to have to do.

I typed feverishly, letting the characters build their own world and relationships as the words flew out onto the paper.

I lost myself to the craft and when my phone went off next to my keyboard, it startled me enough to realize I'd been at it for hours. Four hours, to be exact. And Dallin still wasn't back.

I opened the message app and saw a simple text from him.

Meet us for drinks at Lou's in an hour. Wear something sexy.

Lou's was our favorite place for drinks and dinner; it was off the beaten path and gave off hole-in-the-wall vibes. Which was perfect for our taste.

But going there in something sexy . . . could be trouble.

The crowd was rough, and that made me wonder why Dallin wanted to start trouble.

Was it because he had his two best friends standing next to him? Or was it because he wanted to start trouble with them specifically?

I took a shaky breath, feeling anxious about seeing them face to face after finding everything out, but luckily, Dallin gave me less than enough time to stand around worrying about all of that. I had to shower and get ready if I had a prayer of being there in an hour. Excitement rose in my gut as I thought about what the rest of the evening would look like until I had to get moving.

The first thing I did was order an Uber for five minutes before I was supposed to be there and then ran off to the shower.

I needed to shave.

Everything.

CHAPTER 7

Trey

"This was a mistake," I complained into my whiskey glass. Parker sat across from me at the high top in the back of a crowded biker bar where we waited for Dallin.

One perk to being in the busy Nashville area was that bars opened early for the tourist crowd that was always ready for a drink.

"No, it's not, and you know it," he replied, deadpan.

"Do you really think she was okay with it?" I snapped. "Seriously? Because if you do, you're as dumb as you look."

"Knock it off." He leveled me with a stare. "You're anxious, and on edge, and I get it, but I'm not your punching bag."

"What I am is ready to hit the road again."

"Then you're on your own," he said, leaning back on his stool and motioning to the door. "Because I'm not leaving until I hear what happened up on that trail. I'm sticking around to see what is really offered here."

I shook my head and grumbled under my breath that the only thing Dallin Kent ever offered was betrayal, but Parker ignored me.

He was right, of course.

I was on edge and anxious, taking it out on him, the only person to ever have my back day in and day out. And that wasn't fair.

But it felt like he was getting ready to jump ship too, just like everyone else, and it pissed me off. It pissed me off that Dallin and Reyna were going to be stealing my best friend from me.

I was leaving. No questions asked, and when I did, Parker was going to stay.

I fucking knew it.

And that pissed me off.

"Here he is," Parker said, raising his bottle and catching Dallin's attention where he stood by the door. "Be on your best behavior or I'll kick your ass so hard you can't ride and have no choice but to stay in town for months."

"Hmm," I grumped, but didn't have time to say anything else as Dallin walked up, sliding his black jacket off his arms and throwing it over the back of an empty chair.

Did the man have to look so fucking good, though? It was rude.

And unnecessary.

"Hey," he said, taking a seat between me and Parker at the square table. "Thanks for the invite."

"No problem." Parker smacked him on the shoulder. "Want a beer?"

"Yeah, that'd be great," Dallin said, looking over at my whiskey glass as I tipped it back, draining it.

The waitress ran over when Parker got her attention and eagerly took his order for another round of beers.

"And another double." I raised my glass to her, and she nodded before running to the bar.

"Hitting it pretty hard for noon," Dallin acknowledged, but I didn't respond. Because, of course, the fucker was right, *and* the cause of my need for liquor at noon.

"So." Parker drew the attention to his side of the table as he looked Dallin up and down. "You're alive. And I don't see any cougar scratches chewing up your pretty face."

Dallin smirked, taking a drink from his beer that had arrived at lightning speed. "Nah, I'm whole. Thank you." He smiled at the waitress and then took another pull off his bottle as she settled the drinks around the table before scurrying off to help other customers.

"Don't leave us hanging, man," Parker groaned, staring at him pointedly.

"She took it—" He shrugged with a smirk on his face that I hated. "Surprisingly well."

"Really?" Parker asked with his brows raised before looking over at me. "All of it?"

"Yeah," Dallin sighed. "She thought I was taking her up there to break up with her, actually. And then when I told her I had been keeping a part of myself from her, she asked if it had to do with you guys and that she was getting an idea that something else was going on."

"And what did you tell her, exactly?" I demanded with a glare. The second Dallin's eyes met mine, my shoulders instantly relaxed. My body allowed history to overpower current affairs and my head was battling for control. I didn't want to just give in to what used to be.

But then again, I did, at the same time.

Fuck, I needed another drink.

"I told her everything." He held my gaze, letting his dominance shine through while keeping it calm and gentle. That was always Dallin's special power; he was alpha, but he did it in a way that left you feeling like you had a choice in the matter when, in reality, you were a goner the first fucking time he looked at you. "I told her about Parker admitting his feelings first, and how we spent those first days following that. I told her how we found a comfortable routine in life with the three of us, taking on different towns and enjoying freedom with other women. I told her how even though I was happy with things for the most part, I never felt like every piece of my puzzle was together. And how I came to Nashville in hopes that you two would come with me and we'd find that other piece, that I think we all were without, not just me."

"Did you tell her what you said to me at the shop?" Parker probed, drawing Dallin's gray eyes to him.

"I did." Dallin nodded. "I told her I wanted the four of us to be together, equally. I want us all to be committed and happy and move on from the hurt in the past."

"That you caused," I reminded him firmly.

"Knock it off," Parker snapped, but Dallin put his hand on his forearm.

"It's okay." Dallin nodded to me. "I admit I caused the rift two years ago." He took a deep breath, and I stopped breathing altogether. "I left you guys. And I understand why that hurt. But I didn't do it because I wasn't committed to you and what we had. I thought you'd come with me." He sighed, dropping his shoulders as he looked over to Park and then back to me. "I honestly thought you'd come with me."

"But we didn't, and you still rode away," I prompted him.

"And I got my life together here, setting up something that all three of us could build together, and then I reached out." His eyes widened as he leaned forward on the table. "I didn't call empty-handed, Trey; I'm here." He spread his arms wide. "I'm ready and offering not only myself but this life I've built here. For all of us."

"Reyna's in?" Parker asked like he didn't quite believe it. "She said that?"

Dallin dipped his head and smirked into his beer with his playboy grin. "She said she wants to get to know you both before she agrees to it. But she's—" His grin widened. "Into the idea of it."

Parker smirked, looking over at me and then back to Dallin. "Well, now you have to elaborate on that."

Dallin took a pull of his beer and laced his fingers together around the bottle, relaxed and in charge. I hated his ability to take charge so effortlessly when I always felt like I had to fight for control of everything.

"She told me about your sparring match in the kitchen last night." He stared at me. "And how worked up she got from it, both from the verbal competition and the view while she did it." He nodded to my chest with an eyebrow raised, but I remained silent. "And then how you swooped in and played the knight in shining armor, saving her from the big bad wolf." He looked over at Parker with a wink. "And the view you gave her at the same time." He leaned back on his stool and took a deep breath. "She came into our room after that and woke me up by blowing me hard before climbing on and riding me while I was still asleep. She orgasmed when I called out Parker's name."

"No way," Parker said, slapping his hand on the table with a shit-eating grin on his face. He fucking loved being the center of attention.

"I didn't know I did it; when I finally woke up all the way, she told me to shut the fuck up and rode me like her life depended on it. So when we were on our hike, she admitted why she was so horny last night." He nodded and kept going. "I told her how when I was fucking her last night, I was envisioning her sucking you off at the same time. She couldn't hold it in anymore and begged me to fuck her right there on the trail, which, of course, I did."

"Fuck, man." Parker groaned, shaking his head. "She got off on the idea of being spit-roasted?"

"Shot off like a cannon," he joked before looking over at me. His smile fell and a serious look covered his features. "Want to know what had her coating my cock the most, though?"

"I think you'll tell me even if I don't," I said, even though I was desperate to know what made Reyna tick and cream. Licking my lips, I could not resist the urge to prod Dallin even more. I was hard as a fucking rock in my jeans, and I needed relief, but I was going to let him torture me more, for even a small glimpse into his perfect little sex life with his perfect little girlfriend.

"I asked her what she was thinking about today while I was giving it to her. She didn't want to admit it at first but finally told me she was imagining me laid out on my stomach, taking it from the back by Parker."

"You're killing me, man." Parker reached under the table to adjust himself as he took a long swig of his beer. The bar was so busy and loud no one could hear what we were saying, but talking so freely was like catnip to a couple of hungry tomcats.

And Parker and I were starving.

"I told her I'd give her that anytime she wanted, under one condition: that she lay her pretty thighs open for you to fuck her hard at the same time." He stared right at me like he was daring me to be unaffected by his words. "She came the hardest she's ever come in two years."

"Damn, man." Parker grinned, looking across the table at me. "I knew she'd be hot for the moody shit you threw at her."

"Women always want what they can't have," I deadpanned, staring straight at Dallin. "Doesn't mean they get it."

I tossed back the rest of my drink and tapped the table like I was done.

"Don't you dare walk away right now, Trey," Dallin demanded, breaking from the relaxed and happy attitude he'd had since he walked in, and sliding into the dominating asshole I knew he could be. "That's the one holdup Rey has in this whole fucking thing." He pointed his finger at me. "She doesn't want you to make her feel like she isn't good enough, or to walk away after she invests time into you. She's too fucking good for any of us, let alone you, to just fuck over like that, and she knows it."

"Then why bother?" I snapped back, leaning over the corner of the table, challenging him. "Why even fucking risk it?"

"Because you're worth it," he replied instantly, knocking me back a foot. I wasn't expecting him to say something like that, and he kept going. "Because I've needed you both since I was a teenager, and I'm tired of being half a man without you."

I squinted at him, desperately searching for a tell or a twitch on his face to prove he was lying, but there was nothing there.

Just raw honesty.

And I think I hated that more than if he had just lied to me.

"I have to go." I threw my leg over the stool and stood up, desperate to get away from the intensity of his gaze as something cracked in my chest where my heart used to beat. "I can't be here."

"You can't keep running from it." Parker challenged me with his softer gaze, but a fire still burned behind his brown eyes. "We haven't been whole either since he left, and you know that."

"I haven't been whole a day in my life," I snapped back, grabbing a couple of twenties from my wallet and throwing them on the table. "Don't wait up, Mom," I said to Parker as I pushed past the crowd and left the bar. My bike called to me like a drug, so I obliged, throwing my leg over the seat and dodging downtown Nashville traffic, taking alleyways and side streets until the highway opened up in front of me.

As I drove away from it all, leaving Dallin, Reyna, and Nashville in my dust, I also left Parker behind.

But it had to be done. Because I couldn't get on board with the picket fence life, and apparently, I was the only one standing in the way for the rest of them.

So fuck it.

I'd remove myself from the equation and let them all have their happily ever after.

Fuck 'em.

CHAPTER 8

Parker

"She should be here soon, right?" I asked anxiously as I looked at the front door.

Dallin chuckled lightly and checked his watch. "The hour I gave her expires in three minutes." He dropped his wrist and shrugged. "She's never disobeyed me before."

I grinned and rolled my shoulders. My body felt conflicted, as it fought the urge to chase after Trey and stay put in my chair at the new bar Dallin and I had come to, which was a favorite of Reyna's. I cared for Trey and the relationship we had built over the last twenty years, but I *needed* to see Reyna in the flesh now that she knew the truth about me.

About all of us.

Dallin told us what they had talked about, and how she had reacted to the news, the way her body ignited as she imagined it all, and I needed to see it through.

I needed to see if the connection between us could be as strong as the buildup had been. Her long dark hair, lush curves, sweet cupid's-bow lips, and the innocent look in her bright hazel eyes physically attracted me.

Eyes so bright, they reminded me of Trey.

Fuck.

I'd called him twice since he stormed out of the bar earlier, but he didn't answer.

Go figure.

I hoped he would ride off his frustration and come back, but it was anyone's guess with him. Chances were, he'd ride for a few days before he called, just to give me enough time to worry about him before he returned.

He always said I was an attention whore, but the man knew how to keep everyone thinking about him long after he left.

And not just sexually, because he could do that effortlessly.

"Here she comes," Dallin said, nudging me with his elbow and drawing my eyes back to the door.

And my God, did she fucking come.

Reyna's hair was loose in waves that fell to below her breasts, and a bright red lipstick covered those lips that I'd imagined wrapped around my cock more times than I cared to admit. Dark makeup circled her eyes, making them pop seductively, but it all paled compared to the sexy black dress she wore.

It was tight around her breasts, hugging them as two large hands should be, and then flared around her waist, flowing femininely to the tops of her thighs. She was breathtaking.

And blushing.

She approached our table, her cheeks and the swell of her cleavage tinted pink. She stared at Dallin but gave me shy glances as she pushed her hair behind her ear.

"You passed the test." Dallin grinned at her as he stood up from his stool and leaned down to kiss her. I sat back on my stool with a smirk on my face as he slid his hand into her hair and tightened it into a fist, pulling on it until her head tipped back obediently as she looked up at him. "You're stunning, Rey," he told her, and her body melted further into his. It was magical to watch him work her body and mind over in the way only a longtime lover could master.

It was something I never cared for before because I hardly ever slept with the same woman twice. But seeing them together, moving as one like a well-rehearsed dance, made me long for something similar.

"Thank you," she whispered, smiling up at him as he released her hair and smoothed his fingers through the long locks. I wondered if they were as silky as they looked.

"Now be a good girl and go give Parker a hug for me." Dallin replied next.

As she flicked her hazel eyes over to where I sat leaning back in my seat with my beer bottle in my hand, I felt surprised but didn't show it. Her ruby-red lips parted in bewilderment before she looked back to Dallin for reassurance. He nodded toward me and slid his hand against the small of her back, directing her around the table.

I stood up off my stool as she neared and nearly fell into the deepness of her uncertain hazel eyes as she stared up at me. She sucked her bottom lip between her teeth and nibbled on it.

"Hi," I said, trying to break the ice. I had never been nervous around a woman before, yet with Reyna, I felt like a teenager all over again. "You're the most beautiful woman in the entire place tonight."

The blush deepened on her cheeks and her smile grew. "Thank you, Parker," she replied as I slid my hand around her waist and dragged her against my chest, barely restraining the sigh that tried to escape when I caught the delicious scent of her perfume. Her breasts pressed against my abs as her delicate hands tentatively slid over my shoulders.

The urge to press my lips to hers as I lowered my face against her cheek was nearly too much to contain, but I did. I knew she wanted to go slow and take her time getting to know us, so I pressed my cheek against her hair and gave her a tight hug. I lingered slightly when she took a deep breath against my neck before allowing her to slide back down to her heels and take a step back.

I looked over her head and locked eyes with Dallin's heated ones as he watched me touch his girl. He was almost vibrating with excitement as he winked at me and then pulled her chair out between us at the round table. I didn't miss the way he slid his stool and hers both closer to my side, tucking us all into the corner of the dim bar behind the table.

"Can I get you a drink?" I asked her, as she arranged herself on the stool, crossing her legs at the knee and revealing even more of her thighs to my hungry eyes.

"Yes." She swallowed, looking up at me. "A blackberry margarita would be lovely, thank you."

"I'll be right back." I winked at her, and then because I couldn't help myself, I slid my hand over the curve of her hip as I passed by her, reveling in the way her breath hitched at the contact, and thumped Dallin on the shoulder. "Another one?"

"You know it." He smirked.

I went to the bar and ordered our next round. By the time I returned, Reyna's blush had deepened even more on her tan skin, and she shifted in her seat multiple times as I arranged the glasses in front of us. "What did I miss?"

Dallin grinned, laying his hand on her bare thigh, once again drawing my attention there as I sat down next to her. "I was telling Rey all the dirty things I was going to do to her later tonight."

I groaned, unable to stop it, and took a sip of my drink at the same time Reyna did. Like the alcohol could cool our bodies down from the effect Dallin's words had on us.

"Do I get to at least listen through the walls again?" I looked over at her as her eyes rounded in surprise and her lips parted. "*Both* times last night were hot."

Leaning over, Dallin pressed his lips against her ear. "What do you say, baby? You going to let Parker listen while I fuck your ass?"

Her eyelids fluttered closed, and her nostrils flared as an inferno lit inside my body. This was uncharted territory for us; I wasn't sure if I should push her further or give her a break, but Dallin wasn't taking it easy on either of us.

She brought the rim of her glass to her lips and took a large swallow before tracing the edges with her tongue, getting every drop, and then responding, "It's not as if you'd give me the option to be quiet." She smirked bravely at Dallin. "You always get what you want in the end."

"I usually do," he responded, turning on his stool to face us both completely and leaning his head against his fist propped up on the table like he was relaxed and carefree, whereas I was coiled tight and ready to snap. "But this is about you and what you want. Because if I got what I wanted, Parker would be helping me make you scream tonight, Rey."

"D," I groaned, closing my eyes and shaking my head as I adjusted my hard-on in my jeans. When I opened my eyes, I saw Reyna staring at my crotch and nibbling on her lip again. "I'm only a man and you're making this fucking hard on me, too."

Dallin looked down at where my hand still rested on my lap and smirked. "I see that."

"Jesus," Reyna panted, fanning herself with her hand and staring forward, trying to resist temptation by avoiding eye contact. "We need to find a different topic, or I'm not going to make it through this."

"Fine," Dallin whined with a playboy smirk on his face. "Let's play twenty questions." He picked up his drink and nodded to me. "You guys can get to know each other with your questions, and I'll get to torture you more with mine."

"How is that fair?" I quirked an eyebrow at him.

"Because there are two of you and one of me. Two-thirds of the questions will be tame, leaving only every third question to be naughty. It's the best I can offer at the moment." He shrugged. "Because I'm horny as a frat boy and five of my seven favorite holes to stick my dick into are sitting right here in front of me, flirting with each other and making me so fucking hard I'm dangerously close to coming in my pants. Take it or leave it."

"Who are you?" Reyna smirked over at Dallin. "I've never seen this side of you."

"You don't hate it, though, do you?" Dallin said before looking over at me. "Park knows this side of me, don't you?"

"I do." I nodded, keeping his gaze before looking down at Reyna. "But you were right earlier, he always gets what he wants in the end. So why not?"

Her lips twitched, and she turned on her stool, giving Dallin her back and facing me. We were so close that I had to spread my knees wider to make room for her in between, but I didn't mind it even a little bit.

"Fine." She shook her hair over her shoulder, giving me an unobscured view of her tits, which I took, and then cocked her head to the side. "If you could spend the rest of your life doing one thing, what would it be?"

"You," Dallin chimed in from behind her playfully, and she swatted him with a smirk before raising her eyebrows at me, waiting for my response.

"You went deep first thing," I said, letting the innuendo amuse her before clearing my throat and answering her seriously. "Art," I replied, and she tilted her head to the side, wanting clarification. "Of any kind. Drawing and tattooing have always been my go-to, but I enjoy a lot of other mediums too. So if I had to choose only one thing to do, it'd be art."

"Wow," she whispered in surprise. "Not me?" she added as a joke with a fake pout that Dallin chuckled at.

"I'll let you know after I have you for the first time. My answer could change," I deadpanned, and her breath hitched at my honesty. "My turn," I interrupted, keeping her from saying anything else, and asked her the question I wanted to know. "Why literature? That's your preferred medium of art, but tell me why."

She took a deep breath and rolled her shoulders. "Because when I started writing, I had no idea who I wanted to be. I was stuck in this body, trapped inside my brain, and I felt like I was constantly trying to be two different people and I was unsuccessful at being either of them because of it. So I escaped into writing, where I could let one side of me out and express it while still staying true to that other side of me."

"What are the two sides of you?" I asked, and she grinned.

"The good girl and the *not* so good girl."

"So you live your life portraying the good girl." I nodded at her physical body. "And you let your freak flag fly in the worlds you create inside your head?"

Dallin snorted and nodded. "That's it, exactly."

"I don't portray being a good girl." She huffed good-heartedly with a glare over her shoulder. "I enjoy being good. There's just some times when I feel like I need something else or an outlet for that more adventurous side of me."

"Is that why you fell in love with Dallin?" I quipped, and they both looked at me in confusion, so I elaborated. "He's a bad boy, and he gives that bad girl inside you the freedom she needs vicariously."

She chewed on her lip and looked at her boyfriend. "Well, when you put it that way, maybe." She shrugged. "I don't know if that's why I fell for him or not, but his bad-boy image caught my attention from the start."

"Interesting." I nodded, mulling it over.

"My turn," Dallin smirked, leaning over her shoulder and resting his chin on it. "What do you think your inner bad girl will do once you have three bad boys inside you?"

My jaw clenched as vivid images of Reyna's lush body pressed between ours infiltrated my brain. I saw her taking all three of us into her body at the same time, imagining the noises she would make as we made her orgasm repeatedly until I was once again hard and aching in my jeans.

Reyna looked over at me and then leaned over so she could look at Dallin. "I don't know. But I think I'm interested in finding out." Now it was Dallin's turn to groan and fight his body's reaction to her words. "But since you brought it up, where is the third party of your little boy band? I figured you'd tell me when you were ready, but curiosity is getting the best of me."

"He'll be back," I replied reassuringly.

"Someday," Dallin added realistically. "He took off earlier, who knows when he'll come back, but I know he will."

"How?" she asked, gentling her face. "What if he was right, and this just isn't what he wants? If I'm not what he wants."

"Don't," I commanded instantly, catching the way her self-consciousness bloomed as she spoke her fears. "He wants you, that's not the problem."

"But how do you know?" she asked, chewing her lip. Her lipstick was magic because it never budged, even through all the chewing and drinking. I wondered once again if I could smear it with my cock, though.

"Do you want to know the answer to that?" I raised one eyebrow at her in challenge and she nodded slowly, like she perhaps wasn't so sure after all. I looked over her shoulder to Dallin and licked my lips, catching the way his eyes followed the move and answered her. "Because after you teased Trey with your banter and that sexy lace nightie last night, he was on edge and needy, but his anger was still too potent to give in to it." I leaned forward until my face was right in front of hers, catching her scent again and drowning myself in it. "However, once he heard your moans and pleas for Dallin to fuck you, he couldn't hold back anymore. He bent me over the bed in your pristine and perfect spare bedroom and fucked me like a crazed man, thinking about you and D."

Her chest sank and rose with quick breaths as her eyes glazed over with arousal. "And what were you thinking about while he was inside you?" she whispered, like the words were too naughty to say out loud.

I smirked and laid my palm flat on her exposed thigh, enjoying the way her muscles relaxed instantly under it. "I was thinking about how good it's going to feel the first time I push into your body." Her eyelids fluttered and her lips parted. "How sexy you're going to look coming on my cock with Dallin right there with us." I slowly shook my head. "I came with Trey's cock in my ass, his hand wrapped around my cock, and the thought of you in my head."

"Parker," she moaned, laying her hand on top of mine on her thigh. "You guys make this seem so easy."

"It can be," I assured her. "Physically, it can be easy, and quite rewarding."

"But emotionally?" she asked, looking between me and Dallin, who stared at me intensely. "I'm not interested in just getting something physical out of this. I need more."

"I know." I nodded. "And that's something I'm intrigued to give you. But I've never done it before. And neither has Trey." I looked up at Dallin. "D was the only one brave enough to ever think he deserved more than just sex with someone perfect like you. But I'm willing to try."

She chewed on her lip in contemplation. "I don't know how to give myself to anyone but Dallin."

I shook my head. "It's not about giving anything of yourself away, Reyna."

Dallin added from behind her, "Poly relationships are all about gaining things, baby. Lovers, connections, allies, and freedom."

I agreed. "It's liberating knowing you have options while still being inside something solid."

"Just like that, huh?" She smirked. "Am I just overthinking this because I'm female?"

"Maybe," I joked, and she rolled her eyes.

"You're not overthinking it, Rey," Dallin stated, rubbing her shoulders with his hands. "I knew going into this conversation that you were going to analyze everything possible about it, that's just your personality and how you operate. And there's nothing wrong with it. So take your time and consider it if you want, but know that I don't look at Parker or Trey as competition. In my head, they are inside this relationship, and I want you to explore what they can offer you whenever you feel drawn to them. It's not cheating to me."

"Then I want that for you, too." She looked over her shoulder at him. "I know earlier you said we were solid, and you wouldn't stray outside of us. But I don't think I'd mind if you did." She shrugged. "I don't know one hundred percent, because I've never been in this situation before, but I think I'd be okay if you were intimate with them without me."

Dallin smirked down at her and then kissed her. "We'll take it slow; I promised you that already." He took a deep breath. "We have the rest of our lives."

She smiled against his lips and tightened her fingers around my hand, still resting on her leg, giving me the connection she was worried about making. "Let's do it." She looked over at me. "That is, if you're interested."

I grinned at her, lifting her hand to my lips and kissing the inside of her wrist. She swallowed, and I watched the muscles of her neck move as her lips parted. "I'm interested, Rey." I kissed her pulse again. "Very, very interested."

CHAPTER 9

Reyna

"After you." Parker grinned seductively as he opened the door to the Uber. We stayed at the bar, huddled in our secluded corner while we played a tempting game of twenty questions that turned more into truth or dare without the raunchy dares. I had enough margaritas to feel brave and excited about what the future with Parker and Dallin held for me, and hopeful enough to think that maybe Trey would join, eventually.

I didn't know him like I did Parker, thanks to our evening of exploration. But there was something about him that called to me, even without knowing his story. I wanted him to be a part of this because he was important to Parker and Dallin, and I wanted to give them what they needed.

And they needed Trey.

They also trusted that he'd come back when he was ready, so I had to trust in them. In the meantime, I was going to embrace this new *freedom*, as Dallin called it, and pray that I didn't lose the man I loved over men that I simply lusted for.

But jeez, did I lust for them.

My body had been burning with arousal since Dallin texted me with my instructions to meet them for drinks. Mix in the alcohol, Parker's gentle touches, and Dallin's dirty words, and I was an inferno inside.

As I slid into the back seat of our Uber, sandwiched between the two men, pressed tightly against their bodies, my thighs quivered from pressing them together so tightly, trying to create enough friction to pleasure myself without them noticing.

But Dallin always noticed.

He had his arm thrown behind me on the seat with his fingertips against Parker's neck in the dark back seat. The driver, a young guy with a green Mohawk, was more than happy to ignore us with his headphones in as he drove through the crowded nightlife-filled streets toward our home.

Dallin leaned down until his lips were against my ear and sucked the lobe between his lips. "Put your leg over my knee."

I swallowed as the inferno in my stomach sank lower to the girly parts inside me, and I obeyed. I gently uncrossed my legs and laid one over Dallin's long leg, parting my thighs enough to get cool air against the dampness of my panties. Parker watched me from the other side as Dallin's fingers traced an invisible pattern over the skin of his neck. The touch was intimate and one of past lovers, but I didn't feel the jealousy I would have if it had been with anyone else. It was arousing to watch them touch, and it was just a simple caress of his neck. What would it be like to watch them have sex?

Dallin slid the palm of his free hand across my knee and then slowly down the inside of my thigh as my breath caught in my throat. His fingers traced the outside silk of my panties and he growled, "Fucking soaked for us."

It was ridiculous to be embarrassed, but I kept my eyes on the rearview mirror, waiting for the driver to notice what was happening behind him, but he never once glanced up. The windows were so dark that no one standing on the crowded streets could see into the dark car, but it was still taboo enough to be so close to so many people while my boyfriend stroked the tip of his finger over my pussy.

"Let me help you out here, man," Parker said, sliding his palm under my other leg and lifting it over his knee, spreading my legs wider for Dallin's hand. Feeling Parker's skin on mine while Dallin pulled my panties to the side and ran his bare fingers against my wet clit had my toes curling in ecstasy. "Fuck, I can smell how sweet you are from here," Parker groaned, tightening his hand on my knee and pulling my leg wider while I panted in wild abandon.

"I want you to come before we get to the house," Dallin instructed in his deep growl, sliding a finger inside me, making my eyes flutter closed as my fingers wrapped around his wrist. I rocked my hips, riding his hand without abandon, ignoring the embarrassment that tried to burn inside me as Parker watched.

One look up at him from under my lashes as I rode Dallin's fingers had me parting my lips and moaning. His brown eyes were nearly black from how big his pupils were as he watched us. He licked his lips and worked his jaw back and forth as he stared down at me. "I want to kiss you so fucking bad," he admitted like it pained him.

"Do it," Dallin demanded. "Keep her quiet while I make her come."

I looked back and forth between them, as we all sat on the edge of no return, waiting for Parker to make the move I desperately wanted him to. "Do you want me to kiss you, Rey?" he asked, sliding his hand over my jaw to tip my face to his until our lips were only an inch apart. "Do you want to taste me while you orgasm?"

"Yes." I nodded feverishly. "Please."

"Good girl." He smirked before tilting his head and pressing his lips to mine as Dallin added a second finger inside me. I gasped at how good it felt, and Parker slid his tongue against mine before biting my bottom lip and sucking it into his mouth. "Does your pussy taste as sweet as your mouth, baby girl?" he growled, tightening his hand around the back of my neck and kissing me again.

"Fuck, that's so hot," Dallin groaned, kissing my bare shoulder as I turned my torso toward Parker for better access to his lips.

It had been almost four years since I kissed another man, thanks to a dry spell before I met Dallin, and with my boyfriend's hands and lips on me, encouraging me as I did it, it was all too much.

"Oh my God," I whispered as my jaw went lax. Dallin circled my clit with his thumb, just how I liked, and my orgasm crashed over me like a tidal wave. "Yes," I hissed, rocking on his hand while Parker deepened our kiss, absorbing every moan as I shuddered in their arms.

"You're so sexy when you come," Parker whispered moments later as I panted against his lips. "I could feel your pleasure through your mouth like I was experiencing it myself."

"You're perfect," Dallin praised me, sliding his fingers from my body and leisurely stroking my clit until I jerked and twitched from the oversensitivity. He slid my panties back over my pussy and righted my skirt before leaning against my body and lifting his wet fingers in front of us. "Care for a taste, man?"

Parker groaned and looked at me before lowering his lips to Dallin's outstretched fingers. My soul left my body the second Parker's tongue slid up the length of Dallin's long finger before sucking the tip of his as his eyes closed, and he moaned.

I had never in my life seen something more erotic, and even though I just came, my pussy clenched in anger that she was empty when two sexy men were so near. She was such a needy cunt when she wanted to be.

"I think I just died and went to heaven," I whispered in complete awe as Parker stared at me while he sucked Dallin's second finger clean. I chanced a glance at Dallin and saw his jaw clenched tight as he stared at Parker with such longing in his slate-gray eyes. "Kiss him," I demanded, unsure where I got the nerve or the balls. "Please." I looked over at Parker and then back to Dallin. "I need to see you two kiss more than I need air."

"Can't let the girl suffocate," Parker smirked before something else crossed his face as he stared at Dallin.

Was it uncertainty?

Or nervousness?

But it was gone the second Dallin leaned over me, as Parker met him halfway. I half imagined they would kiss in a macho, manly, aggressive slamming of their lips together like they were fighting for dominance, but they didn't.

It was slow and tentative as they both tilted their heads and explored the motion like they had forgotten how to do it with each other. Dallin's tongue slid against Parker's bottom lip and my arousal spiked as Parker opened to him.

"Oh my God," I panted, sliding my hand brazenly up Dallin's thigh to where I knew I'd find the thickness of his cock. "You're so hard, D," I exulted as Parker growled and covered my hand with his, squeezing it around Dallin's cock. I didn't feel left out as they kissed so passionately, one because I was sitting between them, but two because it didn't feel like a competition between partners.

It was dizzying to feel so included and yet be simply spectating.

I no longer cared about the driver or the crowd on the streets; it was Nashville after all. Weirder things happened every day.

So I let my buzzed brain embolden me and leaned forward to run my tongue up the side of Dallin's neck to his ear as Parker and I massaged his erection. "Fuck, baby," Dallin growled. "If you two keep this up, I'm going to come in my pants."

"Or you could just fill your girl up with it," Parker countered, pulling back to smirk down at me.

"*Our* girl," Dallin corrected him, panting and flexing his hips up into our hands. "Seriously, though, you two have to stop. Rey wanted to take this slow, and I'm about to bend you both over the hood of this car and take turns fucking you."

"I don't hate that idea," I prodded him, but then sighed and leaned back in the seat, pulling my hand free of his cock. "But you're right." I looked over at Parker and smiled apologetically. "I think I let myself take it too far. I'm sorry."

"There's no such thing as too far, Rey." Parker leaned back but put his hand on my knee that I had closed against the other one at some point. "It's just what you're comfortable with, don't apologize. I'm not mad in the least."

"Me either," Dallin added. "Tonight has solidified everything I was afraid to admit for the last two years. This was meant to happen, this way, with all of us. Even if it got messy along the way. Once Trey joins, we'll have it all."

"I can't believe I just did all of that." I shook my head as shyness weighed down on me. Thank God our driver was so used to it that what we had just done didn't even pique his interest enough to watch.

"Did you enjoy yourself?" Parker asked with a raised brow.

"Immensely." I nodded with a shy smile.

"What was your favorite part?" Dallin asked. "Or what surprised you the most?"

I thought about it for a second and then answered truthfully. "How hot watching you two together got me." I smirked and bit my lip. "I didn't feel left out, but I wanted to join in so badly. Like I wanted to immerse myself in the two of you and never come up for air."

The Uber rounded a corner and the neon signs outside Dallin's shop filled the car's interior as we stopped at the curb. "Fuck, it's going to hurt walking up the steps with this," Dallin joked, pulling his jeans away from the very visible erection straining down his leg.

Parker snorted and opened his door. "Not as bad as my blue balls will." He held his hand out and helped me slide from the back seat as Dallin walked around the back of the car. "But I wouldn't take it back for a second." He winked down at me as Dallin pulled me against his side when I shivered from the heat in Parker's stare.

"What happens now?" I asked hesitantly. The door to our home was ten feet away, and the bravado I'd felt in the car ten minutes ago faded with my buzz, leaving me horny and needy, but shy and uncertain.

"Now we go upstairs, order the greasiest takeout on the block, and gorge ourselves until we're too full to fuck and then pass out." Parker nodded surely, and Dallin tipped his head back to laugh.

"I like that idea, but you don't get to pick the takeout, you have terrible taste," D teased him.

"Fuck off." Parker punched Dallin's shoulder as I unlocked the stairwell door with the code. "I have great taste."

"Terrible taste," Dallin argued. "Except in women." He slapped my ass playfully as I started up the stairs ahead of them. "In this single case, you have impeccable taste. But in everything else, you're like a raccoon, literally willing to consume anything."

"I'm not a fucking trash panda, you feral badger," Parker lobbed back, and I giggled at their banter as we walked into the apartment.

The stress of what lay ahead a minute ago melted off my shoulders as they allowed their lifelong friendship to pave the way and ease my anxiety. It was the best of both worlds: friendship and relationship.

I suddenly understood the arrangement that they had when they were nomads so much better.

I also understood why Trey was hesitant to add a woman to the mix when, for two decades, he had just the two guys to enjoy life with.

"I'm going to get sweatpants on if there is going to be junk food ordered," I said as I walked down the hallway to my bedroom. As I slid off the dress and sexy lingerie, trading them for a set of cotton joggers and a semi-thin and revealing camisole, I started planning how I was going to convince Trey I could be good for the three of them.

I'd prove to him I could handle them and their dark, brooding personalities, and convince him to give us a chance.

Because Dallin and Parker thought I was good for them, and I knew they were good for me.

CHAPTER 10

Dallin

"This is pretty sweet, I won't lie," Parker said as we walked through the crowded event center. Nashville's tattoo expo was one of the biggest in the game, and it was an honor to be a host for it. I wouldn't be tattooing too much during the weeklong event, but I would network and meet new clients and other artists as well.

Everyone in our circle of peers knew that Twisted Ink was one of the hottest shops, with an obnoxious waitlist to get work done. They also knew that I had empty chairs in the shop, waiting to find the right new artists to take them.

If I had my way, Parker and Trey would take the seats, but if they didn't, I had no choice but to fill them with other artists because the shop was drowning in work.

"Hey, D!" someone called as we passed a booth, and I saw my friend Jaeger running around his table to me. "What's up, man?" he said, slapping me on the back with a quick hug. He was a small guy who looked better suited for a yacht with his fancy khaki pants and collared shirts than a tattoo shop, but the guy loved ink. And I loved an underdog who had passion.

"Hey." I nudged Parker. "Jaeger, Parker. Parker, Jaeger."

"Hey, man." Parker shook his hand.

"Are you staying long today?" Jaeger asked after exchanging pleasantries with Park. "It's crazy busy already. The staff mentioned that the tickets sold out before the doors even opened this morning."

"Yeah, supposed to be that way for Friday and Saturday already, too."

"Wild, man. Thanks so much for hooking us up with a great spot. The shop needed to pick up, and getting so many fresh faces to interact with right inside the front door is going to be just the thing we needed."

"No problem," I smirked, patting him on the shoulder. "You'd better get back to it." I nodded to the crowded table behind him where a line was forming to look at the digital portfolios laid out on it. The guy had the money, and it looked like he'd spent it on a great booth display to catch eyes. "Have fun, Jaeger."

"Thanks! You too, nice to meet you, Parker," he said and then scurried back to his booth, sales-pitching someone on the way as we headed deeper into the chaos.

"You're not afraid of someone like that stealing your business if you boost him up so high?" Parker asked, putting his hand on my back as he skirted around someone in line. He smelled like fucking sin and looked even better.

Parker always had a pretty laid-back rocker look, keeping it old-school sixties with dark jeans, rolled at the cuffs over his black motorcycle boots, and a neutral-colored tee. Today it was white, and it offset the black of his hair that he kept buzzed short to his head. Last night we ended up gorging on takeout and watching a movie until Reyna fell asleep on the couch between us.

I took her to bed as Parker made his way to the spare room, but it was a fight to keep myself from inviting him to sleep with us, even platonically. Because I knew better, and if he had been in bed with us, something would have happened, and I needed to respect Reyna's speed limitations. But that didn't mean it wasn't hard to keep things PG with him now, either.

It wasn't that I cared if people saw me being overpersonal with a man, or someone that wasn't Reyna. I just really wanted to keep intimate connections with Parker private for now, with Rey included in them like last night in the Uber.

We finally got to the Twisted Ink booth along the back edge of the center and made our way around the line that had built down one aisle and back up the other. "No, I'm not worried." I smirked at Parker as we skirted the table and walked behind the large partition for privacy. "I'm drowning in work as it is. My books are only open two months at a time, and they book up within twenty-four hours each time I open them. I could use the competition."

Lex, the shop's emo Barbie, stood up from her station, taking her gloves off as her client stood up, revealing her bare breasts that Lex had just tattooed as she eagerly ran to the mirror to see the work.

"Jesus," Parker smirked as the woman's fake tits nearly poked his eye out on the way by. "I thought Vegas was wild."

I chuckled and fist-bumped Lex on our way by. "Nashville is the new Vegas. Hey, Lex, how's it going?"

"Fucking wild." She smirked, nodding to the two flotation devices behind us. "Chick wanted her girlfriend's hands tattooed around those tits like she was holding them up for a motorboat." She grinned. "This city never ceases to amaze me."

I nudged Parker. "See what I mean?" I joked and then introduced them. "I'm trying to convince Parker to come join us at the shop."

Lex looked him up and down appreciatively. "I'd enjoy the eye candy."

"Hmm." Parker grinned but didn't give his usual response to flirt back.

"Get back to it and let me know if you need anything," I told Lex.

"You inking anyone today?" she asked with a raised brow.

"Maybe." I shrugged. "We'll see how the day goes."

"Cool," she said distractedly as another woman came behind the partition with Belly, a Buddha-looking man who worked at the shop, wearing a skirt so short you could see both of her ass cheeks. "Yeah, I'm gonna go." She turned and walked away without another word, and we both chuckled in her wake.

"So, what do you want to check out first?" I asked Parker, looking around the center.

"Everything," he smirked. "Show me your life."

It was almost ten p.m. before Parker and I walked back into the stairwell up to the apartment. The day had been chock-full of business opportunities and collaborations between other big-name shops and even newer ones. And Park had been the best wingman all day, fielding clients and crazed fans who just wanted to get close to the artists. All day long, he was at my side, and I didn't realize how much I'd missed the camaraderie between us until I had it again.

He was my best friend, and it felt so good to have him back in my life. And I was going to do everything in my power to keep it that way.

"You think Rey is still up?" he asked quietly as we walked up the steps.

"Why? Hoping for a good-night kiss?" I smirked at him over my shoulder, and he rolled his eyes.

"I just want to see her." He shrugged. "Stupid, huh? Considering I only met her a few days ago."

I stopped at the landing and faced him. "That's not stupid at all," I said firmly, letting the joking fall out of my tone. "I think that's great."

"And it doesn't bother you?" he replied. "That if she asked, I'd ditch your ass and go to bed with her without a second thought."

"I might feel a bit left out if I don't get to even sit in the corner and watch, but I wouldn't hesitate to give her whatever she wanted. Or you. And if privacy was what you guys wanted, I'd give it to you."

"I don't understand you, D." He sighed, putting his hands in his pockets. "If the roles were reversed, and some dude wanted her, I'd lock her away and tell everyone else in the world to fuck off."

"You're not some dude, Park." I stepped forward until we were toe to toe. "I care for you just like I do her. It's not a competition or anything for me to be jealous over."

"You care for me?" he asked quietly, staring me down.

"I know we never talked about feelings or anything before I left." I dropped his stare. "I guess I thought you knew how I felt, after all these years."

"Tell me how you feel," he urged, swallowing.

"I love you." I didn't hesitate. "I've always had love for you, even when we were kids. But it morphed into romantic love after we started hooking up."

"Love," he whispered, like the word was foreign to him.

I felt torn in two different directions as he processed what I told him, so I gave in to my need to reassure him. I wrapped my hand around the back of his neck and pulled him flush to me, stopping only when our foreheads were touching. "I love you, Parker. And I'm sorry that you didn't know that before this moment."

He tilted his head and pressed his lips to mine like he needed physical confirmation of the words, and I willingly fell into the need to give it to him. He groaned when I pushed my tongue into his mouth, remembering the way he always weakened when I asserted dominance over him. His hands fell to my belt, and he hooked his fingers behind the leather, anchoring himself to me until our bodies were flush. I could feel his cock harden in his jeans, pressing against my own as I tightened my hold on his neck.

Our kiss was more turbulent than anything I ever shared with Reyna, and it burned something deep inside me. Calling to the need to be rough and in charge with someone who could withstand that power and wouldn't break under it.

"God, I missed this," he whispered, rocking his cock against me. "But I feel like I'm cheating on Rey." He bit my lip. "Isn't that fucked up?"

"No." I shook my head, walking forward until we ran into the wall, and I pressed him against it hard, covering his body with mine. I growled when his hands slid from my belt to my ass and squeezed, pulling me tighter against him. "She's given us her blessing." I slid my hand from the back of his neck to the front and held him there as I kissed his ear.

"I want to fuck you so bad, Dallin." He groaned, tipping his head to the side. "Fuck!" he cursed, pushing me back as I grabbed his belt. "Wait."

I stood a foot off him, panting like I'd run a marathon as he stared at me with crazed eyes. "What?"

"I don't know." He shook his head. "I just— I think I want her there when we do this again. But I'm not ready yet."

I forced myself to calm down and ran my hand through my hair as disappointment and shame burned through me. "I'm sorry. I shouldn't have pushed you."

"Don't." He shook his head, leaning up off the wall. "I'm just all twisted up in the head over all of this and don't want to fuck it up."

"I get it," I said, stepping back even further, fixing my shirt and rubbing my hand over my jaw. "I'll leave the ball in your court. When you're ready, let me know." I tried to give him a small smile, but it felt weak, so I just turned and opened the front door, breaking the moment completely.

Reyna stood at the kitchen island with wide eyes and a flush up her chest and cheeks, as she tossed her phone down on the counter like it burned her. "Hi." She looked past me to Parker as he stepped in behind me.

"Hi," I said, once again trying for normalcy but failing. She wore a baby pink cropped tank top with no bra underneath, and her lush tits pressed tightly against the fabric, with her hard and prominent nipples.

A pair of tight matching shorts barely covered her ass, and her hair was piled on top of her head in a messy bun.

She was fucking angelic and perfect, and I felt dirty about what I'd just done, even though we had discussed and agreed upon it beforehand.

Parker's rejection made me feel dirty.

And confused. I told him I loved him, and he pushed me away. Did I read this entire thing wrong?

"Are you okay?" she whispered as I circled the island and stopped at her side.

"It was a long day. I'm going to go get a shower and head to bed." I kissed her forehead, unable to taint her perfect lips with mine that still tasted like Parker.

"Okay," she whispered, trying to get me to look at her, but I couldn't. "I love you."

Something hurt inside me from her words, but I pushed it down. "I love you, too."

I walked down the hall, leaving her standing there with Parker, and shut the bedroom door, leaning against it as I struggled to get my head on fucking straight.

I shouldn't have walked away from her like that, after being apart for the entire day. I shouldn't have walked away from Parker like that either, but I didn't trust myself to be sane when emotions were involved.

So I did what I do best, apparently.

I hid.

CHAPTER 11

Parker

Reyna watched Dallin walk down the hallway in confusion before she looked back at me. I could see the hundreds of questions running through her eyes, but she wouldn't voice them.

"I'm sorry," I sighed, shaking my head as words evaded me. "I—"

"Demanded he tell you he loved you and then pushed him away." She raised one eyebrow at me as she dared me to tell her she was wrong.

"How did you know?" Guilt weighed me down at the accusation in her tone.

She picked her phone up with a shrug. "I was watching on the security camera."

That explained the flush covering her body and the way her nipples poked through the thin top she wore. It was fucking tempting to slide my thumbs over both of them to see if they would get even harder. But that was because Dallin had gotten me all worked up moments ago and I had no outlet for the sexual tension for days now.

"I'm sorry you had to see that." I kicked my boots off and walked to the fridge, grabbing a beer and twisting the top off.

"Do you think I'm angry that you guys kissed?" she asked, crossing her arms and propping her hip against the island.

"Are you?"

"Not in the least. I'm horny," she countered, surprising me.

"You're really turned on by us together?" I squinted with speculation, waiting for her to finally admit she was simply playing the part of a willing partner.

"I'm soaked right now." She held her head high. "I was torn between wanting to keep watching you two together and wanting to be in between you while you did it. I was seconds away from playing with myself to ease the ache you were causing."

I clenched my jaw and closed my eyes like they could defend me from her erotic words. But it didn't. Her words were liquid fire to the inferno already burning in my gut from kissing Dallin.

"I can't understand why you're so willing to upheave your entire life for him and what he wants," I admitted. "I can't understand why you're on board with this crazy train."

"It's simple. I love him." She flicked her chin at me. "The same way you do. And I'd do anything to make him happy." She leaned up off the counter. "And having three men totally committed to me and willing to care for me in return is hardly a sacrifice on my part."

I shook my head and then stared off at the closed door of their bedroom. "I don't want to fuck this up."

"What do you want?" she asked.

I looked around their modern apartment and sighed. "This." I looked back at her. "You and Dallin. And Trey." I shook my head. "But I don't know how to get it all without hurting someone."

"Trey," she confirmed with a nod. "I don't have the answers on how to get him on board." She shrugged. "If I did, I would have given them to Dallin the first time Trey walked away. But I don't."

"It's not your responsibility to worry about him or us." I took a sip of my beer. "You're balancing enough on your plate."

"What do you mean?" she asked, and then rolled her eyes. "You still don't believe that I'm on board with Dallin being with men." She shook her head. "Why?"

"It just doesn't happen that easily for men like us," I said. "Men like us don't find women like you, who are not only accepting but encouraging of it after already being in a committed relationship. Women we have found over the years like to fuck us for the fun sideshow high they get out of it, but they aren't looking to commit themselves to it."

I didn't realize how bitter I was about the topic until Reyna started pushing on the wounds of my heart with her gentle comfort and acceptance.

I could tell I was angering her, and I didn't want to. But I needed her to admit finally that she wasn't actually on board with it all, so I could gather the strength to walk away from them before I ruined their happy home. Because I wasn't strong enough to walk away while she kept pretending she wanted this.

"I'm going to give you the benefit of the doubt here because I can see this is a much deeper issue than just me." She uncrossed her arms and slowly walked around the island toward me. "But I will not repeat myself after this moment. And you need to either take my word and believe it or leave." She shook her head. "Because I won't let you hurt Dallin over a doubt you have about me." She stopped walking when she was right in front of me. She took the beer bottle out of my hand and took a swig before placing it down on the counter and wrapping her fingers around my wrist, pulling my hand toward her. I scowled down at her in confusion as she stared at me while sliding both of our hands behind the elastic waistband of her thin booty shorts. My palm pressed flat on her smooth-shaven skin as she slid my hand deeper until my fingers met the wetness she'd tried to tell me was there earlier. I growled, standing up tall off the counter as she rolled my fingers over her soaked entrance, widening her legs to give my hand more room between them.

"Reyna." I locked my jaw tight as my body tried to take over and claim her from the simple feeling of her arousal coating my fingertips.

"Feel me, Parker," she whispered, and her eyelids fluttered closed when I couldn't fight it anymore and circled her clit. "Feel how wet watching Dallin pin you to the wall made me." She bit her bottom lip and pushed my fingers further until I pushed one into her tight entrance, making us both moan.

"You're fucking perfect." I lowered my lips, lowering my lips to hers as she dug her nails into the back of my neck and clung to me as I thrust in and out of her. "So fucking perfect."

She nodded, rocking her hips as I added a second finger inside her and lifted her leg to wrap around my waist, so she was even more open for me.

She moaned and held on as I worked her toward orgasm, pressing my hard cock against her thigh, trying desperately to get the friction I needed to come too. I was frantic.

Spending all day with Dallin like the old days, then the kiss and his declaration, paired with Reyna freely giving me her body to prove to me how committed she was, made me desperate.

I was so close to coming, and she was too; we were both lost in the moment. Eyes closed, lips pressed against hers as we both panted and moaned for more. When she dropped her leg from my hip and backed up, forcing me to pull my hand from her shorts and stand alone, it took me five seconds to realize what she was doing.

"Never hurt Dallin again over me," she panted with fire in her eyes. "Get on board or get out." She swallowed and ran her hand down the column of her neck as she forced herself to calm down. "I really hope you're still here in the morning, Parker, but don't be if you aren't all in. Because Dallin loves you. And we both know you love him too." She stepped forward and pulled my head down so she could press her lips to mine in a quick peck before she turned and walked down the hallway toward her room.

When the wooden door clicked behind her, I stood frozen in the dim kitchen in complete shock. And then I did what any sane man with a hard-on and a hurricane of emotions inside him would do.

I licked her sweet taste from my fingers and walked away from their room to my own. Where I stripped down and jumped in the shower and jacked off, with Rey's and Dallin's tastes on my tongue.

I stood at the stove, flipping the tenth piece of French toast onto the tray before putting it back into the oven to keep warm.

"What's going on out here?"

I looked over my shoulder as Dallin walked out of his bedroom with tight jeans and a black band tee on, while he finger-combed his hair. My stomach fluttered at the sight of him, so I turned back toward the stove to focus on the task at hand before I burned it.

"I'm making all of us breakfast."

"It smells delicious," Reyna's sweet voice called out, and I glanced at her as she walked up to Dallin's side. She had on the same outfit as last night, but this time she wore a matching pink robe over it, untied. They were both fucking tempting on their own but paired together, and my brain was boycotting my decision to cook breakfast at all.

Because all I had wanted to do was crawl into their bed between them and beg for forgiveness.

But I had pride.

And an ego the size of Texas, so I figured I'd start there.

"I hope it tastes just as good," I added, flipping a piece of bacon and hissing when a splatter of grease hit my stomach. Maybe trying to seduce them with my abs while cooking bacon wasn't my brightest move.

Dallin chuckled from behind me, and I shot him a sheepish grin. "Did you lose your shirt?" he asked, crossing his arms over his chest as Rey swatted him on her way to the coffeepot. I'd started brewing it when I got up, so it was hot and ready for her as she grabbed her favorite mug from the shelf above it.

"I was hoping maybe if I flashed you both with my sexy muscles, you'd forgive me for my stupidity. You know, sweeten the deal a little bit." I shrugged, feigning indifference, but in reality, I was a jumble of nerves and anxiety. Reyna had told me to decide, but the entire night and this morning, I was worried they would come out of their room and tell me to kick rocks, that they'd changed their mind.

"Well, it's working on me." Reyna smirked over the rim of her coffee cup and then winked at Dallin, trying to prod him into the conversation.

"How about you, D?" I asked shyly, looking back down at the stovetop. "Is it working on you?"

He didn't respond for a long time, and the longer that went on, the more anxious I got until I couldn't stand it anymore. I risked a glance over my shoulder at him and found him staring at me with a penetrating gaze on his face.

"I told you last night, the ball was in your court," he said firmly.

I nodded, turning the stove off and wiping my hands on the towel I had flung over my shoulder. I leaned back on the counter next to the stove and took a deep breath. "This is me asking if you both will let me stay." I looked between the two of them. "I want this, I told you that last night," I said, nodding to Reyna. "This is me hoping you'll both accept me, and my obvious faults, and try anyway with me."

She bit her bottom lip to hide her smile as she looked at Dallin, waiting for him to respond, so I turned my attention to him, too.

"Do you have feelings for me?" he asked skeptically, with his stoic face in place, giving away nothing.

Do or die. I had to cut myself open like he had last night and admit the truth. "I've been in love with you since I was a teenager, Dallin," I answered honestly, and he sucked a quick breath in. "It just wasn't until Reyna kicked my ass mentally last night that I realized you needed me to say it out loud to know it. Like I needed from you. I'm sorry I didn't say it back in the moment, and I'm even more sorry that I pushed you away."

"Why did you push me away?" he asked.

I shook my head and sighed. "Fuck if I know. Maybe part of me expected you to recant, and I didn't want to be the idiot that got his hopes up." I chuckled and ran my hand over my jaw. "Pretty stupid looking back on it now, I know. But I never claimed to be bright emotionally."

Dallin smirked against his better judgment and his shoulders sagged a little, maybe in relief. "So you're staying? In Nashville?"

"I'd like to stay with you two; the geographic location doesn't matter."

Reyna's lips twitched, and she lifted onto the balls of her feet like her excitement was getting the better of her. "Okay, can you two just kiss and make up already?" She giggled when we both looked at her. "What?" she whined. "I already told you it gets me hot."

Dallin rolled his eyes and chuckled and I smiled, feeling the anxiety that had been building since last night finally melt away.

"How about breakfast?" I said, trying to take the pressure off a public display of affection. We'd never been particularly open about PDA, and I didn't want to force it with him while he was still obviously trying to play it cool. "I've got French toast, eggs, bacon, and orange juice." I clapped my hands together.

"Sounds delicious." Dallin leaned up off the counter, grabbed some plates full of food, and started placing them on the table. "You can stay if you cook like this at least once a week."

I tipped my head back and chuckled, "Deal, man,"

We ate breakfast in relative silence, joking here and there, but mostly, we just enjoyed the peacefulness of the morning.

"Have you talked to Trey?" Rey asked as she wiped her face off with a napkin.

"He finally called me back last night," I admitted. "He was still in Tennessee but wouldn't say where." I rolled my eyes. "I told him I was staying, and that we all wanted him here. But you know how he is, he wouldn't commit to anything."

Dallin nodded, looking over at Reyna. "We'll give him the time he needs to get his head out of his ass," he joked.

"Are you going back to the expo today?" Reyna asked, leaning back in her chair and bringing her knees to her chest. Her skimpy little sleep set was making it hard for me to focus on anything but her.

Dallin replied while I tried to unstick my tongue from the roof of my mouth. "I've got a session this morning at the shop, and then I was going to go back over this afternoon. What are your plans for the day?"

"I have a meeting downtown at two and drinks with my editor after. So I'll be gone until after dinner."

Dallin looked at me. "Why don't you hang out up here this morning with Rey and when I go back to the expo we can meet back up."

The air thickened, and everything around the table slowed down. I held his stare and waited for a sign of challenge from him but found only heat in his eyes. He was setting us up.

"Okay." I nodded, letting him pull my strings, mostly because I was interested in seeing what his endgame was.

"Good." He nodded. "It's settled, then." His lips tugged up into his signature playboy grin as he stood up from the table. "I'm just going to grab some stuff from the office and then I'll be out of your hair." He walked down the hallway, and I heard him opening and closing closets, and then he walked back a moment later. The whole time, Reyna stared at me over the rim of her cup but remained silent.

"I'm going to go take a shower." I stood up from the table and picked up the plates, taking them to the kitchen to escape the tension-thick room. When I looked over my shoulder, Dallin stood over Reyna's chair with his hand gently wrapped around the front of her throat, whispering something in her ear. She took a quick breath in and bit her lip as her eyelids fluttered closed, and I desperately wanted to know what he'd said. I had to walk back through the dining area to get to the hallway bathroom and when I got near, he stood back up and faced me.

She panted in her seat, still clinging to that damn cup like it was her lifeline, and I felt so on edge, unsure of what to do and how to act suddenly. He was playing puppet master, that much was clear, but I didn't know what exactly he expected from us. Or what Reyna expected, either. I knew what I wanted out of everything. But I had to tread carefully, avoiding toes as I stepped.

"I'll see you in a few hours," Dallin said to me, and I nodded, unsure of what to say back. But it turned out he wasn't unsure at all. He closed the distance between us and slid his fingers behind the leather of my belt, pulling me flush to him like I had last night in the stairwell, and then kissed me.

It wasn't heavy or aggressive, but like the kiss we shared in the Uber the other night with Reyna sandwiched between us. I sighed, relaxing into it, and reveling in the way it felt to be in his embrace again after so long without it. I placed my hands on the back of his neck and deepened the kiss until we were both hard and panting before he pulled back and took a few deep breaths with his forehead against mine.

"I need to go take a cold shower," Reyna groaned from beside us and we both turned to see her flushed face as she ran from the room.

Dallin and I both chuckled and separated. "It's going to be a hell of a lot of fun corrupting that girl," I joked, shaking my head.

Dallin smirked and nodded as he grabbed his thermos of coffee and headed toward the front door. He stopped with his hand on the knob and turned back. "Oh, by the way. The water in the guest bathroom isn't working right now." I squinted my eyes in confusion, knowing damn well it did when I took a piss and brushed my teeth before I started cooking breakfast. But the confusion melted away when he added, "Maybe you should go on in and use our shower with Rey. Conserve water and all that hippie shit." He winked and then walked through the door, leaving me unable to question him on it at all.

I felt myself smirking as I walked down the hall to the guest bathroom and turned the knob on the sink. Nothing. And then for shits and giggles, I went to the shower and tried to turn that on, but again, nothing.

"Fucking meddler." I chuckled under my breath and contemplated what to do. I needed a shower, which was clear by the smell of ink still clinging to my skin from the expo yesterday. I could wait for Reyna to get out of the shower and then ask to use hers.

Or I could do what Dallin had suggested and finally get Reyna in my arms.

Before I could talk myself out of it, I stripped out of my jeans and underwear and walked down the hallway with my towel flung over my shoulder. My cock was hard as the cool air of the apartment hit it, and it bobbed as it grew harder with each step toward the woman who had captivated me since I first laid eyes on her.

I knocked softly on the bedroom door but got no reply, so I gently opened it and popped my head in. The room was empty; her discarded sleeping clothes were strewn across the floor like she had stripped on her way to the bathroom. The door to the bathroom was open and the sound of water beckoned me as steam filled the space.

She was naked.

And horny.

And willing.

And I had Dallin's blessing.

I couldn't hold back anymore. I walked across the bedroom and into the tiled bathroom, catching a flash of skin through the frosted glass of the large shower stall. My cock bobbed even more as I smelled the scent of her shampoo in the air. Tossing my towel down on the counter next to hers, I silently padded across the floor and stepped around the half wall at the end, finally getting an unobscured view of her deliciously naked body. She had her back to me and didn't hear me come in.

I stood there and watched her as she tipped her head back and rinsed her hair, biting my bottom lip to stay silent as she groaned frustratedly before placing both hands on the shower wall and sagging into it.

"Just do it," she whispered to herself, shaking her head. "He said you could do it." She groaned again and slapped her hand against the tile. "I can't just walk in there and say, 'Hey, want to fuck me? My boyfriend said it was all right.'" She talked in a silly inner monologue voice, and I couldn't stay silent for long knowing she was at war with herself over me.

So instead I walked forward until she was within reach, and I slid both palms around her waist and pressed my body against hers. She jumped and looked over her shoulder at me. "Dallin sabotaged my shower, and then told me to come use yours." I leaned down and kissed her shoulder, letting my teeth graze her skin, and she shivered, but she didn't push me away. "You don't mind, do you?" I rocked my hips forward so she could feel how hard I was for her.

"I—" She gasped and swallowed as my fingers traced circles around her belly button. "Is your dick studded?" she asked, and I snorted in surprise.

I flexed my hips, letting the barbells tease up her spine and then back down to the swell of her ass and the crease of her crack. "Ribbed for her pleasure."

"Oh my God," she whispered, and put her hand flat on the shower wall again for support.

"Tell me to go and I will," I said, giving her the out if she wanted it. "Or tell me to get on my knees and make you come. Your choice, baby."

"Fuck," she said and pushed back against my cock as one of my hands drifted up to cup her heavy breast. I knew her tits were big, but I had no idea how full they'd feel in my hands until they were spilling out as I started rolling her nipple between my fingers. "Knees." She gasped. "I want you on your knees."

"Good girl." I praised her, biting her shoulder with more force until she squealed and moaned. I lifted her other hand and placed it on the shower wall ahead of her. "Don't move these until you come on my face." I lifted one of her legs and placed her foot on the convenient bench right next to us, opening up her body for me as I kissed my way down her spine, letting my hands massage every inch of skin along the way. I kissed each ass cheek and bit them, before shaking them in my hands, loving the way they trembled. "Your ass is going to look so good bent over in front of me someday while I fuck you hard."

"Parker, please," she whined. "I'm going to combust into flames if you don't touch me where I need you."

"Where do you need me, Rey?" I dropped my head and kissed the backs of her thighs and then toward the inside of them. "Here?"

"Further." She arched her ass, begging for it.

I dropped further and spread her cheeks open, watching as her ass and pussy clenched as I exposed them. "Here?" I kissed right next to her asshole, and she gasped, flinching.

"My pussy," she begged. "Please."

"I will," I smirked. "I'll get there."

I flicked my tongue against the rosette of her ass, and she mewed, leaning her forehead against the tile wall as her legs shook. I growled, pushing my tongue flat against her and dipping it down to her pussy, before dragging it back up and circling her ass again. But I didn't touch her clit. I knew from last night when she used my fingers on herself how much she liked her clit rolled and played with, and I'd give her that, but not yet.

I wanted to hear her beg for it first.

"Twice I've tasted your pussy off of fingers, but now," I whistled, "I'm addicted to the source."

"Yes," she mewed as I pushed my tongue into her pussy and twirled it. "God, you're so good at that."

I kept the teasing trail going up and down for a few minutes before I turned and sat down on the floor of the shower with my back against the wall. I looked up the front of her body and stared into her hazel eyes as I pulled her hips forward and pressed her clit down right onto my waiting tongue. I flicked it and then sucked it into my mouth, making her eyes roll and deliciously sweet moans fall from her lips.

But I still needed her to beg for it.

I sucked her clit into my mouth and pushed two fingers into her pussy, and she flexed her hips, riding my face as I pushed her closer to her orgasm.

"Did you fuck Dallin last night, after you let me play with this sweet pussy in the kitchen?" I asked, distracting her as I reached down and stroked my cock a few times, desperate for release.

"No." She shook her head. "He was upset. And I knew if he fucked me, he'd be thinking about you."

"You were so wet, though."

"I know," she growled. "I had sex dreams all night because of it."

"Poor girl," I mewed, and smirked at her as she cursed and rocked faster. "Let me make you come to make up for it, baby girl."

"Yes," she groaned, and then that groan turned guttural when I rubbed my finger over her ass.

"You like anal?"

"Fuck yes," she panted. "Dallin was the first one to ever fuck me there, and he's so good at it. Which you know."

"I do know." I circled the bud and pushed against it, easily gaining entrance as she pushed back on it. "Good girl," I praised her. "I know exactly how good Dallin feels when he pushes his fat cock into my ass."

"Parker," she moaned, pushing back on my finger more until I had one buried in her ass and two in her pussy. "I'm so close."

"Beg me."

"Please," she cried, and I pulled my fingers free before pushing them back in. "Please make me come. I want it so bad. I've been so fucking horny since you showed up."

"That's it," I groaned, adding a second finger to her ass, and then sucking her clit back into my mouth, biting it between my tongue and upper teeth until she tipped her head back and screamed. Both of her holes clenched down tight around my fingers and her cream coated my tongue with each thrust of them until her body twitched and jerked above me. I pulled my hand free seconds before her legs gave out and caught her as she collapsed, settling her straddled across my thighs with her head buried in my neck while she rode her high. I rubbed my hands up and down her spine, over her ass, and across both thighs as she relaxed, until I felt her smile against my neck.

"Dallin always wants me to ride his face, but I never do," she admitted. "I can never relax enough to enjoy it that way. But with you—" Yet she interrupted herself with a quick shake of her head.

"It was the buildup, baby," I acknowledged. "I could have told you to stand on your head and let me fuck your throat until you swallow my come and you would have."

She snorted and giggled before stilling when the motion rocked her against the barbed underside of my cock, pressed between her pussy and my stomach. "I want to see it."

She pulled back and looked into my eyes, biting her lip before slowly lowering her eyes down to my cock.

I was proud of it, and feeling her eyes on it like a physical caress had it twitching in pleasure even more. "I'm not as thick as Trey or Dallin, but I'm longer."

"And bionic." She smirked. "Can I touch it?"

"Do you want to?" I replied, and she nodded demurely. "Ask me nicely."

Her eyelids fluttered closed, and her hips rolled on their own before she licked her lips and asked, "Parker, can I please stroke your cock?"

"Is that all you want to do with it?" I said, tightening my hold on her hips and rocking her against it again.

She shook her head no, and then leaned forward until her lips were nearly touching mine. "I want to take your cock in every single hole I have. I want to feel these piercings inside me, touching me like no man ever has before."

I growled, squeezing her hips even harder, knowing she'd bruise from it but unable to care. She was spurring me on with her dirty talk, and she knew it.

"Please, Parker," she begged. "Pretty, pretty please, let me stroke your cock and then suck on it."

"Do it," I commanded, unable to say anything else, afraid I'd cover her with come in record time.

"Thank you." She smiled at me as her dainty fingers wrapped around the head of my cock. Her skin was cool compared to my heated flesh, and it sent jolts of electricity straight to my balls. "How do you like to be touched? Around the piercings?" she wondered in uncertainty.

"Over them." I covered her hand with mine and squeezed it around the head of my cock before slowly pushing it down the length. The barbells tugged against her palm and fingers and we both moaned at the sensation. "Just like that, baby."

The warm water from the shower cascaded down her back and kept us both warm as she explored my cock. I put both of my hands on her hips again as she stroked me, getting bolder and braver with each pass. "I'm so fascinated here," she admitted, staring right at her hands.

"You look like a goddess, flushed with your orgasm, stroking my cock." I reached around her and rubbed between her thighs, feeling her swollen pussy and ass. "The first time I take you, you're going to scream so fucking loud. It's going to feel like you're being ripped open and you're going to come so hard from the pleasure and the pain."

"Take me, now," she begged, leaning forward to rub her clit up on the underside of my cock again. I growled and lifted her, letting her wetness coat my cock from root to tip, and she dug her nails into my neck as she rocked against me. "Fuck, Park."

"Not yet," I growled through clenched teeth. "Believe me, I want nothing more than to sink deep inside you. But I want Dallin there the first time I take you."

"God," she moaned, tilting her head back in ecstasy.

"I want him to fuck you first, to stretch you out with his massive cock and coat your pussy with his come. I want you relaxed and silky inside and out the first time you take me deep."

"I'm coming again," she panted. "Fuck, yes!"

"That's it, baby," I groaned, fighting off my orgasm to get her through her second. "Hump me just like that. Take me for a joyride."

"Oh my God," she moaned, coming and coating my cock with her cream until she was limp once again. But instead of letting the high come down naturally, she ripped herself out of my arms and kneeled between my outstretched legs. "How do I get this thing in my mouth?" she asked, tracing her tongue over the head of my cock. "Tell me what to do."

"Relax your jaw," I gasped, fighting for control. I loved that she wanted to know how to pleasure me, instead of just doing some porno-style move that would make her look good. She wanted my pleasure. "Stick your tongue out and cover your bottom teeth with it." She did as I said, and I grabbed a fistful of her hair. "I'm fucking close already, so if you don't want to swallow my come, then come off when I pull," I instructed her, but she simply dropped her mouth over the head of my cock and sucked before pushing down further. "Fuck!" I groaned.

I slammed my head back against the tile wall and grunted when she pushed me past her gag reflex and took me further as her throat opened instinctually. "Mmm." She twisted her head around to lick the top and sides.

"I'm coming," I grunted, tugging her hair, but she shook her head and pressed deeper onto my cock as I roared with my release. My muscles jerked and convulsed as I emptied myself into her stomach and she didn't miss a drop.

She licked her way up my cock, careful of each barbell, and then stared into my eyes as she licked her lips seductively. I pulled her in and slammed my lips down on hers, pushing my tongue into her mouth as she sucked on it. We both groaned and growled as we kissed until it slowed as the passion flowed out of the shower with our orgasms.

"Wow," she whispered against my lips with a small smile. "I can't remember a time I've had more fun on the shower floor than right now."

"Ha." I tipped my head back and laughed as I stood up, pulling her to her feet and into my arms. She rested her cheek against my sternum and wrapped her arms around my waist, simply relaxing into me as we came to terms with what had just happened. After a while, she finally spoke. "I thought I'd feel guilty."

She didn't need to elaborate because I knew what was going through her head. I thought I'd feel guilty for taking Dallin's girl too, but I didn't.

"You don't?"

"No." She shook her head and leaned back to look up at me. "I wish he had stayed, but I'm glad we didn't actually have sex without him, either. So thank you for having restraint when I clearly didn't."

I smirked and kissed her forehead. "Let's finish getting cleaned up, and then we can go snuggle up on the couch and watch a movie until he's done with his appointment. Unless you have work to do this morning." I hesitated, feeling needy and uncertain.

"I always have work to do." She smiled. "But being my own boss means I get to decide when I get a day off. And I think I'm due for at least a morning cuddle session on the couch." She groaned as she reached up for the loofah and soap. "Especially after the whole-body orgasms you put me through. I'm sore now," she joked.

"I'll massage them out later for you." I winked, and she shook her head, soaping up and telling me to turn around so she could wash my back.

And I tried hard as hell not to fall to my knees and ask her to marry me as she did it because she was way too damn good to be true. And only a third of my happiness. I just hoped Trey got his head out of his ass sooner rather than later, so he didn't feel left out by the time he showed back up.

CHAPTER 12

Trey

"*Oh come on, you pain in the ass.*" A sweet voice echoed as I rounded the corner to the stairwell door leading up to Dallin's apartment and came face-to-face with the most delicious ass I'd ever seen before.

Reyna.

She was bent over on the sidewalk, picking up a stack of books that she'd dropped as she teetered on a pair of sky-high heels. Her skinny jeans held her ass in a perfect pear shape, and the floral tank top she wore left no question about the curves underneath it, either.

She was so fucking sexy; it wasn't fair. How was a man supposed to think straight when a woman like that was being offered to him on a fucking platter? "Ugh," she groaned, tripping over a crack in the sidewalk and dropping two of the three books she had picked up.

"Hey," I called, ruining my chance to skirt back around the corner and avoid the whole situation altogether. She swung around on the stiletto heel with panic in her eyes, before teetering back like a slow-motion tower falling. "Jesus," I grunted, lunging forward to catch her before she cracked her head open like a ripe melon on the sidewalk.

"Trey?" She squinted at me in the dark and then her eyes went wide. "You scared the shit out of me." She slapped my chest, hard for a girl her size, before shaking my hands off her. "Don't you know better than to sneak up behind a woman in a dark alley?" She had hardly finished the last word when a hiccup slipped out and she covered her mouth with embarrassment.

"Are you drunk?" I scooped up the offensive books with a half-naked man on the cover that had put her in the situation to begin with and shoved them under my arm, reaching for her as she teetered into the concrete wall once again. "You're a hazard to your health right now, Reyna."

"I'm fine." She hiccupped again and tried shoving me off, but I dodged it.

"Up you go." I dropped my shoulder and pressed it against her stomach as I wrapped my arm over the back of her legs, effectively lifting her, the books, and her drunk bravado in one fell swoop.

"Hey," she cried as I mashed the code that Dallin had given me the first night into the reader and popped the heavy metal door open. "I can"—she hiccupped and groaned—"walk."

"Right." I took the stairs in no time, surprised by how light she was given the amount of curves the girl wore, and opened the door to the apartment. I expected Dallin and Parker to be inside, but only darkness met me as I walked in. "Where are the guys?"

"I dunno." She shrugged upside down and then groaned. "I'm going to puke if you don't put my feet above my head. I mean, behind my head." She grunted as I chuckled at her. "Fuck it. Put me down."

I slid her down the front of my chest, holding her when her heels hit the floor and she started to tip over until she was steady. "Shoes. Off," I ordered, pushing her back onto a barstool and removing the offensive things. "Why do you even wear these awful heels?" I chucked them over my shoulder, bouncing them off the door.

"Careful," she snapped. "Those are Jimmy Choos!"

"Johnny who's?" I asked, simply to push her buttons more, and she rolled her eyes at me.

"My first big-girl purchase as a professional working woman!"

"Is that like a street worker?"

She glared at me. "I really don't like you."

"Lies," I smirked, standing up out of the crouch that made me want to groan out loud thanks to my sore body. I had ridden hard the last few days nonstop, trying to outrun my insecurities or whatever Parker said on the phone the other day, but regardless, I was sore. "You like me, plenty. And that's the problem."

"Why is it a problem?" she asked, resting her chin on her hand on the bar top. "Hypothetically, of course, because I don't like you." I rolled my eyes at her and crossed my arms. "But if I did, why is that the problem?"

"Because you don't even know me. You can't like someone you don't know. And you aren't ready to dive into this life, regardless of what you think."

She snorted and stood up on wobbly legs. "That's not what Parker said when I was riding his face in the shower." She turned and flipped her hair over her shoulder. "But whatever."

She stumbled her way down the hallway as a fire burned through my body from her words. She threw that hook out into the water as I circled, and she thought I'd take it, letting her pull me up like a defenseless little sunfish.

Little did she know I was a piranha.

"Or what he was saying when he had Dallin bent over the kitchen island, fucking him hard for breakfast this morning." She looked over her shoulder before she disappeared into the darkness of her room with a smirk on her face. "But what do I know?"

Cunt.

She had me on the fucking hook like a sunfish, after all.

"They fucked?" I followed her, hating the way my boots thundered down the tile floor in her wake.

I stepped into her dark room and searched for her, but she was gone. Movement caught my eyes as they adjusted to the darkness and I found her in the primary closet, pulling her tank top off over her head. "Hmm. I mean, that's one word for it."

I watched as she reached behind her, unclasped her bra, and tossed it into the hamper on the floor, exposing the length of her silky back to my eyes. The dim moonlight filtering through the blinds glowed off her spine, and I ached to kiss a trail from her neck to the dimples above her ass.

"Does that make you jealous?" she asked as she shimmied her hips and pushed those tight jeans down before pulling them off at the ankle and tossing them into the pile. The dark thong she wore shaped her ass perfectly, making my teeth long to sink them into the supple flesh there. I couldn't think straight as she looked over her shoulder and found me staring at her with a devilish smirk on her perfect lips. "It does, doesn't it?" She grabbed something off a hanger in the closet, pushed her arms through it, and then turned toward me. It was a band tee from a concert Dallin, Parker, and I went to on the road years ago. It barely covered her pussy, leaving half of her ass cheeks exposed like it had shrunk in the dryer a dozen times, and I bit back a groan at how good it looked on her. "Is that why you're so mad?" she asked as she walked forward, leaving herself toe-to-toe with me in the dark of her bedroom, wearing hardly anything, poking a bear that already had a bad temper. "Because you're jealous of them?"

"I'm not jealous of them," I snapped. "Before you, I've never been jealous of another person on this entire fucking spinning rock."

Her eyes rounded slightly as she stared up at me. "What could you possibly be jealous of me for?"

I swallowed, hating that I had said that much at all, yet went on like the darkness and her drunkenness could make it all disappear after I said it.

"You took him."

"You let him go, long before I found him," she retorted.

"I came back for him," I said, and then groaned in frustration and bit my tongue to stop myself from saying anything else.

"What do you mean?" she asked, softening her tone. "When?"

"It doesn't matter." I stepped back, creating distance between us even though I wanted the opposite. Which didn't make a lick of fucking sense, because I hated her entire existence. "It's long gone now."

"No." She walked around me, blocking my way out of the bedroom with a hand on each side of the doorway as if she could physically restrain me. "Tell me the truth."

"Why?" I snapped at her, pressing my chest against her heaving one in challenge. "What does it matter?"

"It matters, Trey." Her eyes searched mine, back and forth. "It could make all the difference to him."

"To him?" I laughed. "You think he needs to know the truth? To know that a few months after he left, I came looking for him, ready to beg him to reconsider. And I found you already wormed into our place like we meant nothing to begin with."

She stared at me with a look of empathy on her face that I hated more than anything else, and then she laid one hand on my chest over my racing heart. Why was I baring everything to her? Why was I unable to stop the word vomit like some teenage girl confessing her feelings to a crush, already knowing it was going to end badly?

"If you meant nothing to him, he wouldn't have called a few weeks ago."

"He called Parker, not me. There's a difference." There was the word vomit again.

Fuck, shut up, Trey!

"He knew Parker would be more receptive to it. You would have hung up on him." She glared at me in argument. "Tell me I'm wrong."

"You're wrong." I pushed her hand off my chest and walked around her toward the living room.

"Now, you're a liar." She padded after me in a hurry. Halfway across the dim kitchen, one of the stools banged into the counter and she hissed in pain. "Ow!"

I flipped around so fast that I caught sight of her falling to the ground, holding her foot in her hand.

"What happened?" I barked, as my fear came out in anger.

"Ow!" she cried again, holding her toes in her hand tight. Through the cracks of her fingers, I could see blood pooling and dripping onto the floor.

"Fuck, Rey." I picked her up and gently sat her down on the counter, flipping on all the overhead lights to see the damage. "Let me see."

"No." She shook her head as tears ran down her cheeks. "Ow! That hurts!" she cried as I pried her fingers free. Her big toe had a cut on the end, and half of her toenail was ripped off, dangling by a thread as she slapped her free hand on the countertop in agony.

"Shh." I lowered my voice, gently setting her foot on a hand towel hung over the stove handle. "Where is your first-aid kit?"

She shook her head, biting her lip as more tears ran down her face. "I don't know." She tipped her head back and cried out to the ceiling. "Why were you running away from me so fast?"

"Rey?"

I didn't hear the front door open, but we both turned our heads and found Dallin and Parker rushing in after catching sight of Reyna in distress.

"What the fuck happened?" Dallin barked, shoving his way into the kitchen. "What did you do?" He looked at me accusingly.

"Fuck off," I snapped. "She stubbed her toe in the dark." I pushed him back when he tried to barge in between us. "Get your first-aid kit, peroxide, and some gauze." He shook me off and tried again, but I held my ground. "Dallin! Get the fucking shit to stop the bleeding!"

"Go, D," Rey said softly, pulling his angry attention from me to her distressed face. "Please, it hurts so bad."

"Fuck," he swore, before storming off toward their bedroom.

"What can I do?" Parker asked, squeezing my shoulder as he leaned in to kiss her forehead. I watched the exchange for only a second before I forced my eyes back to her damaged foot. "Get a bowl of warm water and some paper towels."

"On it." He busied himself doing as I said, and I looked at Rey as she watched me closely with tear-soaked cheeks.

"I'm only crying because I'm drunk," she sniffled. "I'm not a baby." More tears fell down her cheeks, and she wiped at them angrily.

"You have every right to cry. Nails hurt like a bitch when they're torn off," I reasoned with her as Dallin hurried back into the room, opening the kit and laying out supplies. Parker came over with the bowl of water and held it as I lifted her foot off the counter and slowly dunked it into the water. She hissed, grabbing handfuls of my shirt as she bit her bottom lip to stay quiet; I dunked and repeated to clean as much blood from the wound as I could.

"Here." Dallin held out a clean gauze under her toe, careful not to disturb the nail, and handed me the peroxide.

I held the brown bottle but hesitated before I poured it onto her. "This is going to hurt like a bitch," I said evenly, with a slight shrug.

"I guess I have it coming for lying to you," she whispered, chancing a glance at Dallin before dropping her eyes again. "There was no kitchen counter Olympics between them."

I rocked my jaw back and forth as I realized she'd goaded me into the entire conversation with a lie and then shook my head, mildly impressed with her cunning. Suddenly, I didn't feel so bad, and quickly poured a large amount of peroxide directly onto her open wound. It bubbled instantly, and she shrieked, trying to pull her foot out of my hand, but I held on to her ankle with a fierce grip.

"And the shower?" I asked, staring down at her toe. "Was that a lie, too?"

I caught Dallin and Parker sharing a confused look between themselves as she and I had a private conversation right in front of them.

"No," she whispered, tightening her claws into my shirt. "I really did ride Parker's face like a rodeo cowgirl."

Parker snorted and Dallin scowled at me in confusion, but I just silently worked.

"And then she gave me one of the top two blow jobs of my life," Parker added smugly, winning himself a shove from Dallin and a sad smirk from Reyna. "What?" he said dramatically. "I thought we were sharing the perks of our recent days to get him up to speed."

"What was the 'kitchen Olympics' comment about?" Dallin asked, ignoring Parker's playboy smirk.

"Nothing," I argued, grabbing the small medical scissors and nipping the tiny bit holding the nail on and removing it as Reyna jumped in anticipation of pain.

She cleared her throat, finally loosening her hands from their death grip in my shirt, much to my dislike, and then ran them down the top of her thighs. "I pissed Trey off on purpose by telling him you two were fucking like bunnies while he was gone. He tried to take off again, so I chased him and slammed my toe into the stool in my pursuit."

Parker snorted and Dallin's mouth hung open as he stared at his girlfriend in shock.

"What?" she droned on dramatically. "I'm drunk. They overpoured me margaritas at Sal's." She widened her eyes when he didn't relax his shocked face. "They were watermelon margs! What else was I supposed to do? You know I'm a slut for margs."

Dallin finally snapped his mouth shut and rolled his eyes. "How did you get home?"

"A hottie in a Lambo." She popped the *O* at the end and then hissed when I covered the open wound with Neosporin, a little rougher than I needed to. Don't ask me why, but the urge to get her to stop talking about other people's attractiveness was strong inside me.

A very foreign feeling.

"Kidding!" She rolled her eyes. "Uber, like always. I'm not an idiot."

"Just a sloppy drunk," I said under my breath, and she kicked me with her good foot, only inches away from where my balls sat in my jeans.

"Watch it." She pointed her finger at me. "There's nothing sloppy about me, Mr. Grumpy Pants."

Now it was my turn to roll my eyes. I rolled the tape around the gauze bandage and finished up before stepping back and washing my hands in the sink. Dallin helped her off the counter, pausing to kiss her before helping her hop to the couch, where she fell into a pile of soft blankets and pillows.

"So you came back," Parker said with a grin, where he stood against the counter with his arms crossed.

"Yeah. To a complete shit show."

"Stop it." He shook his head seriously. "I'm glad you came back."

I sighed and looked at him, then to Dallin and Reyna, where they sat together watching me. "I don't know why I did, honestly."

"That's okay," Dallin added, gentling his face in that perfected way a dominant did for those he took care of. "Obviously, something inside you wants to be here, or you wouldn't be. So maybe we just work on that for the time being."

I rolled my jaw back and forth as I contemplated it.

"He came back for you," Reyna said quietly on the couch, and I wanted to wrap my hands around her pretty little neck and squeeze until she shut the fuck up. "After you settled here in Nashville. A few months later, Trey came for you." She looked up at him with sadness in her eyes. "But we were together, so he left. That's what he told me when we were fighting earlier."

"Is that true?" Dallin stood up off the couch and stalked toward me. I couldn't quite read the look on his face, but it looked close to shame and regret.

"It doesn't matter."

"It does," Parker bit out. "I didn't know that. Why didn't you tell me?"

"Because he moved on." I flung my hand out toward Reyna. "With a woman. What did you expect me to do?" I yelled to both of them. "Demand he give up that side of himself for us? Beg him to let us be enough for him? We weren't!"

"You were!" Dallin roared angrily as he approached me. "It was never about being enough or not, Trey!" He grabbed the back of my neck and shook me. "I spent two fucking years thinking *you* didn't care *enough* to even fucking try!" His gray eyes were staring deep into mine as his anger boiled over. "Two fucking years of thinking that twenty years meant nothing to you. That *I* meant nothing to you."

"Join the fucking club, because that's how you made us feel when you walked away!" I snapped back, shoving him.

"I begged you to come with me!" He stepped back into my space, and I felt Parker getting closer, ready to get between us if needed. "I begged, Trey." He shook his head sadly. "I couldn't keep living that way, it was killing me."

"I can't change it," I huffed, hating how he was making me feel guilty now after all this time for not showing my face the last time I came to Nashville. "I can't go back and pop out of the bushes and say, 'Hey, I changed my mind!' I just can't!"

"Do you?" he whispered, standing toe-to-toe with me. "Do you want to change your mind now, after all this time?" He spread his hands out to his sides. "Do you want what I can give you now?"

I clenched my jaw and stared at the floor because if I kept staring at his gray eyes, I'd fold. And I wasn't ready for that.

I shook my head, frustrated with myself for being so hung up on him and the hurt at the same time. "I don't know."

"That's not a 'no,'" Parker said gently, putting his hand on my shoulder and one on Dallin's. "Let's take a deep breath and calm down with that bit of truth grounding us for a minute." He looked at me, squeezing his hand up the back of my neck reassuringly. "It's not a 'no.'"

"No, it's not," I agreed, unable to give him more in the moment.

"I can work with that," Dallin said, drawing my gaze back to his. "I made a mistake before." He looked over at Parker. "One I just realized the other night. I never put my feelings into words for you two, because I was afraid it would change something between us." He took a deep breath. "But I love you both, the same way I love Reyna. And I want you here, with us, building a life together. We deserve to be happy, Trey."

"She's yours," I said firmly, choosing to skip his declaration because I couldn't give him one back. "I don't want her." I shook him and Parker off because I needed physical space to keep my emotional space intact. "I'm not interested in a physical relationship with Reyna."

I heard her quick intake of breath from across the room but refused to acknowledge the pain that pierced my chest, knowing I'd just hurt her with my words. I couldn't fold on this. I couldn't give in to my physical desires for her simply to please him. I couldn't lose all of me.

"That's fine," she said after a beat. I chanced a look at her as she stood up off the couch. "Thank you for putting it plainly and making your feelings known." She nodded and turned to Dallin. "I respect his wishes, so we'll find some balance where you and Parker are the only ones involved." I could tell Dallin and Parker both hated that idea, but before they could voice their disagreement, she turned on her pretty face with a quick smile. "I think I should go sleep off this buzz before I throw up the street tacos I ate on the way home. Good night."

She turned from the room and hobbled a few steps before Parker pushed away from me. "I got her." He looked to Dallin. "Figure this out." He scooped her up into his arms and carried her the rest of the way into the the bedroom, closing the door behind him with a resounding thud.

"I don't want to hurt her," I said as the tension between Dallin and me got thicker. "That's not my intention, Dallin."

"Why don't you want her?" he asked, staring at me like he'd be able to tell the lie as soon as I said it.

"I just don't."

"Bullshit, try again."

"What does it matter?" I sighed tiredly. "It sounds like Parker's giving her everything you wanted him to, so what does it matter if I don't?"

"Because I don't want you running around with other women, bringing home something dangerous to us or her," he snapped. "The whole point is to be one unit, together. No outside relationships."

"I don't do relationships, period, Dallin."

He scoffed. "Fucking random women, Trey. That's what I mean."

"So it's fuck your girl or no girls?" I snapped, angrily. "Do you understand how fucking entitled that sounds? You don't get to dictate other people's lives."

"That's the point of a relationship!" he snapped, trying to keep his voice down. "To have something here that makes you not even care what else is out there!" He flung his hand toward the windows overlooking the busy downtown streets below.

I walked forward until we were chest-to-chest. "Then why didn't that work for you here with her?"

He clenched his jaw. "I already told you, Trey, because we're a unit too."

"I'm just not interested in Reyna." I backed up a step, hating that he used the same reason for inviting us into his seemingly happy relationship and risking it all. "Either I'm enough for you this way, or I'm not." I held my arms out at my side and left it up to him to decide. "But make a choice quick or I'll take that as the answer in of itself."

He huffed and glared at me like I was twisting his arm, making him do something he didn't want to do. That would have pissed me off if I didn't feel the same way about what I was doing. But I had no choice.

"Fuck, Trey," he growled, and then closed the distance between us and kissed me. His scent infiltrated my senses, and I groaned at how good he smelled, after all this time. "You're enough," he whispered, sliding his hands under the front of my shirt so he could touch my bare skin. "I'll take you this way, but I won't stop trying to get you to admit you want her to."

My brain was misfiring as he bit my lip and sucked my tongue into his mouth before slowly kissing his way to my neck and biting down hard, marking me. "You can do whatever you want as long as you keep touching me."

"Bed," he grunted. "Now."

I sure as fuck wasn't going to tell him no. Not after two long years.

We fumbled our way down the hallway, falling into walls and doorframes until we made it into the spare bedroom. "Ouch." I cursed as my head bounced off the wall when he pushed me against it.

"Sorry." He smirked, pulling my shirt up over my head before taking off his own. "I haven't done this in so long, it feels like I'm going to snap into two pieces if I don't feel all of you."

"What happened with Parker while I was gone?"

"I've hardly touched him," he growled, forcefully undoing my belt and jeans as he looked me in the eye. "We kissed, first in a cab on the way home from drinks with Rey." He smirked fondly at the memory. "She begged us to kiss after I played with her pussy while he kissed her."

"Jesus," I groaned, laying my head back against the wall as I tried to fight off the excitement that the image was giving me.

"And then I nearly fucked him into the wall at the top of the stairs the other night, but he froze me out."

I barked out a crude laugh. "He froze you out?"

"Yep." He kissed my neck again. "I told him I loved him, and he pushed me away."

"Fuck." I groaned. "That sounds like something I'd do."

He grunted and pushed my jeans down as I struggled to kick off my boots at the same time. "Yet I said the same thing to you tonight, and I have your pants down around your ankles," he joked, and I punched his stomach before successfully kicking off my jeans and underwear. "Damn," he groaned, looking down at my body for the first time in two years. "I didn't realize how much of myself I was forgetting about until right this fucking moment."

I grabbed my cock and stroked it from semi-hard to raging as he watched. "And now you've talked your way into getting your cake and eating it too."

"I'll fucking eat something," he lobbed back, and then wrapped his hand around me, pushing mine off and stroking me with just the right amount of pressure that I loved.

"Jesus fuck." My hips jerked and pushed my cock deeper into his hand as pre-cum coated his palm, gliding up and down with silky perfection. "I'm going to blow my load in two seconds flat."

He smirked and slowly sank to his knees. "Let's see if we can make that happen."

"Dallin," I growled in warning as he pushed me flat to the wall and started sucking me off. "God. Fucking. Dammit." I bit through clenched teeth before burying my fingers in his hair, fisting it, and controlling his pace. "You always were better at sucking my cock than Parker was."

He looked up at me and rolled his eyes. "Yeah, but he can eat pussy like nobody's business."

"Lucky Rey."

"Lucky you, too," he countered, before lowering his tongue to my balls and sucking them into his mouth one after the other. "Turn around." He forcefully flipped me around to face the wall and then pulled my hips back until my ass was presented to him. I usually hated being manhandled, but he knew he was the only one that got away with it.

Still, after all the time that passed, he was the only one to truly have the upper hand over me. Parker and I switched occasionally, but I usually topped. And that worked for us, but it seemed Dallin wasn't interested in taking a cock tonight if the way he was tonguing my ass said anything.

"Where's your lube?" he asked, rimming my ass with his fingers just enough to make me want to push back onto them.

"Parker's bag." I tossed my head back toward the backpack he kept with him, and Dallin opened the front zipper and found it.

I walked toward him and panted as he undid his jeans and pushed them down, kicking his boots off with a thud as we stared at each other. "Take your hair down," he ordered, and I shook it free of the tie it was in. "How do you want it the first time?" he asked, and my brows rose to my hairline.

"The first time?" I smirked before he shoved me toward the bed.

"I'm fucking this ass all night, Trey," he growled against my lips. "So, how do you want it the first time?"

His thick cock pressed against mine and he fisted them both in one hand, nearly making my eyes roll back in my head. "On my back." I stammered out before collapsing onto the bed as he followed. I lifted my legs, opening my ass for him as he popped the lid of the lube open and squirted some on his fingers.

"How long has it been since you've taken it?" he asked, pushing two fingers into me at once.

"Fuck," I grunted, fisting my cock, and stroking it to counter the burn of the stretch. "A few months."

"Good." He watched his fingers working into me, opening them up and scissoring them before adding a third, drawing a hiss from my lips. "I know you said you don't want Rey, and I'm going to let you pretend you believe that. But I'm also going to give you some rules to follow."

"Rules?" I snapped. "Right now? You want to talk about rules?"

"Rule number one," he continued as he coated his cock with the lube and then tossed it aside. "You're never rude to her. Never." He looked into my eyes as he said it. "You want to treat me and Parker like emotional punching bags, fine, but you treat her like that, and I'll treat you like a physical bag and knock the ever-living shit out of you. Understood?"

"Yep." I hissed as he folded my legs back toward my chest and I grabbed the back of my knees to stay open for him. "Got it." I wasn't going to be rude to her on principle. I was a dick, not a monster. "That it?"

"While you're pretending you don't want her physically, you're going to help me give her what she wants sexually."

"Dallin," I growled, ready to object as he lined the head of his cock up with my ass. I forced myself to take a deep breath, because while Parker was a foot long and had the barbells of Satan lining his cock, Dallin was a whole lot thicker, and it was going to burn when he fucked me.

Coincidentally, that was just how I liked it.

"Our girl," he growled, looking away from his cock and into my eyes. "Yes, I'm calling her yours too, because I know she's going to end up with all of us, eventually. But our girl gets hot on the idea of me fucking you guys and getting fucked right back." Fire shot through my balls at his dirty words. "Soaks her pussy right through on just the thought." He pushed forward, slowly feeding his cock into my ass, and I hissed at the pain but kept my knees wide for him. "So when I fuck you, and when I let you fuck me, you're going to be as loud as you want to be. So our perfect girl down the hall can soak her sweet pussy hearing it."

"Dammit!" I arched my back in agony as he pushed deeper past the first ring of muscles and into me. "So thick."

"That's right." He leaned forward with one hand next to my head and his body pressed tight against the front of mine as he pulled back and then thrust in again, making us both moan. "I'm going to fuck you so good, and you're going to let our girl hear just how good I'm giving it to you." He kissed me, burying himself in balls deep and rocking so my cock was pinned between our abs. "Like it or not, you're going to get our girl wet."

"D, stop fucking talking or I'm going to come and kick you out."

He smirked down at me, withdrew, and then slammed back into me, forcing the air from my lungs. "What's wrong, big guy?" He reached between our bodies and took my cock in his hand. "Does talking about making our girl wet and horny get you excited?" He leaned down and kissed my neck, biting me as he started pounding into me. "Good. Because it's going to make the reward of watching you fuck her for the first time that much hotter for me."

"Fuck it," I growled, reaching up with my mouth and biting his shoulder as he pounded into me, making him roar out and then slam into me so hard the headboard cracked against the wall. Fire lit into my balls and spine as my orgasm erupted free.

"That's it," he moaned as I tightened down on him, "Come for me, Trey. Fucking milk me dry."

"God," I hollered, detaching my teeth from his shoulder as he pushed his tongue into my mouth and came. I coated our stomachs with my come as he filled my ass until we were both panting and gasping for breath after such a powerful and pointed exchange between us.

"Fuck, that was good," he moaned, rolling his hips one last time before pulling out and getting off me so I could lower my legs. "I missed you."

I hummed almost incoherently, but I couldn't give up the chance to goad him. "Of course you did, I'm a catch."

He shoved me so hard that I fell off the edge of the bed into a heap on the floor with a flurry of curses thrown his way as he laughed maniacally. I couldn't even be mad, because he'd made a good move, and I'd earned it. I chuckled and stood up, feeling more relaxed thanks to a giant orgasm, and used his discarded shirt to wipe the come off my stomach as he glared at me.

"I need to shower you and the road off me," I said, unsure whether he'd be waiting for me when I got back, but I wasn't willing to ask him to stay.

He said he planned on spending the night, but with Reyna down the hall, I didn't discount his desire to choose her over me either.

"I have to turn the water back on," he said with a smirk as he groaned and stood up, walking ahead of me across the hall to the bathroom.

"Why is the water off?" I asked, watching him kneel in the closet and switch the shutoff back on.

"Because Parker and Reyna needed a push in the right direction to get over their fear of making the first move."

"I don't follow." I stood dumbly as he turned the water on in the large tile shower and tested it.

"She was in our shower when he tried to take one in here, and I was on my way out to a tattoo appointment." He shrugged. "From what I heard when I met up with Parker later, he joined her to conserve water."

"Ah." I nodded, finally following the story. "Hence the face riding and the world-class blow job." I expected him to walk back out of the bathroom, now that the water was all squared away, but instead, he stepped into the shower and tipped his head back, letting the water of one showerhead soak his hair.

"She really can give a world-class blowy." He smiled to himself with his eyes closed. "If you stop standing out there like a statue, I'll wash you up and give you another one. Then you can compare notes when she finally gives you the time of day and blows your mind."

Trouble.

The whole fucking situation was trouble.

But damn if I didn't walk into that shower and come down his throat a few minutes later, as he proved to be a worthy opponent to her reputation.

Only a small part of my brain wondered if I'd ever feel her lips wrapped around me. But an even bigger part of me knew I would. I wouldn't be able to resist her forever if Dallin had anything to say about it.

CHAPTER 13

Reyna

"There it is," Parker said with a smile in his voice as he lay back on Dallin's side of the bed with one hand tucked behind his head.

Groaning, I rolled over to face him, fighting the spins that were trying to make me vomit, and tucked my hands under my cheek. "What?"

"Listen." He still smirked up at the ceiling and looked over at me.

"I don't—" I paused, catching a distinct sound floating through the wooden door of my bedroom. "Is that—?" He nodded. "Oh."

Dallin was moaning and there was a distinct sound of skin slapping now that I finally forced myself to listen for it.

"Yep." Parker groaned, reaching under the blanket to adjust himself. He was wearing only a pair of boxers and having him nearly naked, in my bed, after the events in the shower, I was finding it hard to ignore my urge to straddle him.

Or beg him to fuck me into the mattress. Thankfully, I was just drunk enough still to feel ill, and adding in the throbbing from my busted toe, I was out of commission for the evening.

"Do you want to go join them?" I asked as a loud noise that could only be described as a roar filled the air. My body hummed knowing that Dallin and Trey were hooking up, and I didn't feel jealous or left out, even though Trey didn't want me.

"No way." Parker smirked again. "The sex that's going on in that room right now, and probably for the rest of the night, is raw, aggressive, and no doubt painful for one of them. I have no interest in getting in the middle of that." He rolled over to face me but kept distance between our bodies. "I much prefer your sweet, docile company tonight to all that rage and testosterone."

I chuckled and scooted closer to him. "Is this okay?" I let my fingers brush over the smooth skin on his muscled chest, and he responded by sliding his warm palm over my hip and pulling me even closer.

"This is perfect." He sighed like he was so content to just be in my presence, even though he wasn't getting any sex.

There were more moans and louder slaps of skin before the loud banging of the headboard hitting the wall repeatedly, and then it all stopped. Parker chuckled and looked at the clock. "That lasted about as long as I expected it to."

"What do you mean?"

"That was a quick fuck. Considering that was the first time Dallin has been with a man in two years, and the first time they've been together in that time, it doesn't surprise me it lasted all of ten minutes."

"Who do you think—?" I faded off and shook my head. "Never mind." I giggled.

"Who do I think did the fucking and who took it?" He raised an eyebrow at me in the dark and slid his arm under my pillow, so my head rested on his biceps. He smelled so damn good and was so warm, I loved the feeling of him against me. I nodded shyly, feeling like a voyeur for even asking about something so personal and private. "Judging by Dallin's moans, he was fucking Trey. I doubt after not bottoming in two years that Dallin is just going to jump right in and take that fucking brick with no prep."

I snorted and shook my head at the way he described the entire exchange. He was such a guy, and it was actually really refreshing.

"I think I just had an epiphany," I started. "Now, I'm still filthy drunk, so take this with a spoonful of salt." Parker chuckled at my flub, but I kept going. "I think the reason I'm so okay with Dallin having sex with you and Trey is because we're anatomically and emotionally so different."

"Hmm. Explain further, oh drunk one."

"With you at least, because I don't know anything about Trey's personality other than he's as cuddly as a cactus, you give Dallin that camaraderie and bromance without a ton of girly hormones and feelings involved. He can be rough and crass with you in ways he doesn't allow himself to be with me. Probably because I'd cry." I shrugged and giggled for the hundredth time. "And then with me, he gets the sweet and tender side of him nurtured and returned that I don't think he gets from you guys."

"And the pussy," Parker added nobly. "Believe it or not, there is quite a distinguishable difference in feeling between fucking an ass and a pussy. Never mind that dudes don't have tits and smooth legs usually, either."

"Right." I nodded. "The anatomical differences are things that we literally can't replicate if we wanted to replace each other. I can give you and him femininity when you want."

"It's not a competition, but more of a buffet. Is that what you're saying?"

I chuckled and shook my head. "You make it sound weird."

"Do you want to know how I compared the two the other night?" he asked with a smirk, and I nodded. "Baseball was women, because it was slow-paced and methodical, and football was men because it's brutal and violent with testosterone."

I snorted, tipping my head back and laughing. "You're right, the buffet analogy works so much better."

He squeezed me tight, and I snuggled deeper again, letting the darkness lull me under to sleep. "Good night, Rey," he whispered, kissing my forehead.

"Good night, Parker." I kissed his bare chest and let the watermelon margaritas take me to meet the sandman.

The next morning I walked out to the kitchen, stretching as I went while trying to avoid walking on the end of my toe at all. I stopped short when I got around the corner and saw Trey standing at the coffeepot, watching it like it would brew quicker if he stared at it.

Wearing nothing but a pair of black boxers.

Damn.

His hair was down and wild around his shoulders, dusting the dark tattoos that covered his entire back and arms. He didn't have any on his legs like Dallin did, but he somehow looked darker and more dangerous, even without the extra ink.

He was tall like Dallin, but not quite as muscular as him or Parker, but it fit him better.

"Morning," he said with a thick, gruff voice, without even looking over his shoulder.

I looked behind me like he was somehow talking to someone else, but I knew Parker was still passed out in bed, and Dallin was nowhere to be seen.

"Morning," I croaked, and then cleared my throat. "I didn't expect you to be up so early."

"Why is that?" He finally looked over his shoulder and his eyes fell to my workout shorts and sports bra before he turned around to face the coffee machine again.

"I just—" I paused, realizing I couldn't say *Because you were up all night getting railed by my boyfriend*, so I lied. "Didn't take you as an early riser."

"Hmm." He took the pot out when it finally slowed to a trickle. "Coffee?"

"Please." I walked to the fridge, grabbed the creamer I liked, and met him around the island as he poured me a cup and handed it to me. "Thank you. Creamer?"

He shook his head. "I like it strong." He took a sip of the molten liquid and sighed as it burned off three layers of taste buds from his tongue, and I smirked in surprise.

I added, "And hot." He shrugged with a smirk of his own. I tentatively took a sip of my coffee and hummed happily when it hit my taste buds as he watched.

My eyes were drawn to the very visible bite marks and hickeys that were on his neck and shoulders popping out from under his hair, and my mind tried to imagine what position he was in for Dallin to give them to him when he startled me by talking. "You don't look too hungover this morning," he observed with a raised brow.

I smiled over the rim of my cup and then set it down to grab some fruit out of the fridge. "I'm kind of immune to hangovers. Which is dangerous, because then I never learn my lesson when margaritas are half price."

He crossed his arms over his chest, resting his cup on one forearm as he watched me lay out a bunch of fruit. Under his intense stare, another breakfast idea came to mind, and I turned back to the fridge, putting the fruit back and grabbing things like eggs, ham, and bacon.

"Thanks for helping with my toe last night," I said as I started heating a pan on the stove, which thankfully lit on the first try.

"Sorry, you hurt it because of me," he replied.

"Eh." I shrugged. "Sometimes I can be like a dog with a bone. I shouldn't have tricked you into talking to me." I looked over at him. "Sorry about that and lying to you, too."

He nodded. "Can't say it ended terribly for me."

I knew what he was trying to insinuate, but it felt like he was trying to hurt me with it instead of simply stating a fact. "No, I suppose it didn't."

"Does that bother you?" he countered, taking it one step further as I poured a bunch of eggs into the pan and scrambled them up. I got another pan out and got it heating as I threw some already-cooked bacon and ham into it to reheat it.

"Do you want it to?" I finally asked when I felt like I could do it calmly.

"No," he replied instantly, and I kind of believed him but couldn't be sure.

"You being with Dallin and Parker doesn't bother me," I said, finally answering his original question. "I'm glad you and D ultimately stopped fighting."

"Fucking each other's brains out doesn't mean we've made up and are done fighting," he grumbled.

"Seriously?" I scowled at the pan as I flipped the meat over before preheating the oven and getting the pizza dough out of the fridge. We ate pizza so often that I always had fresh dough chilled and ready to go.

"We don't have to be nice to each other to fuck."

"But wouldn't it make it more enjoyable if you were?" I threw back.

"Nah." He shrugged. "Hate sex is kind of my thing."

I snorted and shook my head. "Then we'd get along great in bed," I said, and then froze with my mouth open in embarrassment. "I mean—" I paused as he cocked a brow up at me, challenging me to keep going. "I meant because you hate me."

"I don't—" he started, but the clicking of the spare bedroom door opening halted his response as Dallin walked out, rubbing his hand over his face before ruffling his hair. He was naked, and his body was covered with marks to match the ones on Trey.

"Morning." He smiled brightly, but I couldn't get my tongue to work, so I smiled back and then turned back to the stove. I felt my face burn bright in a blush as I heard him kiss Trey behind me while I spread out dough on a pan. I buttered it and tossed it into the oven on autopilot as I tried to process what I was feeling. Dallin's hands slid around my bare midriff, and he kissed the back of my neck under where my messy bun sat, and he hummed. "Breakfast pizza? Smells almost as good as you."

I smiled quickly as I caught the scent of sex on his skin and felt Trey's eyes on us from the corner.

"I, uh—" I shook him off gently and stirred the eggs and ham again before wiping my hands off on a towel. "I have to get a workout in before my day gets super crazy." I finally turned around and faced him, praying my smile looked more natural than it felt. "Can you finish the pizza?"

His dark eyebrows bent over his eyes in a scowl as he stared at me silently. "You okay?" he asked quietly.

"Yeah," I said quickly, hating how fake it sounded. "I just have a really busy day and am overwhelmed by it." I shook my head. "Meetings all day and—" I shrugged. "You know how it is."

"Yeah," he said, but he didn't look convinced.

"Thanks." I leaned up on my toes and he turned his head to kiss me on the lips, but I dodged him and kissed his cheek. "I'll probably see you later tonight."

I didn't wait for his reply; instead, I ran to my office and grabbed my laptop bag, shoving everything I could think of on such short notice into it, and then slid a flowy top on over my bra before rushing back out to the front door.

Trey and Dallin both watched me with speculation in their eyes as I threw a small wave their way and ran from the apartment.

My body was in fight-or-flight mode for some reason, and I didn't understand it, but the farther I walked, the deeper the anxiety built inside my gut.

I had to get a handle on my fucking emotions if I stood a chance of keeping it together around the three of them.

Or I'd lose everything.

CHAPTER 14

Dallin

I left the shop an hour ago, unable to even pretend to be useful when my mind was elsewhere. Trey and Parker were setting up rooms they had taken in the shop to see clients in as soon as they were ready.

But I had to get out of there.

I had to find Rey.

She answered my texts with simple one- or two-word answers every time I tried to start a conversation, and the two times I tried calling her, she sent me to voicemail.

Her ruse had been that she was busy today. But after checking the security cameras at the apartment, I knew that she had never returned after her mad dash out the door for a workout, and she wouldn't go to a business meeting in her gym clothes.

So she had lied to me.

And I couldn't think of another time in the two years that we were together that she had done that. We were always one hundred percent honest with each other, since day one, yet today she lied to get away from me and I had a pit in my stomach trying to tell me I fucked everything up.

It was getting late, bars were busy, and the nightlife crowd was building on the sidewalks as I rode through the city, racking my brain to think of where she'd be hiding out.

I tried a few spots she could have been, but each time I walked in, I knew in my bones she wasn't there. I could feel her absence grow the longer I went without settling whatever had made her upset enough this morning to bolt.

I parked my bike on the curb down the street from one of her favorite spots, even though I knew they had closed an hour ago.

Lost in Time, the private bookstore she always came to when she felt like the pressure of writing was making her lose the joy of the story, was mostly dark as I walked up to the front door. But in the back, a single light illuminated the table where Reyna sat, leaning back in her chair with her knees to her chest and an old favorite of hers balanced atop them, reading.

This was her safe space, and she felt like she needed to come here today, to get away from me. As if she could feel my gaze on her, she looked up from the book and locked eyes on me from across the store. I lifted my hand and gave her a small wave, but she didn't move.

Sasha, the owner, was a good friend of Reyna's and would have let her stay late after she closed up. Even though I knew the door would be locked, I still tried.

The denial of access to Rey felt like a physical blow to my stomach. Finally, as if she would rather have done anything else, she stood up and walked to the door, turning the lock and stepping back as I pushed the door open.

I locked it behind me and stood before her, suddenly unsure of what to do or say.

"I'm sorry," she said finally, with sagging shoulders like the weight of the world was on them.

"Can I touch you?" I asked, forcing the words past my dry mouth, and her eyes widened in surprise.

"You've never asked me that before," she whispered.

"You've never lied and hidden from me before, either." I hated the anger that those words caused in my heart.

She swallowed and looked back out the door to the dark streets as tears started pooling in her bottomless hazel eyes. When the first one fell over and ran down her cheek, I couldn't fight the urge to hold her anymore, and I pulled her against my chest.

Thankfully, she came willingly, wrapping her arms around my waist and clinging to me as her shoulders shook.

"I'm sorry," she whispered again.

"Come talk to me." I picked her up and carried her to a large leather chair I usually sat in when we came here. She would read and I'd draw sketches in quiet peace with the smell of old books surrounding us. This was a safe place for both of us, yet I didn't realize it until that moment. I settled in the chair with her in my lap, her head tucked under my chin, and when she was comfortable, I asked, "What happened?"

"I don't know." She shook her head and sighed. "I honestly don't. I've been trying to figure it out all day long and I'm no surer now than I was when I bolted."

"If you want them to leave, just say so." I went for direct and to the point, making it as simple for her as possible. Even though my entire body was conflicted by the idea of telling Trey and Parker that we couldn't be together.

"That's not what I want." She sighed and leaned back to look up at me. "I knew what you were doing last night. And I was fine. And this morning, seeing Trey, I didn't feel jealousy or envy or anything else. Even when I saw the hickeys on his neck and stuff." I cringed slightly, knowing I'd left him marked, and that she had seen it. It was tasteless to throw it in her face like that. And then I came out, naked and hard, covered with marks, not even thinking about her feelings first. "He tried to goad me, I think, asking me if it bothered me that he was with you, and I countered back, asking if he wanted it too. He said no." She shrugged. "And I think he was telling the truth. But then you came out, and you've never looked so . . ." She paused, fighting to find the right words. "Thoroughly fucked and satisfied before." Her eyes misted over again. "And I felt lacking in that moment. Like what I was giving to you before wasn't enough."

"It was, Rey." I sighed, hating that she felt this way.

"No, it wasn't, baby." She shook her head and placed her hand on my chest. "And that's okay. I know now that you have different tastes between men and women, and *logically* I understand that. But I think in the moment, knowing that you got something I can't give you, from someone who openly hates me, left me feeling inadequate and like I was on the outside looking in." I closed my eyes in regret. "I didn't know I'd feel that way until I did, or I would have discussed it with you first. I'm sorry I ran; I just didn't want to admit my faults in front of Trey."

"You are not inferior to him," I said firmly, holding on to each side of her face until she stared right at me. "You are not inferior to either of them, Reyna. I'm so, so, so, sorry that you felt that way today. And I'm even more sorry that I didn't fight you on it at the moment and make you stay so we could talk it through right away. I thought giving you space was what you needed, but I spent the day with them while you were feeling bad about yourself." I sighed and took a deep breath, fighting the panic building. "This is new, for all of us, and I think we're going to have to learn as we go. But I promise you, I want to do better. I want to be better. For you."

"I know, baby." She kissed me, lingering against my lips and breathing like it was the first deep breath she had taken all day. "Me too, I promise to communicate better in the future."

"Okay." I relaxed back into the chair, and she settled back against my chest, letting me breathe her calm scent in. "Did you read anything good today?"

She smiled against my chest and chuckled softly. "Actually, yes."

"What was it?" I asked, feeling like there was something more there.

"It's a new 'why choose' that just came out."

"A 'why choose'?" I asked, not familiar with the term.

"Yeah, a story about a woman who met a guy and fell for him, only to find out he had two roommates he didn't tell her about." She leaned back to look up at me. "Roommates who like to share their toys like good boys." She smirked as the lightbulb clicked over my head.

"You're reading about a polyamorous relationship?" I raised a brow at her in surprise. "Color me intrigued." I shifted her, so she was straddling me and facing me head-on. "What are your thoughts about it? The book, I mean." I smirked at her.

"Hmm." She adjusted herself and slid her hands around the back of my neck as she bit her bottom lip. "Well, I'm not done yet, but there was this one scene that I just finished a while ago." She paused and licked her lips before leaning in to whisper against mine, "Where she was on her hands and knees taking it from behind by her boyfriend, while one friend was underneath her in the sixty-nine position." She tilted and rocked her hips against me and I tightened my hold on her hips to stop her from getting me hard. "Her boyfriend was taking turns penetrating her pussy and then he'd pull out and put it in his buddy's mouth and then go back into her." Fuck it, I was hard. "And she would ride the buddy's face while she was taking it."

"Rey," I growled, letting her rock against me now that I could not hide my desire.

She moaned and moved over to my ear, tracing the shell with her tongue. "They were essentially a human Fun Dip snack," she whispered, talking about her favorite guilty-pleasure candy treat. "The boyfriend was the candy stick." She rocked forward. "She was the bright pink candy powder he dipped the stick into." She rocked again. "And the buddy was the wet mouth that licked the sweet treat clean before he dipped it again."

"I'm going to fuck you so hard right here in this chair if you talk any more," I growled. My girl's ability to talk dirty knew no bounds thanks to her eloquent writing abilities, and apparently, I now had a fetish for candy.

"Wait, aren't you going to ask me what the second buddy was doing during all of that?"

I growled again, unable to even answer her, knowing full well it was going to be dirty, and she was going to tell me, anyway.

She bit my earlobe and reached between us to stroke my cock through my jeans. "He was behind the candy-stick man, fucking him with his hard stick. Pushing him in and out of the other two the entire time."

"Fuck it," I thundered, picking her up and walking her toward the storeroom in the back of the shop. As nice as Sasha's shop was, it wasn't updated with current technology, which meant she had no cameras around. And even if she did, I wouldn't have stopped. "I'll give you a nice hard stick to play with, baby. All you have to do is ask nice." I pushed her up against the wall and pulled her shorts down to her ankles. She giggled and moaned when I dipped my fingers into her pussy and spread her wetness over her clit and pinched it. I opened my jeans, freeing my cock before picking her up under her knees and holding on to her ass with my hands so her feet rested above my biceps. "Ask nicely, baby," I growled as I pressed my cock against her soaked pussy.

"Please fuck me, Dallin." She bit her lip and tore her shirt and bra off over her head, revealing her sexy tits to my hungry eyes. "I want you so bad."

"Hold on." I pushed forward and then lifted her up and down onto my entire cock, coating it with her wetness before I pressed her back against the wall again. "I'm going to fuck you so good, you won't even think about any other sticks."

She giggled, and that evaporated into a moan as I bottomed out and rocked against her clit. "Prove it," she challenged me with a sinister smirk on her perfect lips.

And I did just that.

—

"Tell me about last night," Rey said as she adjusted her bra back over her lush breasts.

I slid my belt through the buckle and raised an eyebrow at her. "Are you sure you want to know about it?"

"Yes." She rolled her eyes. "I told you; I was fine with the act itself. I just wasn't prepared to see the proof of it first thing in the morning."

I caught her as she opened the storeroom door and pulled her flush to my front. "I wasn't thinking this morning, and I promise you I won't be so senseless again."

She waved her hand dismissively. "I want to see you happy, Dallin, I really do. And I know that involves being intimate with them. You can't just keep them locked away in the bedroom and not give your relationship the freedom it deserves. They deserve to have all of you, just like I do; I don't want you treating them like dirty little secrets." She arched her brows at me. "Honestly. Now tell me about your night."

"It was—" I paused, trying to find the right word for it. "Therapeutic?" I shrugged. "Healing? I don't know exactly."

"Okay, tell me what you did, then." She tightened her hold around my waist. "Because I can tell you what it sounded like and what Parker guessed was happening, but I want to hear what you did."

"Does it turn you on or repulse you?" I asked, worried.

"On," she answered instantly without missing a beat. "So on."

Now it was my turn to roll my eyes as I pulled her from the room toward the table that she had occupied all day. "Well, I—" I shrugged, suddenly shy about the whole thing. "We fucked, a lot."

"You fucked him, though, right?" She licked her lips. "That's what Parker guessed was happening considering you haven't done anal in a while."

I snorted and started picking up her stuff and putting it back in her laptop bag. "Sometimes he knows too much for his good. Yes, I fucked Trey." I paused.

"You have to give me more than just that."

I sat down in the chair and pulled her down into the one next to me. "What are you asking for specifically? Tell me what you want to know."

She chewed her bottom lip and then sighed. "I guess I need to hear about how much you enjoyed it. And what you enjoyed about it."

"I enjoyed it," I offered. "I enjoyed being—" I shrugged, trying to find the right words yet again. "Rough, I guess that's the best word for it." She chuckled and covered her mouth. "What?"

She shook her head and flicked her hand. "Parker said the fucking going on last night was raw and aggressive and filled with testosterone. He also said one of you was probably in pain from it." I snorted and rolled my eyes at Parker's ability to make shit weird. "I asked him if he wanted to join you two and he said no way. That he preferred my sweet, calm, feminine nature at the moment, over all of that."

I laughed, nodding. "He wasn't wrong. Trey most definitely felt some pain last night, because I wasn't gentle or nice about it, not after the emotional whiplash he's given me all week." I stood up and pulled her to her feet. "I do have a question for you, though."

"Oh no." She shuddered. "This isn't going to be good, is it?"

I pursed my lips and glared at her until she giggled and waved for me to go on. "I was wondering if you'd be interested in helping me prep my body to be a bottom again sometime. Because Parker's right, that's not something you just jump into after two years off."

Her eyebrows rose to her hairline again, and a flush crawled up her skin. "You want me to help you? I'm surprised you would want me involved."

"I want you involved with everything, Rey. I told you that from the start. If you don't want to be, that's fine, I can take care of it myself. I was just wondering if that would help you feel included and on the inside of things."

She chewed on her thumbnail with a small smile on her lips. "Do I get to put toys in you like you did to me when we first started doing it?" I smirked and nodded. "I get to give you pleasure—" She smiled bigger. "There?"

"Yes, baby." I kissed her lips, seductively. "Does the idea of that excite you?"

She nodded quickly. "Very, very much."

"Then let's get home and get busy."

CHAPTER 15

Reyna

I giggled walking in the front door to the apartment, leaning heavily on the door as Dallin kissed my neck and tried to get his hand down the front of my shorts. "Oh," I gasped, locking eyes on Parker's warm brown ones from the couch. "Hi."

His lips twitched as he turned the television off and put both arms across the back of the couch. "Hello there."

Dallin shut the door behind us and kicked his boots off, tucking them under the bench before nudging me toward Parker. "Park missed you today, too."

I looked between them in uncertainty before Parker motioned for me to come over to the couch, and I went eagerly. Because I had missed him as well. As I tried to sit down next to him, he pulled me onto his lap, straddling his thick thighs, before burying his face in my neck. "You smell like sex, baby girl." He kissed my neck and wrapped his hands around my waist as I ran my fingers up the back of his head. "And Dallin. You and him, mixed, makes me wild."

He pulled out of my neck and kissed me, gently at first, like he was giving me time to shorten it, but I wasn't interested in ending it yet. I put my hands on his abs and leaned into him, pulling a growl from his lips as he deepened it. I felt the couch dip next to us and looked over as Dallin threw himself down next to Parker, watching us with desire in his eyes.

"Do you two have any idea how hot that is?" Dallin asked in a husky voice as he pushed my hair out of my face to see better.

"Yes, but I want to see for myself anyway," I smirked, and pulled back, nodding toward Parker. D didn't hesitate to lean over and pull Parker into a deep sensual kiss that fulfilled every fantasy I'd had since that night in the Uber when I watched them kiss for the first time. This time, I could feel Parker's body react as he hardened even more underneath me. I rocked forward and kissed his neck and then bit his ear as he growled against Dallin's lips, "God, you two are so sexy. I want to see more."

Parker pulled back, laid his head against the back of the couch, and panted before looking between us. "You want to play, baby girl?"

I nodded eagerly and bit my lip. "Dallin wants to play with some toys tonight to prep himself for your ribbed cock." His nostrils flared as I looked over at D with a smile. "Can Parker help us play with your ass, baby?"

"This is your game," Dallin said firmly and confidently, leaning back next to Parker. "You make the rules."

"Where's Trey?" I asked Parker, suddenly worried about being interrupted and having one or both of the guys lured away with his dark appeal.

Parker smirked. "Halfway through an eight-hour piece downstairs." He winked at Dallin. "Emo Barbie set him up with the client from hell and he's going to be there for a few more hours finishing up."

"Great." Dallin rolled his eyes and then licked his lips. "Means he'll be in a fantastic mood when he gets back."

"Well then, let's not waste any of our time right now." Parker effortlessly stood with me in his arms and held his hand out for Dallin, who took it and followed us to the bedroom.

He slid me down the front of his body in our room, as Dallin stood next to him and raised an eyebrow at me. "What next?"

"Clothes." I waved my finger at them both. "Off. All of them."

Both of them grinned wickedly and began stripping for me as I sat on the end of the bed and watched with rapture. I'd been to a few male strip clubs over the years, but these two men, undressing for only me, was better than anything else I'd ever seen. When they both stood naked and hard in front of me, I rose to my feet and sauntered forward. They were both perfection, cut from stone and hardened to rock for me.

Me.

To show them my appreciation, I sank to my knees and looked up at them from under my lashes. "I need to taste you both."

"You won't hear any objections from me." Dallin grinned as Parker ran his fingers through my hair and fisted his cock.

"I need to feel you, or I'm going to lose my mind," Parker groaned, leading my lips to the head of him, where I eagerly took him into my mouth. He groaned and let his head fall backward as his hips jerked. I hummed and relaxed my jaw like he had taught me the other day in the shower, so his barbells didn't break my teeth, and worked him deeper.

I wrapped my hand around Dallin's cock and stroked him as he leaned over and kissed Parker's neck, holding him by the back of it. Parker's chest and face were getting red as I got him more and more worked up before I switched, letting him pop free from my mouth, and diving on Dallin's.

He was a lot thicker, but without the metal piercings, I could still work him down after perfecting the move for the last few years.

"Fuck, she's so good at that," Parker growled, with his fingers still in my hair, pulling me on and off Dallin's cock. "Go deeper, baby," he instructed, pushing me down further on my boyfriend's cock until I gagged and dug my claws into his bare thighs. "Good girl." He pulled me off and then back onto it. He kneeled behind me, cradling my body with his as he forced my mouth up and down Dallin's cock like a toy meant only to be used for pleasure. And it made me so fucking hot to feel used and cherished at the same time.

"Take her clothes off, Park," Dallin ordered through clenched teeth, taking over control of my head as Parker dropped both hands to my shorts and started pulling them down over my ass and to my knees. I shuffled, kicking them off my legs with my panties as Dallin held my head still and pushed himself all the way down the back of my throat and held it there, rolling his hips to stretch my throat out. "Your pussy is coated with my come, and relaxed from getting fucked an hour ago, Rey." He pulled out and I gasped for breath as Parker lifted my shirt and bra, revealing my aching tits to his waiting hands. Parker's cock pressed directly between my thighs as he pushed them wide with his knees and rocked back and forth. He was making me delirious for him again like I'd been in the shower when I begged him to fuck me. "Think Parker can fuck you tonight without tearing you apart?"

"Fuck," I groaned, pushing back against the rock-hard steel of his cock as it nudged against my wet pussy lips. "Yes," I moaned. "But I want to play with you first." I looked up at Dallin through my watery lashes. "I need to see you take a toy before I take a cock, or I'll never get a chance. Because as soon as one of you starts fucking me, I'm not stopping until I pass out."

They both growled and moaned in agreement as Dallin stepped back, walking over to the chest of sex toys he kept in the closet. It was black leather and inconspicuous to most until you opened it up and found an array of toys that we hardly ever used, thanks to my usually boring nature.

But not tonight.

Tonight, we were going to play.

Parker slid his hand around the front of my stomach and down to my soaked entrance and slowly teased circles around my clit. "I'm going to fuck you so good, baby girl," he whispered in my ear as he continued thrusting his cock through my wetness and fingered me. Dallin walked back out with a few silicone toys and the lube I loved, stopping to watch us after dumping them all out onto the bed. "Get on the bed for me," Parker instructed, and I scrambled up, tearing my shirt and bra off to be completely naked like they were, before kneeling in the center of the bed.

Parker grabbed a couple of pillows and threw them down in the center and Dallin crawled over them, lying on his stomach facing me.

"Are you ready?" Parker asked him with a smirk as he kissed his way down Dallin's spine until he stopped right above his presented ass.

"Fuck yes," Dallin groaned, looking up at me as I watched with rapture. "Spread your legs, Rey," he ordered me and I obediently pushed my knees open and he slipped two fingers directly inside me, hooking them so I had no choice but to scoot closer and lean over his back to avoid pain. "Both of you, baby. I need to feel you both."

"Yes, sir," I moaned as he thrust his fingers in and out. Parker spread Dallin's cheeks apart and smirked at me.

"Lube your fingers up, baby girl."

I grabbed the bottle and coated my fingers with a generous amount and then poured some directly onto Dallin's exposed ass, making him hiss from the contact of the cool gel.

"Now what?" I asked Parker in uncertainty. Logically, I knew what to do. Dallin loved playing with my ass, so I was no novice. But he had never let me near his ass before; I always thought he was one of those men who thought enjoying anal play would make him gay.

The joke was on me, turned out he was just denying himself the pleasure because of his guilt over the whole lie the entire time.

"Rub them around in a circle and slowly put pressure on it," Parker instructed, watching me intently as I followed his instructions.

"Fuck," Dallin groaned, and his fingers faltered at their thrusting. "Push them in." I slowly pressed my two fingers into him, going a little and then taking them out and recoating them before going in again. "Jesus," he hissed, turning his head and biting my thigh as I worked them in as deep as I could go.

"I'm coming," I moaned, shocking everyone in the room, including myself. His fingers instantly started thrusting again, rubbing against my G-spot as he pulled the orgasm from my surprised body. "Fuck, fuck, fuck," I moaned, rolling my hips against his hand, rubbing my clit against his palm as Parker pulled my fingers and then pushed them, thrusting them in and out of Dallin.

"You two are fucking killing me," Parker moaned, staring at me as I finally stopped orgasming. My hand never stilled as I fucked Dallin's ass for the first time with them. The sensation was a lot for D, and he withdrew from my body and tightened his hands into fists around the bedsheets but never told me to stop. "God, you're doing so good, D," Parker praised him, leaning over to kiss his shoulders and rub his hands up and down his back as I shifted to kneel toward their legs.

"Rey, put the plug in." Dallin gasped like he was fighting for control. "If you keep doing that, I'm going to come all over your pillow."

"It will wash," I smirked devilishly, twisting my fingers and scissoring them the way I knew he loved to do to me. He growled and spread his legs wide, pushing back onto my hand more. I put one hand on his back and pushed his chest flat while encouraging him to lift his hips higher until he was presented perfectly for me. "Do you want to come?" I asked, willing to push him to that point as I reached under his now-lifted hips and fisted his cock.

"No," he gasped, even as his hips jerked and fucked his cock through my fist further. "I want to come when Parker comes inside you for the first time."

"Dying here," Parker whined dramatically with a wink as he stroked his own cock.

"Plug, Rey!" Dallin begged, and I took the lubed plug from Parker and pulled my fingers out of him until only the very tips remained inside that tight ring of muscles right at the end and pushed the plug in before withdrawing completely. "God!" Dallin roared, tensing under me.

"Make him feel good," I said to Parker, who was already gripping Dallin's cock in my absence and started stroking him. "God, that's so hot, D," I whispered in awe, as I stared at his body taking the wide black plug that always made me feel like I was going to tear into two right before the ache eased at the skinny neck of it. "Just a little bit more, baby." I pushed the rest of it in and heard him ease out a hissing breath as the base settled deep, locking into him.

"Fuck," Dallin said after a while, dropping his body down onto the bed and relaxing his back. He rolled over and looked at me. "How do you feel?" He was nervous about what he'd see in my eyes as he asked that, like somehow I'd be repulsed even though I'd told him the truth the entire time.

"Like I need to have a cock inside me right this second to take away the need that has built inside me from doing that to you."

He relaxed and licked his lips. "I can't wait to watch you two fuck." He sat up, moving gingerly until he knelt on the bed next to Parker. "You ready to make our girl come?"

Parker smirked and nodded to me slowly as he stroked his cock in his big hand. "How do you want to take me the first time, baby girl?"

I lay down on my back and spread my legs, not even bothering to be shy about it before rubbing my clit with my fingertips a few times to ease the burning ache there. "Just like this, so I can see who's fucking me."

Both of their jaws clenched, and Parker pulled me down the bed by my ankles until he was nestled between my thighs. The metal of his piercings lay against my exposed pussy, and I shivered from the contact of it.

"Last chance to back out, Reyna. Because once I'm inside you, I'm never going to stop," he said with seriousness in his eyes as he held himself up over my face, and I shook my head with a smirk. No way was I backing out now. He looked over at D. "You too. Last chance to keep me out of your girl."

"Our girl," Dallin answered firmly, with a nod. "I want you to fuck her good."

"My pleasure," Parker groaned, slowly pulling back until the head of his cock was at my entrance. "Relax for me, baby."

"I am," I whispered.

He chuckled and Dallin lay down next to us, palming my breast and tweaking the nipple as Parker responded.

"No, you're not." Parker put his hand flat on my stomach, right underneath my belly button, and I felt the tense muscles underneath his touch. "Right here. Relax these muscles or I'll never get inside you."

I forced a deep breath into my lungs and laid my head back flat against the bed, feeling those muscles relax under his hand as he pushed the head of his cock inside me.

"Good girl, Rey," Dallin said as Parker pushed and pulled the first few inches of his cock in and out, coating it with my arousal and D's come from earlier.

"So fucking tight," Parker bit out between clenched teeth. "How do you even fit?" He looked at D, who shrugged with a smirk.

"Feels like heaven, doesn't it?" Dallin asked before taking my nipple into his mouth and slowly sucking onto it as he watched where his best friend was sliding into my body.

I felt the hardness of the first piercing and my breath hitched in anticipation of pain, and Parker stilled.

"Right here," Parker said gently, tapping my once-again tense stomach. "Let me in."

I slid my hands up his massive shoulders and rested them there, forcing myself to stare into his deep brown eyes as the metal nudged against me again as he gently pushed, forcing it inside me. I gasped but remained relaxed as he pushed forward to the next one.

"How does it feel?" D asked, flicking his tongue over my hard nipple.

"Okay," I whispered, afraid to breathe too deeply as Parker pushed the second and the third one into me. He was deeper than Dallin had ever been, and he was only three of the four piercings inside. "Mmm," I moaned when the fourth one nudged at my entrance, and he pushed harder, forcing it inside with a bit more intensity.

"You like that?" Parker winked before lowering his lips to mine.

"Yes," I panted, arching my hips as he slid the rest of his cock into me. I couldn't feel the piercings once they were inside me, but I could feel the sensation of tugging when he started to pull out.

"Wait until I really start fucking you," he said, and turned his head toward D, kissing him as he pulled out of me quickly.

I moaned and dug my nails into his shoulders as he came free of me and spread my legs wider as he pushed all twelve inches of himself back in with one quick thrust.

"Fuck!" I moaned, biting down on my lip as intense pleasure burned inside me. "Again."

"Yes, ma'am," Parker smirked, and started fucking me. He watched me intently as he thrust in and out, watching for pain or desire to stop, but he never got it.

What he got was scratches up and down his neck and arms as I clung to him, possessed, and aching for release as the foreign sensation took me over.

"You're taking his cock so well, darling." Dallin praised me in my ear as I moaned Parker's name. The taboo of it all was nearly my undoing, but I needed to feel them both at the same time to come.

"Kiss me," I begged Dallin. "I'm so close."

"I'm right here," he whispered, sucking my bottom lip into his mouth, and Parker moaned. "We're both right here, Rey." I reached between our bodies and fisted his cock, causing his eyes to flutter closed as Parker perfected the rhythm that was driving me mad with desire.

"Up," I panted, tugging on Dallin's cock until he was forced to his knees. "I want you to choke me with your come."

"You're not vanilla at all," Parker smirked, slamming in deep and rocking his hips to rub my clit with his pelvic bone.

"Nope," Dallin replied as he lifted my head off the bed by a handful of hair as I opened my mouth and eagerly sucked him in deep. "She just hasn't been fucked by enough cocks at once to bring the naughty girl out of her."

"Until now," Parker added, lifting my knees to my chest and changing the angle of his cock. "Just wait until you take all three of our cocks at once," he growled. "Not a single hole will be empty." I clenched down hard around him at the thought of it, even as my brain tried to tell him to fuck off because Trey didn't want me like that. In my fantasy world, though, I'd have them all. So right now, I was going to let my fantasy world play boss. "Fuck, you feel so good, baby." Parker leaned over and bit the sensitive skin of Dallin's inner hip bone with a devilish smirk on his perfect lips.

Dallin cursed and pushed deeper. "I'm going to come."

"Yes!" I cried, tightening around Parker's cock as I sucked on Dallin with everything I had.

"Jesus," Parker moaned, "right there with you both."

They both slammed in and out of my body as they chased their orgasms, and it tipped me over the edge of my own. I felt my eyes roll into the back of my head as Dallin's salty taste coated the very back of my throat before he pushed all the way in to come. Parker's hips jerked madly before I felt the warmth of his orgasm coating the inside of my pussy, branding me like a hot iron of ecstasy.

"Oh my God," I gasped as Dallin finally pulled himself free of my mouth and I flopped back onto the bed in exhaustion.

He smirked and gently lowered himself down onto the bed next to me as Parker slowly withdrew from between my legs. The metal of his piercings didn't shock me anymore; instead, I found that I missed the stretch of them when I was empty.

I mewed with my eyes closed, letting my legs fall to the bed as I fought to slow my breathing down.

"I'm going to get a washcloth to clean you up, baby girl," Parker whispered, as he briefly laid his lips against my temple. "Don't go anywhere."

I moaned, not even bothering to open my eyes with a satisfied smile on my face as I felt him crawl off the bed.

"Let me get a head start," Dallin whispered into my ear before sliding down the bed, which was enough to finally open my eyes as he pushed my legs wide and lowered his lips to my aching pussy.

"D," I moaned, shaking my head back and forth. I was so sensitive and raw from the brutality of Parker's fucking that I knew it would be impossible to come again.

"Shh." He soothed me as he gently ran his tongue over the tender spots like he knew where to find them. "Let me taste you two together in one place."

"Mmm," I moaned, letting my legs fall wider as I gently ran my fingers through his hair. He licked and cleaned up the evidence of my and Parker's orgasms, and at any other time in my life, I probably would have orgasmed from the thought of that alone. But at that moment, I was nearly comatose from the turmoil of the entire day and the laundry list of orgasms I'd had since Dallin showed up at the bookstore a few hours ago.

"That's sexy," Parker mused, walking back into the bedroom as Dallin continued to tease me. "So, how do we taste?" he smirked, lying back on the bed beside us as Dallin looked up from between my legs. His lips were wet with our orgasms and the look made my belly burn with something that felt like possession.

But not in the typical way one might feel after their first threesome. I didn't feel possessive of Dallin in response to sharing him *with* Parker. I felt possessive of Dallin in response to *being* shared. Like somehow, being trusted with another man made me want him even more.

It was a mind trip, to say the least, after everything that had happened, and I wasn't in the right mindset to dissect it.

"Like sin and forgiveness, wrapped into one," Dallin finally answered, before lifting himself to his knees between mine and staring down at me. "Like the best damn combination in the world, with just the hint of something else missing off the top."

Parker sighed and gently began cleaning my tender skin as Dallin lay down on the other side of me. "Trey will come around." He looked up at me before tossing the cloth down on the end table, turning off the lamp, and pulling the blankets up over the three of us. "There's no way he'll be able to ignore how right this is for long."

"Hmm." I turned onto my side and snuggled into Dallin's chest as Parker curled around my back. "Let's worry about that when there's sleep and coffee involved. I'm too tired to think about anything past this bed and who's in it right now."

"Whatever you want," Parker said, laying sweet kisses on my shoulder, "it's yours."

"This," I whispered, relaxing into their now familiar blended scents. "I just want this for right now."

CHAPTER 16

Parker

Waking up as a piece of bread in a Reyna sandwich was one of the best ways to start the day. Her silky-smooth skin pressed against mine, her lavender scent swirling around inside my head, and the taste of her sweet spice lingering on my tongue.

Damn.

Her silky thighs nestled my cock, causing it to stir. I was on my back, and she was lying across my chest with one leg thrown over my hip, leaving her wet center snug against the tip of my cock as I hardened.

She let out a sweet sigh against my neck and shifted as my cock started pressing against her clit. But I knew better than to just slide into her and take her again after how hard I had her last night.

Our girl was going to need a few more hours to recover.

And maybe a warm bath.

I forced myself to take a few deep breaths of my own and settle my body before it lit off into an inferno of lust that would be hard to put out, and then carefully slid my body out from under Rey's, eyeing Dallin behind her.

He was still passed out, wrapped around her back, and the longer I looked over at him, waking up next to him for the first time in two years, that lust built inside me again. Groaning silently, I got out of bed, hurrying into the bathroom and starting my plan to romance Reyna after dirty-fucking her in her first threesome last night.

It's all about give and take after all.

I filled the tub with steaming hot water, adding a couple of squirts of bubble bath that sat in a fancy bottle on the back ledge, and then grabbed a fresh towel from the closet. I had no idea if she liked bubble baths or not, but I wanted to try.

When I walked back out into the bedroom, Dallin was propped up on his pillow with his arm tucked behind his head, watching me while Rey still slept in the center.

"Morning," he whispered with a smirk. "Taking a bath?"

I grabbed my underwear from the floor and pulled them on, even though I wanted nothing more than to crawl back into their bed naked. "Thought maybe Rey could use a good soak this morning."

His smirk broadened as he looked over at his sleeping girlfriend. "You always were the sweeter one out of us three."

I snorted and rolled my eyes before walking over to Rey's side of the bed and leaning down to trail kisses over her bare shoulders. "Good morning, beautiful."

"Hmm." She sighed, cracking one eye open and then smiling softly in the gentle morning light. "It wasn't a dream, was it?"

I smiled and Dallin chuckled from the other side of the bed, sliding his hand down under the blankets and onto her ass. "No, baby. You're living in your real-life fantasy land."

She rolled over onto her back, groaning slightly with the effort, and pulled the blankets up to her chin. "Am I supposed to be tender in my fantasy land?"

I shrugged guiltily as I ran my fingers through her hair. "I'm sorry about that, but I do come bearing gifts in a way." I nodded to the bathroom door. "I ran you a steaming hot bath to help ease some of that tenderness before you start your day."

Her brows rose and a dreamy look crested her face. "You did?"

Dallin scoffed. "I run you baths all the time." He flipped the blankets back dramatically, baring her body to the warm bedroom air, and then leaned down to hover right over her face. "But I'll let your goo-goo eyes for Parker slide this time."

She smiled, pulling him down for a quick kiss. "It's just sweet for someone who doesn't know how much I adore bubble baths to draw me one."

"Yeah, yeah, yeah," he whined with good-hearted mirth. "Go get in the tub and I'll start on breakfast."

"Ooh, make me bacon and you can get goo-goo eyes too," she joked as I watched their easy banter, feeling the love between them without feeling like an outsider in it all.

"Bacon and waffles," Dallin countered, and she moaned excitedly.

"If you make me bacon and waffles, I'll let you do really, really dirty things to me after." She looked over at me and I smiled down at her, leaning down to kiss her as Dallin leaned to the side and kissed her neck, making room.

"How about me, baby girl?" I whispered, licking her bottom lip as Dallin blew on her ear. "Do I get to join again?"

"I'd be sad if you didn't," she answered instantly, and then stilled. "I enjoyed myself last night with you both."

"Good." I smiled, pulling back and smoothing my hand over her temple to look into her eyes. "Because I think I'm addicted to the two of you."

She smiled brighter and looked at Dallin. "Go make me bacon, so I can get fucked again." She nudged him dramatically, and he rolled off her, laughing as he went. "Are you joining me in the bath?"

I shook my head, trying to sweeten the disappointment that flashed in her eyes as she stuck her bottom lip out and pouted. "I need to check on Trey." I kissed her once again, pulling her lush body from the bed. "And besides, if I got into that bath with you right now, I'd take advantage of your wetness and you wouldn't get any relief."

"Fine." She rolled her eyes and bit her bottom lip. "Do you think Trey's mad?"

"About what?"

"That you both spent the night with me."

"No." I shook my head. "He's the one who kept things separate, and he's a big boy who's going to have to deal with spending some solo time while we figure this all out between the four of us."

"Okay," she replied, though she didn't sound convinced.

"Go relax. Don't worry about Trey, I'll take care of the big oaf."

"Hmm." She smirked, biting her bottom lip more seductively. "I'm sure you will." She giggled and walked off into the bathroom, shutting the door behind her.

When I headed out to the kitchen, I found Dallin at the island with a cup of coffee in his hand as he watched Trey flip bacon on the stove.

"Holy shit, he cooks?" I joked as I joined them. I was in boxers, Dallin was in a pair of sweatpants, and Trey had just his jeans on, undone and hanging low, showing off the fact that he wasn't wearing anything underneath.

Trey glared at me over his shoulder.

"Figured you three could use the subsistence after last night's mattress Olympics," Trey replied, turning back to the stove.

Dallin looked at me with a pointed smirk and crossed his arms over his chest, remaining quiet. I followed what he was trying to do, so I too kept my mouth shut at Trey's obvious attempt at getting information about last night without working for it.

A long silence passed between the three of us and, as expected, Trey sighed and looked back over his shoulder at us with fire in his eyes. "You're going to make me ask, aren't you?" I raised my eyebrow at him as Dallin shrugged with that playboy grin on his face, and Trey rolled his eyes in exasperation. "Fine, how was your night?"

"It was good," I answered instantly. "Thanks for asking." I walked to the fridge and pulled out a pre-made smoothie as he groaned in frustration.

Dallin laughed and took a seat on one of the stools. "You're going to have to be a little more specific than that if you're looking for information, T."

Trey stayed silent as I drank the smoothie, using the act of flipping the bacon to keep his hands busy as he pretended to contemplate asking when we all knew he was going to fold. He couldn't help it. Even though he continued to act like he wasn't interested in Reyna, he couldn't keep his sexual fascination with her at bay.

"Fine!" he sighed. "Did you both fuck her last night?"

"Define 'fuck her,'" Dallin prodded. "Do you mean, did she take a cock in her pussy and her ass at the same time?"

The glare Trey shot at him would have been enough to melt steel, as Dallin's words did exactly what he knew they would. They excited Trey.

"Well, she let Park fuck that tight pussy of hers." Dallin smirked over at me. "She took those piercings like such a good girl, didn't she?"

"'Good girl' doesn't even begin to describe it." I shook my head, remembering how tight she was. "And the way she put D's plug in for him to help stretch him out for your cock, Trey." I groaned, watching Trey's mouth part as I involved him in the conversation. "She was so fucking turned on by helping him get prepped to be fucked."

"Soaked." Dallin licked his lips, running his thumb over them like he was remembering it right at that moment. "Man, you should have heard her begging for Parker to fuck her harder as she sucked my cock."

"Okay, enough," Trey growled, looking back at the stove. "I get it."

"You don't." I walked up behind him, letting the hardness of my arousal press against his jeans as his hand tightened around the spatula. "You don't get it, not yet anyway." I didn't touch him anywhere else, yet his skin still erupted in goose bumps as he stood still as stone. "But you will the first time she begs you to fuck her deep while D and I give it to her at the same time." I leaned down and bit the meat of his shoulder and sucked on the skin, drawing a deep groan from his lips. "By then, you'll be as addicted to her as we are."

"Fuck off." He shrugged, pushing me backward, and I went with a laugh. I didn't push him too hard, because I knew Trey better than I knew myself some days. And if I pushed him too hard, too fast, he'd bolt and take off again. So little jokes and prods to get him to finally give in were going to have to work.

Because I needed him included.

Completely.

"You interested in tattooing some tits tonight?" I looked up from the sketch pad in my lap and stared at the paradox emo Barbie standing in the doorway to my private room at Dallin's tattoo shop.

"Do you mean tattooing a picture of tits or tattooing on some tits?" I set the sketch pad down and quirked an eyebrow at Lex as she leaned in the doorway.

"On some tits. Chick just walked in and wants a floral piece across her chest, including her nipples."

"Ouch." I shook my head with a smirk. "I'm surprised you aren't jumping at the chance."

She smirked and leaned up off the jamb. "I have plans tonight, or believe me, I'd stay and do it myself." She winked. "They look like a really nice pair of tits, too."

I chuckled and followed her out of the shop. "Lead the way, O great one."

"Hey, man," Trey called from his room across from mine, and I nodded to Lex as she headed back up to reception before walking to his doorway. "You staying?"

"Apparently." I shrugged, looking at the clock. It was only seven, but starting a piece now would leave me working late. "You got plans?"

"Nah." He shook his head as he finished cleaning up his bench. "I'm fucking starving. I think I'm going to head out and grab a bite."

"Why don't you go see if Rey wants to eat? Dallin is at the expo finishing up closing it out. I don't think he'll be home much before me."

"It's not *our* home," Trey argued under his breath with a shake of his head but kept going before I could counter his attempt at diminishing what we were trying to build here. "Yeah, whatever. I'll see if she's hungry."

"Good." I nodded, but as he tried to walk past me through the door, I blocked him and grabbed his arm, halting him right next to me. "Be nice to her," I warned him firmly, not going in any deeper because I knew he was following what I was saying.

"I'll be on my best behavior." He rolled his eyes. "I'd hate to hurt her feelings or something."

"And I'd hate to hurt your fucking brain when I knock it off the wall if you do," I said before leaning in and kissing him quickly. Trey wasn't one for PDA, but I was feeling a bit more open and affectionate from all of Reyna's sweet touches and gentleness. So he was going to have to deal with it, now that this was our new lifestyle.

"Promises, promises." He smirked, surprising me by leaning in and kissing me back. "Have fun with your flowery tits." He nodded toward the front desk, where Lex and my client were staring, both open-mouthed and shocked as they watched our exchange.

"Hmm. Have fun with Rey's," I added as he walked away toward the back door that led to the staircase upstairs.

"Fucker," he grumbled as I chuckled and walked out front.

"Hey, I'm Parker." I shook the hand of the girl with admittedly a nice rack squeezed into a tight tube top. "Lex tells me you want some flowers." She was blond and fake as the day was long, and normally I'd be down to flirt and hook up with a girl like her after staring at her naked tits for a few hours. But she was the exact opposite of Reyna, and nothing stirred inside me like it usually did in a situation like this.

Reyna had gone and gotten me addicted to her good-girl naughty side and left me empty for anything that wasn't her.

"Yup." My client swallowed, finally closing her mouth as I nodded for her to follow me to my room. "I'm Karma," she said, which fit her aesthetic perfectly. As we cleared the doorway to my room and she set her bag down, she smiled at me. "Can I just say how freaking hot that was?" She hooked her thumb toward Trey's room across from mine with a seductive smile on her filler-plump lips. "Like, two sexy macho men getting all hot together." She fanned herself. "I mean that in the most respectful way possible, too," she added.

I chuckled, busying myself with looking at the reference images she had printed out that Lex gave me. "Thanks, our girlfriend and other boyfriend think so too," I replied firmly, leaving no room for questions or assumptions.

Karma nodded with a guilty smile on her face. "Got it." She chuckled. "I saw your portfolio online and knew I needed to get this piece done by you."

"I'm excited to get working on it, so tell me what you want the piece to look like." I dove right into the work, letting the muscle memory from years of tattooing take over the awkwardness as I looked up at the clock once again. The sooner I got started, the sooner I could get upstairs to the three other people I would rather spend time with.

CHAPTER 17

Trey

The apartment was quiet when I walked in, with only the dim lights over the kitchen island on. I toed my boots off and quietly walked through the space, looking for any signs of Reyna as I headed to the spare bedroom that Parker and I shared at the end of the hall.

I wasn't lying when I told him this wasn't our home, but I also didn't want to just voluntarily offer to leave it either. Not when I finally had a piece of serenity after two years of feeling half alive.

When I made my way down the hallway, a warm glow from Reyna's office lit up the space and as I neared her door, I could hear her soft voice drifting toward me.

She was humming a song.

The sound was angelic, drawing me closer like a hymn at the golden gates of heaven. If only I believed in such a place anymore.

I told myself originally I'd walk past the office and straight into the bedroom, but I couldn't convince myself not to look for her as I rounded the doorway.

She sat in her large wingback office chair with her hair piled on top of her head in a cute messy bun and a pair of black-rimmed glasses perched on the end of her nose as she furiously typed on her keyboard.

She didn't hear or see me, and I watched her as she hummed to the radio playing and typed out what I could only assume was some lovey-dovey scene between a gentle, sweet woman and a letterman-jacket-wearing guy who kept his hair styled and his pants starched.

She bit her bottom lip, tilting her head to the side as a devilish smile quirked her lips before a blush crawled up her chest and neck. Maybe she wasn't writing such a wholesome scene after all.

As if sensing me finally, she blinked and then jumped when she caught the dark shadowy figure lurking in her doorway. "Trey!" she gasped, covering her heart with her hand as she pulled her glasses off her nose. "You scared me shitless."

"Sorry," I mumbled, not remorseful in the least. "I was just going to get changed before going out to grab some dinner."

"Okay," she replied, looking past me down the hall. "Is Parker with you? Or Dallin?"

I shook my head. "Parker's still a few hours deep in work, and Dallin was finishing up at the expo. I don't know when he's planning on getting back."

She nodded absently as she chewed on her bottom lip. Almost like the idea of being stuck alone in the apartment with me made her nervous. "Okay, thanks."

"Do you want to come?"

Her eyes rounded and then flicked to her computer screen before she feverishly clicked away from whatever she was working on as she swallowed audibly. "Come?" she squeaked, and the blush deepened on her cleavage above the V-neck cream-colored shirt she wore.

"Food, Rey," I growled, enjoying the way her breath caught, making her chest rise and fall even more, pushing her lush tits into the neckline. Fuck, she had really nice tits. "Do you want to come with me to get some food?"

Her lips parted in surprise, and then she grinned, shaking her head with embarrassment. "Right." She chuckled, turning in her chair to face me. "I don't want to impose on you." She leaned back in the chair and crossed her legs, showing off her lean length under her shorts.

"Impose." I drew my eyes away from the flesh that beckoned to me, trying to calm my stupid horny body as she innocently aroused me. I didn't want her.

At all.

But I was a man, and not at all unaware of how sexy she was. But that was it.

Nothing more.

"I wouldn't have invited you if you would be imposing on anything. But no worries." I shrugged, leaning off the doorframe. "Parker asked me to include you. Maybe another time."

I turned and took a step toward the bedroom when she cleared her throat. "Wait." I looked over my shoulder at her as she stood up from behind her desk and walked toward the hall. "You're right. We should try to get along for Parker and Dallin." She added their names like she wanted to clarify that she was only doing it for them. "I'll go if you're sure you're okay with it."

"I'm good with it," I confirmed. "Let me just get changed and I'll be ready."

"I'll get dressed and meet you in the kitchen." She smiled with a curt nod as she slid around me and all but ran down the hall toward her side of the apartment.

I silently groaned as I walked into the spare room and shut the door behind me, palming my cock through my jeans where it was bricking up from the innocent way she did everything. I needed to get my head on fucking straight or I was going to do something stupid like actually lust after the girl that stole Dallin from me.

"Busy tonight," I mused, opening the door for Rey as we walked into a restaurant she suggested just down the street.

"Wing night," she smirked over her shoulder as she skirted between me and the bouncer, brushing against my front with her sexy black plaid skirt. When she walked out of her bedroom fifteen minutes after disappearing into it, I was incapable of forming words when I saw her.

She wore a short black-and-white plaid miniskirt that gave me serious naughty-schoolgirl vibes and a black lace tank top that showed off the curves of her chest and her slender neck where her pinned-up hair left the skin exposed. She paired the entire outfit with black leather boots that had fringe on the cuff.

She looked both defiantly sexy and innocently pure in the combination. I doubt she had any fucking clue how hot she was; she had that good-girl oblivion to her that would normally spur the cat-and-mouse-game lover in me right on, but I couldn't chase Rey.

She wasn't mine, and I didn't want her, anyway.

So I needed to find some random chick at the bar to give my attention to or swallow my pride and beg Dallin or Parker to come to break the tension between us before I did something stupid.

Like touch what wasn't mine.

"Let's go over there." I nudged her toward an opening at the bar top. She nodded and started weaving her way through the crowd, but every time she'd make two steps toward the bar, someone would step out into her way, and she'd have to go three steps in the other direction to get around them. She was tiny compared to everyone blocking the path, and no one gave a damn to try to be a nice fucking guy and let her by. The crowd was far rowdier than I thought it would be for being a basic country bar, even rivaling seedy biker bars I wouldn't dream of letting her step foot into. "Rey," I called, sliding my hand through hers to pull her back behind me. "Stay close."

"Okay," she said, mystified by the overbearing environment as she slid against my back and squeezed my hand tight as I started shoving my way through. People turned to glare at me or mouth off, but one scowl from me, and most of them turned back around just as fast, choosing not to chance a run-in with my dark bad attitude. "I'm so jealous right now," Reyna called from behind me as she fisted the back of my shirt and pressed her chest against my back, staying close. "They just move right out of your way."

I pushed my way to the opening at the bar and pulled her around my front, caging her in against the bar top and onto a stool as I stood between her and the guy next to her, who didn't even bother to hide his appraisal of her body.

"I'm scary-looking." I shrugged, flagging down the bartender.

"I can be scary-looking." She scowled like she was trying to look intimidating, and I scoffed, chuckling at her attempt.

"Give me an IPA, whatever you have in the bottle," I yelled to the bartender when she stopped in front of us. "And a margarita, blackberry, if you have it." She nodded and ran off to fill the order.

When I looked down at Reyna, her eyes were round in surprise as she stared up at me. "You ordered my favorite drink for me?"

I rolled my eyes. "Don't think about it too much, kitten," I droned. "You said you were a slut for margs after your night out."

She choked on her tongue and then rolled her eyes back at me. "I would never."

"You did," I assured her. "Which is another reason you aren't intimidating at all, either. No one intimidating gets slutty for lime and tequila."

"Oh, yeah?" She scoffed, picking up the glass the bartender set down for her next to my beer and taking a sip. She sighed and closed her eyes, savoring the taste. "You're right, I'm a total slut for a good marg." She moaned around the rim of the glass, and I gripped my bottle even tighter. "But it's so damn good." She giggled, setting the glass down.

"Hmm." I downed most of my beer without tasting it as I tried to get drunk enough to not be so affected by her stupid little mannerisms. I took my phone out of my pocket and pulled up a group message to Parker and Dallin, typing out an SOS.

Me: Park convinced me to invite Rey out to dinner with me. And now I'm sandwiched at a bar way over capacity with your girlfriend wearing some naughty schoolgirl outfit attracting attention from men and women alike while she moans around the rim of a margarita glass. I'm not cut out for this shit. I'm tapping out.

Dallin's response came almost instantly.

Dallin: She sent me a selfie before you guys left. She's more than a naughty little schoolgirl in that skirt, she's a little sex kitten looking to cause trouble. And you're all on your own, I'm tied down right now.

Me: SHE'S YOUR GIRLFRIEND! NOT MINE!

"Everything okay?" Rey asked, glancing down at my phone, where I was angrily texting her man.

"Yep," I groaned. "Let's order some food. What do you want?"

"Hot wings!" she groaned excitedly. "Extra blue cheese and celery."

I clenched my jaw as guys around us looked over at her in response to her sounds, and I shifted to stand behind her stool more as the crowd pushed in even tighter. I waved the bartender back and ordered our dinner. Two orders of hot wings and a glass of ice water to pour down my pants.

I opened my phone again and saw that Parker had finally responded, and hoped he was telling me he was done with his appointment and would be right over.

Wrong.

Parker: And you're our boyfriend. And someday hers too. Suck it up, buttercup. Did you ever stop to wonder if she wore that sexy little outfit to get your attention?

Me: You're both fucking grounded and in the doghouse. If she sucks the sauce off her hot wings like a cock, I'm done. I can only break so many noses in one bar on my own.

Dallin: You can also get her out of there at any point and bend her over literally any surface she chooses on the way home and fuck her brains out for being such a naughty girl.

Me: I hate you both.

"Do you want to leave?" Reyna asked, taking a large sip off her glass as she swayed back and forth to the music on her barstool. "You didn't have to come here with me if you didn't want to."

"Who said I didn't want to?" I replied, pocketing my phone once again and giving her the attention she so obviously was looking for.

"You did, when you buried your nose in your phone and didn't look up for ten minutes straight."

I rolled my eyes at her and took another swig of my beer. "It was two minutes. Max." She rolled her eyes back at me. "And I was talking to your boy toys."

"Oh?" She raised her brows, suddenly more interested and less jaded. "And what did they have to say?"

"That you're a cock tease and I'm a fucking saint for bringing you out tonight looking like that," I deadpanned, and her brows knitted over her nose as she scowled at me.

"What's wrong with how I look?"

"Nothing," I replied with a shrug. "If you're looking to get yourself some dick, and not some wings."

She scoffed, turning to look out over the bar with a flick of her wrist. "I'm not looking to get some dick; I have plenty of that at home waiting for me. Thank you very much."

"Then why bother trying to attract the opposite sex if you're content?"

She turned on me in a rage until she faced me completely, still on her stool. She only came up to my chest, but she had fire in her spine so she faced off with me like she could physically do something about it if I matched her energy.

"I could ask you the same fucking thing!" she snapped, surprising me with the use of the word *fuck*. "I didn't wear this for anyone but myself. I like how I look in it and it makes me feel sexy. Which isn't a fucking crime, ya know." She pointed her finger at me. "And you're the pot calling the kettle black, if you ask me." She flicked her eyes up and down my body with a scoff as she lifted her glass to her lips once again in a huff.

"What's that supposed to mean?" I looked down at my plain white tee and dark blue jeans like I might understand what she was talking about.

"Oh, come on!" she droned dramatically. "You scream sex. Literally and figuratively, because I've heard you getting fucked." She nodded at me with so much sass it nearly bounced her off her stool. "You walk around with your bad-boy looks, your black ink and chunky silver rings, with your crisp white tee and tight jeans that leave absolutely nothing to the imagination about how big your dick is every time it swells. Then you've got all that dark hair pulled up that makes every woman get wet from literally just thinking about pulling it in our hands as you work our bodies into a sexual frenzy! And don't even get me started on your dark and brooding personality to match the bad-boy vibes." She huffed, ignoring how her tirade drew more than one curious look our way. But I was so hung up on her words that I couldn't bother to care about anyone else.

"You said 'our,'" I replied, and she scowled in confusion. The volume in the bar had increased since we walked in, which made it hard to talk privately, so I leaned forward until my lips were at her ear. I didn't miss the way her body froze when my whiskers brushed over her cheek before I elaborated. "You said my hair and bad-boy vibes make women imagine what it would feel like to pull it free in *our* hands. Does that mean you've fantasized about me, kitten?"

I pulled back far enough to see her face in time to watch her swallow purposefully and lick her lips. "Why do you call me kitten?"

She avoided my question because we both already knew the answer to it.

"Because you're as harmless as a tiny pissed-off little pussycat. Your claws and sharp teeth may hurt for the moment, but they don't stand up against a big dog."

She clenched her teeth and tilted her head back to look up at me straighter. "And you think you're a big dog?" Her eyes flicked down my body again. "Like you're so much badder than me."

"I'm the biggest dog in the pound, kitten," I confirmed, leaning forward again until my lips were at her ear. "I'd tear you to fucking shreds. I already told you once that you didn't have what it took to handle me." I pulled back to my full height and took the last pull off my beer, holding it up to the bartender for another one.

"I took Parker's cock, no problem," she countered, making me nearly choke on the liquid as I swallowed. "I could take yours."

"Who said anything about cocks?" I retorted, and her face reddened as she realized her false bravado had made her fall into a trap. "I was talking in hypotheticals. And here you are, once again, thinking and talking about my cock." Her nostrils flared in anger and embarrassment as I cocked my brows at her. "Here comes our food; be a good little girl and eat your wings without imagining they're my cock and I might get you out of here before you embarrass yourself completely by begging me to fuck you."

She tilted her head back and laughed mockingly. "I assure you; it wouldn't be me doing the begging," she countered before turning away from me completely and giving all of her attention to her plate of wings. "God, these look good." She groaned and dug in.

I watched while I organized my plate as she delicately picked up one wing, drowned it in the creamy white sauce, and then devoured it like a wild animal.

It was downright the sexiest thing I'd seen in my entire life.

She ate, ignoring me completely while chatting with people around us, and I tried to let my meal satisfy my hunger, but I came up short. After a while of being ignored, I'd had enough, and I tried to pull her back into a safe conversation.

"Is that your only ink?" I asked, nodding to the small piece on the outside of her forearm above her wrist.

"Yes." She smiled. "Dallin asks me nearly once a week if he can add to it, but that one is enough for me."

"Did he do it?"

"Yeah, a week after I met him." She smirked and shrugged. "I guess I knew then that we were going to last a while."

"What's the significance behind it?" I asked, ignoring the jab she threw at me about the strength of their relationship.

"A quill fountain pen?" She turned her arm to look at the simple black-and-gray pen with a trail of ink spilling from its tip. "I wanted it because I'm an author, I guess."

I raised my brows at her questioningly. "Why didn't you get a book, then? Or a laptop?"

"Why does it matter?" she countered, licking her fingers clean before washing it all down with the last of her margarita. "It's not on *your* body."

I shrugged nonchalantly. "I just don't get it. No one uses quill pens to write anything anymore. It seems silly."

She rolled her eyes and pushed her now-empty plate away. "You can think whatever you want to about me, it doesn't matter."

"So you don't have a good answer, then." I finished my food and stacked my plate on top of hers, hoping to spur her on enough to get a genuine answer out of her.

"Fuck you," she responded right on cue. "You don't know me, Trey."

"You're right, I don't, Rey," I answered honestly, and drank my beer while I watched her stew in her seat.

After a long stretch of awkward silence, she finally huffed and looked over at me. "Cardstock and ink are part of my love language." I raised my eyebrows and watched her closely, waiting for her to elaborate, which she did after a while. "The art of the handwritten note, or letter, is dying." She sighed. "Everyone is so quick to email or text, no one sends things in the mail anymore. Heaven forbid anyone care what their penmanship looks like to send a love letter or something."

"You write love letters?" I asked, turning to lean against the bar and face her.

"I write something to Dallin almost every single day," she answered proudly. "Some days it's a simple 'I love you' on a Post-it, other days it's an elaborate letter on a thick card the color of the panties I'm wearing spritzed with my perfume for him to find in his office when he goes to work." She shrugged. "There's romance in creating something with your own hands for someone you love." She looked up at me finally. "Don't you think?"

I held her stare as I thought about my answer, and instead of responding in a way she would like, I replied in a typical Trey way. "I wouldn't have a clue; I've never loved anyone."

Her shoulders deflated, and she looked at the glass in her hands. "That's a lie, and you know it." She slid down off her stool, pressing the front of her body against mine before picking up her purse. "Because we both know you love Dallin and Parker, even if you do a shitty job of showing it." She didn't wait for my response; I think we both knew I'd tell her to fuck off. "I'm going to pee, and then we can leave and tell Parker we tried his little experiment but that we both just can't stand each other."

CHAPTER 18

Dallin

I poured a protein shake into my cup and walked into the living room, desperate to face the elephant in the room head-on.

"So," I said, throwing myself down into the chair as Parker muted the television while Trey actively avoided my gaze. "What the fuck happened?"

Parker stared Trey down with me, as equally in the dark about it all as I was.

"I told you," Trey said, staring at the silent television like he was watching it. But I knew better because he was on edge and had been watching the front door as much as I had this morning.

Rey took off first thing for a book signing across town and even though I knew the event didn't take place until the afternoon, I let her escape the tension on the lie that she had to get prepared for it.

I just hated that she continued to lie to me to get away from the house. Last night, Parker and I had both gotten home late, and Reyna had already been asleep when I crawled into bed beside her, but Trey had been MIA.

He came stumbling in about three a.m., and from what Parker said this morning, he was in no shape to talk about their dinner date.

But he couldn't hide from it anymore. I couldn't stand both of them hiding and lying to me.

"You told us you two couldn't get along after all," Parker chimed in. "But we're not dumb, so respect us enough to stop lying to our faces, would ya?"

Trey sighed and rubbed his hand over his face, leaning forward on his knees. "What do you want me to say?" He looked from Parker to me. "That I'm an asshole who can't seem to be nice to her for more than a few minutes at a time? And she's catty enough to snap back at every goddamn opportunity?" He sighed. "Is that what you want?"

"If it's the truth," I responded.

"Well, it is," Trey huffed, leaning back into the couch. "I don't know how to make something work for you that I don't want. If it's such a fucking deal-breaker for you two, I'll take myself out of the equation so it can be easier for you both."

"Shut up," Parker snapped, shoving him. "No more running."

"It's not running if I'm solving the obvious problem." Trey stood up in frustration. "Because obviously I'm the fucking problem since you two think Rey is the missing piece in your lives."

"She's the missing piece because we already have you." Parker stood up and stood toe-to-toe with Trey. "If you walk away, you become the missing piece."

"Yeah, well, maybe then you'd start acting like I wasn't the fucking enemy," Trey shot back.

"Enough." I rose from the chair, pleading with them both with my eyes as my chest tightened. "I've never thought of you as the enemy, Trey." I shook my head and sighed. "And I don't want to lose you again. I almost didn't survive it the last time."

His eyes softened, and his shoulders deflated. "Then figure out how to deal with me and Reyna not coexisting." He sighed and grabbed his phone off the arm of the couch. "Because it's not going to happen."

"Where are you going?" Parker asked.

"To look for an apartment to rent." He shrugged. "Because I can't live here in her space. It's not fair to either of us."

"Trey, wait," I said, but I wasn't sure what else to say to give him the reassurance that he needed. Because I didn't know how to make this work if we were all separated.

"I'm not running," he said, walking into my space. "But I'm not convinced this is going to work out the way you hoped it would."

"I know." I nodded, admitting that maybe I'd been wrong after all. "Why don't we all go out and check out some places nearby? Grab a late lunch while we're out?"

"Yeah," Parker chimed in, "it would be nice to have a boys' day."

Trey contemplated it for a moment, and I think he was surprised that I was joining him in his attempt to create space between himself and Reyna. "You sure?"

"Positive." I nodded before leaning forward and pulling him into a kiss. Kissing Trey never got old, because he was so gruff and sharp-edged that it was the complete opposite of kissing a woman, or even Parker, with his gentle nature. It always preluded the intensity of sex with him too, and what I had intended to be a quick kiss of reassurance quickly burned into something hotter as he groaned and bit my bottom lip. He felt that intensity between us too, no doubt remembering how good it used to be between us.

I missed having this freely.

I missed them and the camaraderie between friends who burned for each other sexually too.

"Damn," Parker mused from next to us as Trey fisted the front of my shirt.

"If we don't leave now, we won't be leaving anytime soon," I growled needily.

"I don't see a problem with that," Parker added, sliding up behind Trey and looking at me as I finally pulled back. "Besides, as much fun as I've had with Rey and you, I'm still not quite satisfied."

Trey looked over his shoulder and then smirked at him. "What's the matter, P? Longing for some Dallin dick?"

"Fuck yes, I am," Parker replied. "Two fucking years of longing." He shoved Trey into me, and I easily caught him before he tripped. "Don't even pretend it wasn't worth the wait the other night when you bottomed. We both know no one can fuck quite like D can."

I groaned, tightening my hold on Trey's arms as their banter dragged me back to easier times of fun when we had no responsibilities. "Careful, or I'll fuck you both and completely thwart your plans to find another place to live."

Trey smirked before leaning forward to bite the skin above the hard bone of my clavicle. "It's not like the rentals will all disappear before tomorrow."

Parker's grin turned wolfish as he backed up toward the hallway, pulling his shirt up over his head. "Well, if it's up to me, I'm going to have sex. So"—he paused with a smug shrug as he disappeared into the spare room—"whoever makes it in here first gets the first orgasm."

Trey winked, slowly backing up after Parker. "What do you say, old man?" he joked. "You feeling frisky?"

"Old man?" I scoffed as I pretended to stretch over my head, and thoroughly enjoyed the way his eyes watched my body move and ripple. "We both know I'm in the best shape of my life."

His eyes snapped up from my abs and his body vibrated with energy as he licked his lips. "First orgasm is on Parker, huh?" he said, taking another step.

"Or inside him," I corrected him. "Either way, it's mine." I took off in a sprint, barely making it a few feet before he slammed his giant body into mine, ricocheting me off him and into the sofa. "Oof," I groaned, flipping over the arm of it as he laughed mockingly as he walked toward the bedroom and the reward we both wanted.

Not so fast.

I leaped over the back of the couch and grabbed his arm, slamming him into the wall as I fought to get past him, but he used his unnatural speed to hold on to me before I could slip by. We both grunted and groaned as we fought to tear each other back away from the doorway, bumping into the table that Reyna decorated. I shoved him backward, knocking picture frames off the wall.

"Fucker," Trey grunted, biting my shoulder as I sandwiched him into the wall with my back.

"Correct." I groaned as he bit harder. "I will be the one doing the fucking."

"Lies," he hissed, shoving to get past me by twisting my legs up with his and dropping me to the floor.

"Bastard." I grabbed for him as he leaped over me, catching only the worn fabric of his jeans and tearing them as he got even closer to the doorway. "Ha!" I jeered, ripping his favorite pair of jeans down the entire length until one leg hung uselessly around his ankle.

"You're going to pay for that." He scowled, pushing me back with a wide hand to the face as I climbed to my feet, shoving him aside.

"Yeah, baby," I joked dramatically. "Make me pay."

"Fucker," he repeated and grabbed me when I tried to get past him, before kicking off his jeans altogether as they tangled around his ankles. "You're a poor sport, you know that, right?"

"Me?" I gasped as he threw a punch to my kidney when I pushed one shoulder through the doorway. "Fuck, that's hot," I mused as I caught sight of Parker laid out in the center of the bed, naked, stroking his barbed dick with one arm thrown behind his head like he didn't care who made it through first, as long as he got sex out of it.

"What?" Trey leaned in around my wide shoulders, while still trying to pull me back. "Damn." He groaned, seeing Parker laid out.

"Right." I relaxed my body, trying to trick him into letting go, but he expected my move, shoved me back three steps, and shouldered his way into the doorway. "Fine!" I yelled. "Play you for it."

"Oh my God," Parker groaned from the bed. "You are not playing rock-paper-scissors for the chance to come first."

"Fuck yes, we are." Trey laughed, relaxing and facing me in the opening as he raised his fist. "Rock, paper, scissors, shoot," he commanded.

"Ha!" I cheered. "Rock breaks scissors." I smashed my fist over his fingers and pushed my way firmly into the room. "Now I want my prize."

Parker fist-bumped the air enthusiastically. "It's about fucking time."

"Harder," Parker growled as Trey slammed into him. "Yes."

Parker was bent over the end of the bed with Trey behind him as I leaned against the headboard and stroked my cock, drinking a beer and watching the show.

It was fucking hot as hell, but what I wouldn't give to have Rey included in it.

I lost count of how many times I'd orgasmed in the last few hours, or where. It had been a tangle of limbs and skin since I forced my way through the door, and it hadn't stopped. Two years' worth of time to make up for and the three of us had made it our mission to put a dent in that debt.

"Tell daddy how you like it," Trey teased and Parker clenched his teeth as his eyes rolled.

Parker had taken most of the fucking today, willingly, I might add. But I'd still managed to fuck Trey twice, and he even took it from Parker once, too.

I still had yet to bottom, but the plug I was wearing currently was the largest in the set and it hadn't hurt going in as Trey prepped me earlier, so I knew it was only a matter of time before I begged one of them to take the edge off for me.

"Fuck!" Trey roared, tipping his head back to the ceiling as his hand tightened around the front of Parker's throat, holding himself deep inside. "That's it," he groaned. "I'm fucking empty. I can't come again."

"That makes one of us," I smirked, as Parker hung his head in exhaustion. Trey pulled out and wiped his arm across his forehead to clear the sweat. "I think we need to give Parker some TLC and aftercare." I climbed out of bed and kneaded the tense muscles of his back.

"And an orgasm." He moaned. "You two have edged me for an hour straight."

"Come on," I said, pulling him to his feet. "I'll take care of you in the shower."

"What about me?" Trey complained. "I'm the one that's been doing all the work; I need a shower and it ain't big enough for the three of us."

"Use mine." I shrugged as Parker and I headed for the guest bath. "Just don't use up all of Rey's expensive shampoo," I joked with a wink, and he flipped me off as I disappeared around the wall.

He grumbled down the hallway about finally getting some goddamned peace and quiet as Parker leaned against the cool tile, stroking his still-hard cock. "Why do I feel like I'm missing something important here?" he said.

I chuckled as I flicked the showerhead on full blast, soaking him in icy water before turning it to hot, winning a glare from him.

"Because Rey texted me twenty-five minutes ago and said she'd be home in half an hour," I mused, walking into the shower, shielding his body with mine from the tepid water as it heated. "And how she desperately needed a shower after a long day of meet-and-greets."

His face split into a shit-eating grin. "You're naughty."

"Very." I nodded, leaning forward to drag my tongue up the side of his neck. "And dirty, want to help me get clean?" I grabbed onto his throbbing, studded cock and stroked.

"Only after you get a little dirtier," he growled. "Now get on your knees and apologize for torturing me for the last hour."

"Yes, sir," I smirked, letting him take control. I didn't give it over very often, but Parker had earned it. And besides, the sooner I got him the relief he ached for, the sooner I could sneak across the apartment and spy on what I was hoping was a sexy encounter for Trey and Reyna.

CHAPTER 19

Reyna

"Home sweet home," I mumbled under my breath as I climbed the stairs to the apartment. It had been a *long* day at my book signing, and while I loved interacting with my readers, because I was an introvert, doing public things was hard for me. And I wanted nothing more than to crawl into my bed in a comfy pair of sweats with a tub of ice cream and binge some trashy reality television show that I didn't have to come up with the storyline for.

Well, all that after a shower.

The Nashville heat kicked my ass today, and I had sweat in places no woman liked to be sweaty.

When I opened the front door, I tossed my keys down into the dish and unloaded the bags off my shoulders into a pile on the floor.

"Thank God," I moaned, stretching my shoulders out.

As I toed off my heels, a noise caught my attention from the hallway to the spare bedroom.

Skin.

Clapping.

Loudly.

"Oh." I bit my bottom lip, listening for any indicator of who or where the noise was coming from.

"That's it," a familiar voice called. "Fucking hell, that's it."

Parker.

There was a reply, but it was muffled, and I couldn't discern who it was from. I wanted to go closer and investigate. But something stopped me, and I turned toward my room instead. I would give Parker the alone time he deserved with whoever was with him, and I'd worry about my own needs.

When I walked into my bedroom, I felt the thickness of steam on my skin before I caught the noise of my shower running in the bathroom and nearly groaned with relief at the idea of climbing in with Dallin after a long day.

I stripped out of the tight body con dress I wore to the signing and took my jewelry off at my dresser, nearly moaning from how good the hot water was going to feel on my skin when I got in it.

As I cleared the doorway, I caught Dallin's dark hair through the frosted glass as he stood under the rain head, letting it cascade down over his shoulders.

"I hope you're not partial to that showerhead because I'm calling dibs, big guy," I called, clipping my hair up in a messy bun as I rounded the shower wall.

But where Dallin had been standing a moment ago, a smug Trey waited, making me stop short in surprise.

"Fuck!" I cursed, covering my chest and bits with my arms. "What are you doing in my shower, Trey?"

He had his back to me when I walked in, looking over his shoulder, but as his eyes traveled down my body where I desperately tried to cover up my genitals, he turned to face me head-on.

Head.

On.

I tried. I wanted it written on my headstone someday that I did really, *really* try to keep my eyes above the waist as he stood unashamed and unobscured in front of me for the first time.

But I failed. I was a failure. A dirty, pathetic, aroused, and horny failure that let my eyes fall on the thick cock swinging between his legs, not even hard, yet still intimidatingly thick.

"Oh, come on now, Rey," Trey teased, drawing my eyes back up from his package to his bright blue ones. "I'm showing you mine, you could at least show me yours."

I blinked rapidly, trying to get my mouth to form a coherent sentence. "Out," I stuttered. "Now."

"I would." He tilted his head back, letting the water wash over his long hair as he ran both hands up his abs leisurely. "But I've spent the entire day doing dirty fucking things to Parker and Dallin, and I'm in desperate need of a good shower to ease my tired body. And they're currently fucking in the spare shower, so you're going to have to just get out and wait your turn."

"Wait my turn?" I gasped, glaring at him. "Fuck you."

He chuckled, closing his eyes as the water cascaded down his admittedly delicious body. "I already told you; I'm not interested. And even if I was, I couldn't get hard again right now if I tried." He sighed. "I'm thoroughly sated and exhausted. Not even the most attractive woman in the world could get me hard enough to ride."

His conceited dig at my appearance bristled my irritable attitude, and I fought the urge to pick up the heavy bottle of sugar scrub off the ledge and throw it at his head.

But then a better idea came to mind as he continued to let my favorite showerhead massage his shoulders with blissful arrogance on his face.

Isn't the old saying, if you can't beat them, join them?

I dropped my arms, forcing myself to take a deep breath as the anxiety raced through my body from being naked in front of Trey for the first time and put my bravest face on.

Then I went to war.

I shoved him hard, surprising him as he slid across the slick tile floor into the wall. "Hey!" he snapped, but I ignored him as I turned my back to him and stepped under the magical massaging head.

"I'm not waiting my turn for my shower, douchecanoe." I flicked a glance over my shoulder as the water rippled down my back and caught his eyes locked onto my ass that I may or may not have been pushing up a bit more than normal. "You can stand over there and I'll stand over here."

"Whatever," he growled, grabbing my bottle of shampoo and aggressively squeezing a week's worth of the expensive magic into his hand. "Just try not to get horny from being so close."

"Right." I shook my head, turning away from him as I grabbed my loofah and body wash. "Because I'm the one who's at risk of that," I scoffed.

Though he was right. My body was tight and warm from being naked in the shower with him, knowing I couldn't touch him.

That I didn't want to touch him.

But something about having his eyes on me was turning me on. And from the sound of it, Dallin wasn't going to be in any shape to help me take the edge off in the end. Wasn't the point of letting two more men into my relationship to reap the sexual benefits of all the extra cock?

I was getting shafted in this whole arrangement and not even in the way I needed.

I lathered up my loofah and began washing my body, starting at my neck and working my way down my arms before returning to my chest and slowly taking my time soaping up my breasts. I felt his eyes on my back the entire time, like he was staring through my body to see my front.

Trey was also silent as I worked the sponge down my stomach and over my hips. When I leaned down to run the soap over my legs, I looked over my shoulder and found him standing still as a statue under the auxiliary showerhead on his side of the stall with his eyes lasered in on my ass. "You're staring," I accused mockingly, turning my attention back to my task.

When he didn't reply, I looked back at him as I started in on my other leg. He watched me with his storming blue eyes, his dark eyebrows pinched together. He almost looked angry, and a few weeks ago, I probably would have thought he was.

But I knew him a little better now, and I knew that the emotion burning inside him wasn't anger.

It was something deeper. So I played with it further, turning under the water and facing him head-on, showing him my bits for the first time clearly as I tipped my head back and let the water rinse the soap down the drain. When I finished rinsing my body off, he was still standing there, just staring at me.

"Here." I swallowed past the lump in my throat that was building bigger and bigger with each silent second that passed between us. The air was thicker now from more than just the steam. But he wouldn't comment on it. "Let me help you wash all that sex off."

I rinsed the loofah off and reapplied my favorite soap to it, lathering it slowly as I cautiously got closer to the silent beast watching me. Trey's blue eyes were alive with emotion as I raised the sudsy sponge to his chest and gently circled it over his defined pecs. His jaw clenched tightly at the contact, and he grabbed my wrist, stopping me from moving the sponge anywhere else. His skin was hot against mine and it felt like he was branding me with his soul. Despite that, he didn't speak.

Normally, Trey and I went back and forth with wit and digs at each other. His silence was jarring, and the longer it stretched, the more uneasy it made me.

"It's just an olive branch," I whispered, forcing myself to look into his storming eyes. "To repay you for inviting me to dinner last night." I swallowed. "Even if you did ruin it with your sour disposition."

His nostrils flared as I pulled against his hold on my wrist, but finally, he released me. I dropped his penetrating gaze and stared at his chest as I slowly resumed washing it. As I gently moved my hand across each shoulder and up his neck, I noticed every single muscle in his body coiling tight.

"Relax, Trey. This is supposed to be soothing," I whispered, keeping my eyes downcast as I worked.

He finally took a deep breath, like he was forcing himself to calm down, even though he didn't give away any indication of anger.

"Good boy," I smirked before biting my bottom lip as a sound similar to a growl emanated from his chest when I lowered the loofah to his stomach. "You smell like them," I added, trying to ground us both.

"Are you trying to cover that up with the scent of you?" He finally spoke, though his voice was strained and unfamiliar.

"Is my scent all that unpleasant?" I replied, as his abs twitched with each swipe of my hand.

"I didn't say that."

I licked my dry lips and slid around to stand behind him to wash his back. "I'm not jealous," I responded. "I'm glad you three spent the day together."

I pushed his hair off his neck, holding it to the side, and his entire body shivered as I ran the loofah across the sensitive skin. The heat radiating off his large body felt overpowering in the steamy shower, yet goose bumps broke out over my skin as I watched them rise on his.

"I don't believe you," he finally said, and then sighed. "It doesn't make sense."

"Do you get jealous of Dallin and Parker being together without you?" I replied as I ran the suds down the long lines of his back. How was a back so sexy?

"All the time," he responded, and his answer surprised me.

"Really?" I asked in shock.

"I'm a jealous man." He shrugged. "I always want to be involved, and when I'm not, I'm envious."

I smirked at his back as I cleaned his arms. I still couldn't believe he was letting me wash him; I didn't think he'd let me when I started. But now that he was, I didn't want to ever stop. Touching him like this was intoxicating. I felt like a kid getting away with something I wasn't supposed to be doing, living on the high of it while waiting for the fallout at the same time.

"I guess I can respect the honesty there," I said, clearing my throat as I silently sank to my knees behind him.

Did I mention that Trey had one of the nicest asses I'd ever seen before, too?

Like *plump* didn't even begin to describe it. As I ended up at eye level with it, I started to understand how Dallin was physically attracted to him and Parker in ways that differed from his attraction to me.

I ran the loofah across the back of his calf, and he twisted around to look over his shoulder at me. When he found me on my knees behind him, he clenched both hands into fists and faced forward again. "You don't have to do this," he stated after a moment of silence while I washed the backs of both of his thighs. His legs were parted enough that I could see his balls hanging largely between them and had to bite my bottom lip hard to keep the moan that had been building inside my chest silent.

I hated how affected I was by him.

My body was warm and tingling all over, my nipples hard, and my pussy drenched itself more and more the longer I touched him and shared his space. I ran the sponge over the firm roundness of his ass, taking far longer than was necessary to cleanse the skin simply because I enjoyed touching him.

I wanted him.

Fuck, did I want him.

I wanted to beg him to fuck my throat and then slam me up against the shower wall and fuck my brains out like the dirty girl I was.

I didn't recognize this side of my personality, but something about him called to her.

Dallin had brought out the dirty side of me more often than I thought was possible, but this was more.

This was feral.

It was inhumane how badly I wanted Trey's violence and darkness.

"Turn around," I whispered, through my hazed brain. To be honest, I expected him to refuse. To yell at me and call me some degrading name, or perhaps throw a dig at me about how uninterested he was in what was happening between us at the moment.

That was what Trey from last night and all the nights before would have done.

What he wouldn't have done, however, was turn around and stare down at me where I knelt before him and licked his lips.

But that was what he did.

I looked up at him from under my lashes as I tilted my head way back to see his eyes and swallowed when my gaze had to pass over his cock.

It was no longer thick and hanging between his thighs like it had been when I first stepped into the shower.

No. Now it was throbbing as blood pumped through it, bringing it out from his body and aiming it directly toward my face. Jesus Christ, it was fucking thick.

Dallin had been right.

Trey's cock was shorter than his, but it was massive in girth; the bulbous head was nearly as big as my clenched fist, and I didn't even try to pretend I wasn't staring at it as I knelt before him.

"Rey," he growled, but I couldn't rip my eyes away from his waist. "Get off your knees."

"I'm not done yet." I bit my bottom lip and looked up at him, knowing exactly what image he was getting from me. It was exactly what I wanted him to see.

I wanted him to see seductive me.

I wanted him to want me as much as I wanted him.

I ran the loofah up the front of one calf as he stared down at me with those tumultuous blue eyes. When I got to his thigh, his entire leg twitched as I slowly coated it with the soap. His cock jerked right above my hand like it was calling to me, but I kept my eyes locked on his as I switched legs and cleaned the other one, ending right below his groin.

I could have stopped there.

I *should* have stopped there.

Trey didn't want me, regardless of how hard his cock was from my touch. I knew that.

He'd told me that.

But I couldn't stop if I wanted to. I put one hand on his bare thigh, touching his skin with mine for the first time, and his muscles vibrated under my palm. I ran the loofah across his groin to his throbbing cock and slowly slid it over the thickness, tightening my hand around it as best I could.

He was massive. Feeling it, having the weight of it in my palm, put it into perspective. I'd never be able to take him.

Yet I wanted nothing more.

I cleaned the shaft, twisting the loofah in my palm over his head until he groaned and tipped his head back to stare at the ceiling and then dropped my hand to his heavy balls.

I'd never been one to admire a pair of balls before, but there was something so *manly* about Trey's.

Dallin and Parker both shaved theirs, yet Trey's had a light coating of hair on them up to the base of his cock, and it fit him perfectly. It added to the darkness of everything else about him.

I massaged his balls, not even trying to act like I was simply cleaning him anymore.

Because fuck it.

Fuck it all.

Fuck him and his indifference to me.

Fuck his lies every time he acted like I did not affect him.

Fuck his desire to make me feel small and unworthy of him or the other guys.

Fuck him.

But most disrespectfully at the same time, I wasn't going to fuck him.

I was going to make him wish I did, though.

I rubbed behind his balls with the coarse loofah, and he moaned, biting his bottom lip with his head still thrown back, and the muscles in his neck flinched and clenched as I swirled my fingers on that sensitive area, making his cock jerk and leak for me.

And then I pulled my hands from his body completely and waited for him to finally look back down at me again. When he did, I slowly and seductively unfolded my body from his feet and stood up, staring at him the entire time.

"All done," I purred, swallowing down the fear that tried to burn in my gut as his blue eyes cleared the haze of arousal and replaced it with outrage.

"Reyna," he growled, tilting his head to the side like he was daring me to do what he knew I was about to.

"I'll leave you to it." I glanced down at his still-throbbing cock and then raised an eyebrow as I looked back up at him. "And you tried to tell me you couldn't get hard for even the hottest woman on earth," I smirked. "Yet even ugly old me made you throb." His teeth clenched tight as I placed one hand on his chest and patted the flesh above his pounding heart. "Someday you'll learn to stop underestimating and disrespecting me, Trey."

And with that I turned and walked out of the shower, stopping only long enough to wrap my towel around my body as my heart beat wildly in my chest.

Did I fucking just do that?

I heard the distinct sound of his fist hitting the tile wall behind me as I ran from the bathroom, but I didn't have time to worry over that, because as I walked out into the bedroom, Dallin sat on the bench at the end of the bed.

Waiting for me.

"Let me guess," I said, stiffening my spine. "Trey using our shower was your idea?"

Dallin was wearing a pair of red athletic shorts and nothing else as he leaned back against the bed with a satisfied smile on his face. "Depends." He leaned forward to rest his elbows on his knees. "Did you enjoy your time with him?"

I rolled my eyes, walking into the closet and sliding one of his oversized shirts over my head, desperate for the comfort of it. He followed me into the space as I unclipped my hair and let it fall around my shoulders, watching me in the floor-length mirror. I shrugged, trying to feign indifference. "If you mean, did I enjoy him trying to rile me up while simultaneously telling me how you were so thoroughly fucked and pleasured out that you wouldn't be able to get me off"—I raised one eyebrow at him in the mirror—"then no, I did not enjoy myself." He crossed the space and stood behind me, letting just the faintest amount of skin touch me. "But if you mean, did I enjoy dropping to my knees and rubbing his cock until he was throbbing and aching for me before walking out and leaving him standing alone and unsatisfied"—I smirked—"then yes. Yes, I did."

"You stroked his fat cock?" Dallin growled, sliding his large hand over my hip, pulling me flush to the front of him. "Did you like it?"

I groaned, feeling the heat of his body against my overheated one as my arousal spiked even higher from edging myself into the shower. "Did you let him fuck you today?" I countered, refusing to answer his question because I didn't want to admit the truth to him or myself.

He raised a dominating eyebrow at me in the mirror and fingered the hem of the shirt I was wearing where it fell at the top of my thigh. "The first time I take a cock, his or Parker's, you'll be there, Rey," he stated with such authority my eyes fluttered closed in ecstasy. "The first time I take a cock again, mine will be buried deep inside you, baby. I promise you that," he growled.

"D," I moaned, resting my head against his shoulder as my need burned higher. "I'm so fucking horny."

"Tell me the truth, then." He lowered his lips to my neck and teased my oversensitive skin. "Did you like Trey's cock? Did you like touching him and turning him on?" He flexed his hips against my ass, and I felt the ridge of his hard cock drawing a moan from my lips. How was it possible that he was hard for me after how he spent his day? I heard him fucking Parker when I got home no less than thirty minutes ago. "Did you want him to fuck you right there, just like that?"

"Yes," I moaned, admitting my worst fear. "Yes, I wanted him. Fuck," I whined desperately. "I wanted him to fuck me so hard. I needed it."

"Good girl." Dallin pushed his fingers under the hem of my shirt. "That's my good fucking girl," he praised me. "Show me how wet he made you, baby."

I spread my legs as he pushed his long fingers through my wet pussy, burying two in deep right away. "Fuck," I whispered, fighting for control as the water in the bathroom next door turned off.

"Did you want him like this?" Dallin asked, reaching up to cover the front of my throat with his hand. "You wanted him to take you rough like this, didn't you?"

"Yes," I panted, arching my neck and pressing it into his hand greedily.

He tightened his hold as he finger-fucked me. "You're perfect, Reyna," he whispered in my ear as I coated his hand with my arousal.

"I'm fucked in the head." I closed my eyes as shame burned in my gut. "I'm fucked in the head over a guy who doesn't want me. And it's all your fault."

"I know." Dallin sucked my earlobe as his palm pressed firmly against my clit, grinding against it, just how I liked it. "It's my fault, but don't think for another second that he doesn't want you. You made him hard, just like you've always made me hard. Just like you make Parker hard. It doesn't matter how many times we have you or when we last orgasm, with just a single look from you, we're all throbbing and ready again. We burn for you."

"I burn," I gasped, angrily. "I'm burning. Right now."

"Then be my good girl and ride my face so I can show you just how fucking perfect you are for us," he commanded, pulling his fingers out of me and flipping me around until my back hit the mirror. Dallin sank to his knees and lifted one of my legs over his shoulder as he lifted the shirt I wore over my breasts and looked up at my naked body. He leaned in and took a deep breath against my bare pussy, and I moaned, sinking against him, desperate to feel his mouth on me. "Mine."

"Yes," I panted, nodding, eager for whatever he wanted from me. "Please, D," I begged. "I need to come."

"I'm going to spend the rest of the night making you come, baby." He flicked his tongue across my swollen clit and moaned. "I'm going to give you everything you deserve for being my good fucking girl."

I didn't respond because he dove in, pushing his tongue into me and sucking my clit into his mouth as my hips bucked. I threaded my fingers into his hair, holding his head against me as I rocked into his face, desperate for the release I needed so badly. "Dallin," I moaned when he pushed the shirt up again and started teasing my nipples, pinching and pulling on them as he tongue-fucked my pussy. "Yes, baby," I panted, finally lifting my head off the mirror and opening my eyes.

But I instantly wished I hadn't.

Because standing in the center of my bedroom, staring into the closet, and watching me ride Dallin's face, was Trey.

He was naked, unashamedly watching, and I crumbled beneath his stare.

"Fuck!" I screamed, arching my back off the mirror and throwing my head back again as the biggest orgasm of my life exploded inside me. "Dear God," I cried as Dallin refused to slow down or stop, prolonging my orgasm on and on as I convulsed in his powerful arms. My fingers tightened in his hair until I was sure I was pulling it from his scalp, but he never stopped or pulled off.

He just kept showing me exactly how much he craved me.

When my orgasm finally stopped assaulting me so I could breathe and think again, I opened my eyes and found my bedroom devoid of the ominous figure that had lurked just moments ago.

Trey was gone.

But he had just made me come, without ever touching me.

And I was officially fucked past the point of return.

CHAPTER 20

Parker

Reyna's screams of pleasure ripped through the apartment, stopping me in my tracks as I flipped burgers on the griddle top, drawing every bit of attention I had toward her room.

The room where Trey and Dallin had both disappeared into, as well.

"Damn," I smirked, licking my lips, and forcing myself to stay in the kitchen instead of joining the orgy I was hoping was happening in the next room. "See if I ever volunteer for dinner duty again," I muttered.

"Since when do you volunteer for anything?" Trey called, walking out of the primary bedroom, naked and hard as a rock, with a sour look on his face.

"So you weren't the one making her scream," I mused. "Bummer."

"Fuck off," he grumbled, rubbing a hand over his abs as he opened the fridge door. "I'm guessing that whole setup was Dallin's doing. Again."

I shrugged. "I knew nothing about it."

"Hmm." He pulled a beer from the fridge. "I'm fucking starving."

"You're really not going to tell me what happened in there?" I nodded toward the bedroom once again as Dallin's evil laugh floated out of the dark room. "Or what's going on in there currently?"

Trey sighed, setting his beer down on the island and looking at me. "She—" He paused and looked uncertain. "I don't know."

"Try."

"She—" He groaned, walking around the island with frustrated energy. "She came in, we sparred like we usually do, and then she—"

"Yes—" I dropped my head, begging him to continue.

"She sank to her knees and jacked me off until I was ready to blow all over her face, and then she walked out."

My eyebrows rose to my hair, and my mouth fell open. "Reyna wrapped her pretty little hand around your dick and stroked it?" I asked for clarification. "And then you let her walk out without giving her what you both so desperately need from each other? The fuck?"

He ran one hand through his hair as he walked away toward the spare room. Luckily for me, the burgers were done, so I turned off the burner and followed, desperate for more information on the topic.

Trey angrily stepped into a pair of boxers as I leaned against the doorjamb, crossing my arms and waiting for the rest of it.

"I wanted to. Okay?" he snapped at me. "But by the time I manned the fuck up and went looking for her, she was riding Dallin's face in the closet, and I was clearly not needed."

I felt for Trey; he opened up and let himself be vulnerable to me for the first time in a long time. "Did you make her feel not needed first?" I asked gently.

He sighed, pulling a shirt on with a side-eyed glare at me. "No."

"Liar."

"Whatever," he snapped. "You know how it is between the two of us. We're volatile. One wrong move away from blowing this whole thing up for everyone. For good."

"Or you're one *right* move away from solidifying it for forever," I countered, grabbing his arm as he tried to push past me back toward the kitchen. "Hey." I pulled him to a stop and pushed him back up against the jamb, locking us both into the small space. "It's okay."

He closed his eyes, put his head back against the wood frame, and sighed. "It's not." I waited, giving him time to work through what was upsetting him because he wasn't angry like he usually was after a verbal sparring match with Rey. He was lost. "I'm jealous of her."

I put both hands on his shoulders and tried to let my touch ground him as he cut himself open. "Of what part of her?"

"Of the part of her that so easily has you and Dallin." He opened his eyes and looked at me. "I don't have you that easily. And I've never had D like that."

"You have us both," I reassured him, sliding one hand up his neck and holding him still, forcing him to continue looking directly at me. "You've had us for decades, Trey."

"It's different," he whispered. "She's different."

"She is." I nodded. "That's the point, man. She's different, and she brings different things to the table than we can."

"And you don't see that as a competition?" he scoffed. "You don't feel lacking when you say that?"

I shook my head no and closed the distance between us. "No, Trey. I don't." I put my hands on each side of his face and leaned in. "I've never longed for her more than I do for you or D. But it's different. It's a gentler longing; sweeter." Shaking my head again, trying to articulate my point to push through his insecurities, I said, "I don't crave her like I do you." I leaned in and kissed the side of his neck, right above the collar of his T-shirt. "It's always been do or die between us, since that very first night in that motel all those years ago when none of us knew what the fuck we were doing together." I kissed my way up his neck to his ear. "The first time I felt you move inside me"—I sighed as his body shivered against mine—"it solidified this for me. For us." I ran the edge of my teeth over the lobe of his ear, and he gave in to what I was doing and put his hands on my hips, pulling me tight against him. I could feel his heart racing against my chest. "I felt the same way the first time she took me deep inside her. This thing between the four of us is meant to fucking *be*, baby." I pulled back to look into his eyes, which were dark with longing and uncertainty. "The sooner you stop fighting it, the sooner you can start reveling in it."

"She doesn't want me," he whispered, voicing his fear.

"Listen to her," I said, turning his head to look across the large apartment to their bedroom, which was still dark with the door open. Light noises of ecstasy floated across the space to us. "There isn't a doubt in my mind that Rey is riding Dallin's face right now because of how hot she got touching you." I licked up the side of his neck and he growled deep in his chest. "She probably begged him to get her off because of how turned on you made her. He's just giving her what she needs because she's too scared to ask you for it."

His chest rose and fell with quick pants. "This apartment is turning me into a fucking sexaholic." He flexed his hips, and I felt his hardness growing again, seeking relief.

I chuckled, palming him and giving him a few quick strokes before stepping back and dropping contact with every inch of him. His blue eyes snapped to mine as he whipped his head back toward me, appalled. "The next time you come, I want it to be with her." He started to argue, but I held up my hand and stopped him. "I never call the shots, I'm always happy to just go along with whatever you want to do, the good and the stupid." I said pointedly, "So humor me on this one, please." He clenched his jaw tight like he was fighting the urge to rebut my plea. "The next time you orgasm, I want her to orgasm at the same time. You don't have to be the one making her come, but I want it to happen at the same time, at the same place."

"Why?" he asked.

"Because I think it's exactly what the both of you need," I smirked, and walked back to the kitchen to finish making dinner. "And I want to know right after it happens if I'm not there when it does. Got it?"

He groaned, rolling his eyes at me so hard I could feel it through the back of my own head. "Yes, sir."

"Good boy." I chuckled. "Now come help me make them some food, because we need to feed our girl if she's going to keep that up all night." Her soft moans danced in my ears like a sweet lullaby as I grabbed out her favorite condiments.

This was going to work.

It had to.

"Fuck yes, that's so good," Dallin groaned, wiping the wetness from his lips and leaning back in his chair. "When did you learn to grill burgers that good?"

I threw my napkin at him as I sat back in my chair, stuffed full of jalapeño cheddar stuffed burgers and sweet potato fries. "I had to learn after you left, or I was going to starve."

"Hey," Trey grumped, "I had us covered."

I snorted, and Dallin chuckled. "Spam is not a food group," I countered, winking at Reyna as she giggled with her wineglass against her lips.

"Whatever." Trey rolled his eyes and shook his head.

We all sat around the table, full and happy. Every single person had orgasmed in the last few hours and the tension was low for the first time since Trey and I had arrived in Nashville.

Well, mostly, anyway. Because more than once since sitting down to eat, I noticed a few heated glances from Trey and Reyna, aimed at each other. And the longer that silence stretched between us, the more tension that built.

"So," I said, pushing my plate away. "I think we need a night out."

Dallin raised his eyebrows. "A night out?"

"Yeah." I sat forward, resting my elbows on the table. "Let's hit the town together." I shrugged, looking at Trey and then to Reyna. "You know, like as a couple or whatever we're calling ourselves."

Rey looked to Dallin and then back to me. "Where do you want to go?" she asked.

I shrugged. "I don't care. I'd be good with bowling or Topgolf if that's what you want to do. We can hit up a bar and go dancing, or a movie." I shrugged. "Just something. All four of us."

Reyna smiled and stood up from her seat, walking around the table to me. I scooted my chair back, making room for her as she sat down on my lap, looping her arm around my shoulders. "I like the sounds of that." She leaned in and laid her soft lips against mine and kissed me. It was the first time I had kissed her all day, and I didn't realize how ravenous I was for physical contact with her until then. When she finally came out of her room earlier, Trey and I had dinner on the table ready to eat, so I hadn't gotten this intimacy I needed.

But I was getting it now.

"Let's do golf," Reyna said with a smirk. "We can add some wagers to it and make it fun."

"Oh, really now?" I replied, tightening my arms around her waist as she giggled. "In what way?"

"You'll have to wait until we get there and find out." She kissed me again and then untangled herself from my embrace. "D, call and get us on the list. I'll be ready in ten minutes."

She got up and ran down the hallway with an extra pep in each step until her bedroom door closed.

"You have to be kidding me," I groaned as I watched Reyna clobber yet another ball past anything I thought she was capable of before we got to the driving range.

She looked back over her shoulder at us, gave her ass a little shake as she teed up another ball, and then got back into the perfect golf swing stance, yet again.

And knocked yet another one out of the stratosphere.

"How does she do that?" Trey stood next to me, with his mouth hung open, staring off in awe.

Dallin chuckled, sipping his whiskey, looking far more relaxed than either of us was at the moment. "Did she not mention her dad played professional golf for thirty years?"

I snapped my head over at him as it all clicked. "Dante Delacruz." I spit out angrily. "Fucking hell."

Of course, her father was a PGA legend, and she'd inherited his natural gift for the game. That was also, of course, why she made bets with Trey and me about who could make the best hits tonight.

Bets that we were both currently losing badly.

"What exactly do you owe at the moment?" Dallin quirked a brow at us as Reyna smashed another ball.

We were sitting behind the partition of the bar, watching the shit show unfold before us.

"A back massage and two rounds of drinks." I cursed, watching the numbers on the screen surpass anything I'd hit all night. "Make that three rounds of drinks."

Dallin chuckled, shaking his head. "Trey?"

Trey groaned from beside me, reaching over to take the whiskey out of Dallin's hand since his own was empty on the bar in front of us. "I have to be nice to her." He grumbled under his breath.

"What's that?" Dallin asked, leaning forward like he hadn't heard him right.

"I have to be nice to her," Trey snapped back angrily. "Twenty-four hours straight. Of nice."

I tipped my head back and laughed, drawing Rey's sweet stare as my imagination ran wild. Trey being nice was going to suck so hard for him, but pair that with the stipulation I put on him about his orgasms only coming when hers did . . . damn.

I looked back over at D. "Did I tell you Trey can't come unless Rey does, from now on?"

Dallin's brows rose in surprise and a smirk graced his pretty-boy face. "You did not." He looked over at Trey, who downed the straight whiskey and slammed the glass down on the bar top. "But I'm interested in hearing more about this."

"He can't orgasm again until she does. And he has to be there when she does." I leaned on the bar, keeping Reyna in my peripheral vision in case anyone else was stupid enough to try to talk to our girl while we chatted twenty feet away. "He doesn't have to be the one to give her the big O, but he has to be there for it."

"Interesting." Dallin nodded and licked his lips, turning his gaze to Trey, who still hadn't taken his off Rey. "Have you decided how you're going to get her off for the first time yet?"

"Fuck off," Trey bit out and then sighed. "I'm not giving her an orgasm."

"Why?" Dallin asked.

Trey glared at him. "Nothing has changed here."

Dallin shrugged and stood up as Rey hit her last ball, meaning he was up. "That's not what she said earlier." D stepped right up behind Trey, leaning forward until his mouth was next to his ear, and spoke loud enough so I could hear what he was saying. "When she was riding my face in our closet after your little shower adventure together, she told me that when she had her hand wrapped around your fat cock, she wanted nothing more than for you to push it down her throat. She wanted you to grab a handful of her hair and fuck her pretty little mouth until neither of you could take it anymore. Then she wanted you to slam her up against the shower wall and push it deep into her hot, tight pussy and make her come. She wanted to drain your balls with her body and feel the violence you barely hold back at any given moment around her."

"D." Trey groaned, closing his eyes like he was in physical pain.

"She wants you, Trey. And you want her," Dallin finished as Rey turned off the green and started walking toward us. "Do yourself a favor and give our girl a chance to show you just how fucking good it is with her." He kissed Trey's neck gently, making him shiver. "Stand in her sunshine for once in your life and you'll be a changed man."

I watched the exchange, fighting back an erection at Dallin's dirty words as he and Reyna switched turns.

"Everything okay back here?" she asked, looking between Trey and me.

"Perfectly perfect." I smiled at her. "What do you say you and I go to the bar and start working off some of my debt to you?" I winked.

She smiled prettily and took my hand when I held it out for her. "You're what? Four rounds deep at this point?"

She glanced at Trey, but he didn't look at her as we passed, so I tucked her under my arm to soften that blow to her confidence that I knew would come from his blatant ignoring.

"Be careful stretching the truth, baby girl, or I'll be twelve inches deep inside you before Dallin's done with his turn."

She giggled and moaned as she leaned into me. "That doesn't sound as threatening as I think you were hoping for."

I chuckled and made a space for her at the crowded bar, caging her small body in with mine as rowdy customers fought for the bartender's attention. Luckily, it turned out my girl was a regular here, and she ordered our next round right away.

"Have I told you how breathtakingly sexy you look in this little golf number?" I asked, fingering the hem of her short baby pink golf skirt where it fell right below her ass.

She hummed, leaning into me further. "I miss you." She pouted, biting her bottom lip as she looked up at me. "I feel like I haven't seen much of you the last two days."

"I'm just trying not to monopolize your time. But fuck it, I miss you, too." I leaned down and took a deep breath at her neck. "God, you smell so good."

"Good enough to eat?" she retorted, running her fingertips down my shirt before sliding them barely under the hem to touch the skin of my stomach right above my pants. "Is it selfish of me to want to ride your face right now?" She giggled, and I bit her neck.

"As long as you ride my cock when you're done with my face, baby."

"Mmm." She tipped her head to the side, giving me better access when someone interrupted us, calling to her.

"Rey?" A woman's voice called from our side, making us pull apart. Rey dropped her hands from my body as shock covered her face. "Reyna, oh my God, it is you!"

"Hey, Shae!" Reyna recovered, smoothing on a smile as she turned to the woman. I tried not to let the space she put between our bodies affect me, but it was hard.

"Hey!" The woman walked up, wearing a bright purple jumpsuit covered in sparkles and sky-high heels. She looked from Rey to me and back suspiciously before pulling Reyna into a hug, effectively ending any snuggling we had been doing before her arrival. I took a calming breath and lifted my drink off the bar that had appeared while we were kissing, hoping the ice-cold vodka could calm me down. "Who's this?" The woman, once again, looked me up and down.

"Oh," Reyna said, swallowing quickly. "This is Parker. Park, this is my friend Shae."

"Parker," Shae said, holding her hand out for me to shake. But what she wanted to say was written all over her face, and apparently, she wasn't afraid to say it out loud. She looked back to Reyna. "I feel like a horrible friend, I had no idea you and Dallin broke up."

There it was.

"Oh." Reyna raised her brows and looked at me and then back at her friend, struggling for the words. I left it all up to her, given that this was her friend, and we were in her city. But a part of me was breaking inside with each second that passed without Reyna claiming me. "We didn't break up."

Shae's eyes widened, looking between the two of us before she chuckled lightly. "I'm confused."

"Dallin is my boyfriend," Reyna said firmly, straightening her spine before looking up at me and taking a deep breath. "And Parker is my boyfriend." She slid her hand into mine and squeezed, giving me the contact I needed desperately. Could she tell? Did she see how on edge I was? "Parker, Dallin, and I are in a poly relationship."

She claimed me.

"Oh, dear lord." Her friend gasped, drawing our attention back to her. "I think I'm the most jealous person in the world right now." She fanned herself, relaxing her shoulders as she realized she hadn't just busted her friend cheating in a bar. "Like seriously?"

Reyna chuckled and leaned into me, letting me wrap my arm around her shoulders as I kissed her temple; she continued this exploration of strength on her own, with my physical support wrapped all around her.

"Yes, Shae. Seriously." Rey giggled. "It's new." She shrugged. "But we're finding our rhythm and our footing in it."

"But Jesus Christ, Rey." Shae groaned. "Did you have to have two drop-dead gorgeous men? Couldn't you leave one for the rest of us?"

Rey tipped her head back and laughed. "Shae, you're married. I met Dallin at your bachelorette party, remember?"

"I know that. But that doesn't mean my options are just gone." She waved her hand at me and asked, "How do I convince Tate to do this?"

I chuckled and shook my head. "I have no words of wisdom for you, I apologize."

"Dallin and Parker have been best friends for decades," Rey added.

Shae's shoulder slumped, and she pouted. "I hate all of Tate's friends." She sighed. "I guess I'm stuck in monogamy forever." She chuckled at her joke and Reyna shook her head, smiling. "Well, I'd better get back to my group." She nodded over her shoulder, where a gaggle of women were all dressed to the nines and sloppily trying to hit the golf balls. They were a mess, but they looked like they were having fun.

"Have a good night," Reyna called, waving to the group before turning back toward me and burying her head in my chest. "Jesus Christ."

I ran my hand up her spine, letting her take a few calming breaths after the whole situation, and eventually she pulled back to look at me. "Want to talk about that?"

"Are you mad?" she asked, nibbling on that bottom lip of hers.

"About what?"

"That I stumbled through that whole thing." She sighed. "I was prepared before we got here, I knew exactly what I'd do if I saw someone we knew and how I'd handle it. But then seeing her and having it all happen in real life . . ." She closed her eyes. "I wasn't the smoothest at it."

"Did you tell her the truth?" I asked, hitching my hand onto her hip and leaning her back into the bar, shielding her from the crowd.

"That you were my boyfriend?" she replied. "I mean we didn't talk about labels or whatever—"

"I'm your boyfriend." I cut her off, pressing into her space even more. "I'm your fucking boyfriend, Rey." I leaned down until my lips were a breath away from her parted ones as she struggled to compose herself. "As long as you understand that and admit it when someone asks who I am to you, then I'll never be mad."

"You never asked," she whispered, licking her lips and teasing the edge of mine with her tongue, but didn't kiss me. "To make me yours."

I grinned, adjusting my body so she was pressed flush to the bar and bent backward over the top slightly, pressing her hips forward into mine, where I rubbed my erection over her. "Reyna, I'd very much like it if you'd do me the honor of being mine. We both know I already consume your body when we're together." I ran one finger up her stomach, between her perky breasts in her white tank top, and tapped the spot right over her sternum. "Will you let me claim a part of your heart, too?"

"Yes," she answered with a breath. "God yes, Parker."

"Good." I licked her bottom lip. "Because if you'd said no, I was going to drag you out of here over my shoulder and lock you away somewhere until you gave in and gave me what I wanted." I closed the last bit of space and kissed her, opening her lips with mine as I deepened it, consuming her with my need. "Fuck, I might do it anyway."

"Hmm." She ran her fingers across the back of my neck. "I like that plan." She giggled when I bit her neck and sucked on it before she pulled back to look at her watch that buzzed against my shoulder. "We're being summoned." She smirked, twisting her wrist to show me a text message on the screen.

Dallin: Either fuck him right there or get back here. It's his turn.

I rolled my eyes before pulling back from her body. "Let's give the man what he wants. Maybe then he'll give me what I want tonight." I winked at her as her lips parted in surprise.

"And what exactly is it you want?" She raised an eyebrow at me as I lifted our glasses to carry to the table.

"It has to do with you on your hands and knees." I paused as her pupils dilated. "Taking him in your pussy, and me in your ass."

"Fuck." She gasped as her eyelids fluttered closed.

"My point exactly," I smirked, stepping to the side so she could pass and start walking to the table. I didn't miss the way her nipples were hardened against the fabric of her shirt or how her thighs shook with each step back to the table.

Hook, line, and sinker.

CHAPTER 21

Dallin

"Rey," I called, dragging her eyes away from where they were stuck on Parker as he swung his club. The man was terrible at golf, but he looked good doing it, so I understood her interest. Plus, something had happened at the bar that left them both aroused and needy when they returned to the table. And I planned on taking advantage of that untapped need. "I need your help with something."

I stood up from the table and held my hand out to her, nodding behind me toward the exit.

"With what?" She shook her head, confused.

"Come with me and find out." I raised a brow at her, challenging her to hold out any longer. She bit back a smirk before sliding her hand into mine, letting me pull her from the group as I nodded to Trey. "We'll be back in a few."

He smirked and rolled his eyes. "Is that all it takes you these days, D?"

"With Rey? Fuck yes." I winked at him as Rey blushed. "You'll find out eventually," I added for the hell of it and then tucked her under my arm and led her outside into the humid Tennessee air.

"What are we doing, D?" she asked, sliding her hand into my back pocket as I led her down the street.

"Going somewhere private." I pulled her to the left, walking down a narrow alley that led to a couple of fire escapes and a dumpster. "It's not romantic, but it will have to do."

She scoffed, looking around. "Romantic? You have to be kidding me." She turned and crossed her arms under her large breasts. "I'm not fucking you in an alley."

"I have no plans of taking my dick out, baby," I smirked, grabbing her by the hips and pushing her up against the ladder of a fire escape. "But I do have plans of lifting this skirt and seeing what's underneath."

"D." She moaned as I turned her to face the ladder.

"Hands here." I put both of her hands around one rung, level with her chest. "If you take them off, you lose the game."

"What's the game?" she panted as I kicked her feet apart and pulled her hips back, bending her over at the waist.

"What did Parker say to you that got you so hot at the bar?"

She groaned, laying her head against her arm as she shimmied her hips back and forth as I pressed against her ass. "That he wanted the two of you to fuck me together tonight."

I smirked at the back of her head, thinking about how naughty our guy was. "You want to take two cocks tonight?"

"Fuck yes," she moaned, looking over her shoulder at me, but I grabbed a handful of her hair and twisted her head back around to face forward. "Yes," she hissed.

"You want to be naughty tonight?" I leaned over her body and licked the shell of her ear. "You want to be a dirty girl? Taking it rough and hard?"

"Yes," she moaned, pushing her ass against me harder. "I'm fucking mad for you right now, D. I have been since I walked into the apartment and heard you and Parker fucking in the shower."

"Hmm." I slid my fingers up the back of her thigh, to the hem of her cute little golf skirt, and then higher until I felt the edge of the boy shorts she wore under the skirt. "You have to be my good girl to be my dirty girl."

"Tell me what you want," she begged. "Whatever you want, I'll do it. Just tell me."

"Anything?" I countered.

"Yes."

"Good girl," I praised her, sliding my fingertips under the hem of her underwear, and growled when I found her pussy soaked. "Fucking hell, baby."

"I'm so horny for cock," she mewed, falling deeper into the sweet dirty talk that the guys had brought out of her. Before they showed up, she rarely ever let the spicy words she wrote in her books flow freely from her lips.

Until now.

"Well, this will have to do for now." I pulled my hand free of her shorts and took the secret weapon from my pocket, holding her hair tight as she tried to turn to see what I was doing. "Bend over and hold on to the bottom rung." I slapped her ass, dropping to my knees behind her and looking around to make sure we were still alone. "Now, Rey," I commanded when she hesitated.

She bent over and did as she was told, spreading her legs further as she went until she was bent in half with her ass in the air. "What are you going to do to me, baby?"

"Nothing you don't deserve," I smirked, sliding her underwear to the side and lifting her skirt over her wide hips. "My good girl deserves some pleasure, don't you think?"

"Yes," she panted, eager for more.

I slid the toy I'd brought with me against her pussy lips, letting the cool silicone soak up her juices, and then pushed it against her entrance until her body gave way and let it in. It was shaped like an egg and was pretty big in terms of toys, but her body took it so beautifully. She sighed when it was inside her, swinging her hips back and forth slightly.

"Now what?" she huffed, enthusiastic for more, but frustrated with the lack of progress.

I slid her panties further to the side, leaned in, and sucked her clit into my mouth, drawing a loud gasp and moan from her lips before she pushed back against my face, arching into me. I growled, pushing my tongue deep inside her, loving her taste.

Her body tightened, and she moaned, riding my face backward as she came. She muffled her pleas for more in her arm until I pulled back, gently licking her once more before sliding her panties over her pulsing pussy.

"That's my good, dirty girl," I mused, standing up and pulling her upright with me. I turned her and held on to her as she came down from the high, enjoying the way her body shivered each time her hips shifted with the toy still inside her.

"And this"—she flexed her hips—"do you plan to just leave that there?"

"Yes, I do," I smirked, spanking her ass and pulling her against me. "And you said you'd do anything I wanted you to do, so you'll be a good girl and leave it there. And later, when I give you your next direction, you'll follow that too. Perfectly." I kissed her, enjoying the taste of vodka still on her lips from Parker's heated kiss a few minutes before I dragged her outside. "Let's get back inside before Parker comes hunting you down."

"Hmm," she mused, holding on to me with a smirk on her face. "I like the idea of being hunted by you big, bad wolves."

I growled, cracking my neck as my restraint got smaller and smaller with her and her naughty side. "Inside." I spanked her once again. "Now."

She giggled and skipped inside, high on endorphins and excitement.

I wondered what she would do when she realized the toy inside her had a Bluetooth feature.

"God, you guys suck." Rey joked, checking the scoreboard on her way to the tee once again. "I'm spanking all three of you."

"Hardly," I deadpanned, leveling a stare at her as she bit her bottom lip, knowing she barely had a lead on me.

"Fine, I'm spanking Trey and Parker." She stuck her tongue out at me and took her spot from Trey as he grumbled under his breath about golf's stupidity and grabbed his whiskey before lowering himself down onto the couch next to me.

"I've been known to enjoy a spanking now and again," Parker joked as she got ready to swing, and she pulled it hard, missing the ball completely before glaring at him in surprise. He chuckled, shaking his head, and joined us on the couch, sitting on my other side. She shook it off and recentered herself, correcting her stance. "I just have to come up with a dozen more shocking statements, and I might actually get her to lose," he mumbled.

She hit her ball flawlessly and sent it soaring over the net, taking Parker's hopes away with him as it went.

"Or you could play dirty." I shrugged, sipping my whiskey. He looked over at me at the same time Trey did, wondering what I had up my sleeve. I smirked into my glass and pulled my phone out of my pocket. "I figured you two would need all the help you could get. So I took some liberties with Rey when I took her outside."

"Don't talk sex," Parker groaned. "I've been fucking hard since she walked out in that skirt and I'm counting down the fucking seconds until we get out of here."

"So I shouldn't show you this, then?" I asked, opening the app and flashing it to him before handing my phone over to Trey.

"What's this?" he asked, confused by the graph on the screen with arrows up and down on a couple of different digital settings.

"Push the blue button and find out," I said, nodding to Rey as she set another ball on her tee.

Trey eyed me for a second and then gave in to his morbid curiosity, pushing his thumb down on the big blue button that said *buzz*.

Reyna was halfway through her backswing when the app took over control of the toy buried deep inside her pussy, causing her to shriek loudly and double over, crossing her legs. "Dallin!" she cried, staring at me with wide eyes, holding her hand over her lower abdomen.

"What?" I shrugged innocently and held my hands up.

"Oh, fuck," Parker jeered. "No fucking way."

"I'm confused," Trey said, looking between us and her.

"Go on, baby." I nodded to the range. "You're so close to beating us all for good." I winked at her and nudged Trey. "Hit the green button."

He dutifully hit the green button that said *pivot*, and she nearly fell to her knees.

"Dallin," she groaned, begging me with her pretty fuck-me hazel eyes. "Not here."

"Right here." I challenged her, staring her down. "Now swing," I ordered, dominating her in front of the two men at my sides. "Unless you'd rather concede and let the boys win their bets?"

Her teeth clenched as she held on to her golf club with white knuckles and took a few deep breaths. "I'm not a quitter." She stiffened her spine and turned back toward her tee. "I didn't realize you fought dirty," she snarled under her breath.

I chuckled as Parker shook his head, looking downright feral as he watched her fighting the sensations building inside her. "I'm a very dirty man, baby. You're about to find out just how dirty I can get."

She moaned when I reached over and hit the up arrow on the buzz control, watching the graph spike with the increased vibration inside her.

"Oh." Trey ruminated, leaning forward in his seat and looking between the phone in his hand and our girl standing ten feet away. "You're kidding me."

I shook my head when he looked over his shoulder at me and

nodded toward the phone. "Play with our girl, Trey. Make her lose at her own game."

She lined up to swing, and he set his glass down, holding the phone in both hands, thumb hovering over the up arrow on the buzz control again, and as she lifted the club, he raised it three notches.

She swung, gasping halfway through, yet managed to hit the ball. Too bad for her, it hardly made it off the edge of the platform, automatically knocking her score way down. She glared at him but kept her mouth quiet as she leaned down to get a new ball on her tee. I didn't miss the way she shimmied her hips as she did, like she was trying to relieve the ache inside her as she went.

"Turn it off," I barked, and Trey hit the kill switch milliseconds before she started coming on the toy.

"Dallin!" she barked angrily, with outrage in her eyes. "That's cruel."

"Nah, baby." I shook my head. "That's just evening the score." I held her stare and waited for her to see how serious I was. "No coming," I commanded, daring her to defy me.

"Until when?" She put her hands on her hips. "That's twice today I've wondered if you're the only one who's going to reap the benefits of adding men to our relationship." She tilted her head up and looked down her nose with ire.

"Oh, shit," Parker gasped, shaking his head.

The hair on the back of my neck stood up as I unfolded my body from the couch and stalked toward her. She swallowed and flicked her glance from me to Parker like he was going to save her from me.

"You think you're being iced out, darling?" I stood toe-to-toe with her but refused to touch her. I wanted her truth.

"Maybe," she replied. "Right now I am."

"Wrong," I snapped. "Right now you're being edged so that you're so fucking frantic for an orgasm by the time we get home that you'll be my dirty fucking slut to get it." Her nostrils flared as she looked from side to side to see if any other golfers had heard my threat. "Say the word and I'll turn the toy on so high you scream my name right here in the middle of this building if you want an orgasm so bad." I pushed her hair back over her shoulder and tightened my fingers in the sensitive strands at the base of her neck, pulling them taut. "Or you can be my good little girl, play along with my game, and when we get home, I'll make sure you don't stop orgasming until you pass the fuck out. Which is it going to be, Reyna?" I asked, reveling in the way her pupils were blown wide and her chest rose rapidly. "Are you going to be my spoiled little brat or my dirty little slut?"

"Slut," she whimpered, licking her lips and rising up on her toes to relieve some of the pressure on her hair. "I want to be your dirty little slut, Dallin."

"Good." I smiled down at her, letting my fingers glide through her hair until she sank down onto her heels again. "Because we're crossing over lines we can never go back from tonight, love." I leaned down and kissed her cheek. "And you're going to come so hard when we do it."

"Fuck," she panted, swaying on her feet when I dropped my hands completely from her body and stepped back. "I'm still going to beat you boys." She shook her head. "I never lose."

"Game on, sweetheart," I smirked. "I can't wait to see you deliver on your loss to the boys."

CHAPTER 22

Trey

Reyna's forehead was glistening with perspiration as she stood between Parker and me at the curb, waiting for the Uber. Dallin was squaring up on the tab and purposely taking his sweet time, dragging Reyna's torture out as long as possible.

And I was fucking here for it.

She swayed her hips back and forth, silently trying to make herself come as the busy city life moved all around us on the sidewalk. Parker had the phone, controlling the toy I now knew was buried deep inside her pussy, and I had been aching hard since I realized I held her pleasure in the palm of my hand.

Even if I didn't want her, I enjoyed playing with her.

I was a warm-blooded man after all, and making women squirm had always been my favorite game.

"I hate you both," she gasped, grabbing onto my arm as Parker slid his thumb over one of the controls. Her nails dug into my forearm as she swayed on her feet with her eyes closed and her head tipped back, desperate to come.

"Tell me what it's doing," I said, surprising both of them, but I ignored his amused look my way.

"No." She shook her head, prying one eye open to look over at me. "You don't get to know."

Fucking bold.

I smirked down at her and turned to face her until I pressed right up against her side. She groaned and leaned against me for support. We hadn't touched much since we met, but tonight, she was clingy, constantly grabbing one of us or leaning against us as she rode out the waves of torturous pleasure time and time again. I knew she was desperate and not at all interested in me, but I ate up the contact like a starving dog on a street. I needed it.

I craved it.

Fuck if I understood why.

"Tell me what it's doing, and I'll make Dallin let you come in the car on the way home. Deny me and I'll let him make you wait for it," I challenged her, and Parker chuckled, sliding his finger over the control again.

"Swirling." She gasped, digging those dainty pink painted nails in even further. "It's fucking swirling around and vibrating."

"Steady or pulsing?" I was a fucking moron for asking, but I didn't care at the moment. She'd built this need inside me in the shower and I had denied myself release as well, leaving me nearly as on edge as she was.

"Pulsing." She bit her bottom lip and then dipped her head forward, finally opening both of her eyes. "It's pulsing the way a cock does as it comes, emptying come deep inside me."

I clenched my jaw tight to keep my mouth shut as Dallin came up to us on the sidewalk at the same time our car pulled up.

It was a boxy SUV with party lights illuminated underneath it and strong bass music playing from the stereo system in it. The windows were so tinted, we couldn't see anything about the interior from the street. Reyna looked at Dallin and then at me. "We had a deal."

I nodded to her as Parker handed me the honorary controller in Dallin's phone before opening the back door and sliding into the SUV. "This is going to be good."

"Rey earned herself an orgasm on the way home," I told Dallin, not asking for his permission.

He raised one brow at me and looked down at his minx of a girlfriend, where she stared up at him with big puppy-dog eyes. "Fine, but you have to be the one to give it to her," he replied, staring at me before sliding his hand over her ass and pushing her toward the car. "Sit on Trey's lap in the middle and let him make you come, dirty girl." We stood at the open doorway and watched as Reyna eagerly climbed into the back seat, scurrying across until she sat in Parker's lap, waiting for me to get in next to her.

If she wasn't going to complain about Dallin's methods, I sure as fuck wasn't going to.

Because I wanted to get her off. I needed to feel her come in my arms after watching her get edged all night. I wanted to know what she sounded like up close when she shattered. I needed to feel her break apart in my hands.

"I have one condition," Dallin said, halting me from taking my place in the back seat and waiting until I looked him in the eye before he finished. "When we get home, Parker and I are going to give you both some alone time. And I expect you to make our girl happy while we're gone."

"And what do I get out of playing along?" I retorted, fighting him for control.

"Besides finally getting Rey's body all to yourself?" He chuckled and closed the space between us until we were chest-to-chest, my back to the car so Parker and Reyna couldn't hear what was being discussed. "If you make our girl happy, and I mean, really, *really* happy while Park and I are away, I'll give you what you've wanted since you walked in my front door weeks ago."

I swallowed, hesitant to get my hopes up when he was in the mood for playing games. "Specifics, Dallin."

"Me," he responded. "However you want me, though we both know you love nothing more than bending me over and fucking that thick cock into me deep and hard. My only stipulation is that Rey and Parker are there at the same time."

"Deal," I responded without hesitation. He knew he had me. He knew he held my balls in his hand, twisting them up with expert pressure until I'd be willing to give him whatever he wanted in this entire world. Because I wanted inside him again, after two long years without it. "I'll make her happy."

"Good." He smirked before leaning in and kissing me, ignoring the busy street behind us. "Because I'm aching to feel you inside me. And I don't want to wait another fucking day."

I turned and threw myself into the back seat, sliding over next to Parker as Dallin got in behind us. The driver was some young punk rock dude with a rainbow of colors for hair and pink nail polish. He looked back at us in the mirror. "You guys all set?"

"As long as you keep the music up loud and your eyes faced forward, we're fucking perfect," I responded, staring him down.

He looked from me to Reyna, where she sat on Parker's lap, letting him bite and suck on her neck right above the collar of her tank top, and smiled back knowingly. "I'm not here to judge anyone." He clicked the app on his phone to start the trip. "Party away, my party people." Then he turned the music up until it was vibrating under our seats and the light in the cab went out, replaced with strobing rainbow LED strip lights across the roof that pulsed with the music.

"Hell yes," Dallin smirked, leaning back against the door, and nodding to Rey. "Let's get the party started."

"Come here," I commanded, sliding my hand under Reyna's leg and around her waist, lifting her from Parker's lap and onto mine, straddling my lap, facing me. "Do you want this?" I asked her, hesitating with my hands on her small waist.

"I need to come, Trey," she whined. "Don't overthink it." She rocked her hips forward, looking over to Dallin as she rolled them back, grinding on my hard-on. "Just make me come."

Who was I to deny her demands?

I flipped the app back on, turned the vibe on strong, and then turned on the pivot feature that she described as swirling, before tossing the phone to Dallin. "Oh, fuck," she moaned, tipping her head back as she ground her hips down onto me again. My cock was rock hard and painfully stretching out my tight denim jeans as she rode me, and I was in fucking awe of the show. She found a rhythm, paired with the music and the vibration I knew was pulsating inside her as she chased her pleasure. "I need more," she gasped, sliding her hands up my chest and around the back of my neck, using me for leverage as she worked her hips. "Please, Trey."

I couldn't resist anymore. I slid my hands up under the hem of her tank top and lifted it, baring her breasts, thanking my lucky stars that they were braless under her tight athletic shirt. They bounced free, dropping with the weight of them as I bunched her top under her chin. I'd been mesmerized by them in the shower earlier, nearly swallowing my tongue whole when she soaped them up with her loofah and rubbed them together seductively for me. And now I had them bare and ripe mere inches from my mouth.

And you bet your ass I took a fucking bite.

I leaned forward and held the weight of them each in my hands before dropping my mouth to one hard nipple, flicking my tongue over it before sucking it into my mouth. "Yes, Trey," she moaned, holding my head to her chest. "Suck it, just like that," she begged. "Please don't stop. Please. Please. Please."

"That's so hot." Parker groaned, palming his erection as he watched. "She loves it when you bite them."

I bit one, rolling it between my teeth like Parker said, and she shattered. "Trey!" she moaned, and hearing my name on her lips during her ecstasy nearly had me filling my jeans with come. "You're making me come." She panted, curling forward, and dragging her nails over the back of my scalp, burying them into my hair. "Oh my God!"

She shook in my arms, shivering as her orgasm rolled through her entire body until she sagged in my arms.

"Damn," Dallin growled, adjusting himself in his jeans as Reyna rested her forehead against my shoulder.

"Turn it off," she panted as I ran my hands up and down her bare back.

"No fucking way," D scolded, though he pulled the app up to slow everything down.

"D," she whined. "Please."

The driver cleared his throat, lowering the music a bit. "Your destination is right ahead."

I pulled her shirt down, tucking her fucking delicious tits away, and I didn't miss the way she actively avoided my eyes. When the car pulled up to the curb, Dallin tossed a fifty over the front seat, nodding to the driver. "Thanks, man."

"Hey, thank you!" he called, rainbow hair bouncing as he twisted out his window as Dallin got out. "Here's my card! Text me for a ride anytime and I'll cut the fare in half." He gave D finger guns and clicked his tongue. "Privacy guaranteed."

Reyna groaned, sliding off my lap and righting her skirt as D helped her from the back seat and I followed her. Parker met us around on the sidewalk as the SUV drove off.

"Dallin, please turn it off," Rey whined again, sliding her hands up his back as he keyed in the code to the door.

"Is it keeping you horny?" Dallin asked, opening the door and letting her walk in ahead of him.

"Yes!" she groaned. "I need a break from the constant high."

"Then what are you going to do when our cocks start coming out?" he asked, shocking her enough to turn around and face him at the bottom of the steps. Her eyes found me and flicked back to D, then to Parker, before she shook her head. We all stood in the windowless foyer of the stairwell, with the door locked behind us, waiting for the next move.

I was on fucking edge, horny, hard, and desperate for more. And not at all in the mood for D's games. I needed to fuck. I needed to come.

He'd promised me those things, yet we all stood stationary, so close yet so far away from the bed I needed to fuck someone in.

Someone.

Because right now, if Reyna and Dallin stood next to each other, and each begged for my cock, I didn't know who I'd give it to first. I never would have thought I'd hesitate for a second to have D underneath me again, but now, after having a small fucking taste of her, I was feral for more.

"Take your top off," Dallin instructed her, dominating the space as I leaned against the wall and Parker rested his arms on the metal railing, watching her closely. He had been quiet most of the night, letting her and me figure shit out with Dallin's instructions, but I knew Parker better than anyone else in the world, and I knew he was champing at the bit for some action.

"D." Rey tilted her head questioningly.

Which was mistake number one. She thought because she finally got her orgasm that the game was done. But she forgot that there were three hard and horny men circling her, waiting for sexual satisfaction as well.

He moved quickly, sliding his hand around the front of her throat and pushing her back so she was bending over the handrail, conveniently right into Parker's lap.

"Park," Dallin stated, his intent clear.

"Always glad to help strip our girl," Parker mused, reaching down and sliding Reyna's tank top up over her head. She lifted her arms and helped him get it off completely, standing in just her cute pink little skirt and white sneakers, with those massive tits free and begging for attention.

Rey mewed under Dallin's dominance, gripping his wrist with both of her hands, and Parker reached around, tweaking her nipples, pebbling them up to hard peaks. "Skirt and panties next," D instructed.

And this time Parker didn't even give Rey a chance to comply, reaching around her body and sliding them down her hips to midthigh.

"That will do," D smirked, turning her around to face our buddy. "Mind holding on to her for me?"

Parker grinned. "Don't mind one bit," he said, taking Dallin's place with his hand around her throat. Her eyelids fluttered closed, and she leaned into him as D pulled her hips backward so her ass was popped out, bent at the waist. Her skirt restricted her thighs from spreading, but apparently, D got what he needed out of it. He showered her ass with his hand, spanking her and drawing delicious moans from her lips.

"You wanted to be my dirty slut tonight, didn't you?" D said, pushing his hand between her thighs, playing with her pussy. She hummed her agreement as Parker bent down and sucked on one of her breasts. "You wanted to take Parker and me into your body at the same time, like a good little whore. Filled up and milking our cocks until we gave you our come."

"Jesus, Dallin," she moaned, pressing back against his hand as he started finger-fucking her hard, but shallow because of the toy. "Fuck me or stop toying with me," she cried. "I can't take it."

I could see the panic on her face as she teetered between pleasure and pain from the teasing.

"You want a cock, baby?" D growled. "Beg for one."

"Please fuck me," she gasped, mewling and moaning as he continued to play with her. "Please put a cock inside me. Any hole. I don't care," she cried.

"Good girl," Dallin praised her. "Let's get this toy out and open you up to take a cock. Bend over more."

She bent over the railing more, falling into Parker's waiting arms, and Dallin started working the toy free from her.

Meanwhile, I stood against the wall, feeling like a fucking voyeur as I watched the three of them together. They worked in sync, building the sexual tension among them, and I felt out of place.

I leaned up off the wall, uncrossing my arms, ready to take myself out of the space because it was fucking with my head. I was sinking into my brain, and I didn't fucking like what it was telling me inside there.

They don't need you.

She doesn't want you.

They're happy together.

He left you for her.

You can't give them what she can.

"Don't you fucking dare," Dallin barked, looking over his shoulder at me, sensing my movement without even seeing it. "Don't fucking leave."

I clenched my jaw and looked him square in the eye. "Looks like you have it all covered here." I nodded to where Rey was moaning as Parker dove back down on her breasts, playing with her clit between her legs.

"We had a deal," Dallin argued, standing up with the toy in his hand and turning it off. "You really going to walk away from us now?"

"What do you want from me, man?" I shrugged, exasperated.

"I want you to fuck her," he snapped, closing the distance between us as Rey and Parker froze, finally aware of what was happening on the other side of the room. "I want you to fucking let go of your hang-ups and finally give in to what we all know is building between you," he argued, waving his hand toward Rey, who looked over her shoulder at me.

She was the fucking image of perfection. Naked, bent over, dripping, and begging for release.

But I was still hung up on Dallin, and seeing them together put me on edge.

"The deal was to make her happy. I did that."

"Fuck the deal." He stalked forward and slid his hand over my erection, straining against my jeans, and squeezed, making my eyes close in pleasure. "Tell me you don't want her, and I'll call you a liar. The proof is in my hand, Trey."

I opened my mouth, but nothing would come out. Because he was right, but I was in a mind-fucking trip over it all.

"I want you." Reyna's sweet voice drew our attention to where she stood in Parker's arms, his hands hitched on her flared hips, staring at us. "If you won't admit it, I guess I'll be the bigger person and put it all on the line. For the greater good." She waved her arms around the group. "If you don't want me, then just say so, but I think you'd be lying. I want you."

I stared into her hazel eyes and felt her fear and vulnerability calling to me.

This.

This was what Dallin ached for. The difference between us and her was right here. The vulnerability, and rawness; the tenderness and suppleness of her gentle nature.

It called to me, beckoning me to give in and let someone soft comfort me for once. To rest in her warmth.

I shoved Dallin out of my way, not even aware that my brain told my feet to move until I was halfway across the space. Reyna's eyes widened into big doe eyes as she stared up at me in apprehension, but I was a runaway train, unable to stop or slow down.

I slammed into her, gripping the back of her head in my hand as I kissed her powerfully. She was naked and in my arms for the first time, and I was a goner. I'd never recover from this.

She mewed against my lips before sliding her hands up my abs under the hem of my shirt like she was desperate to feel my skin against hers. I tore at the bindings of her skirt and panties, pushing them down her legs.

"I want you," I growled, frustrated that it took her cutting herself open first for me to finally admit not only to myself but to her and the guys as well. "I've fucking wanted you this whole time."

"I know," she gasped, sliding her arms over my shoulders and holding on to me as I picked her up, wrapping her legs around my waist. "But you hated what I represented, and I understand that."

"Not anymore." I shook my head. "No more."

"Good," Dallin mused as he slid one hand over my shoulder and one down her spine. "Go upstairs and make up for it. We'll be up in a while."

I nodded and climbed the stairs two at a time. I was eager to close this chapter and leave it behind us as we began a new one.

Together.

Reyna's lips were teasing up and down my neck as I walked us through the apartment to her bedroom. I wanted her in her space the first time I consumed her. I wanted to feel like I belonged among all of her.

"Take this off," she demanded, pulling on my shirt as I slid her to her feet at the end of the bed. "All of it." She dropped her hands to my belt as I pulled my shirt off over the back of my head. I took over the belt from her frazzled hands and shoved my jeans down, revealing my aching cock to her hungry eyes. "Commando?" She smirked.

"Sometimes." I kissed her again as her hands drifted down my abs and to the V above my dick, teasing every sensitive spot with her fingernails like she knew the map to them all. "Fuck," I growled, flexing my hips forward as she circled around the base of my cock but didn't touch me where I wanted her to the most.

"Take your hair down," she commanded. "I want to feel it in my hands when you fuck me." I smirked against her lips and pulled my hair tie free, shaking it loose as she stared. "I want your violence," she whispered against my lips. "I want the brutality that I know lies right under here." She tapped my chest, pulling back to look up at me. "I want your wildness, Trey. The darkness you told me that first night that I couldn't handle, I want it all."

"It's yours," I groaned, willing to promise her the sun if she'd just touch me. "I won't hold back, but you need to tell me if it's too much."

"It won't be." She shook her head as she dropped her lips to my sternum and then down my abs as she slowly sank onto her knees. "I crave it, Trey."

"Fucking hell, look at you." She looked up at me from under her dark eyelashes as she adjusted herself at my feet. I ran my thumb over her jaw and across her bottom lip. "You're the most beautiful woman I've ever seen before, Rey."

She smiled and then nibbled on the end of my thumb before she dropped my gaze and let hers fall upon my cock where it leaked, aimed right at her pretty face. "Take it all in, baby." She flicked her gaze up at me and leaned forward to kiss the tip of my cock, letting my pre-cum bead up on her lips before her pink tongue swiped it off to taste. Her eyelids fluttered closed, and she bit her bottom lip. "I'm going to make you feel so good," she moaned.

Then she leaned forward, looking back up at me, and sucked the head of my cock into her mouth, stretching her lips around me and swirling her tongue over the underside. My eyes crossed from how good it felt to finally have her touching me and from how erotic she looked on her knees, taking me into her mouth for the first time.

She hummed, popping her lips off me before spitting onto the head and rubbing her hand down the shaft.

"Jesus, fuck," I groaned, tipping my head back as she drove back down, taking me deeper into her mouth. Her lips were stretched tight around me, trying desperately to fit me down her throat, but I was too thick to make it past halfway down.

But that didn't stop her from giving me the best blow job of my life. She twisted her hands around the part of me she couldn't fit in her mouth and then dropped one to my balls, gently scratching her nails over the tight skin of my balls to my taint and back. I growled something inhuman sounding as I lost control of my desire to tangle my hands into her hair and push her further down my cock.

She hummed her approval as I held her head still and fucked my cock into her mouth, taking it deeper than she did, causing her to gag before she relaxed her throat and took even more. "Good girl." I praised her as she ran her nails down my thighs, creating red gashes in the skin as we found a rhythm that gave her time to breathe between thrusts and kept me from blowing down her throat like some novice. "I don't deserve to touch you." I shook my head, struggling with my moral compass, telling me she was too good for the likes of me. She popped off the head of my cock, fought my hold on her hair, and lifted my cock to suck one of my balls into her mouth before running her tongue behind it, teasing my taint. "Fuck!" I growled.

She chuckled evilly, pushing my legs further apart with her knee for better access, and my eyes rolled into the back of my head.

"And you think I've done something to be worthy of not one but three incredible men in my life?" she scoffed. "It's me that's tricked someone in the karma department, Trey." She watched my face as she used both hands on my cock, twisting them and stroking it. "God, I wanted to do this so bad in the shower earlier." She shook her head. "One more second on my knees and I would have begged to taste you."

"I wanted to fuck you so hard against that wall," I replied, tightening my hand in her hair. "I wanted to make you beg for mercy from how hard I fucked you."

She moaned, "Do it now."

I pulled her to her feet and into my arms, kissing her as I walked us over to the wingback chair in the corner of her bedroom. "You're going to ride me, and then I'm going to make you scream so loud our guys join us to make sure you're still alive." She smirked, holding on to me as I sat down with her in my lap. "But first—" I lifted her until she was standing with her feet next to my hips. "Ride my face."

"Yes please," she moaned, holding on to the back of the chair as I scooted down until she hovered right above my mouth. "Oh, fuck!" she cried when I licked her clit, swirling my tongue around it before sucking it into my mouth. She curled forward, digging her fingers into my loose hair and holding on as she rode my face.

She tasted like fucking heaven, and feeling her body shiver and jolt in my hands from what I was doing was bliss. I put everything I had into it, pleasing her in ways I'd never cared to perfect before her. I listened to her body, watching her cues to what she liked and what drove her wild, and before long, she was thrashing above me, rocking against my face and coming with a scream of ecstasy.

She sank to her knees in my lap as I sat up in the chair, supporting her loosened body as she came off the high. "I can officially say that was my biggest orgasm today."

I chuckled, tickling her side at the cheekiness of that statement as she giggled and squirmed in my arms. "I would take offense to that if it weren't my two best friends that you were comparing me to."

"Hmm. Wouldn't you call them more than just your best friends?" She leaned back and looked at me, pushing her hair back off her forehead.

"What else would I call them?" I leaned against the headrest and gently ran my hands up and down her thighs.

"Your boyfriends." She shrugged.

I mulled that over in my head as she watched me, like she was putting some puzzle together in her mind. "We've never labeled things before. I don't plan to start now."

"Will you label them with me?" she asked. "Now that we've—" She looked down at our naked bodies and winked. "You know."

"First of all . . ." I adjusted her body so that my cock was pinned between her wet pussy and my stomach, flexing my hips to rub against her and make her moan before I completed my statement. "We haven't done anything yet. That was just a small glimpse into what I'm going to do to you." She shivered and rubbed herself up the underside of my cock, enticing us both. Her nipples pebbled hard again as goose bumps covered her arms. "And second of all, I have no plans to change anything, regardless of what I'm doing with you. Or the guys. Though I will admit this is entirely uncharted territory for us."

She took a deep breath and nodded, almost like she was disappointed in my lack of an answer but also understanding it. "I introduced Parker as my boyfriend today to one of my friends." She held my stare and chewed on her bottom lip. "And I admitted I was dating both him and Dallin. So believe me, this is uncharted territory for me, too."

"But you want labels? To define this instead of just letting it be easy and free?" I don't know why, but the pressure to label it was causing my eye to twitch and my heart rate to spike.

"Let it be?" She leaned back, scowling a bit. "Isn't the alternative of labeling it just allowing myself to be someone's fuck toy?"

"I thought the idea of being used aroused you?" I deadpanned, playing off her statement earlier.

"By someone who cares about me," she snapped.

It was in that moment that I realized I'd fucked up.

"Do you think I don't care about you?"

"Can you stop replying with a question each time?" She shifted, sitting back on my legs and creating space between our bodies. "And I have no idea how you feel about me, seeing as you've finally just allowed yourself to admit you were attracted to me."

"Wait." I shook my head, tightening my hands around her waist as even more anxiety raced through my body. I was spiraling from the war raging on inside my head from the entire experience. "You're mad?"

"I'm . . ." She huffed, pausing like she didn't know how to finish her statement. "I don't know what I am." She shook her head, pulling herself away even more and standing up. "I do know I'm not interested in being with someone who doesn't want to claim me in public." She crossed her arms over her chest, hiding her body from me as I sat there dumbfounded. "I get that this just happened a few minutes ago, but it's not new. This"—she flicked her fingers between our bodies—"has been building for weeks now! Can you really say you haven't thought about what the future would look like for us?"

"Of course I've thought about it. I thought it would be the four of us, having fun and enjoying life." I stood up, holding my hands out to the side. "We don't have to scream from the rooftop that we're fucking poly and in an open relationship."

"I don't understand you." She turned and grabbed her robe off the bench by the bed, shielding her body from me and tying it at her waist angrily. "I don't understand how this can work when we want such different things." She was raising her voice and pacing around the room as I stood there, dumbfounded.

Parker would have calmed the situation down, speaking to her gentle side with his own while managing the situation. Dallin would have used that authority in his voice and personality to make her see reason and understand that she was winding herself up for no reason at all.

But me?

I was a fucking menace with absolutely no experience in talking to women or dealing with their feelings, so I did what I did best.

I yelled back.

"So what do you want, then?" I snapped, flapping my arms out in exasperation. "Why don't you start by telling me what the right answer is so I can give it to you? Because I'm going to be honest with you, Rey, I'm fucking lost here."

"I want PDA!" she yelled, matching my volume. "I want you to be proud to call me yours. I want Parker and Dallin to touch and kiss and be comfortable with each other in public without caring what other people think. I want to be touched and kissed by all three of you at the same time."

I scoffed, shaking my head. "You want a fucking fairy tale, but you don't live in a magic kingdom. You live in the real world."

"So you're just going to treat me like a friend? If someone asks you who I am, you'll say what? Your buddy's girlfriend? Then take me somewhere dark and private to fuck me like a dirty whore? I deserve to be treated better than that!"

"Whoa!" I yelled, throwing my hands up in the air. "Dallin called you a slut a handful of times tonight! Don't act like being treated like a whore bothers you."

"Ugh!" she screeched. "You don't get it!" She walked away from me, threw the door to the bedroom open, and walked out.

"You're right!" I roared back, chasing after her. "I don't fucking get it, I don't get how we went from me, D, and Park running a train on you tonight"—I yelled wildly—"which you were fucking begging for, by the way, to you screaming at me about making you feel like a whore in a hypothetical situation that hasn't even happened yet!"

She glared at me over her shoulder as she picked up her phone that magically had appeared on the counter while we were in the bedroom. "So now you're going to throw it in my face that I like the idea of being with all three of you? Seriously?"

I rolled my eyes so far that I saw my brain before holding my hands up in front of me in surrender. "I can't do this." I shook my head.

"What does that mean?" She scowled.

"It means I can't deal with your level of crazy." I turned back and went into the bedroom, picking up my discarded clothes and shoving my arms and legs into them in haste to get the fuck away from the whole situation.

"Oh yeah, that's fucking rich coming from you!" she screamed, chasing after me. "You're the most fucked up out of all of us!"

"Is that so?" I glared at her, feeling my anger rise even more. "Well then, you won't mind if I just take my fucked-up self out of the entire situation!" I screamed back.

"Enough!" Dallin bellowed from behind her in the doorway to the bedroom. Neither of us heard him and Parker come into the apartment, and we both jumped like a couple of kids caught doing something bad. "What the fuck is going on in here?" he sneered, looking from me to Rey and back.

"Ask her," I snapped. "She's all twisted up wanting my cock, but only if it comes with a diamond ring attached to it."

"That's a lie!" she huffed. "You're so goddamned dramatic!"

"I'm dramatic?" My eyes bugged out as I looked at D. "She's distorted in the fucking head over a hypothetical situation in the future that she crafted up on her own, where I somehow made her feel like a whore, and is screaming at me for it."

Parker scowled, trying to track the entire situation the same way I had been a few minutes ago.

"I just asked him what he wanted in the future," Rey huffed, crossing her arms over her chest again defiantly.

"While I was trying to put my cock into her!" I shook my head. "She's fucking nuts if she thinks I'm the kind of man to make declarations for some pussy."

"Enough," D snapped, holding his hand up at me, warning me without words for my tone in her direction. Because that was how this would go.

Right or wrong, she was on a pedestal.

And I was the fucking monster here to ruin her day.

"Never mind." I took a deep breath, feeling everything that had been burning inside me going numb with each erratic beat of my heart. "It's not worth it." I shook my head, staring at Dallin. "I thought this was worth it; wanting her or not sexually doesn't matter. It's not." I shrugged. "I'm out."

"Trey," Dallin warned, cocking his head to the side. I would have normally buckled under his stare, letting him take the lead and call the shots. But for the last few weeks, I'd bounced back and forth on the idea of this all for a reason.

The reason was it just wasn't going to work.

"It's not going to work." I waved my hand toward Rey, who looked at least a little guilty since I said I was out. "I can't bend myself down that far to appease her." I lowered my shoulders and my voice. "This isn't something I can win, so I'd rather walk away before I lose."

I pushed past him, fighting off his hold on me as he tried to keep me in the bedroom until we were in a shoving match, fighting for dominance. His simple attempt to keep me stationary turned into something far more intense as we both let the emotions of the situation bubble up until we were physically fighting.

"Dallin, stop," Rey cried as he slammed me into the wall with his forearm pushed against my neck.

I shoved back, trying to dislodge him, but he was stronger and bigger than me, and even if he'd never used it against me before, I knew I wasn't winning.

"Calm down," he demanded, pushing down harder on my windpipe. "Let's just take a minute."

"No," I growled, kicking his feet, trying to dislodge him. "I've done that."

"Please, Trey." He sighed. "Please don't make me choose."

I gritted my teeth and shoved him with everything I had, dislodging him, and slamming him backward into the other wall. "Because we both know I wouldn't be your pick, don't we," I said, fixing my shirt and wiping away the blood that had beaded up on my split lip. "I need some air." I shook my head, brushing it all off as I stormed down the hall.

"D, go with him," Parker called, and I rolled my eyes.

"I don't need a fucking chaperone. I'm pretty sure I can find some willing pussy on my own," I threw back over my shoulder as I ripped open the front door.

Reyna's small gasp grated my nerves as I flew down the stairs, desperate to get away from her and her infuriating stubbornness.

It pissed off my stubbornness.

When I got down onto the sidewalk, I took a deep breath, letting the toxic air of the city fill my lungs and calm my frayed nerves. I didn't wait for D to catch up as I slid my leg over my bike, but it didn't stop him from doing the same on his bike parked next to mine. The pipes on both roared as we idled at the curb, staring at each other in silence.

"I'm choosing you," D yelled loud enough for me to hear as he slid his nighttime glasses on. "Right now, right here, at this moment, I choose you. But this conversation isn't over."

I swallowed, suddenly unable to find the words necessary to respond to his declaration. So instead, I just nodded, adjusting my position as I flipped up my kickstand. "Then let's ride."

CHAPTER 23

Reyna

"I don't want to hear it," I snapped, crossing my arms over my chest aggressively as I rummaged through the pantry, looking for something sweet and salty to binge on.

Parker smirked at me out of my peripheral and leaned back on the counter. "Hear what? How royally you fucked up tonight?"

I swung around in outrage and stared at him. "I fucked up?" I snapped. "You weren't even there!"

He shrugged, looking unbothered while I was full-on raging still. "I think I got the picture based on what you both said. Plus, I know you both, inside and out, so I'm pretty sure I can figure out who's to blame."

Anger brewed anew inside me as a feeling of betrayal landed heavily on my shoulders. "Well, then I guess I'm the fucking problem here, aren't I?" I cursed, turning back to the pantry and pulling a bag of chocolate-covered pretzels out of the back. "Dallin ran after Trey and you're standing there blaming me for it all." I shrugged even as stupid unshed tears made my nose burn. "Maybe I should be the one to leave."

"Or maybe you should be the one to learn your lesson, so you know not to make the same mistake again," he countered, and I glared at him again.

"You make it sound like I'm some schoolgirl who needs a spanking."

"I think a spanking is exactly what you need." Parker shrugged nonchalantly. "And I think I'm the perfect teacher to give it to you."

"Oh, fuck off," I groaned, hating how my body reacted to the dirty innuendos in his words while also fighting off the anger at his disappointment in me. Because that's what I was ashamed of the most. I was disappointed in myself and how I ended up chasing off Trey with talk of labels and commitments, and hearing Parker voice my fears aloud made me even more insecure in my failures.

"You were naughty tonight, Rey," Parker said in a deep voice that only came into play when he was dangerously on edge with his sexual desires. "You finally gave in to your desires for Trey and then fucked it up."

"I know that!" I screamed, turning on him. "I really don't need you to point it out to me, Parker!"

"No," he growled, walking forward as I tried ripping open the bag of pretzels and taking it out of my hands, tossing it onto the counter before facing me toward the counter again. "What you need is to learn your lesson. I already told you that." He wrapped his hands around my wrists and forcefully placed them flat on the countertop. "You know how much I enjoy being gentle and giving with you, baby girl." He pushed his body flush against my back, pinning me to the counter. "But I also know how much you flourish under a commanding man."

"Parker," I groaned, letting my eyes close as the weight of the night consumed me.

"Shh," he whispered, sliding his hands up my arms. "I'm going to teach you the lesson you so desperately want to be taught, Rey." He kissed his way up the side of my neck. "Don't fucking move an inch without my permission." He nipped my neck, making me gasp. "Do you understand?"

"Yes," I whispered, falling in line with what he wanted. Because he was right, I needed to atone for what I'd done tonight, pushing Trey past limits I knew he wasn't ready to cross. I was consumed with guilt, knowing I was the one to throw our group off balance, and if I had any hope of making up for it, I was going to do whatever it took.

I hated feeling like a failure.

"Good girl," he growled against the shell of my ear as his hands untied the sash at my waist, opening my robe before pulling it off my body completely. "Bend over and put these sexy-ass tits flat against the counter."

My breath caught at the dominance in his voice as my body warmed, replacing the shame and guilt with arousal and desperation.

I instantly followed his instructions, stepping backward and pressing my ass further against his body as I folded at the waist. I sucked in a quick breath when my bare nipples touched the icy stone countertop and then reveled in its smooth texture as I lay flat against it.

"Good girl," he praised me, running his hands down my back and over my ass. "Spread your legs." He pushed my ankles apart with his booted foot over and over again until I was spread wide for him in the bright lights of the kitchen. "Hmm." He stepped back like he was admiring the view. I kept my cheek resting atop the counter and bit my bottom lip to keep from whimpering and begging him to touch me sexually. I was aching for him and his tenderness to prove to myself he still wanted me after my mistakes.

"Please," I pleaded, unable to hold back anymore.

"You want my cock?" he teased, running his fingertips up the back of my thigh until they neared my wet entrance. "Do you think you'd learn your lesson if I just gave you what you wanted without making you work for it first?"

"No," I admitted, knowing he was right.

"Correct." He smoothed his hands over my ass cheeks and shook them. "I'm going to spank you for your naughtiness tonight, Rey." My pussy clenched at his words, but I remained silent. "I'm going to redden this ass and make you count each and every strike until you simply can't take another one." He paused, letting his words sink in as he leaned over my back, covering my overheated naked body with his fully clothed one. "And then I'm going to force my ribbed cock deep into your asshole for the first time until you come all over the place, like the good little girl I know you can be."

"Fuck," I groaned, pushing back against him. Dallin and I had done a little spanking, but never as the main event. It was usually just something he did sometimes when he was going hard from behind. Even though I knew he enjoyed doing it, I was never brave enough to beg him for it before. But that was the old me before he brought Parker and Trey into our lives. "Do it. Please give it to me. Give it all to me."

"You're so perfect when you're my good girl, baby." He latched his teeth into my shoulder and bit before pulling his body off mine. "But I do like your naughty streak, too."

He stepped to the side of my body and ran his hand over my exposed ass as I tensed for the pain I knew would come. But even tensing didn't prepare me for the explosion of stinging discomfort that came from his palm.

"Jesus, fuck," I gasped, throwing myself into the counter in agony. This wasn't the mild spanking that Dallin gave me when he was fucking me senseless. This was a punishment.

"Count, or I'll start over."

"One," I hissed between my clenched teeth, digging my nails into the hard countertop until they bent backward, as he pulled my hips from the counter and back into position.

He laid another slap on my other cheek, and I shrieked as the pain bloomed across my entire ass like his hand had grown four sizes.

"Two," I cried, and before I had even taken another breath, he laid another one down. "Three!" I screamed, unable to hold it back.

"That's my good girl. Let me hear your pain." He spanked me again. "Let me hear you apologize for fucking up."

"Four!" I yelled again, as tears welled up in my eyes. Five and six were fast and hard, covering the tops of my thighs, but seven was where the pain turned into something more intense. I felt a humming dizziness come over my head as I screamed out number eight, and my knees felt weak as Parker's hand came down across my left cheek with a swinging motion that made my entire back end shake from the intensity of it. "Nine," I murmured, trying to stay conscious as my head felt fuzzier with each second. Ten, though—ten was the best and the worst of all. He was a brute and a giver all in one as his hand came down hard against the soaking-wet lips of my pussy. I screamed in horror and pleasure as he plunged two fingers directly into me and lit off an orgasm I didn't even know was building until I rode his hand, grinding up and down on his fingers with zero shame.

The noises his hand was making inside me alone should have sent me cowering in embarrassment. The wet friction gave away any secrets I tried to keep as he pushed me over into a second spontaneous orgasm with his expert fingers. "That's it, baby girl," he groaned, grabbing a handful of my hair and pulling my chest off the counter to change the angle of his fingers inside me. "Ride my hand and give me one more." He pulled his fingers out of my pussy and rubbed them over my clit aggressively as I bucked in his hold.

"Fuck!" I shrieked, pushing back against his hand more as he drew a third wave of ecstasy from my body before I fell limply back onto the counter as his hold on my hair released.

"Stay right there," he commanded, pulling his wet fingers from my body as I panted lifelessly. I heard his boots thudding across the floor before he came back into the kitchen and started stripping off his clothes. I was so tired and emotionally drained that I couldn't even open my eyes as I heard the cap open on the lube he used with the guys. When his fingers rubbed the cold liquid against my asshole, I pushed back, giving him the access he sought until two fingers were buried deep inside me. "Fucking perfect," he growled. "I need my good girl back, Rey."

"I'll be good," I panted, desperate for his cock. "I'll never be naughty again."

He chuckled, slapping the head of his cock against my pussy. "We both know that's a lie." He pushed the head of his cock against my asshole, and I forced my body to relax. "But we both know we're going to enjoy each lesson you force the three of us to teach you."

"I fucked up. He's not coming back. Neither of them will come back."

"He's coming back," he growled, pushing the first barbell into my body, making us both groan. "D will get him back, and when he does, you're going to be a good girl and apologize."

"Ugh," I hissed. "He made me feel"—I paused as the second barbell went in—"casual." I pushed back and took the third metal stud. "That's why I wanted him to label us. So I didn't feel like a toy."

"Oh, Rey." He sighed, pushing the last few inches of his cock into my ass for the first time. "You've got us all so fucked up in the head, you're the puppet master, not us." He pulled his cock out and pushed back in balls deep. "You have far more control than you realize."

"I don't want control, Parker." I moaned, spreading my legs wider as his hand snaked around my body and started rubbing my clit. "I want to be consumed by the three of you. I want to be cherished."

"We will." He grunted as he picked up his pace. "None of us can resist giving you what you want."

"Good." I arched my back as my next orgasm came crashing down on me. "Because I can't get enough of you like this. I'm hooked."

He chuckled, spanking my ass lightly as he rolled his hips. "Just wait until you have all three of us inside you at once, baby girl. You'll be an addict for life."

"I already am," I moaned, reaching back to dig my nails into his thigh as he ground his hips against my ass. "I already fucking am."

CHAPTER 24

Dallin

We rode hard for hours, without stopping or talking about where we were going. He was running; I knew that.

I also knew I shouldn't have taken off on Rey as I did, but I couldn't lose Trey again. I wouldn't survive it twice, and if I hadn't followed him this time, he wouldn't have come back on his own like last time.

I wasn't even sure he would come back this time, but I had to fucking try. I needed him like I needed Rey. I didn't want to imagine losing one of them because of the other; the pain was too much.

He pulled off the interstate an hour ago and finally turned into a lit-up rural motel nowhere near civilization like he knew it was here the whole time. When I parked my bike next to his in the parking lot and took my gear off, he just sat there and looked at me.

"Is this where you came last time?" I asked, looking around the place. It was old, typical of a roadside motel, but it was clean and well-kept.

"For a while," he responded, but didn't move to get off his bike. "You can go back." He watched me closely before I answered.

"I already told you." I shook my head, throwing my leg off my bike with a groan of stiffness. "I'm choosing you right now."

"And what about her?" he asked, avoiding her name like it would keep things from being real. "Do you think she'll forgive you for that?"

I shrugged, groaning as I stretched my back. "I don't know, Trey," I admitted. "I'm hoping so. But I need to be here with you right now."

He scowled like being chosen felt wrong, and I longed to take away the pain that I had put him in two years ago with my actions.

"Look, I'm sorry—" I started, but he cut me off.

"Let's get checked in," he said, standing up like he wasn't sore in the least. "It's late."

He walked toward the late-night office without another word and I sighed, surrounded by the darkness of the parking lot. I took my phone out and sent Rey a text.

Me: We finally stopped for the night. I'll call you in the morning. I love you, Reyna. I'll be home as soon as I can. Trust in me. In us.

I watched the status go from delivered to read, but no response came. I didn't even get the little bubbles that indicated she was replying. After a while, I locked my screen and put it back in my pocket.

She deserved to be silent for a while if that was what she wanted. But I hated the feeling of being torn in two different directions.

Before I could contemplate it for long, Trey walked back out of the office, waving a key in his hand as he walked to a door at the end of the strip.

I followed him, refusing to let his silence grate my nerves like it normally would. The room was clean and didn't smell like piss, so that was a plus.

But as he took off his boots and headed for the bathroom, any positivity I managed to hold on to crashed as he said, "I'm going to take a shower and crash. Pick whatever bed you want, and I'll take the other."

He was closing himself off from me, and with each passing second that lingered between us, the drift grew.

I was losing him.

Fuck, I might have already lost him before I even started up my bike tonight. But I had to keep trying.

So I let him have his space, just like I was letting Rey have hers, as I stripped down to my boxers and crawled into one of the two queen-size beds. Would he join me when he got out of the shower?

Doubtful.

But I refused to just let him slip further away, so before I let myself fall into the exhaustion that was trying to pull me under, I grabbed the four pillows off the other bed and tucked them all underneath my covers.

If he was going to sleep in the other bed, he could do it with a kink in his neck.

I was going to be gentle about the whole thing.

But I wasn't going to be a total pushover.

I was too fucking alpha for that.

So I went to sleep with a Trey-sized pillow body next to me, and Reyna on my mind, listening to the water run.

Sunlight barely crept through the curtains when I rolled over the next time, and I was disoriented and groggy from the brief night of sleep.

I looked across the room to where Trey lay sprawled out on his stomach in the center of the bed with his arms up around his face and his bare foot hanging off the side. His hair was fanned out wildly, air-dried into waves that reminded me of Reyna's lush locks. The sheet covered his bottom half, but I knew he was naked under the thin white fabric, thanks to years of cohabitating with him.

I knew things about him he never had to speak of to teach me. After years of friendship and more, I *knew* him. He was stubborn to a fault, but he was golden to the core when it came to how hard he loved those deserving of his affection. Just like Reyna did.

Did he realize how similar they were? Of course, I was fucked in the head over the both of them.

I looked up at the ceiling, searching for guidance, but found nothing but cracks in the paint staring back at me.

"Fuck it," I whispered, throwing the blankets off and grabbing two pillows from my hoard pile before crossing the space to his bed. "Move over," I growled, shoving my fist into his thigh. He cracked his eyes open and glared at me before seeing the pillow in my hand. He grabbed it quickly and bear-hugged it, giving me his back and dismissing me.

"Go back to your bed, asshole."

But he'd given me the space I needed to slide in behind him on the small queen-size bed. The sheets smelled like him as I pulled the blankets up over us and wrapped myself around him.

"Stop pushing me away," I whispered, holding him as he tried to scoot further away. "Trey, please." I sighed, resting my forehead against the back of his head. "Just stop fighting, for once in your fucking life."

He stilled, but I could feel how tense he was as I clung to him. After a while, he let out a deep breath and I felt his shoulders relax a bit before adjusting himself onto his own stolen pillow.

"Thank you," I whispered, pressing myself even tighter against his back, desperate for physical contact if he wouldn't let me in emotionally.

He grumbled something into the pillow that sounded a hell of a lot like *Go fuck yourself*, but I ignored his attitude.

I'd spent almost three decades ignoring his attitude once I realized he used it to keep people at arm's length.

Not anymore.

I was done living just out of reach of what I wanted most.

What I needed.

Hours later, a knock on the door woke me up. When I cracked my eyes open, the sunlight was bright, indicating it was midday, though I was anything but eager to get out of bed anytime soon. My body ached from riding last night, having not done it like that for years.

A knock sounded at the door again and I looked down at where Trey lay, still bear-hugging his pillow with his back to me, but pressed against my side as I lay on my back.

"Guess you're not getting up." I groaned, pulling myself out of bed.

"Ignore it, and whoever it is will go away," he murmured into the pillow.

"How has that worked out where I'm concerned?" I threw back as I opened the door, finding a young maid, with her key in the lock, ready to enter. "Sorry." I held my hands up as she jumped back a few feet. "Didn't mean to scare you."

"Uh—" she stammered, looking down at my nearly naked body and then into the room. From this angle, I knew Trey's back was visible, but as I looked over my shoulder, following her gaze, I saw that his bare ass was visible too. Jealousy flared in my chest as she got far too much of a good look at my guy.

I chuckled and stepped to the side, blocking her view of his firm ass, and forced her attention back to me. "Can I help you?"

"Right." She blushed, looking down at my feet and then blinking rapidly as my morning wood caught her eye. "Uh, are you checking out today?" she finally asked. "You're only paid up through this morning."

I smirked and looked back over my shoulder, letting my naughty streak fly as I called out to Trey, "What do you think, baby? Want to stay another night?" He groaned, flipping the bird over his shoulder as I chuckled and turned back to the poor maid, who was even more scandalized. "I think my snookum needs some more rest; I kept him up most of the night." I leaned on the doorjamb and crossed my arms.

"You didn't get any noise complaints about us last night, did you?" Her eyes widened, and I heard Trey snort behind me. "He's a screamer sometimes." I shrugged and called out to him, "I told you to bite the pillow harder, baby."

This time I was rewarded with a pillow to the back of the head as the maid backed up, clearly not wanting to be a part of whatever was happening inside. "Just stop by the front desk before two and pay for the night, or the manager will call the sheriff," she stammered as she grabbed her cart and pushed it away quickly.

"We'll pay up, thank you!" I called after her with a cheery smile and a wave before shutting the door and throwing the bolt to lock it, laughing.

Trey lay on his back, now using my pillow as he absently rubbed his hand over his abs while watching me.

"Remember that time in Pasadena?" I asked, walking toward him. "We fucked Parker so hard he put a hole in the wall with his fist and the night manager broke in, expecting to see the three of us fighting and tearing his place up," I smirked.

"And instead he found Park spit-roasted between the two of us at the same time that I came into his mouth." He shook his head with a slight grin on his face. "That man was never the same, I'm sure."

I threw myself down onto the bed next to him and leaned up against the headboard. "Parker or the manager?" I joked.

"Hmm . . . Both."

I smirked, remembering that night like it was yesterday. "We had a lot of fun on the road, didn't we?"

Silence fell between us as the elephant in the room got larger. "It was never the same after you left," he finally responded. I looked over at him but had nothing worthy to reply with as he continued. "Parker sank deep into his head." He sighed. "It took months to get him to even talk to me." He looked over at me in the dim, muted sunlight. "I think in a way, you're his soul mate. Or part of it. And you ripped that away from him when you left."

"I never meant to hurt him, or you," I admitted. "But I was hurting. More and more every day that we went on with life the way it was."

He swallowed and looked back at the ceiling. "I never thought of it that way. That you were in pain. I just always focused on our pain in your wake."

"I didn't want you two to know I was unhappy because a large part of me thought that I'd move on and get over it after a while. Like maybe I'd stop wanting more."

"But you didn't."

"No," I replied. "It felt like part of my soul was missing."

"And then you found Reyna."

"I never felt like I was choosing her over you guys, but I understand how you could have felt that way." I validated his biggest point, daring to keep bringing up old wounds since he was willing to talk finally.

"I didn't." He sighed, running his hand through his hair. "I mean, I did, until I saw you with her. *Really* saw you with her and got to know her myself."

"And now what do you feel?" I reached out and slid a lock of his hair through my fingers, desperate to touch him and feel close again.

"And now I feel—" He paused and thought about it for a while. "Like I fucked everything up by refusing to give her what she needed." He looked up at me again. "What you needed."

"What happened?" I asked. "I want to know what happened in that bedroom last night."

He shrugged and raised his eyebrows in uncertainty. "She wants the world for you and Parker. And me too, I guess. She wants everyone to be happy, loved, and treated right by the world while we live happily in some weird little bubble of polyamorous bliss."

"She's good-hearted like that, that's why."

He smiled sadly and nodded, before sitting up to rest his back against the headboard next to me, with his shoulder brushing mine. Suddenly, the small bed didn't bother me so much when it kept him in my personal space.

"She's good in general, man." He shook his head. "So fucking good. I know that, and I can't fault her for it." He groaned. "Believe me, I wanted to hate her for being so nice in the beginning. But her kindness was just infectious and I couldn't. Though when she sasses me, I get the urge to punish her." He smirked, staring off at the wall at the end of the bed.

I nodded, understanding his feelings. "Why did you leave last night?"

He sighed. "I don't know. I think I was just running from the bullshit."

"Haven't you learned that doesn't ever work out well?"

"Yeah, well, I can't say I'm always levelheaded around her." He looked over at me. "Or you, for that matter."

My body warmed when his blue eyes landed on mine and held my stare. "I'm in love with you, Trey," I admitted, once again. "I don't want to lose you."

"I don't want to be the bad egg in the group," he confessed. "What if she and I go at it like that all the time?"

I raised my eyebrow at him. "Like you haven't gone at it like that with me and Parker over the years too?"

He rolled his eyes. "It's different."

"How?"

"Because when you and Parker piss me off, I can punch you or fuck you into submission."

I snorted and shook my head. "Well, you have never gotten me to submit to you, with violence or sex."

"Either way, I can't do that with her."

"You're right, you can't," I agreed. "But there are other ways to deal with disagreements, Trey. Like adults do every day."

"Like I know the first fucking thing about being an adult." He scoffed.

"Maybe it's time you learn." I looked back over at him and put my hand on the blanket on top of his thigh. "We've got a real chance at something good here, man. I want you to let yourself have it. You deserve to have it all."

He sighed and I felt his muscular thigh tense beneath my hand. "You and Parker have always thought so much more of me than I ever have."

I leaned over, sliding my hand across the side of his face and tipping it my way until we were nose to nose. I had held off on being overly physical, but I couldn't hold off anymore, I needed to touch him.

"You are worth it, Trey. You always have been," I whispered, staring straight into his eyes, hoping that he'd finally fucking believe me. Believe in himself.

He leaned into me. "I fucked up."

"We'll fix it. Together," I countered, shutting down his excuses.

"I don't think we can."

"We can!" I argued, pulling his body over my legs until he straddled me. He was naked and on display like this, and I didn't even try to pretend not to notice the way his cock bobbed against our stomachs as he settled his ass down on my thighs. "I promise you; we can fix it. She was wrong, too. It's going to take some give and take. But a week ago you didn't even want to admit that you wanted her; you both were just acting like we could be three separate couples cohabitating under one roof. But you moved past that and admitted the truth to yourself and her. We can get past this, too." I tightened my hand in his long hair at the back of his head, pulling his forehead against mine as he put his hands on my chest. "I promise you, Trey, we can make this work."

"I want to." He groaned as I slid one hand around his hip and pulled him closer to me, sandwiching his cock between our abs. "I really fucking want to, D. I just don't know how."

"Let me help you." I rocked him again and his eyelids fluttered as his head tipped back. I took my hand from his hair and wrapped it around his fat cock, stroking him from root to tip and running my thumb over the pre-cum that leaked. "Lean on me for what you need, baby."

"Okay." He flexed his hips, pushing his cock into my hand further. "I'd agree to just about anything right now to keep you touching me."

I pulled my hand away from his cock and spanked his ass, and he groaned in frustration. "Go get that bottle of lotion from the bathroom."

He rolled his eyes at me but leaped from the bed and went for the complimentary bottle of cheap lotion left on the bathroom counter for us at check-in and then came back out. I slid my boxer briefs down and kicked them off, stroking my cock as he stood at the edge of the bed and watched. "Get back up here," I ordered him, patting my thigh. "We don't have lube, so this will have to do for now."

I pulled him back up onto my lap until his cock was pressed against mine between us and took the lotion from him. I uncapped it and poured a generous amount into my palm as he watched, panting in anticipation.

"Why did we always let Parker be the prepared one?" He groaned.

"Because Parker's kinky as fuck and always brought fun stuff to the party." I smirked, wrapping my hand around both of our cocks, sliding my lotioned palm up and down. "God, damn," I grunted as pleasure raced up my cock.

"Mmm," he moaned, gripping both of my shoulders for support as I found the rhythm we liked, making him flex his hips to get what he wanted from me. "Just like that," he growled.

"I can't wait to feel you inside me again." I leaned back into the headboard further, arching my hips to press against him further before sliding my free hand down to grip his balls and massage them.

"You want me to fuck you?" he asked like he didn't believe me.

"You know I do," I responded, tightening my hold on our cocks. "But I need Rey there. So this will have to do for now."

"God." He tilted his head back again and his abs tightened. "I'm going to come."

"Thank god," I groaned. "Been fighting off my own for hours now."

He chuckled and then moaned, "Don't stop."

"Come for me," I demanded, twisting my hand around us both as I slid my slick fingers past the bottom of his balls to his taint and massaged him there. "Come for me, Trey."

"Yes!" he hissed, and then with the first twitch of his cock, I let my orgasm loose, coating both of our stomachs with come as I kept pumping us.

"Holy fuck," I grunted, laying my head back and panting from how good it felt to have him like this.

"Hmm." He leaned forward until his lips were right in front of mine. "I haven't said it back," he said, and the blood in my veins froze cold in anticipation as I tried to remain calm. "But I guess I've been in love with you for years, too. Just been too stubborn to admit it to myself."

I kissed him, consuming his lips as he held on to the back of my neck and gave it right back, taking everything I was willing to give to him. When we finally pulled apart, we both caught our breaths with uncertainty filling the space, until he broke the silence and spoke.

"I love you, Dallin. And I love Parker too. And believe it or not, I'm falling for Rey too." Elation filled my system from his declaration. "But I'm not ready to run right back and settle it all." He sighed. "I want to be selfish for a day or two."

"Selfish?" I asked, wondering what he meant.

He nodded and slid back off my thighs before standing up next to the bed. "I want to stay here tonight, at least. I want to reconnect with you before I try to build this whole thing with her." He sighed. "I know you're itching to get back to her and Parker, and so am I, to be honest. But I need us to be solid before I can commit to giving her everything she needs." I stood up off the bed and stared into his eyes as he continued. "I need to know you aren't going to take off again. Or choose her over me and Parker if she gives you that ultimatum."

"I'm not going anywhere, Trey," I confirmed. "And she's not going to give me that ultimatum."

"How do you know?" he asked skeptically.

"Because Parker is going to take this time to show her exactly what went wrong and how to fix it."

He rolled his eyes, walking toward the bathroom. "You sound so sure."

I followed him as he turned on the shower and let the water warm up. "I am. Have you ever known Parker Hurst to miss an opportunity to teach someone a lesson and go all alpha? A sexy little minx at that?"

He paused, eyeing me in the mirror as he grabbed washcloths from the rack. "Maybe you're onto something."

I chuckled as he stepped into the shower, and I took my place behind him in the steamy water. "I'm onto it, all right." I wrapped my hands around his waist and slid them up and down his toned abs. His muscle mass was smaller compared to Parker and me, but the lean masculinity fit him so well, and it drove me wild. "If I were a betting man, I'd bet that Parker has her all twisted up right now, withholding sex or using it against her until she's begging him to bring you back to her to make up for what went wrong."

He scoffed. "As if she'd apologize. Besides, I was the one in the wrong."

"Maybe," I admitted, sliding my hands down over the front of his thighs, rinsing away our orgasms from his skin as he leaned back into me. "But she looks so goddamn good on her knees begging for forgiveness. So let her beg if she wants to."

"Fuck," he groaned, reaching behind him to stroke his wet hand over my still semi-hard cock. "I had her on her knees, my cock down her throat, and I fucked it up."

"Hmm." I kissed his neck before wrapping my hand around the front of his throat. "Then let's get your head on straight so you're better suited to see it through when we get home."

"How are we going to do that?" he asked with a smirk in his voice.

"How about you get on your knees and show me just how bad you want all of us together? Then we can run to the pharmacy down the road and buy some lube, so I can nail you into the fucking headboard until you're too sated to say something dumb to her when we get back."

"Fuck yes." He tightened his hand on my cock before turning and kissing his way down my chest until he knelt at my feet. "Show me how to be a good boy," he smirked, before lifting my cock out of the way and sucking one of my balls into his mouth, swirling it around with his tongue until stars danced in my vision. "I want to be so fucking good for her."

CHAPTER 25

Reyna

Four days.

Four fucking days Dallin and Trey had been gone so far, and I'd been on edge every second.

Dallin called twice and texted a few times, telling me he loved me, that Trey was just working some of his frustrations out on the asphalt, and that they'd be home soon. But a part of me feared I'd lost Dallin for good when Trey walked out.

Dallin had already survived the pain of losing Trey once, and I didn't know if he'd be willing to do it again.

Even for me.

"Stop it," Parker said from the doorway, breaking my dazed gaze out the window. I was sitting at my desk, lost in thought over the two men missing from our apartment and being so unproductive; my editor was ready to show up and kidnap me until I gave her the next section of my work in progress.

I rolled my eyes, leaning back into my chair. "Stop what?"

"Stressing," Parker said, walking into my office looking like he had just gotten off a runway in his tight black jeans and white cotton short-sleeve button-up that was undone and exposing his muscular chest and abs. "I can see your wheels turning from here."

I rolled my eyes again and sighed. "I can't help it."

"They're coming back."

"How do you know that?"

"Because Dallin said so," Parker responded instantly like it was a clear-as-day observation. "Dallin has never lied to me, so I won't start doubting him now."

"Yeah, well, he's lied to me," I grumbled under my breath, crossing my arms over my chest as my salty attitude got the best of me.

"About what?" He sat down on the edge of my desk, crossing his ankles and looking effortlessly sexy. So sexy I was considering taking a bite of what he was offering, but for some reason, the last few days had been fucking with my head and I hadn't been able to let myself use his wondrous skills for some sexual relief. It was like the longer we went without Dallin and Trey here, the less likely I was to ever orgasm again. No matter how hard Parker tried. And God, was he trying.

It was a real fucking mind trip, and I was desperate to get off it.

Or off in general.

"Nothing," I groaned. "It's nothing."

"Tell me, Rey," he insisted. "Let me into this big giant brain of yours."

I glared at him and ended up smirking at his playboy grin as he watched me, waiting for me to open up to him.

"The day D told me about his past with you, he promised me he'd never leave me," I admitted, feeling even more insecure as the words passed my lips. "That he and I were a unit and at the end of the day, it was us against the world, no matter what I chose to do about his needs."

"And then he left with Trey." Parker nodded. "Leaving you behind and abandoned."

I sighed, deflating into the chair. "It sounds ridiculous when you say it out loud like that. It's not like he left me completely alone and unattended to." I gave him a small smile. "But yeah, that's how it feels, nonetheless."

"I get it," Parker said gently, walking around the desk to a reading chair by the window and lowering himself down into it. I didn't miss the way he scanned the street as he did so either, looking for any sign of our missing boyfriends. "Your feelings are valid."

I snorted, shaking my head. "You should teach D that phrase," I joked.

Parker chuckled. "He's not the best with feelings, but he's far better at them than Trey is."

I groaned. "Don't remind me."

"How's work coming?" he asked, nodding to my blank computer screen like he could see the emptiness through the back of it.

"Ugh," I groaned again, closing it. "It's not. I'm blocked."

"Writer's block?" he asked, and I nodded, "Well, I don't have any tips for unblocking writer's block, but I think you're blocked in other ways too." He raised an eyebrow at me, mentioning my fresh trouble in the bedroom.

"Don't rub that in." I scowled at him.

"I'm not." He held his hands up. "I'm also not taking it personally, though it's extremely hard not to do with my overly big ego and small cock." He chuckled when I glared at him even harder. "I'm here to give you a solution. Hopefully," he added with a smirk as he stood up.

"A solution?" I squinted warily.

"Yep." He nodded. "I ran out earlier and picked you up some stuff to help with the *situation*." He walked out to the hallway and picked up a pink satin gift bag tied together with a red bow on top. I raised my eyebrows curiously as he carried it back into the room. "There are only two rules to accepting my marvelous gift."

"Rules?" I chuckled. "I don't like the sounds of this at all."

"Rule number one," he continued, ignoring me. "You have to open it immediately after I leave for my ink appointment in a few minutes, and you have to use it immediately upon opening it."

"That's two rules," I deadpanned.

"It's one." He waved his finger around in the air. "They go together."

"Okay, so I have to open it and use it right now." I nodded. "And rule number two?"

"Rule number two is—" He leaned over the desk until he lingered right above my face. "You have to use every single thing inside that bag and you cannot give up until you finish. No quitting."

My lips parted as I shook my head. "I'm confused."

"You won't be once you open it." He handed me the bag, which was surprisingly heavy in my hands. "But no peeking until I'm gone."

"And why do I have to wait until you're gone, exactly?" I asked.

He stood up and winked at me. "Because you need to figure out everything that's going on inside your head, causing your block." He smirked. "And only you can do that. I obviously can't." He rolled his eyes. "Even with my fancy cock."

I chuckled, shaking my head again. "I'm even more confused now than I was before."

"I know." He leaned back down and gave me a chaste kiss. "I have to go. I want you to enjoy yourself while I'm gone." He turned and walked out of my office. I sat in silence and listened to him open and close the door to the shop stairwell and then to the thumping of my heartbeat in my ears.

"What the hell?" I mused, pulling the tie of the gift bag open and looking inside. "Oh, that bastard."

"This is stupid." I muttered under my breath as I glared down at the contents of Parker's "present" laid out on my bed.

One thick vibrating dildo that looked suspiciously like Trey's cock. Check.

One rose-shaped clit sucker that my smut groups on social media raved about. Check.

One pair of twist-on, nipple-stimulating fake piercings. Check.

One aphrodisiac aromatherapy candle. Check.

One sexy-time playlist crafted by no other than Parker himself. Check.

One handwritten card with *explicit* instructions for what to do with each item. Check.

Oh yeah, can't forget the three shooters of Fireball in the bottom of the bag too.

A part of me wanted to throw all the offensive items back into the bag and say *Fuck that*. But another part of me desperately wanted to rid myself of this emotional and psychological mind block that was now affecting my sex life. Like a big part of me wanted that. So even as I groaned, feeling my face redden with the ridiculousness of it all, I gave in to my curiosity.

I lit the candle, pleased with the scent that started arising immediately before setting it on Dallin's side of the bed. I crossed the room to the windows and pulled the wooden shutters closed before drawing the thick linen curtains across to mute the rest of the light. Next, I plugged the thumb drive into the speaker system in the entertainment center and cranked it up, letting the seductive strumming of an acoustic guitar vibrate through my body like the hum of my heartbeat.

I closed my eyes, reminding myself I was home alone and completely safe in being vulnerable, and let the music sway my body around the space, loosening up my tense muscles as I moved. Slowly, I unbuttoned my sheer black top, feeling the texture of each button slide through the closures before letting it slide off my arms and pool on the floor. Next,

I toed off my sandals and shimmied out of my jeans, swaying my hips to the music, letting a man with a rich voice serenade me about desire and pleasure.

I cracked the top off one of the fireballs and tipped it back, hissing with my exhale as the cinnamon burned its way back up. People can say what they want about tequila, but it's a hundred times smoother in a margarita than any whiskey I'd ever drunk. Mixed or straight.

I took my bra and panties off, stood at the side of the bed, and looked down at the toys, wondering which one I was more excited about playing with first. But I didn't want to rush. I had no need to.

Parker would be downstairs at the shop for hours if I had to guess. And who knew if my boyfriend would ever return to me or if he was off driving into the sunset with the third man I lusted after as I contemplated self-sabotage.

Nope. I shook my head, twisting the cap off another whiskey shooter and tipping it back, cringing harder than I did the first time and shaking my head like it would rid my tongue of the taste.

I picked up the velvet container holding the twist-style nipple jewelry and walked into the closet, flipping on the light and staring at my reflection in the mirror. Waves of loose dark hair framed my face as the arousal, fueled by the whiskey, flushed my cheeks and burned in my belly.

I was beautiful.

I knew that, realistically, anyway. But feeling it, like I did at that moment, didn't happen very often for me.

Parker did that. He gave me the chance to feel beautiful and sensual when I was feeling so detached mentally from my physical being, without me even having to ask him to.

He was a good man.

I needed to reward him for being a good man to me. It took some trial and error, but I finally convinced the nipple rings to twirl around my hardened buds, making them even harder as the blood pooled slightly there against the cold metal. Small diamonds decorated the metal circles around them and I instantly liked the way the shimmer looked in the mirrored light.

I took my phone out and posed with one hand tousling my hair, with my head tipped back and my hip jutted out to accentuate my curves in the way I liked, and then I took a couple of pictures.

When I got one I approved of, I sent it to Parker.

Me: I think I may need a body piercer to make these a permanent thing.

I chewed on my bottom lip as I watched the message go to read and then as the bubbles of his reply popped up instantly.

Parker: Be my good girl, and I'll pierce them for you tonight. I can't wait to hear your scream when I pull on them as I fuck you. You're breathtaking, baby girl.

I smiled and then replied, feeling brazen from the whiskey and the desire.

Me: I'll be your good girl. So good, you won't be able to believe it. Now off I go to fuck myself with your toys.

Parker: Good girl. I want your bedsheets soaked when you're done.

I set my phone down on the dresser, choosing not to reply as the warmth of the whiskey spread down my limbs. My bed and those toys were beckoning to me, begging to be used by me to come.

I needed to come.

It was torture having Parker by my side 24/7 without being able to get out of my head long enough to orgasm. But I felt so good right now, I wasn't going to waste my opportunity.

I crawled into the center of the bed, rereading the note Parker wrote to me, dirtily explaining what he wanted me to do with the toys and what he wanted me to say and do while I did it. Then I took the pillowy petaled toy, holding it in my palm as I clicked it on, and smiled when it tickled my flesh.

I ran the buzzing toy across one of my nipples, letting the sucking tip tease the puckered flesh, and moaned, arching my back into the sensation. "Yes," I whispered, relaxing into the comfort of my bed. The music had changed to a steady thumping bass song with sexy lyrics about a headboard hitting a wall and angering the neighbors. It was perfectly Parker.

I spread my legs, letting his presence into the room with me as I sank deeper into my buzz. He did this for me, helped me even when I needed more than he could physically give me, without letting it make him jealous or envious.

I thought of him and the way he controlled me in the kitchen the night Dallin and Trey left. I remembered the way he took command of my feelings and thoughts and left me with just the physical need inside me, carrying the burden of my guilt for me and relieving me of it.

I gently pressed the toy against my clit and bowed my back off the bed as intense pleasure jolted through my soul at the first contact. "Oh my God!" I panted, dizzy with bliss as I adjusted it and found the perfect combination of pressure and intensity until it caused me to orgasm within minutes of lying down.

"Yes, yes, yes," I moaned, rubbing it in circles around my clit as I pinched my nipples and reveled in the pain and pleasure mingling there.

This.

This was what I needed.

I needed me. I needed to take back control of my body and my mind to feel in sync again. The toy played with my clit while I toyed with my nipples, breaking through the invisible barrier of another orgasm again quickly after the first.

As I panted in bliss and shock, I took the toy off and stared at it like I was going to discover the cure to cancer from it and smiled at the ceiling. Parker managed to break my block and reconnect my head and body together as one in only a few minutes.

But as I lay there, wondering what happened next, I saw the thick cock-like toy lying alone and unused. Rule number two was that I had to use every single thing inside the bag.

And I was trying to be a good girl, after all.

I'd hate to start breaking rules again already. I smirked to myself.

To be honest, I wanted to know what it would feel like to take something so thick deep inside me. It was thicker than Dallin, but not as long.

Just like Trey.

And if I would never have the real thing, I might as well fuck the toy and at least feel that fullness, even if it wasn't firsthand.

Which was no doubt why Parker purchased this dildo out of all the options available out there. He was a smart man, after all.

I bit my lip, looking around the room like someone was going to bust me fucking the toy that mimicked Trey's cock and judge me for using it in his place. But that was stupid, and I was desperate to feel him inside me. I'd come so close that night, I'd rubbed my clit against his shaft and was seconds away from lowering myself down onto him, taking him deep for the first time.

He was the last cock I wanted to take for the first time ever.

So fuck it. I picked up the dildo and ran my fingers over the realistic veins and ridges of it, feeling my soaked pussy spasming like it was begging to be stretched around the girth in my hands.

"If you insist," I murmured to myself as I grabbed the lube and poured some over the tip, rubbing it in like I was rubbing Trey personally, pleasuring him. "Here goes nothing, big guy."

CHAPTER 26

Trey

I climbed the stairs, silently ascending into the apartment. I didn't know if anyone was home, but I knew who I was hoping wasn't.

Reyna.

Not because I didn't want to see her bright hazel eyes and the sweet dimples in her lush cheeks. Or her supple body as she shimmied around the kitchen, cooking for us. Or even hear her infectious girly giggle when Parker would tickle her feet when he rubbed them on the couch while they watched their trashy reality TV, which Dallin and I couldn't stand. Even if we sat there with them anyway, desperate to be near.

Because I wanted to see all of those things again.

Desperately.

In the weeks we'd spent with Dallin and Reyna, Parker and I had ingrained into their world. Into their lives.

And I hadn't realized how deep-rooted I was in it until I wasn't. Until I was hundreds of miles away on my bike, with Dallin riding next to me, willing to walk away from everything for a while to choose me.

That was when I realized I was fucking stupidly engrossed with their life here in Nashville.

With him *and* her. And Parker too.

The farther away I got, the emptier I felt. The more on edge and angsty I felt, even with D at my side.

It didn't matter without Rey and Parker. Dallin had gone and embedded us both into their world until we no longer made sense outside of the foursome we'd built. Even if I'd done a fuckwad job of messing it up with Rey that night after golfing.

God, I was such a fucking moron.

Which, of course, Dallin knew. And that was why he'd chosen to come with me instead of staying with his perfect girlfriend and our perfect boyfriend, who dutifully stayed behind to wait for me to realize my stupidity.

None of that was why I didn't want to see her now. I didn't want to see her now because I was wrong to leave, and even more wrong to take Dallin with me. In the moment, I chose selfishness and took what he was willing to give to me.

I knew his disappearance hurt Reyna, and I knew she'd be less than thrilled to see me, the man who stole him away for four days, in her home at the end.

Especially because he wasn't with me now upon my return. When we got back to town, he went straight to the shop to put out some fires that had built in his absence.

Leaving me to face the pissed-off princess in the tower alone.

Unless, of course, Parker was up here with her, willing to play buffer.

But as I cleared the threshold, every hair on my body stood up on alert at the atmosphere inside the apartment. Parker wasn't home, I could tell right away.

But Rey was.

I could feel her in the air.

On the air, like a weighted scent, lingering for me to inhale and soothe the beast inside me. But on the edge of her flowery scent was the sharp scent of something else.

Sex.

The curtains in the living room were drawn shut, and her bedroom was dark to the left of the living space. But she was in there.

I could hear her, almost as clearly as I could feel her.

My skin pebbled up with goose bumps, my muscles rebelling against the fight-or-flight reaction of being in her space again.

Run to her.

Run from her.

Give in to her.

Hold out on her.

My body and my mind were at war.

Before I could consciously tell my feet to move, I slowly and silently crossed the distance between the front door and the dark opening to her bedroom. Her and Dallin's bedroom. Where I didn't belong.

I had no business within the walls of her space, yet as I paused in the doorway, I felt like I was home for the first time in decades.

But then I saw her.

And everything else faded away as I mutely watched her, lost in her world, oblivious to the monster lurking at her door.

Jesus fuck, she was perfection.

Her body was coiled tight in euphoria, laid out on her back with her legs spread wide, facing the door as she fucked herself with a thick dildo. It was dark in the room, lit with only a single candle on the bedside table; some crooning sex song that Parker would have loved played on the speakers. Even through the low light, I could see the perspiration coating her bronze skin as she writhed back and forth in the center of her bed.

She moaned out a low growl of pleasure as her free hand gripped the rumpled-up bedsheets in a tight fist before she dragged her pointed nails across them like she was marking the skin of her lover's back.

But she was alone.

Except for me.

The voyeur.

The last person on earth to deserve the show I was getting as she masturbated.

"Fuck," she panted, twisting herself around on the bed until she was on all fours facing the wall, giving me an unobstructed view of her pussy, stretched wide around the thick dildo as she worked it in and out. The thing looked mammoth in her tiny hand, though I knew it was about the same size as me.

Was she thinking about me as she took the fat cock? Was she imagining how it would have felt to feel me push deep into her body that night before all of our baggage got in the way?

"Please," she whined, holding on to the top of the headboard as she knelt, legs still spread as she worked the silicone dick. "Please, please, please."

I was rock fucking hard in my jeans, desperate to take the toy's place as she panted and cried out in . . . frustration?

"Fuck!" she sneered. "Just come!"

She wasn't talking to me, of that I was sure. But was she talking to herself? Demanding that she come on the toy? Was it really not getting her off?

She sighed, stilling her hand that had been pumping as she tipped her head back and took a deep breath. I watched her face in the reflection of the decorative mirror hung above the bed. Her hair was tangled and damp at her temples, but I'd never seen her look so beautiful.

When she opened her eyes, she stared at her reflection with something that looked like disappointment or anger.

Until she caught my presence in the mirror and gasped silently, popping her plump lips apart in surprise. "What are you doing?" she snapped, quickly replacing her shock with ire.

"Watching your show." I leaned against the doorjamb, feigning indifference as I reached down to adjust my erection in my jeans. Her bright hazel eyes flicked down to my movement and then back to my face.

"It's not for you, now get out!" she sneered, looking away from me completely, but not shielding her body or removing the dildo from her tight pussy. A pussy I longed to taste.

"Is that really what you want?" I asked. "Because it sounded to me like you wanted to come." I tilted my head in challenge, drawing her eyes back to me. "Having troubles?"

"Fuck off." She straightened her spine and finally removed the toy, dropping it to the bed between her spread knees. "Didn't you get enough 'willing pussy' on the road?" She threw back my words from that dreadful night in my face.

"I didn't get any pussy, Rey," I admitted, being honest, as I took a step into the bedroom that smelled like her and sin.

Heaven and hell.

Angels and devils.

"Liar," she huffed, and then her shoulders sagged. "Never mind, it doesn't matter. Get out."

"No." I got closer to the bed as she watched me like a hawk in the mirror. "I didn't want any pussy on the road, because it wasn't yours." I stopped at the end of the bed. "I fucked up, Rey. I'll admit that." She swallowed, and I watched the muscles of her throat work, reminding me what it looked like to watch her suck my cock deep down her throat. "I freaked out when you demanded more from me than just what I could give to you with my body. But that doesn't change how I feel about you."

"You hate me," she retorted. "You said I was crazy."

"After you called me crazy," I reminded her with a raised brow. "But I don't want to fight with you."

"Then what do you want?" She squinted in the low light. "Where's D?"

"Working." I nodded to the doorway. "Stuff he couldn't put off after being away unexpectedly. But I don't want to talk about D right now." I slowly kicked my boots off, leaving them at the end of the bed as her eyes rounded in uncertainty in the mirror again. "Right now, I want to give you so many orgasms that you forget your fucking name."

"Trey." She cocked her head as her eyelids fluttered like she was battling within her head. "You hate me."

I moved up the bed on my knees until I was inches from her back, her lush ass nearly cradled against my cock as it hardened even more from feeling her body heat through my jeans. "Wrong." I trailed my fingertip up her arm and across her shoulder before wrapping my hand around the front of her throat and pulling her back into my body, closing the distance. "I want you. But I want more than just your body, Rey."

She gasped, arching her back as she leaned into me as her grip tightened on the top of the wooden headboard. "What do you want?" she repeated.

"You." I tilted her head to the side and bit her neck. "Under me." She moaned, and I moved down to her shoulder. "On top of me." Her entire body shivered as I tightened my hold on her throat and turned her head to the other side, exposing her neck again. "Beside me." I licked up the column of her throat, over the pulse point that was beating erratically, to her ear, where I whispered, "Committed to me." I sucked her earlobe into my mouth and slid my free hand around her waist until it was flat against her quivering stomach, with my fingers inching down to her needy cunt. "Mine, Rey. I want the label and the title. I want the burden and the gift of it all." I slid my hand down lower as she wrapped one hand around my wrist, urging me further. "I want the four of us. I need us."

"Yes." She sagged into me when my fingertips brushed over her soaked clit. "Promise me."

"I promise," I hissed, circling her clit and then pinching it between my pointer and middle finger.

"Promise me you won't leave again," she begged. "I can't fucking take watching you walk away again, Trey."

"I'm not going anywhere, baby," I promised, trying to reassure her against the insecurities that I'd planted inside her. "I'm yours. I'm theirs." I kissed her neck. "Be mine."

"Yes!" She moaned, arching her hips so my fingers went deeper toward her entrance. "Please, Trey. I need you so bad."

"Do you?" I teased. "Is that why you're in here, all alone, riding a dildo shaped like my cock?"

"Yes." She rocked her hips against my cock, rubbing me up and down her thick ass. "Parker's doing," she panted. "He bought all of this." She waved her hand around the messed-up bed. "He planned it to help me get over the mind block you caused."

I chuckled. "I blocked your brain? Were you so hung up on me?"

"Asshole," she cursed, but I could hear and see her grin in the mirror. "For your information, Parker has been trying to make me come for days, but I haven't been able to get out of my head and orgasm. No matter how hard the poor guy tried. You were fucking with my head by being gone, and by taking Dallin with you."

"Hmm," I growled. "It strokes my ego to know he couldn't make you come while you were thinking about me, to be honest."

"Well, to be honest, right after you left, he fucked me so hard in the ass I came all over the entire kitchen," she sassed, making me freeze solid as I imagined what she was describing. "After he spanked me for being such a naughty girl and made me fall into something called subspace, and *then* I came out the other side a good girl."

"Fuck," I growled, bending her forward over the headboard until her ass was presented to me. "He spanked this perfect ass for starting shit with me?"

"Yep." She swayed her hips, looking over her shoulder at me. "I couldn't sit down for two days straight. Never mind how bad my asshole hurt from him railing that raw too."

"Reyna." I smoothed both hands over her lush ass, imagining it reddened and hot from my palm, and then opened the button of my jeans to give my poor cock a break. She chuckled at me sexily and pushed back until her ass cheeks teased the tip of my cock over the top of my fly. "I want to watch him fuck this ass sometime." I twirled my finger over her rosette. "I want to hear you scream when you come around him."

"Can I scream when you fuck me?" she fired back. "Please, Trey. I need to be fucked by you. This dildo wasn't cutting it."

An idea sparked inside my head as I eyed the discarded dildo still lying between her legs. "Maybe it was the operator of the toy that wasn't cutting it."

"Are you saying I was doing it wrong?"

"Maybe," I smirked, grabbing the toy and enjoying the weight of it in my palm. "I guess we should see if it was a user error or not." I looked up in the mirror where she was staring at me and held her gaze. "Hold on to that headboard, kitten, and don't let go."

She hummed with arousal and nodded. "Whatever you say, big guy."

"Daddy," I growled, running my hand up the long line of her spine to her hair and grabbing a handful. "Right now, I'm your fucking daddy."

"Oh God." She moaned, spreading her legs wider when I hitched the tip of the toy against her pussy lips and coated it with her wetness. I didn't touch her anywhere but where my fingers tangled in her hair, and the space made it feel more exciting. I pushed the toy into her loosened pussy until the end was just sticking out enough for me to grasp, and then I flicked the switch on the end, reveling in the way she moaned and swung her hips. "Jesus."

"Do you have a God kink, baby?" I asked, pulling the toy out and pushing it back in. "You keep calling for him."

"Would you prefer I summon Satan?" she replied, dropping her head between her arms as I started fucking her.

"Now you're talking about my people." I smiled into the darkness. "Did you think about me when you took this cock deep the first time?"

"Yes," she replied instantly without hesitation. "I knew it was close to your size, and I finally knew what it would have felt like if we'd kept our mouths shut the other night."

I laughed, pumping her extra hard for her honesty. "We both could have handled ourselves differently, baby."

"Mmm," she moaned, rocking her hips. "Why won't you just fuck me?"

"Because I'm enjoying watching you take this toy like a good girl." I leaned over her back and whispered in her ear. "Why? Do you want me to fuck you?"

"Yes!" she begged. "You know I do."

I chuckled and then spanked her ass, pushing her forward with the force of it. She screamed and moaned as I did it. "That's daddy's good girl."

"That's it," she cried. "I'm so close, Trey."

"Come for me," I demanded, reaching around her body to her clit and rubbing it. "I want you to come so hard you lose your mind before I slide into you for the first time."

"Oh, shit!" she mewed. "I'm coming, don't stop. Fuck me. Jesus, just like that." Watching Reyna Delacruz come apart at the seams with an orgasm was probably the best thing I'd ever witnessed before. The usual straitlaced good-girl-next-door giving in to her carnal desires and letting go of her inhibitions, begging for cock, and soaking my hand was unlike anything else. Even after the other orgasms I'd given her and watched rack her body the other night, before it all went to shit.

This was different.

This was new and healed.

Fresh.

"Roll onto your back, I want to see your face when I taste your pussy tonight," I commanded, pulling the dildo from her body and tossing it on the floor. She'd never need it again after tonight.

After tonight, she'd have all three of us whenever she wanted us. No more hiding or holding back.

She flipped around, slowly, swaying on her knees before sliding down onto her back against the pillows. When she rested back with her arms over her head, panting, my eyes fell on her juicy breasts, heaving with each breath.

That was when I saw them.

"Did you—?" I paused, unable to process what I was seeing.

She smirked devilishly as she slid her dainty little fingers over her full breasts and tweaked the jewels sparkling around the peaks of her nipples. "Pierce them?" She shrugged. "No, but I'm considering it. I think Parker wants to see me studded like he is."

I growled, lowering over her body to inspect the feminine jewels, and sure enough, they were a twist-on kind. "Say the word, and I'll pierce them for you. Any fucking day. Any fucking place."

"You do body piercing?" She hummed as I flicked my tongue across one nipple, watching it glisten in the candlelight.

"Who do you think took care of Parker's dick?"

She groaned. "Why is that so hot?" She threaded her fingers into my hair, taking out the tie and sliding it over her wrist. "Your hair feels good tickling my body like this." She smiled with her eyes closed.

"It will tickle your thighs when I eat your pussy, too." I slid down her body, kissing my way over her stomach and across each hip bone before folding her thighs back toward her chest, opening up her sweet body.

"Lord, have mercy." She hissed when I flicked my tongue over her swollen clit, tightening her fingers in my hair until she was holding it like handles. Dallin always had his hands in my hair when we were fucking, but feeling her feminine fingers tangled in it gave me shivers.

"I already told you, I'm the devil, sweetheart." I pushed two fingers into her, scissoring them and curling them toward her G-spot.

"I don't care who you are as long as you stop teasing me and fuck me." She winked, curling forward when I sucked on her clit. "That's good. So good."

I grinned and pulled up, stripping my clothes off as she stared up at me. "I need to be inside you, Rey." Crawling back up her body, sliding my cock through her wetness like she had done that night in the chair next to the bed. Her eyelids fluttered as she rocked her hips against me, eager to take me deep.

As I pushed the head of my cock against her opening, she placed one hand against my chest and made me pause. "Wait," she grinned. "Does this make you my boyfriend?"

I gave her a one-sided grin as I took both of her wrists and held them down above her head with my hands and pushed into her body, slowly, giving her inch by inch of my fat cock until she stopped breathing altogether. "This makes us bonded for life, Reyna." Her plump lips parted on an O when I rolled my hips, rubbing her clit when I was buried completely. "I didn't jump at the idea of calling you my girlfriend because it doesn't do justice to what this is. This bond between you, me, and the guys goes far deeper than some twenty-first-century title that's handed out every single second to undeserving bastards."

"Trey," she whispered, staring at me with moisture in her eyes.

"This is for life, kitten." I pulled out and gave it back to her. "This is more than all of that."

"Yes," she hissed, clawing at my hands with her nails as I slid my fingers through hers, linking them together as I fucked her. "God, yes."

"Now be my good girl and scream so loud our guys come back up to investigate," I commanded, slamming back down into her body as she threw her head back and moaned loudly. "That's it, baby, give me everything you've got."

CHAPTER 27

Parker

I ran the tattoo machine across the skin, watching the line work take shape as I neared completion on the piece. My client had sat like a rock for three straight hours, and I was thankful for it because I needed to get the fuck out of the shop.

I loved that Twisted Ink was a shop that let artists rent their space, giving them the control to set their schedule without having to commit to standard business hours.

I had an early appointment that took up all morning and into the early afternoon, and then a gap for lunch before finishing up the day with the piece I was working on.

And then I was fucking out of here.

With every passing minute, I wondered what Reyna was getting into upstairs. Was she using the toys like I wanted her to? Was she coming? Was she thinking of me? Or better yet, Trey?

My cock thickened in my jeans for the hundredth time since I left her upstairs hours ago, and I was ready to say fuck it and just tattoo with it hanging out instead of pinched in my jeans.

But something told me the big bald-headed MMA fighter in my chair would knock my head off my shoulders if I pulled my cock out for the rest of the session.

"And we're done," I said loudly, startling the man, who looked suspiciously like he'd fallen asleep while I tattooed his side. Beast mode activated. "Let me wipe it up and take a look."

I cleaned the art, proud as fuck of the giant memorial piece he'd requested, and then let him check it out in the mirror.

"Thanks, man, looks just like my mama did when she was alive," he said, stiff-lipping it as he admired the piece.

"No problem. You can sit in my chair anytime you want work done. That was the easiest three hours I've had in a long time." I smirked, fist-bumping him as he put his shirt back on.

"Oh, I'll be back. And I've got buddies who are always looking for fresh ink. This town can't keep its talent, so keep your phone on."

"Got it, man." I nodded. "Thanks again." I walked him out to reception, squared up with him, and then headed back to my room to finish cleaning up. As I wiped down the last surface with disinfectant, I felt a presence behind me and looked over my shoulder to see the man I'd come all the way to Nashville for to begin with.

"Hey." I stood up and faced him, taking my gloves off. "Did you just get back?"

"Hey," Dallin said, leaning up off the doorjamb and walking into my room, shutting the door behind him, closing us in alone. "God, I fucking missed you." He crossed the small space, and I held my ground as he pressed his body flush against mine, sliding both hands around the back of my neck and hitching me even tighter to him.

His lips were hot and needy as he kissed me, and I gave in to it, feeling so many emotions pour from them as he deepened it. An inferno lit inside me with each brush of his tongue against mine, paired with the possessive touch of his hands as they skimmed over my arms and back, pressing me against the wall.

I groaned, fisting his shirt as he fought with my belt, opening it and pushing his hand down the front of my jeans. "Already hard for me?" He smirked against my lips. "Or was this for our girl?"

"Our girl," I grunted as he fisted me. "Always our girl," I smirked as he tightened his hold on me and bit my neck. "Okay! Okay!" I conceded, flinching under his grip. "Both of you."

"That's better." He loosened his hold and stroked me just how I liked. "Did you miss me?"

"Fuck yes," I groaned, tipping my head back and holding on to him as he worked me over. "Tell me you brought Trey home with you. For good this time."

"I brought him home. He's in. All in," he replied, and his words moved like sludge through my brain. "I sent him upstairs hours ago to seal the deal. Neither of them has come down screaming at each other and they haven't burned the place to the ground yet, so I'm guessing things are going well up there."

"Oh, fuck," I growled. "Oh, fuck." I pushed him back a step and panted, trying to collect my thoughts. "Hours ago?" I looked at the wall and tried to do math in my head with the one brain cell still getting blood flow not robbed by my raging hard-on. "Oh, fuck."

"What?" He paused, catching on to my worry. "What's going on?"

"I set Rey up to get herself off before I came down here just over three hours ago."

"Huh?" He shook his head, taking his hand from my pants. My dick protested the idea, but my brain was winning the war.

"You leaving fucked with her head." I shook mine, scattering the last of the fog. "She couldn't get off the last few days, no matter what I did." I widened my eyes. "And believe me, I did *everything.* So I set her up with toys and atmosphere and scents to hopefully get her over the mind block the two of you put in her head when you pulled out of town without a backward glance." His face darkened at my jab, but I rolled my eyes and pressed on. "It fucked with her head, man; I'm telling you. But that was three hours ago, and you're telling me you sent him upstairs, without a clue what he was walking in on."

"Oh, fuck." He groaned, rubbing his hand over his face. "You think it went well?"

I shrugged, pulling my pants back up on my hips, buttoning them and my belt back up. "I don't know. But we'd better get up there in case she has him tied to the bed, shoving her stilettoed foot up his ass for all his trouble or something."

Dallin snorted and nodded. "Probably a good idea."

I tossed the rest of my supplies away and grabbed my phone and keys off the shelf, but when I woke my phone up, I saw I had a message waiting for me. "Wait up," I called, as D paused with his hand on the doorknob. I clicked the message, seeing it was from Rey, and then swore as the video thumbnail came up. "Oh, fuck."

"What is it?" D asked, sliding to my side and looking over my shoulder as the dark video started. It was Rey, but she wasn't the one taking the video. She was bent over, in the center of her bed, on her hands and knees, moaning and crying out in ecstasy as I recognized Trey's cock slamming into her wet pussy from behind. "Oh, fuck." D repeated the only phrase we could come up with in the last thirty seconds as we both watched the two of them fuck.

"*Who's your fucking daddy now, baby?*" Trey asked on the video as he fisted his tattooed hand in her hair, pulling her head back and slamming hard into her again.

"*You are,*" she cried. "*You are, Trey.*"

"*That's my good girl,*" he praised her, lowering the phone so the flash showed the glistening of her pussy wrapped tight around his cock with each pull from her body. "*Tell Parker and D whose pussy this is.*"

"*Yours.*" She gasped as he let go of her hair and peppered her ass with his palm, rippling the flesh in between each thrust.

She screamed and moaned, pushing back into his lap each time he bottomed out before he leaned over her back, holding the camera in front of her face so we could see her and him as they fucked. He looked positively rabid, hair loose and wild, with a look of pure dominance in his eyes.

And her.

God.

Reyna was breathtaking. Her cheeks were flushed, and her eyes were glassy as she stared into the camera.

"Whose pussy?" Trey smirked before biting her ear, tugging the lobe with his teeth.

"Daddy's." She moaned, shivering, and biting her bottom lip. From this angle, we could see her tits swaying with each punishing thrust, and the sparkling jewels in her nipples glowed brightly in the video.

"Did you fucking pierce her nipples?" Dallin growled in my ear.

"No, but she wants them done now. And so do I," I responded, watching her face morph into one of pure bliss as she came, screaming Trey's name repeatedly until he roared, bottoming out again and holding still inside her. He leaned back up, taking the camera with him to show where he was buried deep. He grunted in the background before slowly pulling out of her and lowering the camera until we had a close-up view of her throbbing pussy.

"Show them whose pussy this is now," Trey commanded. "Show them, baby."

Her muscles contracted a few times and then the milky white of his come dripped out of her slightly gaped pussy. "Jesus Christ," D moaned, fisting himself as we watched Trey claim the pussy we were both obsessed with.

"Sorry, fellas." Trey flipped the camera around so we could see him in the dimly lit room. "But she's mine now." He winked and shrugged as Rey's melodic giggle sounded from the background. "You have no one but yourselves to blame, either." He smirked. "Have a good one."

"Fucker." I growled as the video closed and went back to the message thread.

"When did he send that?" D asked.

"Half an hour ago," I barked, pushing past him through the door.

"I'm going to put them both over my knee for being teases," D cursed, chasing after me as I cleared the stairwell door and flew up them, two at a time.

"Get in line," I challenged him with a good-hearted smirk. It was everything we wanted from them, and it felt so fucking good seeing it finally be delivered. But I needed to be a part of it. I needed to see it with my own eyes, feel it with my skin, taste it with my tongue.

Hell, I'd settle for a seat in the corner, to be honest.

As soon as I cleared the doorway to the apartment, I heard Trey's moans of pleasure coming from the bedroom. Dallin shoved me aside as he chased after those noises, crossing the threshold of the bedroom milliseconds before I did.

Fuck.

Trey lay on his back in the center of the bed with Rey grinding in his lap, riding his cock like a pro in a bull-riding competition. Her head was tilted back, hair piled high on top, and her hips swung expertly, giving them both exactly what they needed. She caught us in the doorway, looking at us in the mirror over the bed, and smiled sexily.

"It's about damn time," she moaned, circling her hips again. "I was trying to hold off my orgasm for when you guys finally got here, but I was getting so close I didn't know if I'd be able to do it." She looked over her shoulder finally and held out one hand to us. "Come to me."

We didn't waste a second, stripping off our clothes as we crossed to the bed and crawled up.

Trey looked like the cat that ate the canary as he held on to her lush ass, lifting her so we could see his cock buried firmly inside her. "I think she's hooked for life," he said arrogantly.

"I'll hold him down," I said to D. "You fill a sock with bars of soap."

Trey tipped his head back and laughed as Rey questioned us both with her eyes before shaking her head and looking back down to where she was impaled on a cock the thickness of a tree log.

"This is how this is going to go," she panted, resting her hands on Trey's chest and lifting her ass and dropping it even harder. "I'm going to come. And then I'm going to get off this cock and let my poor kitty rest for a while." She looked at me with a pout. "She's tender." I chuckled and nodded, knowing just how hard Trey could fuck and they'd been at it for hours now. "Then"—she turned and looked at D on her other side—"you're going to give me what I want most out of anything else in this world."

"And that is?" he asked, with darkening eyes as he pushed an errant lock of hair over her ear.

"I'm going to sit back and watch you get fucked by these two." Her eyelids fluttered closed before opening again. "I *need* to see you take their cocks into your body."

I chuckled. "Whatever she wants, she gets."

"Whatever you want," D agreed.

"Oh, this is going to be fun." Trey nudged D with his fist.

"Careful, or I'll let Rey use that monster-sized dildo on your ass instead," D grumped, eyeing the discarded dildo on the nightstand next to the bed.

Trey tipped his head back and laughed into the ceiling. "That wouldn't be a threat if you two didn't have such puny, pathetic-sized dicks."

"Fucker," I growled, reaching under Rey's ass to twist one of his balls until he gasped and held his hands up in submission.

But apparently, the change in the angle of his hips was what Rey needed to light off her next orgasm, moaning incoherently as she rocked back and forth in his lap.

"That's daddy's good girl," Trey praised her, focusing on her again after our ball-busting. "God, you feel so good wrapped around me when you come."

Rey blew some of her bangs back and dismounted, collapsing onto her back next to him on the bed to catch her breath.

I didn't waste a second before leaning down and kissing her hello. "Did you enjoy my presents?" I asked, tweaking one of her nipples, still wearing the gems I'd bought her.

"They were perfect." She smiled dreamily at me. "Got the job done."

"Wrong," Trey squawked annoyingly as he stood up off the bed and ran his hand over his chest. "She was fucking herself hard with that dildo, but couldn't get off until I did it for her."

Dallin snorted as he lay down next to Rey and kissed her sweetly. "Guess size doesn't matter after all." He poked at Trey. They got into a small shoving match, where D ended up getting tossed off the bed completely into a heap on the floor and Rey giggled, curling into me.

"Enough," she called after D grabbed one of Trey's ankles and flipped him off his feet onto the floor next to him. "Stop delaying what we all want."

"She's right." I nodded to her, kissing her nose and detangling myself from her limbs. "The girl wants to see some ass fucking." I held my hand out for D and helped him up, and when he was on his feet, I pulled him flush to the front of my body. "And I'm desperate to get into that ass after all this buildup." His cock jerked against our stomachs as mine hardened. He leaned in challengingly and stopped with his lips right against mine, but not kissing me.

"You want to fuck me first?" he asked, running the tip of his tongue across my bottom lip.

"You know I do." I closed the distance and pressed my lips against his, kissing him slowly, coaxing the passion we used to have for each other out of him until his hands were wrapped around the back of my neck, anchoring me to him even closer. "Fuck, I've missed how good it feels to be like this with you."

He reached between our bodies and lined our cocks up, rubbing us both in his hand as he kissed me deeper.

"I still remember how it felt to kiss you that first time," he growled against my lips. "We were a couple of dumb kids running off alcohol and testosterone, fumbling around like idiots."

"It was so bad," I chuckled, biting his bottom lip when he started playing with my piercings. "But so fucking good, too," I groaned.

"I fucked you into that bed so hard, I was afraid I broke you after the sex-crazed high ended."

"I came so many times, I thought my balls would never be the same."

"And then I entered the chat," Trey said, sliding up next to us.

"And we started all over again," D smirked, turning his head and leaning in for a kiss from Trey. D slid his hand into Trey's hair and pulled him in close to our bodies, creating a triangle. I leaned over and bit Trey's neck, sucking on it as he grabbed one of my ass cheeks and squeezed.

It felt so good to be with both of them again like this; I didn't even realize how badly I missed it until I had it within reach again.

"Mmm." Rey's sexy voice floated into my ears from the bed, and I looked over at her. She was lying in the center of the bed propped up on the pillows watching us with such carnal hunger in her eyes it nearly masked the love in them too.

She absolutely loved this. There was no mistaking it. No feeling of her just pretending to keep Dallin in her life. She loved this side of us all just as much as when we gave her our attention. I never imagined finding a woman who could accept us for who we really were deep down.

I never thought I'd have it all.

Yet here I was, with everything I'd ever need in one room.

"Still want to just spectate, baby girl?" I challenged her as she bit her bottom lip and shifted her legs back and forth in the center of the bed. "It looks like you might want to play, too."

Her chest rose and fell, her hard nipples like little buds on the ends of her lush breasts beckoning me to take another bite of them. I fucking loved her tits. And her pussy. *And* her ass.

I loved everything about her.

I loved her.

The thought sent me reeling as D and Trey both descended on me. Trey kissed me like he always did, powerfully, with a roughness that left me feeling sore and hungry for more. And Dallin ran his hands up and down my body, teasing me with touches not quite where I needed them to be.

"I don't know," Rey finally responded, and I cracked one eye to see her around Trey as she started playing with her nipples. "Maybe you should show me some more so I can make up my mind." She smiled so fucking pretty at me, I would have given her the world for a glimpse of her perfect smile.

"You heard our girl." I pulled back from Trey. "She wants to see more."

"More?" D looked over his shoulder at her. "Like this?" He watched her as he slowly sank to his knees at my feet before turning to look up at Trey and me as we stood over him. "How does this look, sweetheart?" He asked her as he fisted us both, stroking us with long, slow sensual pulls of his palm.

"Uh-huh," she murmured absent-mindedly, crawling to the end of the bed to see better. "That's working."

"And this?" D asked, leaning forward to take the head of my cock into his mouth and suck on it like he was trying to steal my soul.

"Yep." She nodded quickly, spreading her legs to kneel and watch, still playing with her gorgeous tits. "That too."

"Fuck," I groaned, tipping my head back as pleasure rolled through my body. "Just like that, D. Your fucking mouth should be used for nothing else but this." He smirked as he lowered himself down to suck on my smooth balls and massage them as he kept stroking me.

"Look at our girl," Trey whispered, sliding his hand up the back of my neck to turn my head back toward Rey.

"Baby," I growled, watching as she chewed on that plump bottom lip and rubbed slow, leisurely circles around her clit. Her legs were spread wide under her, and I wanted nothing more than to watch her taking a cock while D sucked mine, but she said she was sore.

"What if I changed my mind?" She spoke quickly, blinking like she was breaking the trance.

D fell backward, creating a space between our bodies like he was burned, and fear raced through my soul. Did she not want this after all? Had I read it all wrong the whole time?

"No!" she gasped, crawling off the bed and falling to her knees next to D. "Not about this." She hurried, running her hands up his chest and circling them behind his neck to pull him in close before looking up at Trey and me. "I don't change my mind about wanting this." I relaxed a bit and so did D, but I was still reeling. "I mean, what if I changed my mind about just wanting to watch?" She smiled sweetly at D as he sagged into her touch, relieved. "I didn't think it was possible, but I'm so fucking turned on right now," she whined, leaning into D and gently stroking his cock as she swayed back and forth on her knees like she was trying to rub herself with the air. "I want to help you take them."

"I love you," D growled, burying his hands in her hair and kissing her like his life depended on it. "I don't deserve you and your love."

"Shut up and show me just how much you love me." She kissed him back. "Show Trey and Parker how much you love them, too."

"Park," Trey growled, clearing his throat like it all overwhelmed him. "On the bed." I lay on my back in the center of the bed as Trey continued giving orders. "D, keep sucking our guy. Get him nice and hard so he can fuck you."

D rolled his eyes at Trey's demands but did what he said. He kept his gaze locked on mine as he knelt between my feet and laid kisses up the inside of my thigh like Rey liked to do, and I jerked and twitched under his touch. "Damn, D," I complained. "Don't be a tease."

He smirked and then gave me what I needed from him, sucking me into his mouth again as Trey and Reyna stood at the foot of the bed, watching.

Trey laid his hand on D's back and pushed his shoulders down, so his ass was up in the air, and handed Reyna the bottle of lube. "You know how to prep him?" he asked her.

She nodded, and D's eyes darkened as he stared up at me.

"Parker taught me how," she added finally, running the lube over her fingers before pouring it onto his exposed ass. "You with me, Dallin?" she asked as she started rubbing her fingers over his hole.

"Right here," he responded, fluttering his eyelids as pleasure consumed him.

"Suck my cock while she fucks your ass with her fingers," I demanded, tangling my fingers in the wavy hair on top of his head. I knew he was going to get anxious about being a bottom again after so long, so distracting him was the only way to help him.

He groaned when she turned her wrist and penetrated him, but he opened his mouth and let me push my cock inside like a good little fuck toy.

Watching Dallin Kent bottom was something meant to be celebrated. It was magnificent seeing his dominant alpha side give way to someone else and fall submissive.

"You're loving this, aren't you?" Trey asked Rey as he stood behind her and played with her breasts while she played with D.

"Yes," she moaned, thrusting her fingers in and out. "Are you ready, D?"

"Are you?" he asked, looking over his shoulder at her. "I need you."

"I'm here." She crawled up the bed as I slid out onto the floor and took the bottle of lube from her. "What do you want?"

"I need to fuck you. I need to be inside you," he growled as he watched me lube up my cock, like he was torn between wanting it and not.

"I think I can handle that." Rey smiled and leaned in, kissing him, soothing the worst of the anxiety trying to worm its way into the room. "I mean, it's a tough job, but someone has to do it."

"On your back," D demanded between clenched teeth as he fought for control. "I won't be gentle, though. I can't be when I'm with them."

"I can take it," she purred, lying on her back and opening her legs for him as she rolled her clit and one nipple in her fingers. "God, I'm so fucking horny for this."

He grabbed her ankles and jerked her down to the end of the bed aggressively, making her gasp and moan before he sank into her without a second of hesitation, burying his cock balls deep into her pussy and hissing from the pleasure of her body wrapped around his.

I knew exactly what he was feeling in that moment, because there was nothing else like the feeling of sliding into her for the first time; feeling her body yield to our invasion and accommodate us was magical.

"Yes, baby." She groaned when he started rolling his hips, rubbing her clit with his pelvic bone to work her up to the onslaught she was about to get from him.

"Park," he growled, and I slid my hand up his spine as I held my cock by the base, aimed directly at his ass. "I need you."

"Right here." I hummed as he stilled when I pressed against him. "God, I'm going to come so fucking fast, D," I growled, already fighting off the tingles of pleasure without even being inside him yet.

"I need you to fuck me hard," D begged, so uncharacteristically for him.

"I got you, baby," I reassured him as I pushed into him, forcing my way through the tight ring of muscles at the entrance of his ass. "Mmm," I growled, unable to hold it back. "Fucking tight."

Dallin grabbed Rey's wrists and pinned her hands above her head, widening his knees to sink deeper, and then pushed back against me. "Park, don't tease me." He demanded. "Fuck me already."

"Yes, sir." I groaned, grabbing his hips and slamming deep inside him in one thrust. He tipped his head back and roared an animalistic sound that reminded me of a lion's growl as it stood above a kill. He was reduced to nothing but nature's instincts as I pulled out and slammed into him again. My piercings snagged on the way in and out, blinding me with pleasure as he groaned repeatedly as he took it.

I looked over his shoulder and saw Reyna's wild eyes as he rocked into her pussy, taking my cock and giving her his. And it was nearly my undoing.

She fucking loved it. She was as crazed as he was as she fought the hold he had on her, simply out of instinct.

"Take that cock, Rey," I praised her, as I brutally fucked our guy sandwiched between us. "Give it to her, D. Fuck her so good. She's going to come all over you.."

Trey had his hands running up and down their bodies, unable to keep them to himself as he lost himself to the sight before us, too. He didn't have any smart-ass comments or jokes to make as he witnessed something powerful between the four of us.

"I'm coming," Rey gasped, clawing at D's hands as she tipped her head back and screamed when D started moving his hips on his own, pushing himself back onto my cock and then deep into her pussy. "Fucking hell!" she cried. "Don't stop. Please don't stop."

"Never," D promised. His entire body was coiled tight and ready to snap, but he forced himself to hold off as she got her pleasure from him.

"I love you." I leaned over his back and bit his shoulder, pushing him in deep to her and holding him there as I rocked my cock in and out, forcing him to still as her eyes rolled and fought the pleasure he gave to her. "D, God," I moaned. "I fucking love you both so much."

"Park," he cried, reaching back to grab my hip as I ground my cock in circles inside him, stretching him out as best I could for the monster waiting for his turn next to us. Trey was watching with his hand wrapped around his cock, champing at the bit for the pleasure he knew he'd get when he took D again. "I'm coming."

"Good boy," I growled, pushing him further into the submissive role as I topped. "Take that fucking cock and fill her pussy up with your come." I didn't recognize the Dom coming out in me as I pushed him down further, but I reveled in it. Rey's eyes were so full of love and adoration as she kissed D's neck and stared up at me, still pinned beneath us.

"Fuck!" Dallin bellowed, and I felt his ass tighten as his cock twitched, pumping our girl's pussy full of his come, as he spurred my orgasm on, milking me with his body.

"Take it." I pulled back and slammed into him a few more times as my entire body tensed up and shivered. I couldn't see anything as my eyes screwed shut from the overwhelming pleasure coursing through my body, and nothing outside of my physical touch mattered as the biggest orgasm of my life carried on and on.

"Oh my God," Rey cried, finally pulling her wrists free of D's grip as she wrapped them around his back and held him to her chest. "Oh my God."

"Are you okay?" Trey asked, pausing as the only levelheaded one at the moment to check on her.

She nodded quickly, taking his hand and squeezing it, unable to say anything more as emotion overtook her.

I pulled my cock out of Dallin, reveling in the post-orgasm pleasure and pain of my piercings tugging on the withdraw until only the head was still inside him.

"Let me see." Trey stood next to me, watching D's ass as I pulled free, leaving him gaped with the white evidence of my orgasm dripping from him. "Fucking hell." He groaned, stroking his cock.

"I'm done," D groaned, pulling out of Rey and rolling to the side in a heap, landing on his back with his arm thrown over his face as his chest rose and fell quickly.

"Same," I smirked, lying down next to Rey, who had an equally smitten look on her face as she curled into his side, pulling me toward her back.

"How do you feel?" she asked D.

"Horny," he said, without removing his arm from his face. "I don't fucking know how. I think that was the biggest load of come I've ever pumped from my body before." He pulled his arm down far enough to look at Rey with one eye. "But still."

She giggled. "I'm glad you enjoyed it."

"Mmm." He growled, finally dropping his arm all the way and looking at Trey, who stood solo at the end of the bed with a raging hard-on and a less-than-amused look on his face. "Ready, big guy?" D asked.

"You fucking know it," Trey responded instantly. "Are you?"

"If I'm going to take that cock"—D looked down at the monster turning molten purple from how hard it was—"I need to do it while I'm stretched and relaxed."

"Good." Trey stepped forward and lifted D's thick thighs, folding them back toward his chest without asking permission. "Because I'm going to fuck this ass so hard," Trey growled with a slight shake of his head, "the neighbors are going to call the cops for a welfare check from the noises I'm about to make you make."

D licked his lips, watching as Trey poured a generous amount of lube onto his cock and coated it. "Rey."

"Yeah, baby?" she purred, rubbing her hands over his chest as his cock twitched excitedly against his stomach.

"Be a good girl and ride my face, so I don't wake the neighbors."

"Mmm," she moaned, jumping to her knees, eagerly willing to help him. He lifted her onto his face without preamble, pulling her down flush to his mouth and sucking her clit into his mouth as Trey lined up with his ass.

Rey reached down and held on to his knees for him as Trey pushed inside, making Dallin hiss. "Fuck, you're fat," he cursed, arching his back as Trey smirked and pushed deeper, forcing his cock in.

"Yes, D," Reyna moaned, rocking her hips as he squeezed her ass cheeks. "Trey, come here." She leaned forward and kissed him as he slid the rest of the way into Dallin.

I lay on my side and watched the three of them find their rhythm. Trey started sliding in and out, making Dallin curse and make noises unrecognizable as human. Reyna and Trey kissed hungrily, as she rocked her pussy on D's face, and watching them both use him for their pleasure was so hot.

"Do you feel used?" I asked D, sliding my hands into his hair and pulling on it to tilt his mouth toward Reyna's clit.

"Mmm" was his response as she started bouncing on his tongue like a good girl.

I chuckled and winked at Trey as he savagely fucked our guy. "How does he feel?"

"Like fucking heaven," he admitted with a smirk. "Thanks for opening him up for me."

I shrugged. "Anytime."

"Fuck off," Dallin argued from under Reyna as she chuckled.

"Oh, poor baby." I fake pouted and leaned over to suck the head of his cock into my mouth, tasting Reyna's sweet pussy on it and groaning at my mistake. Because I had meant to tease him with a quick head play, but I managed to entice myself to suck him off simply to taste the mix of them coating his cock.

"Parker." Dallin cursed, dropping Reyna's ass and sliding his hand over the back of my head to push me down further on his cock. I laughed to myself, getting on my knees and taking him to the back of my throat and giving him whatever he needed in the moment.

"Fuck all of you," Trey growled. "I'm going to fucking blow from how hot you all look right now."

Rey teased, "Do it, daddy. Fill him up and take what you've wanted for so long."

"Rey," Trey groaned in warning as he slammed into D harder, rocking him forward and down my throat even further as Reyna moaned at the jolt too. "Be careful or I'll bend you over and fuck your ass."

"Mmm. Promises, promises—" She gasped and then screamed as Dallin bit her clit and spanked her ass hard. "Oh God, just like that."

"Beg me," Dallin growled from under her, taking back control as she tried to push him down further into the submissive role by using Trey against him.

"Please, God, please, Dallin. Do it again."

"Good girl," I praised her, using my fist to stroke Dallin as I sucked her nipple into my mouth and bit it at the same time Dallin bit her clit and spanked her again, pushing her headfirst into an orgasm that ignited D and Trey into their own.

The next several minutes consisted of moans and groans of pleasure as each of them came, finding ecstasy in their bodies and then exhaustion on the other side after a marathon of sex.

And I fucking loved every single second of it. I had my guys and our girl all together for the first time, and I was never looking back.

CHAPTER 28

Dallin

Peace.

That was the first thing I felt when I woke up the next morning. It was a deep peace that settled into my bones and soul all in one, leaving me calm and relaxed.

The second thing I felt was the knot in my neck from sleeping on the edge of the bed all night with Parker's bony elbows in my back. That one sucked a bit.

I rolled onto my back, groaning silently as my muscles protested, and lay silently, not wanting to open my eyes yet to find out it was all a dream.

But then I heard something, and the hair on my arms stood up as I listened to it from the darkness behind my eyelids.

Whimpers.

My eyes flew open, adjusting to the dim light of the sunshine outside through the curtains before I sat up and looked over to the other side of the bed and found Parker's head buried between Rey's thighs as he feasted on her for breakfast.

"Damn," I growled with deep gravel in my voice. "That's a hell of a way to wake up in the morning."

Rey looked over at me and smiled sleepily. "I thought the same thing." She arched her back and moaned, running her fingers over Parker's short hair, pushing his face harder against her pussy.

He finally pulled up and looked at me, licking his lips as he slid his fingers into her body in his tongue's wake. "Morning." He smirked. "Didn't mean to wake you."

"I'd be offended if you didn't," I responded, and then watched as Trey stirred on Rey's other side, cracking his eyes open and looking at the two of them in the middle of the bed. "Nice of you to join us."

He leaned up on one elbow and watched the sensual sight with a gleam in his eye. "What did I miss?"

"Nothing much," Rey responded. "I woke up just a few minutes ago to Parker tasting your come from last night."

"God," I groaned, scooting across the bed to be closer to them. "Why is that so fucking hot?"

She grinned and leaned in for a kiss, which I gave willingly.

Morning breath be damned, I wanted her.

"I'm so close," Rey whimpered against my lips, digging her nails into my neck. "He's so good with his tongue."

"You want to come on his tongue?" I asked, sliding my fingers down her chest to her nipples and tweaking them as Trey leaned in on her other side, kissing her neck and circling her clit with his fingertips as Parker finger-fucked her.

"Yes," she moaned. "I'm such a selfish bitch." She smirked, still feeling like the spoiled princess we'd made her into last night.

"You can start leveling out the score," Trey countered, leaning down to suck on her nipple as he looked across her body at me. "What do you say, D?" He flicked his tongue across the tight bud before biting it. "Think it's time to play a game with our sexy little girlfriend?"

"I think that's a fabulous idea," I agreed, reveling in the way her entire body shivered at the prospect. Parker slapped the inside of her thigh with his palm and slid off the end of the bed.

"Get up, baby girl," He ordered as Trey and I met him at the end of the bed and stared down at where she lay still with her legs parted and sex appeal dripping from her eyes.

"What are you going to do to me?" she asked, leaning up on her elbows to stare at the three naked and desperate men watching her like their next meal.

"It's not *what* we're going to do to you," Trey cautioned as he rubbed his palms together. "It's about *who*."

She raised an eyebrow at him and then slowly crawled to her knees on the end of the bed. "I'm confused."

"How do you feel about the game hide-and-seek?" Parker asked, and I could feel the excitement of times past bubbling up in my veins.

"Hide-and-seek?" she asked, speculatively. "Like the kids' game?"

"Similar," I responded. "But with bigger stakes."

She bit her bottom lip and looked at each of us. She was nervous.

Good.

I always was the best at smelling fear in the dark.

"Game is easy," Parker started. "We'll leave the apartment and wait in the stairwell. You get thirty seconds to find a place to hide inside this apartment. And when your time is up, we come to find you."

Her eyebrows rose. "That's it?"

Trey chuckled. "Not even close." He reached out and ran his fingers down a lock of her long hair before snaking his hand into the length and twisting it tight at the base of her neck, pulling her forward until her breasts were pressed against his chest. She gasped and panted as he held her right in front of his lips. "You'll be naked when we play, and it will be dark. And the first one to find you gets the prize."

"What's the prize?" she whispered.

"Their pick, and you can't refuse."

"And if I win?" she retorted, looking away from his serious blue eyes to mine. "What do I get?"

"How do you think you're going to win?" I smirked, "It's three-on-one in a three-bedroom apartment, baby."

"You get sixty seconds." She dug her nails into Trey's chest until he loosened his hold on her hair so she could look at me fully. "Sixty seconds from the time the front door opens to find me, and if no one does, then I win. And I get to pick the prize."

"Deal," Parker said, without conferring with us, and spanked her ass loudly before wrapping his hand around the front of her throat, effectively pulling her out of Trey's hold and into his arms. "You'd better hide with a bottle of lube, because when I find you . . ." He slid his fingers down her stomach and rubbed her clit until she mewed in his arms. "And I will be the one to find you. I have something special planned for this pussy."

She moaned and let her eyelids flutter closed as he kept circling her clit before he abruptly let go of her and pushed her backward onto the bed, where she landed in a smiling heap. "Game on, boys."

Parker smirked and walked out with Trey and his maniacal laugh following him as they headed for the stairwell, naked and hard.

"There's something you should know." I stood there as she turned her attention back to me and licked her lips. "We've played this game for years, baby." Her pupils dilated. "Chasing each other through the darkness has been a favorite of ours, and each time the stakes get higher, and the game gets hotter." I leaned down over her body and pushed two fingers into her pussy and one straight into her ass, which was wet from Parker's attention a few minutes ago. "But out of the three of us, it is usually me who wins. Because there's a side of me you've never seen before, Rey. A side that preys on the scared in the dark and makes them my victims." Her pussy tightened around my fingers as the blackness of my words penetrated her brain. "Once I unleash this monster on you, there's no putting him away again."

She slid her hands down my sides, gripping my steel cock and stroking me, pulling me forward until the tip traced the wet lips of her pussy and hitched at her entrance where my fingers were buried. She pulled me further until my cock slid in with my fingers, something we'd never done before, and both of us groaned at the new sensation. She leaned up and bit my ear and whispered, "When I win, Dallin, it's you who will be the prize. For the three of us to fuck together again." She rocked her hips and took me deeper, tightening her muscles around my cock and fingers until I almost forgot who was topping. "Game on."

I smirked and pulled free of her body, staring down at her sexy body on display for me. My cock glistened with her wetness, and I licked my fingers clean as she played with her clit, watching me. "Game fucking on."

"Ready or not, little red, here we come!" Trey sang from the front door as we walked back in. The apartment was dark, but the air was alive with electricity as we shut the door behind us, locking it.

Parker slid the dining room table across the floor and pinned it against the front door with a smirk on his face. "In case she tries to escape."

I chuckled, but there was no humor in my voice when I did it. Because I was alive for the first time in years.

I hoped she ran. I hoped she tried to escape from us so we could chase her. I imagined the look of terror in her eyes as she looked over her shoulder, sprinting away from us, but knowing we were right on her heels. My cock thickened even more as I played it out in my head.

"We're losing time," Trey said, walking into the apartment. "Let's find her."

Parker took off down the hall toward the spare bedroom, and I went toward the main, leaving Trey in the living space, tearing at the pillows and blankets in the large baskets on the floor, eager to find her.

I quickly checked in the obvious places—under the bed, in the closets, the shower—but I knew she wouldn't choose anywhere like that.

"Come out, come out, wherever you are." Trey's villainous voice wafted through the apartment, and a shiver of excitement ran over my body. He loved this just as much as I did. What bad guy didn't like a good game of chase with the pretty little bunny?

I could sense her fear. I imagined her tucked away somewhere, with both hands pressed over her mouth to keep silent as we stalked her.

I needed to find her.

My watch said fifteen seconds. But I wasn't on her trail.

I left the main, running across the living space where Trey had the couch tipped over, looking under it, and met Parker as he ran into her office.

"She's got to be in here," he said, with wild eyes. "I can feel her."

"She's here," I agreed, shoving open the closet as he pushed aside the pile of boxes from behind her desk that were delivered last week. "Somewhere."

When he shoved the last box, a large one used to ship the new bookshelf she ordered, it didn't slide across the carpet like the others did. It twisted a little under his force, and he looked at me over the top with a smirk.

Trey cleared the doorway after coming up empty-handed and watched as Parker ripped open the top of the box.

"Fuck!" Rey screamed as he reached inside, unfolded her from her hiding spot, and pulled her out. She flailed, squirming and fighting his hold on her as her fear and adrenaline mounted. She landed a hard blow to the top of his foot with hers and he grunted, loosening his hold on her just enough for her to wiggle by him, but she didn't account for me standing there, ready to intercept her.

I grabbed both of her wrists and pushed her up against the wall, pinning them high above her head as her chest heaved with excitement, drawing my eyes down to her perfect breasts. "Hmm." I reached down with one hand to tweak one of her nipples. "What do we have here?"

"You didn't find me in sixty seconds," she gasped, kicking her knee out, trying to hit me in the nuts as fight-or-flight took over her good sense.

"Wrong," Trey quipped from behind me. "Fifty-seven seconds, to be exact."

"Lies," she hissed.

I slid my free hand down her body and cupped her cunt, running my fingers through her wet folds before burying three deep into her pussy. "Don't act like you aren't dripping in anticipation for what we're going to do to you," I smirked, dodging her teeth as she lunged for my lips with them.

"What *I'm* going to do to you," Parker corrected, sliding up beside us. "Were you a good girl and did you bring your lube?" he smirked.

She swallowed, flicking her eyes between the two of us wildly. "Why would I need lube for my vagina?"

Parker smirked, shaking his head as he leaned forward and kissed her ear. "Because you might be wet enough to take one big cock into your pussy with no problem. But when I push inside you in a few minutes, I won't be the only one buried deep inside that sweet, tight kitty."

She gasped, and my cock jerked at the idea of her taking two cocks inside her pussy at the same time. "You're too big," she panted. "All of you."

"Correct," Parker added, leaning up off her to tweak her nose. "Which is why this is my prize, and not yours." He winked. "It's going to hurt, but it's also going to make you come so fucking hard you'll be bowlegged for days."

"Parker," she whined, desperate for leniency.

"Next time, you'll do a better job hiding." I cut her off, pulling her off the wall by her caged-in wrists. "Where do you want her, buddy?"

"On the couch," Parker replied, rubbing his hand over his whisker-covered jaw as I led her out and tossed her down onto her butt on the couch. She stared up at the three of us with nervousness in her eyes, but I knew better than to think she wasn't the least bit excited about this, either. "Now," Parker started, "I'm not a total monster, so I'll let you have a little say in this." He stroked his cock and her eyes dropped to the studs on the underside as he manipulated them. "I'll let you choose who gets to fuck you with me, though I think we all know you're not going to pick Trey," he joked, and Trey snorted, knowing there was no way she was going to willingly take his fat cock next to Parker's the first time she did DVP. "Under one condition." Parker held his finger up, and she raised her eyebrows. "If you get on your knees and take our cocks in your mouth like our good little slut, I'll let Dallin fuck you with me. If you don't, then you're taking Trey the first time."

She rolled her lips together like she was fighting a sarcastic retort, but she wasn't in any position to challenge him on it. I saw the second she decided to play along with his game, as he was the winner, after all.

She plastered a sweetly sick smile onto her face and gracefully slid off the couch onto her knees at our feet. She looked up at us seductively from under her lashes before sliding one hand up my thigh and one hand up Trey's thigh, leaving Parker free of her touch in the middle before she leaned forward and traced the end of his cock with her tongue. "Whatever you say, sir," she cooed, batting her lashes at him before looking over at me. "Do you want to feel Parker's ribbed cock against yours inside me, baby?" she teased, circling the base of my cock with her hand and squeezing.

"More than I want my next fucking breath," I replied instantly.

"And you." She turned her attention to Trey, stroking his thickness in her small hand and driving us both mad. "What are you going to do with your cock while they fuck me, daddy?"

She purred the taboo name they both apparently loved, and he closed his eyes and tipped his head back in pleasure as she teased him.

"Keep talking like that and I'll find something for your mouth to do," he growled.

"Yes, please." She hummed before leaning forward and sucking Parker's cock into her mouth, twirling her tongue around the head of him as she stroked us. She worked him up and down before switching hands and positions, sucking on all of us and getting us worked up even more.

I knew what Parker was trying to do with the impromptu head jobs, even if he didn't tell her. He was getting us all close, so that we didn't last long to prolong the experience. He knew that keeping it short and sweet would be better for her in the long run, and this was his way of protecting and caring for her while keeping her thinking she was the powerless one.

"You're such a fucking Dom." I groaned as she deep-throated me, looking at Park. "I know what you're doing."

He smirked, tightening his fingers into her hair and pushing her deeper onto my cock. "Just taking care of our girl."

She gagged and gasped as he pulled her off and then to her feet by the bun in her hair.

"Do I get to get fucked now?" she purred, running her wet fingertips down to her pussy and circling her clit.

"Is that what you want?" he asked, and she nodded eagerly. "Then be a good girl and straddle D on the couch."

I didn't hesitate to take my place, laid down on the couch with my cock standing up tall and ready for her hot pussy. As she threw her leg over me, I saw the anxiety in her eyes trying to take over her brain. I held my cock up for her and she sank onto it, hardly hesitating to accommodate herself to the invasion like she usually did, probably thanks in part to the nonstop sex we'd been having lately. When she was fully impaled on me, she rocked forward and leaned her hands on my chest for leverage.

"Come here, pretty girl," I said, sliding my hand around the back of her neck and bringing her down to lie flat against my chest to kiss her, trying my best to silence the fear in her brain. "If you want to stop, just say the words and we'll stop."

"Okay," she whispered as Trey handed Park the bottle of lube and he coated his cock with it.

"Cock out, D," Parker instructed, and Rey rose, letting me fall free of her body. Parker poured the cold lube onto my cock and then stroked it, coating me and teasing me in a way that only he could. "You ready to feel my cock against yours?"

"Fuck yes," I groaned as he lined me back up with our girl and she sank down onto me again, rising and falling a few more times to spread the lube out inside her. "Good girl," I praised her, holding her stare. "Keep your eyes right here, with me."

"I love you," she whispered, as Parker climbed up onto the couch behind her and kissed her back.

"How about me?" he asked, leaning over her shoulder. "Do you love me?"

"I do." She smiled, turning her face and letting him kiss her lips before freezing as he slid his fingers into her pussy against my shaft. "Mmm."

"Relax for me, baby girl," he cooed, pressing the head of his cock against the base of mine and pushing forward to penetrate the tight ring of her muscles. "I'm going to make you feel so good, Reyna."

"Fuck." She groaned when the head of his cock slid inside her, tensing under the invasion before she took a deep breath and relaxed her muscles again. "So tight."

"You're not kidding," I growled, fighting off the urge to slide out and slam back into her. I could feel the hard ridge of Parker's first piercing as he pushed in deeper and bit back another growl as it stroked against the underside of my cock on its way in.

"How do you feel, Rey?" Trey asked, walking around to the side of the couch and kneeling beside us. He ran his fingers through her messy hair and pushed it away from her face lovingly as she struggled to speak. "Focus on us, baby. Stay present with us."

"I'm trying." She moaned when the second piercing slid in. I knew she wasn't being overly affected by the studs in this position, but the thickness of each inch was no doubt pushing her past limits she didn't know she had until she met me. "Fuck, it feels so good," she moaned, closing her eyes and biting her bottom lip.

"Let me help you make it feel even better," Trey said, sliding his hand between our bodies until he reached her clit, and then started rubbing it just how she liked.

"Yes," she groaned, pushing back against Parker and me, taking us faster than he planned. "I want it all," she begged. "Fuck me, P." She opened her eyes and looked down at me. "I'm so fucking hot knowing he's stroking your cock right now."

"I'm close already," I admitted.

"Do you like it?" She looked over her shoulder to where Parker stared down at her ass, watching his cock disappear deep inside her next to mine. "Is this what you were hoping for, Park?"

"Yes," he panted. "Fuck yes." His hands tightened around her waist and then he pushed faster, burying himself in balls deep before pausing and letting her body adjust to us both. "Fuck, you feel so good."

Trey kept playing with her clit with his hand and then leaned down and kissed me. "This is so hot." He reached around her body and cupped my balls, rubbing his fingertips over my taint. "Like really fucking hot." He leaned around so he could see where we impaled her together.

"Let me help you." I smirked at him, dropping my hand off Rey's ass and gripping his hard cock where it bobbed between his knees next to us. He groaned and pushed his cock deeper into my fist as Parker lightly spanked Rey's ass.

"Hold on tight, baby," he warned her, and then pulled out; the friction against my cock pulled me out with him, and I rocked my hips to withdraw until just the head was inside her still and then plunged back in, timed perfectly with his thrust, and filled her right back up.

She screamed and moaned as we fucked her hard, pushing her over the cusp of an orgasm within the first ten thrusts. She dug her nails into my pecs and swore a slurry of curse words I'd never heard from her before as she rode us, rocking her hips in time to take us deeper and harder as she climaxed. I felt the wetness of her orgasm coating our dicks as her pussy loosened around us again, sated for the moment.

"I'm close," Parker gasped, every muscle in his chest and neck taut as he fucked her. "You?" He looked over her shoulder at where I was fighting for control at the same time.

"Right there," I grunted, and Rey rolled her hips, rubbing her clit against Trey's fingers.

"Make me come again," she cried, turning her face to Trey and taking the kiss he gave her. "Please, make me come again."

"Good girl," he praised her, holding her tight as she came on his fingers again with our cocks deep inside. "Milk them dry, baby. Drain their cocks."

"That's it," Parker yelled, spanking Rey hard, and I felt his cock jerk against mine as he started coming. It was all I needed to spark my orgasm, and I followed off the edge with him as we filled her pussy so full our come dripped down my cock and onto my balls with each thrust.

"Fuck!" Rey screamed, digging her nails in deep again as she came around us once again. "I'm done," she gasped. "Enough, I can't take any more."

"Okay," Parker panted, pulling out and taking my cock with his as we gave her the break she needed. "Easy, baby girl." He ran his hands up her back as she collapsed into my arms completely, going limp and weak. I held on to her, kissing her damp temple as she panted, coming down from the high of it all.

Eventually, she pulled back and looked at me. "Was that as good as you hoped it would be?" she asked.

I smiled at her and kissed her plump lips. "Better, baby," I admitted. "Every single thing has been better than I could have ever imagined."

CHAPTER 29

Reyna

I sat at the kitchen island, stirring my cup of tea a few days after Dallin and Trey returned from their impromptu bike trip. My head swam with all the changes that had taken place in my life over the last month since Parker and Trey arrived on our doorstep for dinner. I'd been under the impression back then that they were just D's friends, in town for a visit and crashing with us because it was easier than finding a place to stay in the busy tourist district.

Man, had I been wrong.

But I wouldn't have changed any part of it, now looking back. Even if I'd doubted everything I thought I knew about myself those first few weeks.

It had tested my relationship with Dallin, for sure. I had felt inadequate and selfish a few times, as he struggled with his need to pull Trey into the equation even through his own reservations and hang-ups.

And don't even get me started on the guilt I felt the first time I had sex with another man while still desperately in love with D.

It was like grieving something and celebrating something at the same time, but I had no idea how good it would be for us at the time.

Looking back, God.

I was a completely different woman. Loved by not one but three incredible men who brought out different parts of myself with their own differences, and it was so fulfilling to feel so nurtured and complete. Even if it took three men to make me feel that way.

I had never even realized I was missing so much of myself until Parker and Trey brought a new side of me to life.

And having Dallin's unwavering love and support through it, even his insistence on it at the beginning, was invaluable.

"Hey, pretty girl," Dallin called from the front door as he walked in, tossing his keys and wallet down in the dish. I smiled up at him as he walked across the space and leaned over the island to kiss me. "What are you up to?"

"Thinking." I smirked again and hid my smile in my cup as he leaned his elbows onto the stone top and watched me.

"About what?" He raised one brow with a playful smile on his lips.

"About how good life is right now," I admitted. "And how it feels too good to be true."

D sighed and nodded once. "I can relate. But I'm trying to keep that doomsday feel from taking over. Any way I can help you do the same?"

"Hmm." I wondered if there was anything specific he could do for me. "Actually." I sat up straight. "There is."

"What is it?"

"Do you have plans for the rest of the day?" I asked, not wanting to tell him what I needed from him before I knew what he'd be giving up to give it to me. Because he would give it to me. Without hesitating. That was just Dallin's nature, where I was concerned.

"I'm actually free of any plans today." He smirked, raising one brow at me. "Now tell me what you want."

"You." I slid off my stool and rounded the island to his side, sliding my hands around his tight abdomen as I squeezed between him and the counter. "I need some you time." I put my hands in his back pockets, pulling him to me even more. "Maybe a date at our favorite spot?" I asked hopefully. "A couple of hours together uninterrupted should help ease some of this anxiety in me."

He smiled, sliding his hands around my waist and holding on to me as he leaned down and kissed me. "Can I rail you in the office again, like last time?" he asked, speaking of that time he came searching for me at Lost in Time, my best friend's quaint little bookshop. The time when I'd lied and run from him all day until he came and found me.

Just like he did during hide-and-seek the other day.

I felt a rush of adrenaline and warmth spread through my body as I remembered how excited and afraid I'd been to play with the three big wolves, hungry for their next meal in our apartment.

"Does that excite you?" He hummed, running his nose down the side of my face. "I can smell your need like I can smell your perfume."

I moaned, leaning into his touch. "I have a better idea," I replied, panting and digging my nails into his ass through his jeans.

"Than getting railed?" He scoffed, biting my neck. "Can I rail you as well as your other idea?" He flexed his hips and pressed his growing erection into my belly. "I really want to feel you wrapped around my cock right now."

"More than you want to chase me down in the dark before you force your cock into any of my holes?" I mewed, and his entire body stilled against mine and tightened, every muscle locked tight as he dragged his face out of my neck and looked down at me.

"What are you saying?" he asked in a lethally deep voice as his gray eyes dilated until they were black.

"I want to play a game," I whispered, feeling nervous and a bit stupid for asking to be terrorized by him for his pleasure.

But it was for my pleasure too.

He growled and wrapped his long fingers around both of my wrists, pulling them behind the small of my back and pinning them there in one hand. He crouched down until we were eye to eye. "Be very, *very* careful here, Reyna. Don't ask for something you aren't prepared to get."

"I want it." Pulling on the hold he had on my wrists, he tightened his grip, pinning them further behind me, making my breasts arch up into his chest. "I want you guys to chase me like you used to do to each other." I licked my lips, and his eyes followed the motion until his own tongue coated his lips. "I want to be your prey and your prize."

"Rey," he growled, pressing his lips against mine in a feral kiss. "I'm a different man when I'm in that world."

"I want to meet him," I replied instantly.

"He's not a good man."

"Then I want to feel the stain of his touch on my skin." I pushed my hips forward again, and he stood back up tall so I could press my belly back into his cock.

"You're too much of a good girl to be ruined by him, baby." He closed his eyes as I rubbed him through his jeans with my body, unable to remove my hands from behind me.

"You don't see it, do you?" I said, leaning up on my tiptoes to lick the pulse point on his neck before sucking it into my mouth and marking him as he pressed his neck in tighter against my teeth like he craved the pain of my mark. "I'm already ruined. You ruined me when you let another man touch me for the first time," I whispered, kissing my way down his neck. "Now I crave that taboo more than ever. The forbidden and wrong." I pulled my hands up, making me fall back to my toes. "I thirst for what you can give to me, D. Give it to me."

"You want us to chase you through the darkness like a defenseless animal?" he growled. "What happens when we find you? Because we *will* find you, baby."

"If you find me, you pick the prize," I all but begged. "Whatever you want, it's yours."

"You want to be our good little girl, don't you?"

"Yes," I panted, humping the air, desperate to feel his body back against mine.

He wrapped his free hand in my hair, pulled my face up against his, and bit my bottom lip, "Then get on your knees and show me how bad you want it. Show me you deserve to see that side of me."

I had never fallen to my knees so fast in my life. I gasped when my bare bones bounced off the cold wood floor, but it didn't stop me as I ripped at his belt and button, tearing them open and freeing his rock-hard cock into my waiting palm.

"No," he barked. "Hands behind your back. Show me how good your little mouth can be." I crossed my wrists behind my back and leaned forward with my mouth open and tongue sticking out. "There she is," he praised me, fisting the base of his cock and slapping the head of it against my tongue. "Swallow my fucking cock, Rey."

I moaned as I swirled my tongue around the head of him and then spit on it, staring up at him from under my lashes as I pushed my mouth down over him. He instantly pressed against the back of my throat, filling it with his thickness and making me gag.

But he fucking loved that.

So I pulled off, took a deep breath, and did it again, going further and further, over and over. I used every single trick I knew, with only my mouth as I worked him over. His hands were both tangled in my hair as he rocked forward, pushing his cock deep into my throat and holding it there, longer each time.

Tears ran down my face from the torment, and he was getting more feral as he watched each one roll onto my chest.

I put my all into the blow job, focusing on nothing but his pleasure, when I heard the door open into the kitchen behind me, though I didn't stop.

"Whoa," Parker groaned as Dallin's fingers tightened in my hair, forcing me to stay focused on only him. If only he knew I was already right there with him. "What's going on here?"

"I don't know, but I think I'm going to like it," Trey added as they stopped next to us.

"Rey wants to play a game tonight," Dallin said between clenched teeth. "Hide-and-seek."

"Oh, fuck," Trey growled as Parker whistled through his teeth. I felt someone kneel behind me, and then body heat encased me along my back and sides as Trey wrapped himself around me. I grabbed a handful of his shirt in my hand, still held behind my back, and dug my nails into his tight abs as Dallin fucked my throat. He hissed and slid one hand around the front of my throat, putting even more pressure on D's cock each time he went deep. "Are you going to be a good girl or a dirty girl tonight?" he asked into my ear, running the tip of his tongue over the rim and making me shiver.

I was panting, desperate for pleasure as I gave it to Dallin with Trey wrapped around me and Parker standing at D's side, watching it all.

D let me pull off his cock long enough to respond. "Dirty," I gasped. "I want to get dirty tonight." I looked up at Parker as I panted. "Stroke his cock for me, please?" I pleaded, batting my eyes at him until he smirked, already willing to give in to me if it meant touching D.

He turned and wrapped his large hand around D's cock, stroking him with the wetness of my saliva as Dallin moaned deeply. "You like that?" Parker asked D.

"Fuck yes," D replied as I watched in rapture. Seeing D with these two beautifully sexy men would never get old for me. Seeing their masculinity melt away to something else that fell between sensuality and alpha dominance made me weak with desire.

"You enjoy watching them, don't you?" Trey spoke into my ear as his hand tightened around my throat. "You like seeing D with us, like this."

"Yes," I said, nodding as best I could around his hand. "So much. It makes me so wet."

"Did you hear that, D?" Trey called, gaining D's eyes from where they'd been locked on Parker's hand, stroking up and down his cock.

"Our girl says watching you two makes her wet; do you think she's telling the truth?"

D shrugged with a devilish smirk on his face. "Only one way to find out."

I didn't even have time to process his words before Trey let go of my throat and slid both hands to the cuffs on my pajama shorts at my thighs, where they were spread as I knelt, and ripped them clear off me into two pieces. "AH!" I screamed from the violence of it, and then moaned when he cupped my bare pussy, suddenly exposed.

"Fuck," he growled against my ear. "Soaking wet." He bit my earlobe and then patted my thighs. "Squat on your feet, legs spread."

I hopped up off my shins to my feet and spread my legs wide, so I was open and exposed how he wanted me to be. "Now what?" I panted.

"Now you're going to stick that pretty pink tongue out again and let D fuck your throat while I fuck this pretty pussy with my fingers and make you both come at the same time."

D chuckled, turning back to face me as Parker slid behind him, wrapping his arms around his waist to cup his balls and kiss his neck as I eagerly accepted his cock back into my mouth. My thighs started burning as Trey teased my clit and then pushed his fingers into me, but he expected that, and slid his legs underneath mine, cocooning me in and supporting my weight perfectly as I leaned back into his strength.

"You take my cock so good, baby," D crooned, smoothing his hands over my hair and holding my head still as he fucked my mouth. "Such a good girl."

"Our dirty little girl," Trey corrected. His fingers were making wet sounds as they plunged into me at a weird angle, and I was too aroused to be mortified.

"Ours," Parker finalized, as he watched from over D's shoulder, still massaging his balls in time with my blow job. "Our perfect. Good. Little. Dirty. Girl."

"Yes, she is," Trey praised me, biting my neck and tweaking my nipples through my shirt as his fingers hooked and found my G-spot. "She's close too, aren't you?"

"Mmm," I choked out around the thickness in my mouth, and nodded.

"Me too." D quickened his pace. "You suck my cock so good, Reyna. Like a perfect little slut."

That was it. I tightened my hands in Trey's shirt as my entire body snapped like a rubber band, arching into his hand, and taking the entirety of Dallin's cock down my throat in my distraction as my orgasm took over.

"She's coming," Trey growled. "Fuck, her pussy is so tight right now."

"I'm coming," D bellowed, tipping his head back in ecstasy as he brutally fucked my mouth, spraying his come across my tongue and throat.

"Don't swallow it," Parker commanded. "Hold it on your tongue."

D flexed his hips a few more times, filling my mouth so much that it spilled out over my lips thanks to my inability to swallow it per Parker's instructions. Trey kept his fingers in my pussy as he leisurely circled my clit repeatedly, prolonging the orgasmic bliss as long as he could.

When Dallin finally pulled out, Parker sank to his knees in front of me, taking his place, and pulled me in for a kiss, taking Dallin's come into his mouth as he tangled his tongue with mine. Trey pushed my body into Parker's as Dallin growled at the display from above.

It was the hottest kiss of my life.

Never mind the messiest.

But it was so taboo and so hot I was vibrating with arousal even after the incredibly high orgasm Trey had just given me.

When Parker finally pulled back and smiled at me, wiping his thumb over the last drips on my chin, his eyes were glazed over with arousal. "I'm going to have so much fucking fun chasing you tonight, baby girl."

I smiled sleepily, leaning into him as my knees finally gave out and I sank onto the floor in a heap. "I'm going to be easy to catch if you keep my legs this Jell-O during the game."

"She's onto us," Dallin said with a satisfied smile as he tucked himself away into his boxers but didn't do up his jeans. And he looked so fucking sexy. "Come here, baby." He leaned down and picked me up in his arms, carrying me out of the kitchen and to the bedroom.

"Where are we going?" I asked, leaning my head on his shoulder as Parker and Trey followed us.

"Bed," D replied, laying me down in the center of the pillowy bed as he kicked off his jeans altogether and crawled in next to me. "We're all going to take a nap before the game tonight."

Parker slid in behind me and Trey in beside D, wrapping his arms around him as the post-orgasm bliss weighed me down in tiredness.

"I could go for a nap." I smiled sleepily, turning to face Parker as D rested his hand on my hip and let Parker hold on to me under the warm blankets. "I think I'm going to need my rest for what comes after the game more than I will for the game itself."

"You're onto something now," Trey quipped with a smile in his voice as I let Parker's powerful arms and steady heartbeat pull me under completely.

My breath came in quick pants as the surrounding darkness was blinding. I couldn't see a single thing at first, as the headlights of my car faded and left the four of us in blackness.

"It's so dark," I whispered, knowing Parker was somewhere to my right, but having lost track of the other two guys as we walked around the clearing. The more time that passed, the more my eyes finally adjusted to the darkness, leaving me able to make out the stars above us and the distant glow of city lights over the horizon.

"All the better to hunt you in, my dear." Trey's evil voice surprised me right at my ear and I jumped, screeching in fear as he wrapped his muscular arms around me, immobilizing me.

Parker and Dallin chuckled from around us, as I could just make out their silhouettes.

"Tell me." Trey nibbled on my earlobe. "Do you have any panties on under this sexy little dress?"

The white sundress I wore was thin and did little to ward off the humidity in the night air as my skin dampened.

It would make me an easy target in the dark, but that was the point. I wanted to be hunted and found. I wanted to be taken.

Owned.

Possessed.

Kept.

"You'll have to win the game to find out," I countered over my shoulder to Trey, and pulled out his arms as his calloused hands started traveling up my thighs to where panties would be if I were wearing any. I was a whore.

But again, that was the point. I didn't have a bra or panties on under the thin cotton, and with the rain clouds above us threatening to dump at any moment, even in the dark, the dress would still be indecent when it was soaked.

Which just added to the excitement of it for me.

My guys, on the other hand, all wore black and dark colors as they stalked around me in a circle, like they were circling their prey.

"Game is simple," Dallin said as I finally could make out his face in the dark thanks to my slowly adjusting eyes. "You get a two-minute head start. You can run or hide, but when those two minutes are up, we get to chase you." He licked his lips and his teeth glowed brightly in the darkness like a wolf when it was getting ready to attack. "And we won't be gentle when we find you."

I raised my head, challenging him. "I don't want you to be." There was no point in countering them with my demands if I won because I wouldn't be victorious tonight. Yet, in a way, I'd be the one feeling triumphant when it was all said and done.

"Safe word," Parker added in from my right. "If things get to be too much, or you get lost or want to stop for any reason at all, your safe word is *red*."

I snorted and then covered my mouth with my hand to stifle it. He stalked toward me with a menacing look on his face. "Do you have a problem with my safe word?"

I shook my head and fought for control of my emotions thanks to the adrenaline rushing through my body. "Just all the Little Red Riding Hood innuendos." I shrugged. "Red. Got it. But I won't be using it." I declared, "Do your worst to me."

He growled and cracked his neck.

Trey slowly hopped back and forth on the balls of his feet as he smirked in the darkness, and Dallin just stared at me with hunger in his eyes.

My men were feral.

And all mine.

"Go, Little Red," Dallin said with a single eyebrow raised. "Run."

My heart rate skyrocketed as I turned around and bolted without a backward glance. My little white sneakers squelched in the dewy grass as I tore through the manicured lawn of the park we were in, before breaking through the barrier into the tall brush lining the edge of the expansive forest that we hiked every week.

I knew that was why Dallin chose this spot to chase me in. I knew it like the back of my hand, but so did he. He knew the places I liked to hike, and the places I avoided.

So I obviously ran left inside the thick brush line, heading away from the meadow grounds that held special little attractions like rock castles, gardens, and ponds, and instead ran toward the thick woods of the hills. The place I hated the most. The place that always made me feel like a wild animal was lying in wait, stalking through the woods after me when we were here.

God, look at me now. A wild harebrained creature, running for my life from three wild animals hunting me down.

If I had a chance to put any space between us, I had to do it quickly, because they were machines compared to me, and they'd eat up the distance as soon as they were free.

As if on cue, thunder rumbled above me as I climbed in elevation, and the lightning flashed across the sky above the trees. It was magical, eerie, and terrifying all at the same time.

Being in a forest of hundred-year-old trees during a lightning storm was probably the worst idea I'd had in a while, but it didn't matter. I was wild with need and adrenaline; nothing could stop me now.

"Fuck!" I screeched as I spiraled in midair, having caught my toe on a low root sticking out of the ground. I slid across the cold forest floor on my hands and knees, and pain ricocheted up my wrists and across my palms from the impact.

But I never stopped. With the momentum of the fall, I rolled, got back to my feet, and took off without ever halting.

"Little Red!" A haunting voice called from down the hill as I used a thick branch hanging off a tree to propel myself up the hill that was now a near-straight incline toward the sky. "Where are you?"

It was Trey.

Fuck, that was hot.

But I didn't stop. I kept running, using every branch and rock to claw my way up.

They were bigger than I was, with a million more pounds of muscle, but the space between the branches and the ground was small, leaving barely enough space for me to duck and run. Which meant it would slow them down.

My palms burned with each abrasive surface that dug into it from my fall, but I kept going.

The icy cold drops of rain started hitting my skin through the trees about halfway up, nearly evaporating right off my skin as sweat combined with them. I was on fire.

An inferno burned inside me, yet I shivered from fear as the darkness encased me on all sides.

My breath was rapid, and I paused to listen to my surroundings, terrified I'd hear the heavy fall of boots at my heel, but there was nothing.

They weren't near yet.

But then Parker's caramel voice echoed from the surrounding trees. "Baby girl," he sang. "I'm coming for you."

My heart was going to beat out of my chest and I was going to die from cardiac failure. I could see the headlines in my head.

BEST-SELLING LOCAL ROMANCE AUTHOR FOUND DEAD IN POPULAR TOURIST ATTRACTION. SUSPECTED CAUSE OF DEATH? FEAR.

No.

Not me.

My guys wouldn't let that happen to me.

But damn, if they didn't want to eat me like Little Red either way.

"*Rey-na.*" A deep voice echoed from all around me, leaving me unable to tell the direction of origin as panic took full control of my body. It sounded like Trey, but with a hint of wild twist in it.

I turned to the right and took off parallel to the ground, running across the hillside, slapping tree limbs and brush out of my way as logical reason left my brain.

Run.

Escape.

Hide.

The words played on repeat inside my head as I ran. Rain pelted my skin harder with each passing minute. My soaked dress was clinging to my legs and tangling my feet up as I sprinted. My side burned with a cramp from running so hard for so long, but I still didn't stop.

A clearing was up ahead, indicating that I'd made it to one trailhead, and I searched in the driving rain for the hollowed-out tree I'd admired once on a hike to this elevation.

"Where are you?" I whispered in panic as I ran my hands around the trees near the clearing. "Come on, you're here somewhere."

"Little Red!" Trey yelled, and it sounded like he was mere feet behind me. "I can smell that sweet pussy," he jeered. "God, you're going to taste so good on my tongue in a minute."

I nearly squealed with delight when I found the tree I was looking for and dove inside. The cavern was big enough for me to sit on one side, hidden from the opening, but I could see out to the woods and clearing.

"Baby girl!" Parker called again, and I held my hand over my mouth to keep silent. It sounded like he was right on the other side of the tree. I heard a twig snap in the opposite direction and gasped, closing my eyes as I fought to stay silent and control my body.

Where was D?

He had been silent the entire time, and I knew that was part of his game.

God, the man had been feral since exposing yet another side of himself to me. How many other parts had he kept hidden over the years from his partner? What if I wasn't enough to fulfill them all for him?

I'd been lucky enough, up to this point, to be fully on board with the two big revelations about his character: his bisexual side and his primal kink that apparently both Parker and Trey shared.

A dark figure slowly walked in front of the tree opening, and I pressed myself into the darkness even further, clamping my hand down over my mouth even tighter. I couldn't tell who it was from my crouched position, but it was too close for comfort.

I prayed that he'd keep walking by, and after a few seconds I got my wish. He moved on, walking out of sight as Trey's haunting voice carried through the wilderness once again, beckoning me to give myself up to him.

"I promise I'll make it feel so good for you, kitten," he promised.

But I knew better. Because Trey had darkness in his soul, and it would hurt if he found me.

Even if I liked it.

"I'll keep you all to myself," Parker declared, throwing out his own offer. "I'll make them watch as I torture you with pleasure, making you come over and over again before I finally get off myself."

I smiled against my hand, desperate to give in to his sweet side. My Parker was a pleasure Dom. He loved getting me off and doing it sweetly, the spanking in my kitchen aside.

That had been a page out of Trey's and Dallin's books. And it had been so good, too.

"Come on, baby girl. I know you want to give in. I know you want me to find out what's under that little dress," Parker added, sounding even closer.

Before I could even contemplate giving in to him though, the figure from before shut off any moonlight coming in through the opening as he reached in and dragged me out of my hiding spot by my upper arms.

I screamed a primal bloodcurdling scream out of fear as I thrashed in his arms, desperate to get away.

Fight-or-flight consumed me.

I didn't know which one of them had me; my senses were going haywire as he spun me around in the darkness and moved away from the opening to the thickness of the forest, taking me deeper. His hand covered my mouth as I thrashed, fighting his hold on me like a banshee.

Movement caught my eye to my right as Parker stepped out from behind a tree with a wicked smirk on his face. "Fuck, I really wanted to win this one."

"Serves you right for winning in the apartment the other night," Trey added, walking out from the other direction.

Fuck.

That meant D had me.

I started fighting anew, kicking my legs and swinging my arms wildly, desperate to rid myself of the monster on my back while also fighting the urge to bend over right in front of him and beg him to fuck me.

I was warped in the fucking brain because of the three of them.

Dallin pushed me against a wide tree, pressing my face into the rough bark of it as he kicked my feet apart and pressed his front to my back. "I win," he growled against my ear, and I shivered from the menace in it.

"Dallin," I panted, digging my nails into the bark of the tree to ground myself as I fought the urge to fight him even more now.

"My little slut," he growled, biting my ear and rocking his hips against my ass. God, he was so hard. "I told you I'd find you. I'll always find you."

My eyelids fluttered as pleasure and excitement pulsed inside my body. I sagged into him, pressing back against him as my desperation won against my dignity.

"Rope," he barked a second later, and any relief of being found froze to ice with my blood in my veins.

"What?" I gasped, fighting his hold on my head so I could look to where Parker and Trey stood, but he pushed harder, keeping me immobilized.

He wrapped both hands around my wrists and forced me to bear-hug the tree, and then I felt other hands take his place around the thick tree trunk before a soft rope slid over my wrists and tightened almost painfully.

"Fuck, your perfect skin looks good in a red satin rope," Trey growled from the other side of the tree as he did up the rope. Dallin let up the pressure on my head and body, stepping away from my back completely.

I whipped my head around to find Parker staring at me from a few feet away with his hand on his erection, slowly rubbing himself through his wet jeans. He smiled at me and tilted his head to the side. "You're perfection, Reyna."

"Dirty perfection," Dallin said from behind me like a monster in the dark, and I jumped, almost having forgotten that he lurked there, controlling my fate. "A dirty little girl who loves to be spanked, apparently," he added.

I swallowed, trying to figure out the endgame here. A rope wrapped around the back of my knees, pulling them tighter to the tree as Trey tied it on the other side.

They tied me to the tree, leaving me immobilized and terrified.

And wet.

I was dripping fucking wet, and not just from the rain.

My body shivered as I tried to look at Dallin, but he kept dodging me, keeping just out of my line of sight like a mythical creature, somehow making him more terrifying without his familiar features on display to remind me of all his kindness over the years.

"What are you going to do with me?" I asked, pressing my forehead to the tree, giving in to his game and taking a deep breath, fighting to control my body's reaction.

"I'm going to make you beg for mercy," he whispered in my ear, once again right against me. His fingers trailed up the back of my thighs, starting at the tight rope line to the hem of my soaked dress. "I'm going to spank this perfect ass until you fall into subspace and drift nearly unconscious." My eyelids fluttered closed at the prospect of finding that weird lull between consciousness and sleep that Parker had put me into that night. "Then I'm going to fuck you so hard that you wear my marks for weeks." His fingers slid over my bare ass cheeks, and he groaned.

"Dallin," I whimpered, pathetically. "Please."

"Trey," Dallin called, backing up off my body and sliding further behind me. "Our girl isn't wearing any panties. Why don't you take a look?"

"Gladly." Trey slid into Dallin's absent space behind me and then sank down to his knees behind me. I sagged into the tree, suddenly glad for the bindings holding me upright. He lifted my dress and bunched it at my waist, exposing my bare ass. "Hmm," he growled, grabbing each cheek in one of his big hands, and then shaking them. "Ripe like a peach." Then he spread them wide and leaned in so close I could feel his breath against my ass. "Give daddy a taste, sweet girl."

He dived in with his tongue, flicking it over my ass and then down to my pussy, growling as he went. "Fuck," I moaned, bouncing my head off the bark in sweet agony. "Yes."

He hummed as he tortured me, on his knees in the wet forest as he tongue-fucked me toward bliss. "Do you want to come on daddy's tongue?"

"Yes," I cried, nodding desperately. "Please, Trey."

"Hmm," he growled, pulling his tongue from my pussy and biting my ass cheek. "Wrong answer."

"Daddy!" I gasped, anger and shock waging war inside my head. "I'm sorry. Daddy. Yes, daddy."

He stood up and pressed himself against my back, pinning me to the tree with his weight. "You were never going to get off right now. We both know big daddy Dallin wasn't going to let you off that easy." He chuckled before biting my shoulder. "But your taste on my tongue is going to keep me satisfied for a little while longer while he plays with you."

"Please," I begged, closing my eyes to fight off the sudden desire to cry. "I need it."

"I know." He slid his fingers down the length of my crack and found my waiting heat, plunging three fingers deep inside my pussy and making me melt into his arms. "But D won the game, so he makes the rules. But don't worry, baby, I'm going to make you feel so good when he's done with you. You're going to scream my name so loud, Broadway Street will hear you."

I growled ferally as he pulled his fingers from my body and then stepped back, leaving my back cold and wet in his absence.

"Fuck!" I screamed in frustration.

CHAPTER 30

Trey

Her scream vibrated off the surrounding trees, and I smiled in the darkness. Parker looked downright feral as he stood on the other side of the tree, rubbing the erection in his pants, waiting his turn. "Let Parker have a taste," I called out, as Dallin stepped back into her space. D paused and looked over at me questioningly. "He needs a taste; he won't survive an entire session without one." I nodded to where our friend was hanging on by a thread.

Dallin looked to Parker and then nodded to our girl. "Have at it," he offered, and Parker jumped forward, pausing only when Dallin held his finger out in his direction. "She doesn't come," he warned. "If she does, you don't get to the rest of the night."

Parker smirked evilly as he nodded. "Got it, boss."

I wasn't sure what Parker was going to do, but when he undid his jeans and pulled his cock out, crouching just enough behind Reyna and slamming into her without a second's hesitation, her screams of agony caught me off guard.

He smashed into her pussy, holding her throat in his hand as he bit her shoulder, thrusting less than a dozen times before tipping his head back and roaring as he filled her with his come.

Dallin's eyebrows rose, surprised to see how close to losing control Parker had been before letting him use her for his pleasure.

Parker pulled out of her body without any preamble and stumbled back a few steps, not even bothering to put his cock away as come dripped out of the tip still.

Reyna glared at him with daggers and snarled, "Bastard."

Parker chuckled and nodded guiltily. "If you had given yourself to me, I would have made you come three times by now." He tsked with his tongue. "No one to blame but yourself, baby girl." He backed up as she lunged forward with her teeth, desperate to clamp them onto some part of him out of revenge.

He walked over to my side to watch the show again, a little calmer.

"You good?" I asked, looking out of the corner of my eye before giving Reyna my attention again as Dallin ran his palms over her lush ass.

"I was going crazy there, man." He shook his head. "I can't explain it."

"She has that effect on us all," I admitted, trying to reason with him.

"Yeah," he chuckled, "him especially." He nodded to Dallin as he reared back and laid a forceful slap to her ass, drawing a startled scream from her lips.

My cock hardened even more as her flesh rippled and her body fought her bindings.

"One," she whispered after a breath, following the directions he'd given her.

"Fuck, I'm going to get hard again," Parker groaned, stroking his still-exposed dick as Dallin peppered her other ass cheek, drawing another string of screams from her lips.

"Four." She gasped, sagging into the tree. "Five."

"I'm going to marry that girl," I said, not even caring who heard. "I'm going to lock her down for the rest of her life."

Parker chuckled while Dallin panted behind our girl, with a wild look in his eyes as her words started slurring as he made her beg for another.

"Same, man." Parker held his fist out for me to bump and I shook my head, doing it while never taking my eyes off our girl. "She's bloody fucking perfect."

"I can't believe I almost missed out on this."

"I just thank the divine who intervened and put the two of them on the same path that night two years ago."

I nodded, struggling to find the anger that I used to feel when I thought back to seeing them together a few years ago when I came back for D. It didn't exist anymore because in its place was the love I'd found for her after getting to know her.

"Nine," she moaned, as her head lolled off her shoulder. "Please, can I have another one?"

"You're such a good girl," Dallin praised her, giving her the tenth slap and sinking to his knees behind her, spreading her cheeks and tasting her like I had. "Fuck, you're so sweet." He pushed fingers into her cunt, fucking them up into her as she sagged against the ropes helplessly, moaning and begging to come.

I took my place next to her and kissed her shoulders, rubbing them to ease the discomfort of being bound around the tree as he pushed her over the edge of her orgasm. "You're so perfect, Rey," I whispered into her ear, as Parker took her other side. "Come for D, baby. Be our good little slut and come so hard."

She was screaming incoherently, begging and pleading as D nodded to us, and we instantly cut her free. He caught her before she fell and carried her over to a downed log the size of a couch and laid her on her back over the natural curve of it, letting her head hang off one side while her legs parted instinctively as he pushed his jeans down, desperate to be inside her.

"I'm going to fuck this pussy so good," D growled, lining up as I stood over her head and played with her perfect fucking tits through her soaked dress. I needed them in my mouth, so I ripped her dress open, exposing them to my hungry tongue, and took a bite as D sank deep inside her.

"Fuck, you're so sexy," Parker praised her, straddling the log next to her like he was sitting on top of a wall. He held her thighs up and spread them wide as Dallin brutally fucked her. I sucked on her nipples, biting them just how she liked, and pinched them until they were rock hard against the icy rain that soaked us all.

She slid her hand up my crotch until she wrapped her hand around my cock and fought with the zipper. I took pity on her, not even bothering to pretend I didn't want her touching me, and helped her free my cock. She pulled me by it until I straddled her face and pushed deep into her mouth.

"Fuck," I groaned, bracing my hands on the log on each side of her waist as I thrust in and out of her mouth.

"That's such a good girl," D rasped. "Suck Trey's cock so good, baby." He took her legs from Parker and pressed them back toward her chest, folding her how he wanted. Parker took the opportunity to fill his hands with one of her breasts and her clit, strumming it perfectly in time to Dallin's deep thrusts until she was pushing me out of her mouth and screaming to the treetops again.

"I need to fuck her again," Parker said, stroking his cock next to her tits, zoned out on the lush mounds as they swayed with each thrust D gave to her. "Like I *need* to fuck her." He leaned down and sucked one nipple into his mouth. "Can I fuck you, baby girl?"

"Get the fuck in line," I growled, pushing my cock down her throat again so she couldn't tell him yes, because I knew her, she'd always tell Parker yes. She was soft for his sweetness.

But I needed to silence her niceties with my darkness.

"Oh my God," Rey cried, reaching up blindly and fisting Dallin's shirt. "Make me come, I need you to fill me up. Give it to me," she demanded, and any resolve he had evaporated.

His thrusts became even more punishing, her golden skin reddened from the abrasiveness of the log underneath her with each rocking motion. But she never safe-worded or cried out for mercy. No, not our girl.

Our girl held on to my thighs and braced herself so she could meet each of his powerful thrusts while she sucked one of my balls into her mouth and then licked my taint, like a fucking pro.

And D lost his ever-loving mind. He grabbed her breasts, squeezing them in his hands until the skin turned molten and angry, and held her where he wanted as he slammed home one last time and bellowed into the night air on his release. She was right there with him, chasing him through bliss and begging for even more.

"Over here." Dallin nodded to a spot that was cleared out underneath a giant pine tree. He picked her up, effectively pulling her off my cock again, and I growled intensely at him, daring him to fucking try it again. But he just winked at me. "Careful, or I won't let you have her pussy while Park takes her ass."

"Oh, shit." Parker hopped off the tree eagerly, giving chase to the duo as Dallin held her up, still impaled on his cock as his come leaked down onto his balls.

"Take your jacket off and lay it down for her knees." Dallin nodded to the pine-needle-covered forest floor, and I took off my bomber jacket, fanning it out and making a spot for her before lying down on it on my back. My cock stood up like a tree in the forest, ready and desperate to feel her warmth strangling it.

"Come here, Little Red." I held my hands out as D set her on her feet next to me. She smiled sweetly as she nearly collapsed in my lap, but managed to straddle my hips with her knees on my jacket.

She was a mess. Her dress was ripped down to her belly button, and the skirt was twisted up above her hips, leaving her tits and cunt on display. Mud streaked her hands and legs from running during the chase, and she had leaves and debris in her wet hair.

"You're the most beautiful woman in the world," I whispered to her, pulling her down to press her cold nipples against my warm chest. "You want to take Parker and me together?"

"Yes," she moaned, biting her lip and nodding to me. "Do you want to feel him inside me at the same time?"

"Fuck yes, I do," I smirked, lifting her hips just enough so the head of my cock could nudge against her pussy opening. "Sink down onto me, Little Red. Take the big bad wolf's big cock."

She moaned, doing what I said and taking me deep in one smooth thrust. Dallin's silky release coated her pussy for the invasion, and she felt so good, swallowing me up. "Coming in hot," Parker joked from above as he lowered himself to his knees behind her, rubbing his hands up and down her ass as I started thrusting into her. I heard him lubing up, always the boy scout coming prepared with his trusty bottle of ass-fuckery fun. "Hold still, baby girl," he said as he pressed his cock against her ass, and she stilled.

"Look at me." I drew her attention to my eyes and forced her to focus on just me. I dropped my hips and let most of my cock come out, so Parker had room to fit. "Deep breaths with me." I inhaled and so did she, before leaning down to kiss me.

"Kiss the fear away," she whispered against my lips, and I did just that.

Parker pushed inside her ass, going slowly past each barbell, until he was balls deep. His balls were so fucking big they hung down against mine and sort of massaged them each time he thrust in and out. "You like that, daddy?" he smirked over her shoulder, sensing the pleasure he was giving me without even trying.

"'Bout as much as you do," I grumbled, sliding my hands back over Reyna's hips and pushing up into her in time with him.

All three of us groaned.

"D," Rey gasped, looking around for him in the darkness. "Where are you?"

"I'm here," he called, kneeling at her side and pushing her wet hair back affectionately. "Do you have any idea how sexy you are taking them both deep into your body like this?"

"I need you too," she begged, licking her lips and looking down at his still-undone jeans. "Can I suck your cock? Please?"

He groaned and ran his thumb over her bottom lip as I tweaked her nipples and Parker bottomed out hard. "Whatever you want, it's yours," he finally conceded, like he had wanted this moment to be just between the three of us, while he sat to the side. But that wasn't how she liked it. It was always all of us.

All the time.

"I want three cocks inside my body at the same time." She smirked with naughty mischief and stuck her tongue out, waiting for him to oblige her; even so, he hesitated.

"Come on, big guy." I reached between his knees and found the head of his cock, hard and poking out against the top band of his underwear, thanks to his impressive length. I wrapped my fist around him and pulled him free, stroking him in time with my thrusts into Rey's pussy. "Look at how he's leaking for you again already," I mused, rubbing my thumb over the head of D's cock, collecting the come that beaded up there.

"Taste it," Rey whispered, and Parker chuckled behind her, leaning over her back so he was close and part of the conversation.

"You want Trey to suck D's cock?" Parker quipped, and Reyna nodded with a nervous look on her face. "If you want it, I want to hear you say it," he declared, pushing her further out of her comfort zone.

"I want to watch Trey suck on Dallin's cock." She looked up at Dallin, biting her bottom lip. "Is that okay?"

D smirked and nodded. "Whatever you want," he repeated.

I grinned, already knowing I was going to wrap my lips around his cock if she wanted me to. It wasn't like I hadn't given him head before, even if it wasn't something I did often.

"Whatever she wants," I echoed, and pulled him forward by his cock, still in my hand and leaking more now as he stared down at me. "Fuck my mouth for our girl, D," I said, then swirled my tongue over the head of him, while still thrusting into Rey, a little slower as I focused on D's pleasure, too. I teased him with just the tip of my tongue before he pushed the head into my mouth completely, filling me up with his thickness right away.

Rey's eyes were mesmerized as she watched us like she wasn't even paying attention to the two cocks fucking her pussy and ass at the same moment.

Until her eyes rolled, and she orgasmed, tightening around us both.

And I was done. I let my head fall back onto the ground as Parker's thrusts changed tempo, speeding up as he neared his orgasm and I fell over the edge of mine.

"That's it," Rey moaned. "Fill me up."

"Fuck." D was stroking his cock now that I was incapable of sucking on him anymore. But Rey took my place, opening her mouth as the first burst of come erupted from the tip. "Take it, baby," D commanded her, holding her jaw open with his thumb on her bottom teeth as he covered her tongue with it.

"Jesus," Parker chirped. "How the fuck did I last the longest?" he joked, having spent himself at some point during all the other coming. He slowly withdrew from Rey's ass and collapsed on the forest floor next to me with a smug look on his face.

"Um, probably because you came like five seconds into the whole thing," Rey deadpanned, glaring at him as she gently stood up, pulling her dress down and covering her bare breasts as she shivered.

"Sorry about that." Parker winked at her and rose to his feet. "Would you forgive me if I told you I packed you a fresh change of warm clothes in the car?" He shrugged his jacket off and tossed it over her shoulders, shielding her from the worst of it.

"You did?" She stared up at him dreamily and I rolled my eyes and groaned as I got to my feet. "You're so sweet, Parker."

He grinned his megawatt smile down at her, and Dallin shook his head knowingly.

"Was it as good as you remembered it to be?" I asked D, who nodded slowly.

"I think it was better." He looked at Rey with Parker's jacket and beefy arm slung over her shoulders, tucked into his side. "I think everything these days is better."

"I agree." She winked with that just-railed-seven-ways-to-Sunday dreamy look in her eyes. "But can we go home and take a hot shower and spend the rest of the night in bed?"

"Hmm." I scratched my jaw. "Only if you wash my hair with that jasmine shampoo of yours." I grinned. "It smells amazing."

She chuckled and took my hand in hers as we turned to walk out of the woods and back down to the car. "I think I can handle that."

EPILOGUE I

Reyna

"Breathe, kitten," Trey said for the hundredth time.

"I am breathing, asshole," I snapped, squeezing the cushioned seat beneath my ass with my fists, wishing it were harder so maybe the pain of squeezing it would distract from the pain Trey was inflicting on me.

"Almost done."

"Thank God," I groaned, staring at the wall over his head like I could disassociate from it all if I pretended he wasn't even here.

"Done," he said, standing back and staring at his work of art. "They're going to lose their fucking minds." He shook his head with a smirk. "How do you feel?"

"Like I want to stab metal through something important on you for revenge," I threatened, arching my back and testing the movement to see what hurt and what didn't.

"Hmm." He stared at my two brand-new piercings with thick lust in his blue eyes. "I'll let you pierce whatever you want if I get to be the first one to slide my cock between those sexy tits once your nipples heal." He groaned, "God, you're so sexy."

"Not now," I whined, sliding off the bench in his tattoo suite and walking over to the mirror to see. I twisted side to side a couple of times as the light glinted off the two new diamond-studded barbells through my poor nipples. "Wow." I hesitated, as the pain faded and excitement took its place. "They look—" I tilted my head to the side, trying to come up with the right word as Trey slid his arms around my stomach and rested his chin on my head. "Hot."

He smirked and gently cupped the weight of my tits in his hands as he admired his work again while simultaneously fondling his favorite part of me. "The guys are going to lose their minds," he repeated.

"Let's go give Parker his birthday present."

"Let's." He helped me put my loose sleep tank back on and then opened his suite door and held my hand as we crossed the dark and empty shop toward the private stairwell that led to our place upstairs.

The four of us had lived together for six months now, and today was Parker's birthday, so I finally folded to my bad-girl desire to get my nipples pierced and let Trey do it for me as one of my gifts to our favorite sweet lover.

Trey walked into the apartment ahead of me, yelling for the guys to come to the living room while shielding me from their view.

"What's up?" Parker asked as he came in. "It's rude to steal a man's girl on his birthday."

"I think you'll thank me later," Trey joked. "Both of you sit down on the couch and close your eyes."

I could almost feel Parker and Dallin look at each other in confusion before I saw them move to the couch from around Trey's shoulder. When they were settled with their eyes closed, we joined them in the living room. I bit my bottom lip and gently kneeled on the couch in Parker's lap, straddling his thick, muscular thighs. "Keep your eyes closed," I commanded, sliding my hand over Dallin's arm to ground him with us, including him.

"I'll do whatever you want me to do, baby girl," Parker smirked with his eyes closed as his big hands rubbed over the swell of my ass in seductive circles.

"I did something for your birthday present." I hesitated, worried about their reaction now that I'd permanently altered my body for them. Parker had been the one to get me the twist-on nipple rings, and it had been such a big hit with all three of the guys that I knew I had to pull the trigger and pierce them. Not only had they loved them, but I also loved the look of them, too. I just had to keep reminding myself of that as they throbbed in pain.

"Did what, exactly?" Parker scowled a bit, hearing the trepidation in my voice, and Trey chuckled from the other side of Dallin, where he sat, enjoying the show.

"Open your eyes," I whispered, and both he and D opened them, looking at me in confusion. I lifted the edge of my sleep tank and held it out for him with a small smile on my lips before shimmying my shoulders to draw his attention to my nipples. "Open your present and see what it is."

Their eyes flicked down to my breasts and Dallin hissed audibly, squeezing my hand as Parker's mouth popped open in surprise, but he remained silent. He tilted his head to the side, like he was daring me to be lying to him before he slowly, and gently, thank God, lifted my shirt to reveal my bare breasts.

"Holy fucking shit," Parker finally whispered, staring right at my nipples. "You pierced these?" He squeezed my hips like he was restraining himself from touching them. "For me?"

"Mm-hmm." I nodded, looking at Dallin, and shivering when I saw the hunger in his eyes as he looked between my chest and my face. "Do you like them?" I asked them both.

"Fuck yes," Parker groaned, and I felt his arousal under my ass. "But you realize I won't be able to touch them for weeks. Months maybe."

"I know." I nodded. "I guess you'll just have to find other parts of my body to touch in the meantime." I smiled when he leaned forward and kissed me, using his signature sweet and sensual touch to steal my breath and cause shivers of excitement to cover my entire body. When we finally parted, I whispered against his lips, "Happy birthday, baby."

"Best birthday ever," he whispered back, and then pulled back and looked at D. "You're quiet."

"I'm giving you a moment," D replied through clenched teeth. "Because when I finally make my move, I'm not letting either of you near her for hours."

Exhilaration crackled through my body as I lifted my shirt off all the way, tossing it onto the floor before holding my hands out for D. He took the opportunity and pulled me off Parker's lap with a strong grip around my waist and set me on his thighs, pulling me forward until I sat directly on top of his erection.

"What do you think?" I asked, running my hands up his chest and around to the back of his neck, anchoring myself to him.

"I think I've never been more fucking amazed by you in my life." He slowly shook his head. "And I think I'm jealous as fuck that you let Trey do it without me."

"I wanted to surprise you," I whispered, trying to soften the blow. "Don't be mad."

"'Mad' isn't the word, sweetheart," he growled, leaning in to kiss the flesh of my breast, trailing his tongue down between them without ever touching the sensitive wounds. "Feral," he said, biting his lip, leaning his head back against the couch cushion, and swallowing. The muscles of his neck worked in that sexy manly way that always made me tingle, and I shifted in his lap. "I'm positively feral for you right now."

"Fuck," I moaned, jumping in his arms as a sudden vibrating ignited inside my pussy. "Trey!" I gasped, snapping my head around to look at him as Parker and Dallin followed suit.

"What?" Trey shrugged with a shit-eating grin on his face and his phone in his hand. "I was feeling left out." He tapped his thumb on his phone screen, and I moaned a throaty, deep growl I didn't even know I was capable of making as my head tipped back. The combination of vibrations and pulses was atomic inside me. "Oh," he laughed. "Did she not mention that she fought the pain with endorphins and orgasms while I pierced those sexy nipples?" He flashed his phone screen to the guys.

"I'm going to kill you," I moaned, shifting on Dallin's erection to rub my clit against the hardness as desire once again filled my system.

"I have an idea." Parker smiled as he kissed my shoulder.

"I'd like to hear it, birthday boy," I whimpered as I dug my fingernails into his arm, clinging to him.

"It involves you, laid back, coming on that toy you love to wear so much." He nodded to the spot between my legs that I was actively rubbing against D. "And the three of us taking turns fucking each other to release some of this pent-up feralness." He winked at Dallin, who shrugged, unbothered by his jab. "As Dallin put it so plainly. That way, we don't hurt your pretty new piercings."

"I like the sound of that," I purred, excited to watch the three guys play. "Under one condition." I gave a sultry look to all three of them before I continued. "You can't hold back. I need to see you all fuck like you do when I'm not around."

Trey smirked, already nodding as the other two contemplated it for a bit longer. "I'll fuck 'em hard for you, kitten," Trey agreed.

Parker snorted and shook his head. "It's my birthday." He stood up, pulling me to my feet as Dallin snatched the phone out of Trey's hand and turned the settings on the toy down so I could stand up. "If anyone is going to be taking it rough, it's you, pretty boy."

Trey and Parker headed toward the bedroom, stripping their clothes off as they went as Dallin pulled me into his arms, careful to avoid any friction against my tits as he leaned down and kissed me. "I love you," he whispered against my lips.

"I love you, too." I smiled, leaning into him and taking a deep breath. "Thank you for bringing them into my life."

He smirked and rolled his eyes before slinging his arm over my shoulder and pulling me toward the bedroom after our two mischievous boyfriends. "I think you've been a saint to deal with all of us, for sure," he joked. "But you're welcome, nonetheless."

"Do me a favor?" I purred, sliding my hands around his waist.

"Anything."

We just cleared the doorway to the bedroom, where Trey and Parker were both pulling my favorite throw pillows off our new custom bed that was the size of two king mattresses put together in a rich mahogany wood frame with posts and white linen drapery hung above it. I loved how romantic the bed looked, and the guys loved how much room they had to sleep with all four of us in it, even if they were usually cuddling around me, anyway.

"Come on, you two," Trey called, pushing his pants down and stroking his thick cock as he eyed us up. "I've got some primal kinkery to work out on someone." He smirked, and Dallin rolled his eyes.

"He put two needles through my nipples with a smile on his face," I deadpanned. "Make it fucking hurt for him." I kissed Dallin's neck as he tipped his head back and laughed boisterously. "At least a little."

"You got it, sweetheart." He kissed me deeply, using his tongue to tease my lips the way I loved before nibbling on them. "I'll make him beg for mercy before the night is through."

"Good boy." I smiled against his lips.

"What are you two chatting about over there?" Parker asked with a questioning glance as he kneeled on the edge of the bed.

"Oh, just how if you hold Trey down and help Dallin make it hurt for him for hurting me, I'll give you the best birthday blowy of your life."

"Hey!" Trey scowled, putting his hands on his hips in outrage. "You wanted them pierced!"

"Deal!" Parker yelled as he leaped off the bed and onto Trey's back, knocking him straight to the floor under his weight.

"Fuckers!" Trey yelled, fighting back as Dallin walked over and grabbed his ankles, twisting his belt around them with lightning speed.

"Just stay still and we'll make it quick." D chuckled.

I crawled up on the bed and lay back, watching the three of them horse around like a bunch of teenage boys who had a lifetime of shenanigans ahead of themselves and a couple of decades of history to fall back on.

And I felt at home as a piece of it.

EPILOGUE II

Dallin

"Bro, you can't be serious," Trey groaned as we walked down the street toward the jeweler's.

"What the fuck is that supposed to mean?" Parker snapped angrily from my other side as I simply rolled my eyes.

"This place is too mainstream for Rey," Trey scoffed. "She's too—" He paused. "Unique." He shook his head. "No, that's not the right word. Eclectic?" He groaned, throwing his arms up in frustration at the game of word twister he was playing with himself. "This ain't it."

"I just want to look." I kept walking forward.

"She deserves something that's not on every other finger in the fucking world," Trey argued.

"What do you recommend, then?" Parker quipped. "Should we go find her one made of a fork at a flea market that no one else in the world has the exact same kind of? Rey deserves a fucking diamond the size of Texas for putting up with our asses. I support this decision, D."

I chuckled, shaking my head again at their ridiculous banter, wondering how the fuck we ended up here. But as I reached for the door handle to go inside, Trey pushed my hand away and blocked my path.

"Dude," I snapped, getting angry. "We talked about this." I glared at him. "At length. We're proposing. Sooner rather than later."

"I know that, fuckwad." Trey glared back. "Cookie-cutter shit ain't it, though."

"You don't even know what they have." I tried reasoning with the black cloud blocking the door. "I just want to look and see what options we have in the first place. This whole thing is unconventional; we don't know how we're going to make it work in a single piece of jewelry anyway."

Trey held my stare but didn't move. "It doesn't feel right getting it here. I don't think you understand how strongly I feel about this."

I took a deep breath and forced myself to take his input into account, given that he was a quarter of our relationship, and his feelings were important.

"Okay," I sighed. "What do you suggest, then?"

"Custom-made rings." He pulled his phone out, and Parker groaned next to us, leaning against the window to the shop as he waited to hear Trey out. "There's this shop right here in Nashville that works with you from the very beginning through the process to create a masterpiece for your girl. I'm talking from the stone size and cut and shit to the band material and design and setting, everything." He was talking quickly and using his hands animatedly as he flicked through some pictures on their website.

"You're really pressed on this." I held his stare until he dropped his phone and nodded.

"I owe everything in the world to our girl, D." He swallowed and took a deep breath. "Without her, and her grace and complete faith in me, I wouldn't have this." He looked from me to Parker and back. "I would be alone on the road without even Parker anymore." His dark eyes were full of emotion as he all but pleaded with me. "I just think she deserves more from us in this commitment than for us to walk into a big chain store and pick out some generic ring that we had no hand in making."

Parker crossed his arms and shrugged at me when I looked at him. "He kind of has a point."

I scoffed and ran a hand over my face. "I agree. Reyna deserves the world and the stars above. I just didn't realize that this felt so impersonal until you threw your hissy fit," I joked with Trey, trying to lighten the mood. "Where is this custom shop?" I nodded at his phone.

"Across town." He smirked. "They're open until seven."

"Not that you planned this or anything." I rolled my eyes, turning away from the big chain jeweler's and walking back to where we parked our bikes on the street. "Lead the way, daddy," I said, calling him the nickname Rey used on him when he went all predator on her.

"But let's hurry," Parker added, throwing his leg over his iron horse. "I have a sexy date tonight that I need to get spruced up for." He winked, rubbing it in that he was whisking Rey away for a night of sweet and sensual romance at a swanky hotel downtown with a spa and elegant room service. What he didn't know, though, was that Trey and I had broken our cardinal rule of uninterrupted individual time within our poly relationship, and booked the room right next door while also secretly extending his reservation through tomorrow night as well.

He could wine and dine and fuck our girl ten ways to Sunday tonight, but when the clock struck midnight, Trey and I were breaking in and taking our places with our divine girl and our sweet guy, and neither of them was walking out of that expensive hotel without a limp of some sort in two days.

EPILOGUE III

Trey

"Will you tell me where we're going?" Reyna asked, fussing with the edge of her blindfold for the hundredth time since I put it on her at the apartment.

"Not yet." I took her hand and kissed her knuckles. She looked incredible in a tight red dress that hugged her delicious curves like a second skin and made me ache to remove it for her with my teeth.

"I can't run, you know that, right?" she huffed. "This dress is impossible to run in, so if you're planning on dropping me off somewhere in the woods and playing with me, I'm going to be really mad."

I chuckled and pulled her Jeep into the parking lot of the swanky hotel we thought of as our special place within Nashville for nights away. Parker stole her away a few months ago intending to twist her up in all sorts of Kama Sutra positions all night long, but Dallin and I were waiting for him right next door, with our own plans for the two of them.

My body tightened at just the memory of listening to the two of them crying out in pleasure as Dallin and I edged them for hours before sinking into their bodies simultaneously.

"Trey?" she said, drawing my attention back to the present as she looked at me even though her eyes were covered. "Did you hear me?"

"The only place I'm chasing you tonight is over the edge of ecstasy the first time I push inside your perfect body," I reassured her, and her shoulders relaxed a little.

"Are you trying to romance me, Trey Myers?" she asked with a smirk on her bright-red-painted lips.

What I wouldn't do to smear her pretty lipstick right now.

My phone buzzed with yet another text from D, making sure we were on track for the master plan.

"Is it working?" I asked, turning off the Jeep and leaning over until my lips were hovering right beneath her ear so my breath could tickle the sensitive flesh there.

"Yes," she whispered, smiling into the darkness she didn't even know surrounded her.

"Good. Let's go so I can woo you the rest of the night." I pressed a chaste kiss to her neck and then got out of the Jeep before she could question anything else and walked around to her side. On cue, the side entrance to the hotel opened, and Parker stood silhouetted in the bright hallway light as I helped Rey get out of the Jeep. "Careful," I warned her, and then pressed her body into my side, holding her tight as we walked up the pathway to the private entrance. Parker stayed silent as I pushed the button on the elevator, standing behind us like an ominous figure.

But I knew better than to think he'd stay that way for long.

As we walked into the elevator, he stood behind us, watching us in the reflective mirrored walls as the car started ascending to the top floor.

"Are we in an elevator?" Rey asked.

"Maybe." I toyed with her as I watched Parker lean forward and silently press his nose into the side of her neck on her opposite side and take a sniff. "Ah!" she shrieked, finally feeling his presence, and then melted into his touch when he chuckled in her ear and pressed himself against her back. "Parker," she panted as the fear receded. "What are you doing here?"

"I thought I'd pay Trey back for interrupting our night away a few months ago." He ran his hands down her body and growled. "My God, Reyna, you look divine in this dress."

"Mmm." She leaned into him while keeping her hold on me tight. "Wait until you see what I wore underneath it," she teased.

I reacted instantly, pulling her out of his arms and spinning her around until her back pressed against the wall with my body caging her in. "You wore something special for me, kitten?" I growled, and her red lips parted as she pushed back against me. "Care to divulge what it is?"

"You'll have to wait until after my show," she purred. "I guess Parker can watch too."

"Show?" Parker pushed his way in against the wall and nibbled on her earlobe. "What show?"

"The striptease I planned for tonight." She bit her bottom lip. "Lap dance included."

I growled and pressed my erection against her stomach. "Change of plans. Parker, get lost."

"Not on your life," he argued, and wrapped his hand around the front of her throat. She still couldn't see anything, and I think that heightened everything for her and us as she panted in our arms. "Dallin is going to go feral for you tonight, baby girl."

"Mmm. I was hoping D was here too." She bit her bottom lip and then ran her hands down the front of our bodies to our erections and squeezed. Before she could take it further, though, the elevator stopped, and the doors opened, revealing the very feral and dominant man waiting for us in the suite's lobby with a dark look on his perfect face.

"Change of plans," I growled. "I'm keeping her and her sexy lap dance for myself."

"Reyna," Dallin called gravely, and her body melted further.

"There's plenty of me to go around, boys." She hummed seductively, pushing us both back off her. "Can I take this off yet?" Her hand rose to the blindfold, but Parker caught it and pulled it back down.

"Almost, baby girl." He kissed her cheek. "It will be worth it, I promise."

She lightly chuckled and let us lead her from the elevator and into the suite. The boys had been busy, I'd give them that.

The suite was covered in flower petals and sensually scented candles that reminded me of the way Reyna's skin smelled when she was horny, causing me to draw a deep breath in.

"Where are we?" she whispered in awe, taking in the atmosphere through her other senses.

"Almost," I said, placing her on the spot in the center of the large living room that had been transformed for this moment. "Okay." I lifted my fingers to the tie behind her head and loosened it, gently pulling it free of her face before taking my spot next to Dallin in front of her.

I watched her eyelids flutter as she adjusted to the light in the room and looked around. Her chest rose in awe as she took it all in. "What in the world?" she whispered, looking between the three of us and then back out over the romantic setting.

"We thought maybe we could spend the evening romancing you, the way you write all of those swoony book boyfriends doing all the time," Parker announced with a grand show of spreading his arms, like she could miss the display.

"I knew you read her books when no one was looking," I whispered, and Dallin elbowed me in the gut.

"Duh," Parker tossed back. "How else do you expect me to keep coming up with new ways to get you two out of the doghouse all the time?"

"Enough," Dallin barked, making Reyna giggle into her hand as her eyes got misty. "Sweetheart." He held his hand out and pulled her into our circle. "There's something we've been trying to find the right way to ask you for quite some time."

Her eyes rounded as she looked up at him before they flicked to each of us in uncertainty.

"We can't seem to agree on anything, ever," I started, taking her other hand and running my thumb over her knuckles. "But the one thing that hasn't faltered for us, even when I was trying to be a stubborn asshole and hide it even from myself, was how much you mean to us."

"How perfect you are for us," Parker added.

"How blessed we are to have you in our lives, every single day," Dallin finished. "Which has brought us here."

He licked his lips and pulled the black leather ring box out of his pocket that Parker had picked out, and we all three slowly sank to our knees in front of our woman.

She gasped and covered her mouth with her hands, as tears rolled down her eyelashes and onto her blushed cheeks.

"Reyna, my love," Dallin swallowed.

"Kitten," I added with a smirk, as she let out a breathy giggle.

"Baby girl," Parker inserted.

"Will you do us the honor of committing the rest of your life to the three of us, promising to keep us a solid unit of four for however long the almighty deems us worthy of this life?" Dallin asked, and Parker and I stayed silent, none of us breathing as we waited for her response.

She sank to her knees in front of us, nodding as she started sobbing harder, and we all engulfed her in our arms, desperate to feel her body against ours like it would help make it feel more real.

"Yes!" she cried after a while, pulling back and kissing each of us before wiping away her tears. "Yes, a million times over."

"Thank God!" Parker cheered.

"And Satan," I added, drawing another giggle from her lips at our inside joke, before Dallin rose, pulling her to her feet and into his arms.

"I know legally we can't do this the way we want to," he explained as we all stood in one embrace. "But without you, we don't exist. You're the very center of our lives, and however it's recognized by the law, we'll know, from this moment on"—he slid the ring out of the ring box and put it onto her left ring finger as more tears started anew—"that you belong to us, and we belong to you."

"Oh my God," she cried, looking down at the custom piece I'd demanded to be made for her when Dallin and Parker first started looking for rings. Because by that point, I'd already been looking for one for months. I knew that day in the woods, our very first game of hide-and-seek, that she was the only woman I'd ever hold in my arms, ever again. And I was ready to commit to her.

And the ring we designed displayed that perfectly.

Three bands of platinum metal twisted together, all three encrusted with bright white diamonds to one point in the center where a giant round stone was set, handpicked by the three of us to match the beauty in Reyna's eyes, sat, twinkling.

"It's perfect." She looked up at us. "I've never seen anything more perfect in my life, you guys."

"Nailed it." I fist-pumped the sky before pulling her out of Dallin's arms and into mine. "It was all my idea."

"Jesus Christ," Dallin groaned as Parker slapped his forehead in exasperation, but I didn't care. Because it made our girl smile.

"I love you," she whispered, kissing me deeply, and my body ignited again to the inferno that had been burning in the elevator, but she slid from my arms before I could caveman-carry her to the bedroom without them. She did the same to Dallin, and ended with Parker, giving us the attention we desperately ached to get from her after such a momentous occasion. "Can I tell you a secret?" she whispered tentatively, stepping back to stand in front of us all. "I feel a little silly now, in hindsight."

"Uh-oh." I cocked my head to the side, and Dallin raised his brows at her, and Parker prepared for the worst.

"I did something today," she admitted, chewing on that bottom lip as she looked at Dallin. "And I think you're going to be a little mad at me for it."

I felt the shift in Dallin's body through the air, without ever taking my eyes off Rey as she twisted her fingers together in front of her as our new ring glowed brightly in the candlelight.

"What did you do?" D asked deeply, not sounding like himself at all.

"I—" She hesitated and took a deep breath. "I had a private session with Lex this morning," she rushed out on the exhale. "While you three were busy setting this all up apparently."

"Lex." Dallin growled, taking a step forward. "So help me God, if that woman touched your skin with a tattoo machine, I'm tearing her limb from limb." He took another step, wrapped a hand around the back of Reyna's neck, and pulled her to his chest. "And I'll spank you so fucking hard you won't be able to sit down for a week."

Reyna ran her hands up his chest, trying to soothe him as the monster inside him took control at just the thought of someone else tattooing her untouched skin. I, on the other hand, hardened to a fucking brick, thinking about seeing new ink on our girl.

"Where is it?" I asked, smiling devilishly down at our girl, knowing she was about to get a punishment, but that it would be so worth it to reward her after, depending on what ink she got.

"What is it?" Parker questioned, with a dark brow raised over his almost-black eyes.

"That's the fun part." She gasped as Dallin's hand tightened in her hair. "You'll have to let me do what I planned to do in the first place to find it."

"The striptease?" I asked, shrugging off my jacket instantly and looking around for a place to sit. "I got a lap for you to grind on right here, kitten."

She giggled but turned her attention back to Dallin, who hadn't moved or spoken since his original threat. "I got the purple Möbius symbol of polyamory on my ribs," she said tentatively. "With your names on each side of the triangle, signifying exactly who holds my heart."

"I need to see it," he demanded. "I was supposed to be the only one to ever brand your skin." He closed his eyes like he was fighting a war. "You let Trey pierce you, and now you've let Lex ink you." He shook his head.

"I want more," she purred. "I've got a whole Pinterest board going with ideas. I want your brand, Dallin. I promise. I just wanted some way to display the significance of what you three mean to me, and maybe that's because you three have been so extra over-the-top affectionate the last few weeks." She waved her hand around. "Probably because of this whole plan, and it made me want to do some grand gesture without even knowing what you were planning." She sighed, looking up at him with her big doe eyes of innocence. "Can you forgive me?"

"Depends." Dallin finally released his hold on her and stepped back, pushing off his jacket like I had before, grabbing one of the couches and sliding it back to the center of the room and sitting down in the center.

"On what exactly?" Rey asked cautiously, and Parker rubbed his hands together, already catching on ahead of her.

I selected Parker's sex playlist on my phone, which was connected to the Bluetooth surround sound system in the suite, and the bass-driven tempo built for fucking pulsed around us.

"On how fucking good of a lap dance you can give," he replied darkly. "Because if you're any good at it, I might take away some of the punishment I'm going to give you for this little stunt. But if you're bad"—he shook his head slowly as he ran his finger over his bottom lip—"we're going to leave this hotel, and all of this romance we've planned for you, and we're going to go directly to the shop, where each of us are going to tattoo our names onto very visible places on your body. To signify who fucking owns it."

Her entire body shivered as she looked at Parker and me before taking a deep breath and letting her fingers slide up the length of her dress from her thighs to her shoulders as her eyes fluttered closed, letting the music drive her. "Then it's a good thing I took pole dancing classes in college," she admitted, surprising us all. "Because, baby, I'm going to blow all of your minds with how good I can move my body before I take you all deep inside it."

"Game on, kitten," I challenged her, nodding for her to start as she walked forward and laid her ass directly against my erection, as I leaned forward and spoke into her ear. "First one to beg for an orgasm loses."

She chuckled devilishly and rubbed her ass over me, making my eyes nearly cross with pleasure. "Game on, daddy."

EPILOGUE IV

Parker

"Can you believe that shit?" Trey grumbled as I carried the box up the steps like he was the one doing the heavy lifting. Good thing I liked to work out.

"Whatever, man." I shook it off. "Do you know what the hell is going on up here?" I asked, eyeing the drywall dust lining the stairs to match the hundreds of footprints up and down them that the handymen had created all day.

Rey had kicked us out this morning at seven a.m. and told us to stay away until she gave the all clear, but wouldn't tell us what the hell she was doing.

And I was on edge.

Men were in our house.

With her.

Alone.

And I didn't fucking like it one bit.

"No idea." Trey popped a piece of gum in his mouth. "But Lex is involved and that can't be fucking good."

I whipped around right outside the front door on him. "Lex is involved? You knew this and you're just now telling me?"

Trey scowled. "I didn't know you didn't know that." He scoffed. "You work in the same fucking shop as I do. She's been up and down all day, completely useless. She even passed on piercing a pair of tits and said she was too busy up here. How did you not catch on?"

"Uh, because I was working!"

"What are you girls yelling about?" Dallin asked, climbing the stairs from the exterior door. He had been out of the shop all day doing marketing work with a new tattoo magazine and looked dead on his feet.

"What the fuck is all of this?" He eyed the dropcloths and paint buckets lining the steps.

"Did you know Lex was helping Rey with this project she had going?" I tossed the box down on the floor at my feet, frustrated and on edge. Dallin's face fell as he looked at us. "Trey knew but didn't bother sharing that information."

"Jesus fuck." Trey groaned. "WE ALL WORK TOGETHER!" he yelled. "I can't help it that our wife befriended the crazy chick that *you* hired." He jabbed his finger in Dallin's chest.

"Fuck off," D cursed, pushing him away and making him fall into me, tripping on the box at my feet.

"Get off, man," I snapped, angrily pushing him back toward D.

"Hey!" Trey barked, going all dark, crazy serial killer on us. "Fuck off, yourself."

But I couldn't hear anything else they were saying, because when I bent down to pick up the box that was delivered down at our front door when we got permission to come upstairs, something had fallen out of the hole that Trey's boot caused in the side.

Dallin and Trey went silent around me as they saw what I picked up, staring at it like I couldn't understand what it was.

"Is that—" Trey asked, cocking his head to the side.

"A spreader bar?" I pulled it out of the box completely, and sure enough, red leather cuffs were attached to a sturdy metal bar that extended out to almost three feet. I spun it in my hand before Trey ripped it out and Dallin kneeled to read the label on the box. "Is it for us?" I asked, thinking the delivery man had the wrong address again.

"To Reyna Kent," he growled, using our wife's new last name.

All of our new last names, well except for Dallin, since it was his to begin with.

"The fuck?" Trey mused.

Dallin ripped the box open and dumped the contents out on the floor, sending an array of sex dungeon BDSM paraphernalia scattering across the tile.

Whips.

Chains.

Restraints.

Floggers.

Paddles.

And a lot more sat at our feet as we stared mindlessly at it all, confused beyond words.

"Oh!" An excited squeal came from the front door and we turned, realizing Reyna had opened it while we stared in scandalized shock at the contents of the box. She wore a black satin robe that fell to the top of her thighs, but I couldn't tell from where I stood if she had anything on underneath it or not. "My box came after all! The app said it was delayed, yay!"

"Your box?" D questioned darkly. "Full of BDSM toys?"

"Yep." She smirked at him. "Pick it up and bring it inside and I'll show you what I've been up to all day."

To say we scrambled would be an understatement. We picked it all up and ran inside after her, dumping the ripped box onto the couch as she stood in the hallway to her office and the spare room.

"So I hope you boys don't mind, but I did a little renovating in the spare room today," she said excitedly, as she stood on the balls of her feet.

"What did you do?" I asked.

"And why did you have Lex's help?" Dallin added.

"And when can I spread your fucking legs with this spreader bar?" Trey contributed, and Dallin and I groaned at his stupidity.

Reyna winked at him seductively and pulled the sash free on her robe, revealing a black leather harness-style piece of lingerie strapped around her lush body. Her nipples and pussy were the only bits of her actually covered, and as she did a slow turn on her toes, I realized the thing was crotchless and hugged her ass like a pair of hands. The ink that covered her side and one thigh still made my mouth water, even though I'd tattooed some of it there. When we'd met, she only had one small piece on her arm, and now she was covered with our art, and each piece was significant to us and our relationship.

"Jesus, Mary, and Joseph," Trey cursed, and I fought to not swallow my tongue completely. I'd never seen our girl in anything so dark and dangerous before, and she looked divine.

"To answer your question, you each can pick one thing from that box to bring into the spare room with you." She pointed to the box like a prim schoolteacher, but I couldn't tear my eyes away from her body in the black ensemble long enough to care about what item I picked.

"What for?" Dallin asked, fighting for control of the situation like he usually did.

"Be a good boy, pick your toy, and you can find out," Reyna sang temptingly.

"Got mine!" Trey held up the spreader bar and walked until he was right in front of her like he was at the head of the line. "Can I know what the secret is now? It's kinky, isn't it?" he asked.

She giggled and leaned up to kiss him before looking back at Dallin and me. "Are you two not interested in my surprise? Even a little?" She pouted, spurring us into action.

D grabbed a riding crop from the box and I grabbed a rigging system I knew would bind her hands behind her back and her ankles folded up behind her ass, attached to her wrists.

Hogtied and pliable.

My cock grew down my pant leg and I walked toward her and her sexy little outfit as she smirked and licked her lips.

"Good boys." She turned and walked down the hallway, crooking her finger for us to follow her. "I want to formally introduce you to our new playroom." She opened the door to the spare room that just this morning had held a spare bed we didn't use anymore, and some boxes from a storage unit Trey and I emptied when we officially moved in almost a year ago. But now, it was unrecognizable.

Deep blood-red paint covered the walls, and thick black drapes blocked out any light coming in through the windows, giving off a dungeon feel thanks to gold sconces on the walls and an elaborate golden chandelier hanging in the center.

There was still a bed, but it wasn't the one that was here this morning. The one sitting against one wall had a black leather headboard and giant golden rings for anchor points on all four corners atop black satin sheets.

"Oh my God." Trey whistled, walking in ahead of us as we slowly took in the entire room.

Various sex benches and furniture took up space across the room, and in the center, there was an elaborate black leather swing that I could imagine Reyna lying back in, strung up and helpless as the three of us bounced her on and off our cocks, weightlessly.

Along one wall, a pegboard waited with empty hooks for the toys we found at the door when we walked up.

"What do you think?"

"You turned our spare room into a sex dungeon?" Dallin asked, cocking his head to the side as he fingered the smooth leather of the crop in his hand.

"A playroom," she countered, walking up to him and sliding her hands over his wide chest, pressing hers against it. "Where you three can let your wild animals free and play."

"Rey." He clenched his teeth, making the muscles in his jaw flex as he fought for control. I recognized the look on his face, and it wasn't one he showed her very often.

"The woods are fun," she purred. "I love being chased by you, but there are times I want to see that beast here, in our home, but you never let him free." She looked over at me and Trey. "I want you all to have a space to be yourselves, and have the tools to enjoy yourselves, with no limits." She smiled prettily. "Because I know, as much as I like playing Little Red, you all like being the big bad wolves far more."

"Fuck, woman," I growled, unable to contain it any longer. "Do you have any idea how sexy you're going to look, strung up from the ceiling with this." I held the rigging up in my hand. "Defenseless and open for our cocks?"

"Mmm." She slid up against my body and kissed me. "I can't wait for you to show me." She looked down at the straps in my hand and licked her lips. "How is it that all three of you picked out the toys I selected specifically for you without me telling you?"

"Because we're predictable." Trey shrugged. "You know I love pushing you past your limits." He nodded to me. "And Parker gets off on tying you down and forcing orgasm after orgasm from your body until you're begging him to fuck you." He looked at D and smirked. "And Daddy Dom Dallin over there loves branding your thick ass with his hand, until you're delirious for cock. Easy picks, kitten."

"Hmm." She pursed her lips and tapped her chin like she was contemplating something. "Predictable, huh?" She walked over to a set of drawers and pulled something out, hiding it behind her back as she walked back to us. "Well, did any of you expect me to buy this?" She pulled a thick strap-on dildo in a bright pink harness out from behind her as she cocked her head to the side. "Because I'm ready to make the three of you start begging me to fuck you like you make me do all the time." She winked. "So who's going to be the good boy who gets to use his toy on me first after I make you come with this cock in your ass?"

BONUS NOVELLA

TWISTED ROAD TRIP

ROMANCE OR BUST

Reyna

I had my phone perched on my desk, with my assistant Lucy on speakerphone, prattling off the details of the book tour I was leaving on tomorrow. It was a huge deal; my publisher was holding back nothing in terms of costs, and it was going to be a massive rush of adrenaline in each city.

Yet I couldn't quite muster the energy to be excited for it. It was like there was a dark cloud hanging over my head that got bigger with each minute closer to leaving.

I didn't want to go.

There, I said it.

I wanted to stay in the little bubble of newlywed bliss I was in and ignore the rest of the world for a little while longer while I enjoyed my husbands. They were so much fun to enjoy.

But my wants didn't stop the responsibilities that were already in place, and it felt like a runaway train, with no way off.

"So, with the changes, you'll start in Jacksonville and then do the East Coast stops, before flying out for the bigger events."

"Right," I replied on autopilot. "Got it."

Lucy went on. "And I've changed all the hotel accommodations into suites, because I know how stifling the guys can be. So I figured a single room and one bathroom wouldn't cut it."

"Right. Thanks."

"No problem—oh!" She paused as she flipped through some papers on her side of the line. "The con in L.A. agreed to Trey's demonstration during your panel. In fact, they're actually feral for the guys being onstage with you. I've even had requests from other signings for interactions with the guys being added, but I figured I'd let you feel that one out as you go."

"Trey's demo—" I blinked away my distraction, trying to remember what the hell she was talking about as the rest of what she said clicked. "Wait, what?"

"Huh?" She paused. "What?"

"What demo?" I sat up in my chair. "What are you talking about, having the guys involved?"

"The changes—" She hummed, waiting for me to remember. "The email you sent me three days ago demanding that I rearrange your entire book tour so all three tall, dark, and handsome men could join you for the entirety of it."

"I—" I shook my head, clicking through my email to find the email she was referencing. Though it was marked as spam in my folder, so her replies were all hidden until I searched for it. "They didn't."

"Oh God," she groaned. "I'm going to kill Trey!"

Lucy got annoyed by the mere mention of Trey's name, thanks to his insane ability to pester her and drive her nuts.

"They're coming with me?" I leaned back into my chair as a silly smile crossed my face. "For the full two weeks?"

"All of the stops. Driving the first leg, and then flying with you to the last few." Lucy sighed again. "Tell me that's okay and that I don't have to redo what I've just worked tirelessly for days adjusting. I will, of course, that's my job. But I'm going to demand a bigger Christmas bonus from Trey's account if I do."

"It's fine." I chuckled. "It's better than fine, actually. I've been in such a funk about leaving and I guess they decided to take matters into their own hands."

"Oh," she replied with relief, "I'm guessing you're about to go thank them for the thought."

"You know me so well," I said, standing up from my desk as I headed out of my office. "Talk to you later!"

"Make Trey suffer a little bit first!" she yelled out after me as I walked down the hall, and I laughed in response.

I headed down the private stairwell to Twisted Ink, my husbands' tattoo shop below, and entered into the chaotic loud heavy metal music and busy lobby. Thankfully I had gotten dressed before working in my office, though it wouldn't have been the first time I came to the shop dressed in my bathrobe or worse.

Lex was at the front desk, chatting with some clients and other artists when she clocked me walking through the space. "Hey, girl," she called, propping her hip against the desk. "You look like you're on a mission."

"Do I?" I smirked. "Looking for my husbands."

"Anyone in particular?" she joked with a wink and then nodded back toward the suites. "I'm pretty sure they're all in D's space having a chitty-chat."

"Uh-oh." I rolled my eyes. "Wish me luck."

"You go bust those balls, girl," she called out with a cackle.

I didn't stick around to tell her I was more likely going to rub them for their good idea; she'd just gag and make some comment about Trey being an ogre.

When I got to D's suite, I didn't knock as I slid the door open, finding my guys lounged out around the big room eating lunch and conversing.

"Hey, beautiful." Parker stood up and greeted me, giving me a kiss on the cheek and closing the door behind me. "To what do we owe this pleasure?"

He was being sweet, the same overly sweet version of himself that he had been for days. It was almost as if he was trying to win some brownie points before he needed them.

"Oh, I don't know." I turned on him, enjoying the way his eyes widened when I wrapped my arms around his neck and slid my body against his. "I'm trying to figure out which one of you I'm going to suck off first for your dirty little trick."

"Me!" Trey cried out from behind us as he threw his plate to the side. "It was my idea!"

"Trey," Dallin said, smacking him as I looked over my shoulder to our dominant bossy husband as he dropped his laid-back legs off the stool and stood up, with that slow powerful grace of his. Parker pulled my back into his chest as Dallin prowled toward me and Trey pouted. "What are you talking about, Little Red?"

My thighs clenched at his dirty little nickname for me, but I stared up into his powerful stare. "Lucy told me you're coming with me. Is it true? All three of you?"

He grinned as Park chuckled from my shoulder, letting his hands roam my hips. Dallin stopped right in front of me. "Is that okay with you, darling? Can we crash your vacation from us and follow after you like three little lost puppies chasing after our favorite treat?"

"Mmm," I moaned, sliding my hands over his massive chest and tilting my head back to look up at him. "I didn't realize how fucking badly I wanted you with me, until she let it slip." I shook my head, "I was dreading leaving, and felt like such an Eeyore, so blessed with an amazing work trip, while wanting to stay home instead."

"We know." Parker kissed my neck as Dallin kissed my lips. "That's why we wanted to surprise you."

"I can't wait to have you three at my disposal for two whole weeks. Just us."

"Why wait until we leave to use us?" Parker asked from my neck. "We could start right now."

"I think I like that idea." I grinned, pulling myself out from between their two massive bodies, and found Trey looking feral and pouty in his chair across the room. "I'm going to start with the man who no doubt would have stowed away in my suitcase, either way."

Trey's face darkened as a sinister smile teased his lips. "You know it, kitten. Nothing was going to keep me away from you for two weeks."

"Good," I purred, straddling him as I started unbuttoning my shirt. "Let me show you just how much I appreciate the thought and effort you put forth for me, daddy."

Dallin growled from behind us as I heard the lock in the door slide closed. "Play your silly games, Rey. But you're going to thank us all before you leave this room."

"With pleasure," I purred again, looking over my shoulder as I slid to my knees between Trey's. "My fucking pleasure."

"That's it," I snapped, blowing my bangs out of my face. "You're not going."

Pulling the leather harness from my suitcase with a glare, I flung it at the bedroom door.

"Did you pack the nipple clamps?" Trey's voice called out from the hallway like he was asking about socks.

"No, Trey," I yelled back, "I didn't pack the nipple clamps because this is a *book tour*, not a dungeon crawl."

Appearing at the doorway, shirtless as usual, hair damp from the shower he took instead of helping me pack, with zero shame and his signature dark smirk. "You're the one who wrote about being tied to a headboard and used like a toy. I was just going to help you with more inspiration."

"I don't need help with that."

"Rude," he muttered, disappearing again. "I'm getting the spreader bar."

I turned back to my suitcase to get back to packing, when I heard a crash from the kitchen. "Parker! What is going on out there?"

"I dropped your Smut Queen mug," he yelled back. "Well, technically I decapitated it."

"You broke the crown?" I yelled. "That was the whole aesthetic!"

"I'll glue it back on. Probably."

I groaned and dragged my hands down my face. A moment later, a coffee cup appeared in front of me, held by Dallin, calm and sinfully dominant as always. His tattoos peeked out from beneath the sleeves of a too-tight white shirt and somehow he looked as good as he smelled.

At the door of the closet sat his compact bag, packed and ready to go without a flare of drama like the other two were giving before eight o'clock in the morning.

"I made your coffee," he said, kissing my temple. "Extra sweet with vanilla, just how you like it when you're about to explode."

"I'm not about to explode," I grumbled, sipping the coffee and instantly feeling it relax my shoulders. "Damn, that's good."

Dallin tilted his head. "You hissed like an actual cat at Trey for touching your checklist."

"He wrote 'Don't forget the lube' in permanent marker on it."

"He's not wrong," Dallin said with a slow smile. "To be fair."

I hated how hard he made it to stay mad at them when they were being all over the top, hot, and unhelpful.

Then I changed my mind as Trey walked back into the room, tossing a coil of rope into a duffel bag marked *Event Supplies* and winked. "What's the over-under on Rey flashing the hotel window guy again?"

"That was one time!" I snapped. "And he shouldn't have been looking."

"That man saw the pearly gates of heaven that day," Parker called from the kitchen.

"You're going to see them too if you don't get packed so we can leave in twenty minutes!"

Twenty-eight minutes later we were finally packed and downstairs in the private garage. Originally, I had rented a cute white SUV with all the bells and whistles to drive up the East Coast for the first leg of the trip. But since the change to plans happened, so did the rental car.

And in that cute little SUV's place sat a monstrosity of a black van, taking up two parking spots with the cringey wrap on it that Parker insisted on.

Romance or Bust, in dripping pink letters, coated every side of the thing. It was packed with boxes of books, swag bags, my signing outfits, our luggage, and a tote labeled *Hotel Fun*.

I didn't look inside it before it was loaded into the van. I was too afraid. And equally excited.

Trey was leaning against the passenger door, wearing aviators with no sense of urgency as he watched me walk toward him. "Shotgun's mine," he said when I got close.

"You're navigating." I crossed my arms.

"That's not how shotgun works."

"I will throw you into traffic."

He opened the door, and I tensed, ready to jump in like an irrational teenager fighting a sibling for the front seat instead of a grown professional adult talking to my husband. The man just had a way of riling me up that much.

Instead of fighting me for the spot, he slid his hand over my back and helped me up into the seat, before leaning over and kissing my temple. "We're proud of you, kitten."

Dammit. That got me.

Settling into the seat with a sigh, I glanced behind me to where Parker was sprawled out across the back row already creating a playlist he called *Backseat Debauchery*, as Trey sat in the seats backed up against the front row. Dallin organized my favorite snacks into an incredibly efficient compartment system between us.

We were ridiculous.

We were also late.

"First stop, Pine and Ink Books." Dallin winked from the driver's seat, and my nerves tangled with excitement, letting go of the anxiety and frustration I had been feeling moments ago as I screamed at them all like a banshee to get out the door. "You ready?"

I looked at him, at all of them.

Parker's sunglasses were perched on his head, and a protein bar stuck out of his mouth like a cigar. Trey tossed a bottle of lube into the cup holder like it belonged there. And Dallin looked at me, steady and dangerously sexy from behind the wheel, as if he'd drive us into the fires of hell if I asked.

"Oh I'm ready," I said, smiling. "Let's raise some hell."

With the windows down, the playlist started playing, and the wind tangled my hair as we hit the road.

Romance or bust.

THE D-TRAIN

Dallin

Pine and Ink was a funky indie bookstore that smelled like paper and herbal tea. There was a tattoo shop next door with a connecting doorway and a handwritten sign that said *Cash Only* and a black cat sunbathing in the front window.

Every employee of the bookstore was either pierced, queer, or wearing a shirt that said things like *I came for the tattoos, stayed for the monster smut.*

One even said *Smut Peddler in Training.*

Rey fit right in, instantly. They were her people, her fans, and the people she connected with most in the whole world.

Before we even got in the front door, Reyna was surrounded by readers with her arms full of swag bags and books. I tried to help, but she was halfway through setting up her table before the guys and I even got all of the boxes inside.

"She's in her element," Parker muttered from beside me, leaning against a table with a poster of her latest book cover blown up behind him. Trey was charming two of the bookstore employees with his mix of sarcasm and danger.

I wouldn't be surprised if he didn't end up at the tattoo shop before we left.

But I didn't move.

I just stood there and watched her.

I watched her work. I watched her socialize. I watched her *thrive.*

It hit me like that sometimes, quiet and out of the blue, that I got to love that woman every day. The woman signing bookmarks with glitter pens and responding to people calling her a smut dealer was the same one who cried in my arms the night she hit publish on her first real book.

The same one who read her filthy rough draft scenes out loud in a voice sweet enough to ruin a man.

And she was out there in the real world now, confident, shining.

Mine.

Hours later, she was still signing with the same energy as the first book she opened when we first arrived. Parker and Trey were mingling with the employees, but staying out of her way as I held my post in the crowd.

Watching her.

"She really is something, isn't she?" a woman next to me said. She was a reader, mid-thirties maybe, holding a stack of Rey's paperbacks and blinking like she was staring at the sun as she looked at my wife. "Are you . . . one of them?"

I arched a brow at her. "One of who?"

Her face flushed and she pulled a handheld electric fan out of her bag and aimed it at herself. "Sorry. That came out weird." Giggling, she went on. "I mean one of the guys she writes about. You know, the inspiration behind the ink. The *husbands*."

"Guilty," I said with a half smile. "First husband, most patient. The one who makes sure everyone eats something and gets sunshine."

"I knew it. You're the Dallin."

I blinked. "Wait, there's a character named Dallin in her books?" I knew her books forward and backward, but I had never seen my name in one of them before.

She must have hidden that.

The woman next to me blushed deeper. "I mean, she changes the names, but at one of her events, she used your name." Clearing her throat, she pressed on. "But you're the quiet one who ties her to the chair with her own silk robe, right? That's the scene she got from you, she said."

Christ.

I pressed a hand to the back of my neck as I looked over at my wife, charming everyone. "I, uh—yeah, that's me."

The reader clicked the fan higher, and I inwardly groaned at the whole exchange. "I knew it. Tell her she created a cult following for you. We call ourselves the D-Train."

Jesus. I didn't even know how to respond, so I just nodded with wide eyes, and the woman chuckled and walked away back in line, whispering furiously with her group of friends.

When they all looked over at me and fell into a fit of giggles, I found Parker's gaze across the room and nodded to him to switch.

I had to get out of the room before I used my wife to work my embarrassment out on and gave the women a firsthand demonstration of just how well my pretty wife begged, all tied up for me.

The event ran for hours, even going past the end time as the line showed no sign of ending. Reyna signed every book with flair, posed for photos, and gave away limited-edition bookmarks that said *Romance or Bust: Signed. Sealed. Spanked.*

By the time I got her back into the van, her voice was hoarse and her hands were clamped around two frozen ice packs to relieve the strain.

"You were incredible." I cheered for her as I slid into the driver's seat beside her. "They adore you."

"They *adore* you," she teased. "I saw at least three people try to take your picture from across the room. One even told me there's a cult following, hungry for you."

"Let them be hungry," I murmured, watching her mouth as her smile turned teasing. "You're the only one I want to devour."

"What if I want to do the eating?" she countered, lifting a brow.

I tightened my grip on the wheel. "You want to be stuffed tonight, darling?"

Her smile turned wicked as Trey and Parker got in behind us. "And eaten. In that order."

Parker poked his head up between our seats with a devilish chuckle. "Are we talking about food or—?"

We barely made it to the hotel in one piece.

Parker and Trey were taking turns playing with Rey in the back seat, teasing me the whole time with every moan and growl as we crossed the city.

But that had been the point of the van after all. Not only did it have room for all of her stock, but it had large bench seats that faced each other in the back, with blackout tint.

It was perfect to play in.

They could have their fun with her on the way there, but once we got to the hotel, I'd get my fill.

I left Parker and Trey to get the bags and park the van as I carried Rey to our suite, and the second we were inside I slammed the door shut behind us. I was tempted to throw the privacy lock to keep the guys out while I had my way with her, but I knew it would be hotter for her if they were there for their turn when I was done.

She thrived on being the center of attention, and she deserved it tonight.

Her sweet, breathless laughter cut off when I set her down on the bed in the primary bedroom, stopping when I fell to my knees in front of her.

"I watched you all day," I murmured, fingers sliding up her thighs, pushing her dress up inch by inch. "Being adored. Worshipped. Wanted."

There had been more than a few men who showed up to meet the woman behind the stories, and I wasn't convinced their intentions had been completely platonic.

It had driven me wild with need, watching everyone get a piece of her all day long.

She opened her mouth, but I gripped the back of her knees and pulled her forward until her hips brushed against my face. "Now it's my turn."

"Yes, D." She moaned as her head fell back when I kissed my way up her thighs slowly, possessively.

"No cameras. No fans," I said against her skin. "Just me, devouring you."

Ripping her panties off, I got to work on her needy body, pushing my tongue into her and sucking her clit with practiced, obsessive perfection. I knew her.

I knew what she needed.

Her hands tangled in my hair, pulling me into her as she rode my face from below, begging me with her words and her body. "Please, D," she gasped, falling back on the bed after coming for the third time. "I need to be filled, remember? I want to be stuffed."

"I got you, love." I stripped off my clothes and removed hers as I lifted her body up the bed and onto the pillows. "I love you, Reyna."

Her hazel eyes fluttered open to look up at me as I slowly sank into her body, making her lips part and her neck work to swallow as she sighed with each inch. "God, I love you, D."

I could have slammed into her body, taking what I was ravished for, and settling that animal inside me that wanted her in every way, as quickly as possible.

But I was too overcome with admiration of her to give in. Not yet.

Instead, I slowly fucked her, dragging my body against her clit and playing with her pleasure points as she cried out from under me, dragging her nails across my back and neck as she came again and again.

The only thing better than being written into one of Reyna's books was getting to make her feel like every filthy fantasy would never be enough without this in real life.

I VOLUNTEER AS TRIBUTE

Parker

There was a particular kind of feral energy in a room full of romance readers, and I was living for it. It was the third stop on Reyna's bestseller book tour, and this time, we were at a romance-specific book con. Rey was one of the bigger-named authors attending, and the energy was wild.

It smelled like perfume and sin, with the air around everyone buzzing with excitement. There were no fewer than three different women in the audience wearing shirts that said *Book Boyfriend Collector* like it was a competitive sport.

Spoiler alert—Reyna could win it blindfolded. Literally. There was video evidence on Dallin's phone.

Reyna was onstage, seated on a panel of authors who all wrote various flavors of debauchery. One was a monster romance queen who wore tentacle earrings. One of the others wrote mafia. And one just read a scene about a priest doing things that probably required an exorcism to get the stains out of the kneeling bench.

Then there was Rey.

Our girl.

She was sunshine and sin, curves for days, lips glossed to hellish perfection, and wearing a leather blazer with a lace corset underneath. We bought her that blazer but had zero intention of her keeping it on for long.

Glancing to my left, I saw Trey leaning forward in his chair, dark sunglasses on indoors like the broody menace he was. To my right, Dallin had his arms folded and his jaw clenched, probably already counting the seconds until he could get her alone.

Me? I was grinning like a man about to start something naughty.

Because I knew what was coming.

News had been spreading through the social media grapevine that Reyna Kent's very own dark and dirty reverse harem was shadowing her around her events. And the response had been insane.

And of course, I was more than willing to control her social media, fueling the fire and building the buzz every chance I got.

Our girl deserved all the hype she could get for these events, given that I was sure it would be a long, long time before Dallin let her out of the house for another tour.

The moderator held up one of Reyna's books—that one—as she addressed our pretty wife. "You're known for your emotionally driven poly romances with a heavy dose of kink and trauma," she said. "This scene in particular went viral for—" She paused with a smirk, looking out over the crowd. "Well, you'll see."

When she read the page number aloud, the crowd went wild.

Somewhere to the left of us, a reader shrieked. Someone else yelled, "Chapter fourteen ruined my marriage—in a good way!"

Reyna was already blushing, not in a shy way, but flustered. And that was my favorite dose of Rey.

The moderator cleared her throat.

"He tied her wrists behind her back with the belt that used to hold his suit pants together. Now it held her upright—bare, breathless, trembling. Her other lovers stood at his side, watching from the edge of the bed. Together they had eyes like wolves, waiting to feed."

Someone gasped. Someone else fanned themselves with their badge.

Reyna shifted in her seat. "Well, that sounds—familiar." She chuckled, and the crowd followed her.

Trey leaned over and murmured, "That was your belt, wasn't it?"

Dallin's teeth flashed in a slow grin. "Sure as hell was."

Raising my hand and drawing attention to our row, I announced, "For the record, I was the one who said 'We're not fucking you. We're claiming you.' But who's keeping track?"

Our pretty wife covered her face with her hands and groaned. When I rose to my feet, the crowd all turned my way, as I asked loud enough for the whole room to hear, "Do we get a live reading too? Because I brought props."

A ripple of laughter broke across the panel as Reyna flipped me off and mouthed *I hate you.*

Which the four of us knew was code for *You're getting ridden until you can't walk tonight.*

We made it through the rest of the panel and the signing that followed, without any major meltdowns occurring. Though twice, Trey had to leave to cool down.

He was on edge and more angsty than usual, if you could believe that. When they opened the floor to questions, readers pinpointed in on our wife and asked questions like "How do you balance three very different men in one relationship?"

And mentally I responded with all of the ways I planned to *unbalance* her when we finally left.

By the time we got back to our next hotel suite, the door wasn't even hardly open before I had Reyna's back against the wall, fingers on her throat, stripping the leather blazer off her body and my lips absorbing her gasps.

"Are you really going to keep up the act like that wasn't on purpose?" I asked, voice low against her ear.

"What are you talking about?" she stammered.

"The scene. The reading. You let them use that one, out loud, in front of us. Don't act like you didn't know what it would do to us."

Licking her lips, she breathed, "What are you going to do about it, Parker?"

Instead of answering, I pulled off her and took the book from her bag, flipping right to the scene before pushing her plump ass in those painted-on jeans down into a chair in the living room. Sitting prim and proper in the highback chair, she looked just like she had onstage again.

Though without the blazer, her tits were on display, spilling over the cups of her corset. Almost tempting me into taking a bite.

Trey appeared beside me, calm but dangerous. No one needed to be told how on edge he had been. We all saw it.

Dallin kicked the door shut behind him and locked it, putting the *do not disturb* sign out.

"Page two thirty-eight," I said, unbuckling my belt. "We're going to act it out. Line for line."

"And if I say no?" Reyna asked, her voice firm and daring.

Kneeling in front of her, I looped my belt around her wrists and tightened it behind her back. "Then we skip to chapter fifteen." I smiled, and her lips parted. "Do you remember what happened in that one, baby girl?"

"Fuck." She groaned as I kneeled behind her, fastening the leather to the chair. Black leather, cracked in the middle from age and use, cinched just tight enough to make her shift in her seat.

Her lips parted and her thighs were pressed together tightly.

"You're blushing," I murmured, back in front of her again. "I thought you liked a live audience."

"There *is* no live audience," she said, tilting her chin defiantly.

"Oh, kitten," Trey drawled, circling around her back. "There always is."

She jerked as he slid his hand into her hair, tipping her head back. She couldn't see him, not the way she was tied, but her mouth fell open like she was ready to take whatever was coming.

Our good little attention slut.

"You like to share these depraved and dirty moments with complete strangers, using your fancy words and delicate craft to make people orgasm from fantasies we make come true for you. The least you can do is let us play them out too."

"Parker," she moaned, then whimpered slightly when Trey tightened his hand in her hair.

Dallin stepped into her line of sight, slow and controlled, dragging a chair over with that deliberate calm that meant he was plotting something terrible and poetic. Opening the book to the flagged page, he read aloud, his voice deep and even.

"He crouched between her knees and said, 'You remember the rules?'"

"She nodded. He tsked. 'Say it.'"

"'Don't come unless you tell me to,' she whispered."

"Sound familiar?" I asked Reyna, placing my hands on her knees.

Swallowing, she shook her head slightly. "Nope. Never heard of her."

Trey laughed behind her, low and dark. "Liar."

I slid her legs apart slowly, dragging my palms up her inner thighs, and Reyna's breath stuttered in her chest like she was caught between being a smartass and submission.

"Parker—" she warned.

"Page two-forty," Dallin continued, unfazed. *"She was already wet, thighs trembling, the threat of three pairs of eyes on her making her ache like a whore in church."*

Trey growled, "Damn, baby. You wrote that line for me, didn't you?"

"Stop reading it like it's poetry," Reyna bit out. "I can't focus."

"That's the point." I grinned.

Her blazer was long gone, and the corset top she wore under it, teasing little glimpses of skin and snatched waist all day, was on display for her men. Her wolves.

I dipped my fingers under the cups of her top, brushing against her hard nipples before I started unclasping the thing, inch by inch, revealing her body to us.

"Tell me you want it," I demanded.

"I think you're doing a great job even without my words," she breathed.

I pinched, just hard enough to make her hiss. "Say it."

"I want it," she snapped. "I want all of you. Every filthy thing."

Trey kissed her temple as he slid his fingers around the front of her throat. "Good girl."

Dallin set the book down and stepped forward. "Let's give her the rest." Untucking his shirt with that dominant precision, I started in on her jeans, peeling them off her as she rocked her hips to help.

She was seeking, desperate for our touch.

Trey stroked her hair like a reward. "Think she'll last the whole chapter?"

"She better," Dallin said, opening his belt. "Or she doesn't come at all."

"Rude," Rey muttered, and then gasped when Trey's hand tightened around her throat. But I could hear her moan.

"Realistic," I replied, licking a slow trail up her thigh, just to make her gasp against his hand again.

Taking our time, we teased her.

One mouth on her throat, one between her legs. One voice in her ear, reading her own filthy words back to her, page by page, line by line.

Orgasm by orgasm.

Writhing against the chair, she panted with her hands clenched tight behind her back. Her hair stuck to her forehead and cheeks, yet she had never looked more beautiful.

Every time her breath hitched just right, Trey commanded, "Not yet."

Every time she started to beg or tighten on my tongue and fingers, I pulled back.

Every time she almost tipped over the edge into ecstasy, Dallin tightened his grip on her control.

And when she finally said please—broken, breathless, and ready to burn for us—we let go of the chapter.

Time to write a new one of our own.

NEXT STOP: NOWHERE GOOD

Trey

The silence struck about thirty minutes after we left the convention in Myrtle Beach. Parker passed out in the back with his mouth open like he was dreaming of pussy and Pop-Tarts. Dallin drove with one hand on the wheel and one arm stretched across to Rey's seat, like he owned the road and her spine.

And Reyna?

She was quiet. Which was never good. Not quiet like that, anyway.

Staring out the window, I pretended I wasn't watching her reflection in the glass. But I was just faking it.

She had her hoodie pulled up, one knee tucked to her chest, and earbuds in, but they weren't playing anything. That was her signature look when her brain was going places she wouldn't say out loud.

Perhaps she was just coming off the high of the event yesterday. Perhaps she was just tired.

Or perhaps she was replaying what that reader said to her in the buffet line this morning at breakfast.

"I just love how imaginary your books are. They're so far from reality and not at all real, but it gives us all something to escape into when we don't want normal."

I watched her fake a smile and nod, before setting her empty plate down in the bin and settling for a coffee instead.

Then I watched her eyes flick to us—her *real* men—and I knew right then that the comments had landed like a punch.

While Reyna was known for her ability to craft spicy delicious goodies for her readers, there was more to her than that. Under the jokes and the fiery sass, she was soft.

She wanted to be believed in. She wanted to be taken seriously, and that comment made her feel like a joke.

It made her feel like *we* were a joke.

We stopped for gas on a desolate back road between cities. It was one of those towns where the diner was the only place open past eight, and the gas pumps still asked if you wanted a car wash that wasn't even operational anymore.

I told Dallin I'd drive the next leg, and he nodded, too tired to argue.

We were on our way to Pittsburgh, and still had a few hours before we would make it to our destination.

If I was lucky, we'd make it before I imploded.

Reyna walked into the gas station to pee, and Parker followed her like a lost dog, no doubt hoping for a candy bar and a quickie in the bathroom if he played his cards right.

Leaning against the van, I watched the sunset leak orange across the sky, trying not to pick a fight with the ghosts in my head.

I tried to remind myself that we weren't always like this.

There were fights in the beginning, spurred by jealousy, missteps, and bad communication. Usually, all on my behalf. There were nights I slept in my tattoo suite downstairs, because I didn't know how to say, *I feel too much and not enough all at the same time.*

But now Dallin kept it all together with that scary calm order of his. Parker made everyone laugh, distracting us with his charm and chaos. And Rey, our girl, our glue, she held all the pieces like they didn't cut her palms when she carried them.

Sometimes, though, I wondered. Did she ever look at us now and think that she could have had it simple? She could have had quiet. She could have had easy.

She could have had that with Dallin.

The gas pump clicked off and I slammed it back into its spot harder than necessary.

"You good?" Reyna's voice broke through the haze, and I turned to find her standing there, arms crossed and head tilted.

She was watching me, in that way I hated like she could see through me to the other side if she tried hard enough. And no amount of asshole remarks or snarky attitude would block her.

"You tell me," I said.

"You've been chewing on your cheek since we left the city," she replied, narrowing her eyes at me in accusation.

"Maybe I'm just sick of people acting like our life is fake," I grumbled, letting my frustration out, aimed at her.

Because I was an idiot.

But she was used to me at this point in our relationship, and she didn't rise to it like she used to. Sometimes I wished she would.

Stepping closer to me instead, she replied, "It's not fake, you know that."

"Do *you*?" I snapped, and then the silence between us stretched.

Her mouth opened and closed until finally she said, "That's not fair."

Nodding, I deflated. "No. It's not."

And then she did the thing that broke me. The one thing that I never could prepare for, because I never anticipated it when I was being a dick to her. She reached for me.

Not demanding anything. Not for dramatic flair. Just—a touch. Two fingers on my wrist, feather light. "I don't need them to believe in us," she said. "I need *you* to."

My throat tightened and I leaned in, pressing my forehead to hers like she was the only clean air left in the world. "I believe in *you*," I whispered. "Even when I hate the world."

She kissed me, like it was an answer to it all. Like a truce. Like a promise she didn't have to make because she already kept it every damn day.

Back in the van, Dallin was out cold in his seat, and Parker was snoring into a bag of M&M's as Reyna curled into my side with her hand on my leg, like she was plugging me into something warm and vital.

Her.

I drove us into the dark, the three people I loved the most asleep and trusting of me.

Still here.

Still real.

Still mine.

Checking into our hotel went awry, and it being after ten didn't help the matter. Our suite wasn't available, some mix-up on their end, and we were stuck with a single room with a queen bed and a pull-out couch.

But we were all exhausted, and Rey had a big day at another signing in the morning, so we dealt with what we had.

Parker followed me into the room and shouted, "Dibs on top," before face-planting into the center of the bed, face down, and falling asleep. The man slept all day long and was already claiming the bed. Fucker.

Dallin was quiet while we checked in; he had been the rest of the trip. He was the kind of tired you felt in your bones—driver tired, peacekeeper tired, control keeper tired.

He gave Reyna a kiss and hit the shower, closing the door behind him without a word.

Which left me and Rey, in a room lit by a flickering bedside lamp, and the blue glow of a muted television stuck on the Telemundo channel.

I took a seat in the corner chair, elbows on my knees, chewing on the thought that hadn't left me since the hotel that morning.

What if I was just the kink?

Not the soul. Not the softness. Not the one she clung to when she was scared or hurting. Just the fire she used to stay warm.

Just the sharp edge she liked to press against until she bled.

Silently, Rey crawled across the mattress toward me, still in her shorts and hoodie, bare legs brushing against the sheets as she climbed over Parker with soft, focused eyes. "Don't shut down on me, Trey."

"I'm not," I replied, regarding her without moving toward her like she wanted me to.

"Don't lie to me either," she demanded firmly.

Sighing, I ran my hand down my face and gave in. "Do you ever wonder if people look at us and think—you settled for the sideshow instead of the main act?"

"Do you think I did?" she asked, avoiding my question.

I glanced up at her and really saw her. Her hair was messy, her eyeliner smudged, and she looked exhausted. But she also looked so fucking here. Present. Grounded. Not wavering or going anywhere. "No," I muttered. "But I'm not exactly known for thinking clearly when I'm spiraling."

She moved closer, kneeling between my knees and gripping the arms of the chair so I couldn't look away. In that moment, only she existed.

"You're not just the edge, Trey. You're the anchor."

I huffed out a bitter laugh. "You're really going to look me in the eye and say *I'm* the stable one?"

"No." She shook her head. "I'm saying you hold weight I don't always see until it cracks your spine."

Fuck. That one landed.

I swallowed as she went on.

"You want to know the truth?" she asked, softer now. "If I'd only written you in the book, readers would've called you unrealistic. Too loyal. And too intense. Too deep." She urged, "Too much. But that's what makes you mine. I never wanted quiet. I wanted you. I wanted the fire in the middle of the ocean during a storm. I want it all, Trey."

Pulling her into my lap, I buried my face in her neck before I did something embarrassing like break open and leak out my pain. She didn't flinch. Instantly, she climbed onto me, wrapped herself around me, and let me feel her weight.

Her real weight, the kind I could carry, the kind I want to.

"I don't need them to get it," she whispered. "I just need you to believe that I'm not going anywhere."

I didn't reply. Instead I kissed her. Hard. Messy. Desperate.

And she gave it right back.

We didn't undress each other, we tore. We ripped apart the barriers between us. Her hoodie hit the floor, my shirt ended up who knows where. Pulling my pants down far enough to straddle me, she pulled her shorts to the side and widened her thighs. Her nails dug into my shoulders like she wanted to mark *home* into my bones.

She rocked against me as I pushed my cock through her wetness and into her, forcing her to take me as I gripped her hips like she was slipping through my fingers.

"You're mine," I growled against her lips.

"Then take me like I am," she challenged me.

I did.

She tipped her head back as she rocked in my lap, forcing my cock to stay deep inside her as she rode me. I knew Parker was on the bed behind her, but I'd tear him limb from limb if he tried to interrupt us.

I was never against sharing her with my men, but tonight, right now, I *needed* her.

I wouldn't survive if the connection was severed.

"Please, Trey," she whispered, pushing my head back into the chair with a hand on my neck and forcing me to look into her eyes. "Give me everything."

I fucked the doubt out of both of us. It was rough, raw, and not at all pretty. There was nothing performative in it, no games, or tricks. Just sweat, panting, and two people who loved each other too hard to say it softly.

When she came, she whispered my name like it was a spell, as though if she chanted it just right, her wish would come true.

And I came with my face buried in her neck, whispering my chant like a prayer.

Stay.

WILDERNESS

Reyna

I didn't know who actually booked the cabin in the Appalachian Mountains, but they were getting head for dinner, for sure. We had four days before we had to be in L.A. for the biggest book signing of my career, and the pit stop just felt—right.

The second my feet touched the hardwood floor, it hit me. The smell of pine and cedar, the hush of the woods surrounding the house, the way the floor creaked like an actual *home* instead of a cookie-cutter hotel suite with blackout curtains and corporate carpet.

The quiet settled into my bones like it was where it had been meant to live forever.

Part of me never wanted to leave. I wanted it to last forever.

When we left the hotel in Pittsburgh that morning, Trey had written me a note and left it on the dash of the van for me to find. I thought we were heading to the airport, ditching the van, and moving on to the glitzy part of the tour.

Instead, Dallin drove us out of the city and into the woods as I read Trey's note.

No signings. No panels. No people. Just us.

And maybe a little rope.

And standing in the center of the massive cabin, with its exposed-beam ceiling, floor-to-ceiling stone fireplace, leather chairs, and heavy fur throw blankets, I never wanted to leave.

"Oh baby, there's a hot tub." Parker whistled, walking back in from the back deck with a naughty grin. "Imagine all the ways I'm going to make you come in there."

I smiled and let his carefree mood wash over me.

Dallin walked in from the garage, carrying Trey's mysterious bag of fun, and winked at me. "I'll get the towels." Because that was who he was, our caretaker, our compass. And I was going to spend the next few days thanking him for always keeping us steady.

"You good?" Trey asked, setting down the wine he unpacked from grocery bags that were waiting for us when we arrived.

I nodded. "I will be."

Leaning in, he brushed a kiss against my temple in a sweet softness so different from his norm. "We're going to make sure of it."

Instead of jumping straight into the hot tub, we congregated on the plush carpet in front of the fireplace, eating snacks and being goofy like a bunch of teenagers. We shared a bottle of wine, a box of crackers, and a block of cheese Parker couldn't identify but kept slicing into like a game of Operation.

"I wish I knew who you were as teenagers," I mused after a while, looking away from the dancing flames to my men. "All of you."

I leaned against Dallin's chest, where he was braced against the couch and his fingers continuously brushed over my scalp, down my long hair and back. We were all at ease, and I almost regretted breaking through that with my statement.

But not enough to take it back.

"No, you don't, babe." Parker grimaced with a smirk. "I didn't know what deodorant was, and Trey was soft and sweet. We were totally gross."

I smiled and let his humor chill me out, but Dallin's hand tightened in my hair, gently pulling my head back to look up at him behind me. "We would have loved you back then, just the same," he said with fierce conviction. "But we never would have earned you. And that would have been a goddamn travesty."

"Sometimes I feel like the unworthy one," I whispered to him, and instead of countering my feelings or proving how wrong he thought they were, he simply kissed my doubts away.

"Did I ever tell you about the first tattoo I ever did on someone else?" Parker asked mischievously, to break the tension.

"No."

"Or better yet," Trey added, "how he fucked it up, royally."

"Oh no." I giggled, sipping my wine.

"I had a drunk guy want the word *breathe* stamped on his ass cheek." Parker started with a chuckle. "But I think I was drunker than him, to be honest."

"Uh-oh," I laughed, and Dallin chuckled behind me.

"I remember that." He added wistfully, "You got fired the next morning. Day two."

"I forgot the *e* at the end and had shaded in the other stuff he wanted, so I couldn't go back and add it. All I could do was make an exclamation point out of the designs and called it a statement piece, sending him on his way!"

"Oh my God, stop it." I laughed, holding my sides as tears rolled down my face. "So you're to blame for the three of you taking to the road instead of settling down so early."

"Pretty much," he joked. "After that we kind of hopped shops for a while and then said fuck it, let's ride."

"Was the guy mad?"

"Fuming." Trey smirked from where he lay on the floor looking like he was asleep the whole time. "Came in the next morning and yanked his pants down in a tirade." Peeking one eye open he looked over at me, he said, "His ass was almost as ugly as Dallin's."

"Oh, fuck off," Dallin cursed good-heartedly, tossing a cracker at Trey, who managed to catch it with his mouth and chewed it triumphantly.

A peaceful silence fell on us again, as we snuggled and watched the flames dancing before I started feeling restless in the serenity of it all. My skin started to feel tight and hot as we all just relaxed.

None of us did much of that in life, let alone together.

"Well." I detangled Dallin's fingers from my hair as I stood up in the center of the group. "I think I'm ready to take this party into the bedroom." I bit my lip and held my hand out to Parker, who eagerly took it and rose to his feet. "I'm going to go take a shower and then I want to play."

"Do you remember the first shower we took together?" Parker asked seductively, running his hands around my waist.

"The one Dallin tricked us into?" I raised a brow at the man on the floor, who simply shrugged. "Yes, I do."

"Do you remember what I told you when I found you, fighting with yourself about giving in to your carnal needs?"

I chuckled and pretended to contemplate it. "Something about you getting on your knees."

"I said, tell me to go and I will. Or tell me to get on my knees and make you come." He growled, leaning down to kiss my neck in that spot I loved so much. "And you told me to get on my fucking knees, baby."

"Hmm," I moaned, and then pushed back, forcing space between us. "Then be ready to get on your knees when I get out. Because I want all three of you tonight."

Stepping out of the bathroom, wrapped in a towel, I found all three of them waiting for me. Shirtless, barefoot, and quiet.

Trey sat on the edge of the bed with the rope coiled in his hand; Dallin lit candles one by one, basking the room in the warm glow and aromatic scents, while Parker held one of my books, opened to a page I forgot I even wrote as he read.

"She wanted to be touched like a devotion, not a demand."

"And they worshipped her accordingly."

I froze, standing on the edge of a promise that felt like a threat and a reward, all wrapped into one sinful night.

"Let us take care of you," Dallin said.

Nodding, I gave in to their plans, eager to feel them on my skin and in my heart at the same time. I dropped the towel. They didn't rush me. They didn't tease me. They touched me like I was something sacred.

And I felt bare in a way that had nothing to do with my skin.

Dallin moved first, as usual. And I welcomed his comforting presence on the cusp of something monumental. He teased his fingertips down my arm, barely a whisper against my skin, and then the other arm. Then to the curve of my waist.

He was in no rush, he gave no commands. Just giving me his touch, honest and worshipful.

"Come here," he said, and I did. Sitting on the edge of the bed, he pulled me between his thighs, bracketing me with his arms. D's warm lips kissed my sternum, just above my heart, as he whispered against my skin, "You're so loved, Reyna."

It broke something inside me. "I know," I breathed through the painful love burning in my chest. "I know, I just forget."

"You don't have to remember alone," Parker said from behind me, voice soft and loving in his gentle caressing way. "We're here to remind you. Always."

Trey took his place at my side, laying his hand on Dallin's shoulder as he pushed my hair over my shoulder and kissed my neck. I melted into Dallin's strength as if the brief contact of their lips on my body were enough to wreck me.

Or mend me.

I couldn't tell anymore.

"Turn to me," Trey demanded, low and calmly. "Let me tie you."

Not because he wanted control, but because they knew I needed to let go.

Trey used the rope to bind my wrists together in front of me—not to restrict, but to *hold* before laying me backward in the center of the bed. As soon as my skin touched the duvet, Parker's hands were pushing my legs wide as he kneeled between my thighs, running his lips and tongue over my bare stomach and down to my core.

"Yes, baby," I purred, melting into his touch and arching my back into it as Dallin lay down next to me, pulling my hands above my head and pinning them to the mattress.

D whispered every filthy thing they wanted to do to me, but it wasn't about *possession.* It was about presence. He was telling me how they were going to worship me.

Parker growled as he took a long lick. "I love when you let me start."

"God, yes," I groaned, widening my legs and bending my knees. As Parker went down on me, Trey and Dallin kissed every inch of my exposed body.

My ankles, my knees, my thighs, my breasts, my neck, my arms. Each press of their mouths was slow and sure, trailing fire across my skin that was still damp from my shower. Their hands cradled me like I was breakable, as if I was more than just a thing to fuck or fulfill.

I was helpless in their arms, desperate and begging for more of themselves.

Dallin kept my hands pinned as he whispered praise I could barely hear over the rushing blood in my ears. "That's it, baby, let us take this from you. Let us fill you back up."

Trey's hands stroked down my stomach, flat and warm, and when he leaned in to whisper in my ear, it wasn't sharp or dirty.

It was reverent.

"You don't have to be strong tonight," he promised. "You don't have to be anything to the rest of the world in this room, kitten. In here, you're ours. To cherish. To worship. To take care of."

I came with tears on my cheeks and their names on my tongue. They didn't stop, though.

Parker bit the inside of my thigh as the guys shifted on the bed, releasing my arms and flipping me onto my hands and knees. My wrists were still tied, and I fell onto my elbows as Dallin lay against the headboard cradling my jaw in his hand as he pulled his cock out.

And I had never wanted to suck him more than I did at that moment. Teasingly, I ran my tongue around the crown of his thick cock as hands skated over my upturned ass. I didn't know who it was, and in a way I didn't care.

I just wanted to be held by them.

"Suck it, Rey," Dallin said, pushing his thumb into my mouth and pulling my lower jaw down. "Lose yourself in us."

I held my jaw open as he fed his cock into my mouth, pushing it against my reflex and making me gag as Trey's fat cock pushed into my body from behind. I groaned, widening my hips and changing the angle of my jaw as I bobbed up and down on Dallin. I didn't care how I looked or sounded as I slurped, gagging and drooling all over him as Trey slowly fucked me from behind.

He was driving me mad with his restraint, using slow, deep thrusts to ruin me. He was being so damn careful with me, and I tried to force him to break free by pleasing Dallin erotically. And it worked, because as Dallin lost his hold on his own restraint, tangling his hands in my hair and forcing my head up and down, my pussy soaked Trey's cock and he growled, spanking my ass and slamming in deep.

I hummed. I moaned. I screamed when I came, and Dallin pulled me off his cock as his balls tightened against my hands before he could finish in my mouth. "My turn," he said firmly, before he slid off the bed and pushed Trey away from me.

I glanced over my shoulder as Dallin took his place and watched that dark stare as he gazed at my pussy, lining up and pushing himself in roughly, making me cry out in pleasure.

There was nothing better than watching my men lose themselves to me. No one else could make them slip like I could.

No one else could give them what I gave them.

"Come here, baby girl." Parker pulled me up, pushing pillows beneath my upper body as he and Trey both knelt at the head of the bed. "Suck us off, while you take D's big cock."

He didn't have to tell me twice. Eagerly, I sucked Parker's long barbed cock into my mouth, hollowing out my jaw, and held still when he fed me more until it was in my throat. He was so deep, and Dallin was fucking me so hard, it felt like they'd meet in the middle somewhere in my guts.

And I fucking loved it.

"My turn," Trey growled, turning my head to his cock, still wet with me on it, and I turned my head when he tried to push in deep and bit the side of his shaft, drawing a slur of curses from his lips.

"Only if you fuck me like you need me," I demanded, staring up at him as I licked a trail over the red indent of my teeth before sucking him into my mouth.

His eyes were feral as he painfully took my hair in his hands, holding my head still as he pushed in deep, using me for his own pleasure while D gave me mine.

They used me like that, the three of them, trading places and filling my body up, forcing me to come over and over again as they fucked me. I was delirious from their measured thrusts and deliberate kisses. Each hand and word sounded woven into the kind of love no one wrote about. Not because it wasn't hot.

But because it was real.

Because it was fucking holy.

"I need a break," I cried, ripping my mouth away from D's cock as Parker's cock pulled on my insides with each punishing thrust. "I need a minute."

They both paused, and Trey's hands instantly lifted me from the same position I had been in for what felt like hours, untying my hands and laying me on my back.

I could see the concern on their faces as they stared, chests heaving, testosterone pumping, and cocks hard still. Each of them had come, yet they were all hard still, working in tandem to please me like a goddess on a throne, but I was ready to call the shots.

"I didn't say you could stop," I gasped, stretching my body and groaning before I grabbed the rope Trey ripped off my wrists. "Give me your hands."

Trey's eyes darkened but he didn't hesitate to hold them out in front of himself as I tied the same knots around him until he was restrained like I was, and then I slid off the bed, creating an empty space in the center.

"On your hands and knees, daddy," I purred, daring him to deny me.

"Fuck," Dallin growled, stroking his dick as he watched Trey get onto the bed in my place, folding himself exactly as I had been for the last hour. "How do you want us, Red?"

I gave D a push toward the head of the bed. "Mouth." Then I nodded to Parker. "Fuck him."

"And what are you going to do, princess?" Parker asked with a grin as he grabbed lube from the tote, pouring a generous amount over his cock.

I took the bottle from him and squirted some onto my fingers before reaching around my body and rubbing them over my ass. "Prep."

"Jesus Christ," Trey groaned as Dallin turned his face and pushed his cock in deep, taking it as Parker lined up with his ass.

I had needed a break from the fucking, but as I watched my guys fuck, that break wasn't going to last long. Nothing was hotter than watching the dominant men I married bottom to each other, especially when they did it at my insistence.

Too often they focused on me, forgoing their own bisexual needs and getting complacent with who they fucked. Not tonight.

I kneeled on the bed at Trey's side, playing with myself as I watched my men fuck with that savage strength they only used on each other when I wasn't around. It turned me on so fucking much that before long I was needy again.

I locked eyes with Dallin over Trey's head, and a sinister grin pulled at his lips as I started coming on my fingers. "That's it, darling," he praised me, reaching over and rubbing my clit for me as I fucked my pussy and ass with my fingers.

"Good girl," Parker growled, bruising Trey's hips with his big hands as he slammed into him. "Fuck, you're so damn sexy, Rey."

"Cock," I gasped when I could finally breathe again, scurrying up the bed to straddle Dallin's lap backward. I squatted over his cock that was wet with Trey's spit, and he held it up for me to lower my ass down onto as my other men watched.

"Take it, baby," Trey demanded as he leaned forward and licked my clit as I pushed down onto D's big cock. "So fucking perfect for us."

"Your turn," I gasped, shimmying my hips and forcing D to scoot down the bed until I could lie back against his chest with my legs spread.

The burn from the angle was almost enough to make me come again, but I held off as Trey pulled himself off Parker's cock and slammed into my pussy, forgoing a warm-up period as I screamed, filled with the two fattest cocks I'd ever seen.

I bit Trey's neck when he started fucking me hard, and he returned the favor when Parker pushed back into him.

"Dammit," he growled, grinding his cock into me as Dallin lifted my ass just enough to get room to thrust. "God, that's so good."

My dark and broken man lay against my chest, with our strong and delicious husbands sandwiching us together as they fucked us.

"I'm going to come," I gasped, digging my nails into Parker's chest when he leaned over Trey's back to go deeper. "I'm going to squirt."

"Cover me with it, kitten," Trey demanded, arching his back to thrust his cock into me each time Parker fucked him. In time with Dallin's short thrusts I saw stars and screamed, coming over them, coating them with my orgasm.

Through the blaring echoes in my ears, Dallin's groans and Trey's curses followed Parker's savage thrusts until we were all a pile of ecstasy and blinding pleasure. Then nothing existed but the four hearts beating wildly in a heap of bliss.

Slowly, bodies moved and untangled from each other, but Trey wouldn't pull out, even growling at Dallin when he tried to get us apart to clean us up.

Instead, Trey rolled us onto our sides, clinging to me as I clung to him, letting our men care for us the way true loves did.

And then they joined us in bed.

I was spent. I was sore. I was soft in a way I never let myself be. Curled on my side, wrapped in arms and limbs and muscle and warmth.

And in that stillness, in that breathless, heart-wrecking quiet, I knew.

I wasn't just loved.

I was worshiped in the way I'd never be able to write into any story that wasn't ours.

IN EVERY CHAPTER, I CHOOSE HER

Dallin

Big cities all smelled the same—concrete, car exhaust, street vendors hawking hot dogs and knockoff sunglasses, and body odor.

Los Angeles was no different, yet in a way there was a scent of excitement in the air as we walked through the skywalk to the convention center. Although I would have given anything to stay at that cabin for another week or two, secluded and away from the world, this was right where Reyna belonged.

As a star, playing a role in her very own movie.

She was buzzing beside me, trying to pretend she wasn't panicking as we walked into the massive convention center. But I knew all the signs: her grip on her phone was a just a little too tight, her pace was too fast, and her teeth continuously dragged across her bottom lip like she was trying to hold back a scream.

The convention was the biggest of her career yet. Hundreds of authors and thousands of attendees. As much as she enjoyed the indie bookstore and quirky panels at the other signings, this was the main stage. And even though she had dreamed of a day like this for years, I knew what she was secretly telling herself.

She was an impostor.

She'd somehow tricked her way here.

She wasn't one of the "real" authors.

But I'd be damned if she walked out of the convention at the end of the day feeling that way. Not on my watch.

Her table was front and center, stacked high with her books. Every spicy, soul-ripping, sin-filled one of them. And behind her table hung a long banner reading *Reyna Kent:* New York Times *Best-Selling Author*.

I was so fucking proud.

Rey stopped cold when she got to the table, reading the banner. "I thought it was just a *USA Today* hit," she said softly. "Is it a fluke?"

"No fluke," I corrected as I stepped behind her, hands settling lightly in the dip of her waist. "You broke into it. With stories you were scared to publish, this one specifically, you thought it was too much. But look at you fly, baby."

She turned to look at me, wide-eyed. "You did this?"

I shook my head. "Everyone already knew, darling. I just confirmed it with a new banner."

She fought to keep her tears at bay, but they welled up and perched precariously on her lashes nonetheless. When she reached for my hand, I let her hold it. She could hold on to me for as long as she wanted.

It didn't take long before the lines rushed through the front door, forming at different tables, readers desperate to meet their favorite authors in person. Including Reyna.

Readers held copies of her latest book, *Claimed By Three: Hard Ink, Soft Hearts*, and others from her backlist. Rey was full of grace and gratitude, signing whatever they brought with them, never turning anyone away, and working through the line so everyone had a chance to chat with her face-to-face.

One woman wore a shirt that said *I want a Dallin (And the others too)* and asked me to sign it.

Rey giggled, handing me the marker and urging me forward to make the reader's day. It was wild, and surreal, and I was so fucking happy for our wife. But I could see the fatigue on her face as the end of the first signing session came to a close.

"Hey." Parker nudged me from where he leaned against the wall behind her table. "Think she needs a break?"

"She needs food, and water," I mused. "And an orgasm."

He snorted with a devilish wink. "Did I mention I came prepared?" Pulling his hand from his pocket, he flashed me a personal favorite toy of his, and then put his hand back.

"You brought your vibrating cock ring to the convention?" I deadpanned, even though it was fucking genius.

"I figured the more times we can get her off in the least amount of time, the better."

He had a point.

Our girl deserved it.

"Fine." I leaned up off the wall. "Give me five to find somewhere quiet, and then bring her to me."

"And who's going to watch the table while she's gone?" he asked, even as we both looked over at our Sweeney Todd–flavored Fabio of a husband signing books like he had anything to do with writing them.

"Let Trey hold it down for a few."

Parker chuckled. "You've got four minutes before I pull her away, and then I'm fucking her wherever we land if you don't find somewhere private."

"On it." I walked away into the convention and out into the hall. I perused the different rooms, filled with readers and staff, desperate to find somewhere that would do the trick. And then I did. "Bingo."

I texted the directions to Parker and stood guard at the door outside the nearly deserted freight entrance that the convention was using to store stock for the event. With a convenient freight elevator marked *out of order* with the doors jammed open, loaded with a pallet of books.

My wife's books, to be exact.

"Parker, what are you doing?" Reyna's confused voice echoed as they came down the corridor, rounding the corner and finding me standing there, waiting for them. "D? What's going on?"

My wife looked like a sex goddess, in a tight pencil skirt with thigh-high stockings that had the words *Good Girl* sewn into them; her feet were laced into black sharp stilettos with velvet ribbon tied up her legs. And her top? Jesus fuck, the red lace top hugged her lush tits and delicious curves like a second skin.

She was begging to be fucked, just by dressing that way for us.

Tempting us all day long.

"Ten minutes, darling," I replied, before walking backward into the elevator. "How many times can we make you come in that time?"

Her eyes widened and her lips parted as Parker pulled her into the elevator with a chuckle as I pulled the wedge out of the door, leaving it between them so I could get my fingers between to open them back up when we were done with her.

"I can't do this!" Reyna hissed even as her thighs squeezed together as she stood. "I have to go back."

"In ten minutes," I repeated, lifting her by her waist and setting her on the pallet of shrink-wrapped signed stock. As soon as her ass was on the top, I pulled her legs wide, pulling her to the edge. The height was perfect, and I watched as she stared at Parker in disbelief as he pushed his jeans down, slowly stroking his cock to hard before sliding the ribbed cock ring over his length.

"Oh my God," she whined, but lifted her hips as I pulled her red lace panties down her legs and pocketed them. The same panties that nearly got ripped in a game of tug-of-war this morning when she tried to put them on in front of Trey to begin with. He ended up on his knees behind her, thong pulled to the side, eating her ass and fingering her pussy until she came for a consolation prize.

"You're going to stay still and take it," I commanded, "You're not allowed to do anything but come. No touching, no begging, no thinking." I moved and let Parker take my place between her silky thighs, where he instantly knelt down and spat onto her spread-open pussy. There was no time for foreplay.

Not when she had a time crunch.

"God," she moaned, biting the back of her hand when he bottomed out in one brutal thrust, before turning the ring on to max. "Fuck!"

"Yes, dear." Parker smiled, leaning forward, holding the ring against her clit as he started circling his hips.

She didn't even try to hold back or deny herself what she wanted; instead she dug her nails into my arm where I stood at her side, wrapping her other hand around the back of Parker's neck, and angling her hips how she wanted and moaned. "God, you feel so good, baby."

"Tell me how good," Parker growled, giving short thrusts and then rubbing her clit with the toy again.

"So good, I'm going to come already," she moaned, pinching her hard nipples through the thin fabric of her shirt. "Oh God, fuck yes!"

"That's it," I praised her, pushing her hand aside and tweaking her nipples. "Come for him."

"Mmm," she moaned, tipping her head back and rocking her hips in time with his, riding him like a toy for her pleasure. "Just like that. Don't stop."

"She's going to come again, D," he groaned, pulling her arms around to the small of her back, banding them there as he started slamming into her roughly. "God, she's shaking. I love it when you fucking break for us, Rey."

"That's good," I cooed, wrapping my hand around her throat and squeezing as she rocked faster. "Good girl coming on Parker's cock, I want to see your pussy cream all over it for me."

"Fuck!" she cried, biting her lips to stop from screaming as he pushed her headfirst into another orgasm.

"That's it, let it go. We're yours, baby girl," Parker moaned, and I could tell he was close. Even though he was trying to just please her, Reyna's body was far too sinful to ignore how damn good she felt wrapped around his cock. "I'm going to fill you up, and then Dallin is going to take his turn."

"Oh my God," she cried, digging her nails into his neck as her tits jiggled with each punishing thrust.

If someone was out in the corridor, they'd hear what we were doing. And if they peeked through the crack, they'd see it.

That just added to the high for me, though.

I pulled my cock free, stroking it slowly as he erupted, filling her pussy up and giving her another orgasm in the process before he pulled the ring off, slick with their release, and slid it over my cock.

"Give me more, D," Reyna demanded, widening her legs and rubbing her pink swollen clit while we switched.

"You want me?" I challenged, lifting her off the boxes and slamming her into the wall before impaling her. The angle was perfect to let gravity hold her against the toy and she screamed, muffled behind my hand as I savagely fucked her. "Come for me, Little Red. Coat my cock with it so I can feel you on me the rest of the day. Give me something to hold me over until tonight."

Voices out in the corridor echoed around the space, and Parker quickly fastened his jeans and stood with his back at the door, blocking anyone from looking in.

"Shh, baby," I whispered, slamming into her as she started coming on my cock. In the middle of her orgasm I stopped moving, grinding the toy against her clit as she clawed at me in ecstasy, coming again before the first one even stopped completely. "Take my come," I demanded, as her sharp little teeth bit the flesh of my palm and I fucked her harder, just how she liked until my heart felt like it would explode in my chest if I didn't stop and take a breath.

"Good girl," Parker praised her quietly, coming to her side and pushing her hair back from her damp forehead. "You did so good."

"I'm not done with you yet." I pulled out of her, and she whimpered, stumbling on her jelly legs as I bent her over the pallet. "Don't move, Rey."

I knelt behind her, spreading her thick ass cheeks apart, and saw the proof of our orgasms coating her swollen pink lips, dripping down onto her clit. "D," she moaned, looking over her shoulder.

Parker leaned around me, snapping a picture of her cream-filled pussy, and whistled. "Trey's going to go berserk when he sees what he missed out on."

I knew what she wanted. She knew what I needed.

Our girl loved it when we cleaned up our messes when we were done.

So I licked her clean, teasing her once more into another powerful orgasm before gently backing down and helping her slide her useless panties back up her legs. They were so thin, they never would have held back one load as she stood on her feet all day, let alone two.

But it didn't matter.

She'd feel us for the rest of the afternoon; every time she shifted, or bent over, she'd remember who she belonged to.

Just how I liked it.

HAPPILY. STILL. ALWAYS.

Reyna

The apartment above Twisted Ink was quiet when we walked in. Too quiet. Too still. There was no buzz of the book tour halls, the crinkle of swag bags, or the shriek of readers asking Trey to sign their tits.

It was just us and our stupidly cozy living room that smelled like testosterone and lavender air freshener.

I dropped my bag at the door and stood there, overwhelmed by the weight of it all. The tour was over. I did it. I survived the nerves, the chaos, the panels, and the elevator. Oh God, the elevator.

And all that was left was home.

Only it didn't feel like the end of something like I had imagined it would.

It felt like something new.

My guys filed in behind me, carrying bags from the rental car, one by one until they were done. Dallin threw his keys in the bowl, Parker immediately pulled his shirt off and stretched like a cat in heat, and Trey walked straight to the fridge, pulling out beers for everyone like nothing happened.

But something did happen.

Everything changed.

I changed.

I ended up on the couch wrapped in a blanket, curled between Parker's legs with my feet on Trey's lap, all three of them talking about the shop and what they'd start first when they returned the next morning.

I knew I should be exhausted after all the travel. For a homebody who stayed local to Nashville as much as possible, the two weeks on tour was a lot.

Instead, I felt alive. Not buzzing or burning with adrenaline alive, though, just *settled*.

"Do you want to unpack tonight, or tomorrow?" Dallin asked, brushing his fingers over my knee from the other side of Trey.

Shaking my head, I said, "Never."

Trey chuckled. "Tour burnout?"

"No," I replied honestly. "But something weird happened while we were gone."

Parker looked over my head, brow raised. "Yeah?"

"I think I started believing it."

"Believing what?" Dallin asked.

"That I deserve this," I whispered. "The readers. The stories. The love. You guys."

There was a pause and then Trey was the first to speak. "That's not weird, kitten. It's the truth."

I smiled at him, but didn't say anything else as the comfortable silence blanketed us.

I knew I'd end up in bed with them in a few hours, my guys tangled around me, and we'd probably all sleep like we hadn't in months.

But as I pulled my laptop off the table and opened a blank document, I typed the first line of my next book.

I thought I'd have to choose—between being the story or writing it. But it turned out, when the love was real, you got to have both.

ABOUT THE AUTHOR

A.M. McCoy is a dark romance author whose books feature tumultuous relationships with happy endings. McCoy lives in Western New York with her husband, their two kiddos, and a blessedly obese and challenging beagle. When she's not chasing down the four of them, she's locked away writing stories she loves.